MW01286274

"In *Oil and Water*, two w̶̶̶̶̶ unfinished business bet̶w̶e̶e̶n̶ ̶a̶ ̶t̶e̶n̶ ̶y̶e̶a̶r̶-̶o̶l̶d̶ ̶a̶n̶d̶ ̶a̶ ̶b̶i̶g̶ ̶o̶i̶l̶ ̶c̶o̶m̶p̶a̶n̶y̶. From scene to gripping scene, P. J Lazos packs this environmental thriller with intrigue, suspense, and well-fueled imagination."

—Jan Groft, Author of *Artichokes & City Chicken*

"*Oil and Water* is described as "an environmental murder mystery," but there is far more to this book than murder and mystery. *Oil and Water* … is close to an epic … [as] it delves into the author's deep concern with the state of the planet's environment. The "McGuffin," as director Alfred Hitchcock called the device or thing in which a plot revolves, is a technology that promises to solve the world's energy needs and pollution problems … . Unseen forces are trying to steal the invention, which … is similar to an actual technology still being perfected. Lazos does an impressive job explaining the science to the lay person … [and] writes especially well in describing her characters and using them to set the chapter moods. It's well worth a dive into *Oil and Water*."

— Peter Durantine, Author of *The Chocolate Assassin*

"You won't find an environmental story more thrilling to read than the character-driven novel *Oil and Water* by P.J. Lazos. From one chapter to the next, Lazos keeps you on the edge of your seat as she transforms a murder mystery into a dramatic narrative of a fight to the finish to save the earth from the degradation caused by fossil fuels. Everything you would want in a thriller is inside the covers of *Oil and Water*: intrigue, mystery, coincidence, love, envy, greed, and yes, in the end, hope."

— Sandra Fluck, *bookscover2cover.com*

"Lazos weaves an endearing tale of the Tirabi brothers and their sister who bravely face down evil forces out to steal what's theirs. Intelligent and resourceful, the family members are led to meet key players of a powerful oil company seeking to assure its survival. When pure motives collide with materialistic greed, the world of the Tirabi's combusts. Lazos writes one suspenseful sentence after another, never letting her grip relax until the last, satisfying page."

— Donna Walker, bookscover2cover.com

"A taut, timely, ecological thriller that shows P. J. Lazos' ability to blend a wide-ranging cast of well-defined characters with a fast-moving plot that moves with ease back and forth between Philadelphia, Houston and Iraq. There is murder, there is a "bulging, engorged moon," there is an oil spill, a wounded duck. A young boy comes up with an invention that could change the world, that could turn trash into cash, that could convert waste, even old love letters, into oil. Will the oil industry resist this chance to make the planet blue again? Read *Oil and Water* and find out."

— Wade Stevenson, author of *Moon Talk* and *One Time in Paris*

OIL AND WATER

[Handwritten inscription: "Tanya, Thanks for keeping us in line! You're amazing."]

P. J. LAZOS

Also by P.J. Lazos

Six Sisters

DEDICATION

For my husband, Scott Eberly, perhaps my greatest teacher.

Thank You, Friend.

Thanking people should be the easiest part of writing a book and yet, it's not. Why? Well, in this instance, the first draft of *Oil and Water* was written about thirteen years ago, and in between then and now I edited the manuscript at least four times, beefed it up, cut it down, pasted it back together, started as close to the "inciting event" as I could without losing the integrity of the document, subjected it to scrutiny by various critique groups, let it languish for months, sometimes years at a time while I worked on other things, and then shredded it again before sending it out to publishers and agents where it garnered interest at times and fell into darkness at others. When I got tired of the search for the perfect representative, I decided to become her. Whether I have succeeded magnificently or failed miserably is a subjective matter, but I do know I have tried, sometimes with grace and sometimes with everything but, to bring this most heartfelt work out into the world, and maybe drag some environmental awareness along with it in a fun, non-threatening, non-judgmental manner. Okay, maybe the teeniest bit of judgment, but I am an environmentalist after all and old habits die hard.

I loved writing this book. It was my first novel and I finished the first draft in nine months, but like all infants, it needed time to grow and change and discover. Frankly, I think I've held onto it longer than I should have the way a mother is conflicted about seeing her children grow up and leave the nest. You want the best for them. You want to see them succeed, but it's a scary world and there are so many potential pitfalls. Whatever. I'm setting it free so I can begin my next project. Closure only works in your favor when you actually finish something.

Often many hands contribute to the success of a project, and to that end, I'd like to give my thanks and warmest regards to the following people. If I left you out, it was inadvertent and I seek forgiveness in advance. Thirteen years is a long time, and lots of people have passed in and out of this book's life in that time. So here goes. Thanks to:

Clay Tully, for your brilliant, innovative spirit and creative spark. You are a national treasure. My fab friends, and stalwart readers, critics, and Important Persons without whom I'd undoubtedly be lost, my BFF, Debbe Bosin, Rita Lazos and Jean Blevins (who bless me from above), Stacey Lazos — sisters!, Gayle Materna, for your innate wisdom and good humor, Randy Myer, Mary Maddox, Adele Greenberg and Rosina Rucci. Duncan Alderson, Kerry Loughlin, Peggy Rushton, Lisa Graham, Harvey Freedenberg, Clemson Page, Brenda Witmer, Peggy Frailey, Carolyn Sherzer, Sandy Arnold, Terry Shuman, Keith Strandberg, and the rest of the Rabbit Hill Writers who were subjected to raw, rough, and sometimes incomprehensible chapters of this book — thanks for hanging in there. Dinty Moore for your professorial insight. Dave Eberly, Sr., Lin Stainbrook, Susan Eberly, John Casadia, Mark Sibley, Russ Swan, Jeff Hoffman, Kelley Prassad, Stefan Friend, Jill Gamber, Jodi Bosin, Deana Terry, Piper Templeton, Peter Durantine, Wade Stevenson and Jan Groft for your comments and kudos. H.G. Reifsnyder — I probably wouldn't have ever started writing if not for you. Gaspare Perrello for your editing and intellectual support. Bob Puzauskie for answering my endless design questions. The real and indefatigable paladins of the OSC world, Glen Lapsley and Vince Zenone, who deal daily with oil and other hazardous waste spills so that our "waters of the United States" might remain safe and usable, and who never tired of my endless questions about all things mucky and murky. Jim Self and the MA peeps for raising the bar on collective consciousness and buoying me along in the process. Sandra Fluck and Donna Walker, true angels walking around in human garb, for your editing and proofreading skills and your knowledge of proper comma and ellipses usage. Sandra Fluck and Justine Bugaj, and their wonderful brainchild, bookscover2cover.com for serializing *Oil and Water* on their website. Janice Kim for the beautiful cover painting of the Philadelphia skyline. Andrew Goldman for use of the original photo, for your wonderful cover design work, and for chair dancing with me. My kids, Morgan, Ian and Arianna who were little cherubs when I started this novel, and now, thirteen years later are full blown angels. My husband, Scott Eberly, for sharing all the best stories from his commercial diving days, the endless Knowledge Transfer Sessions regarding, among other things, the differences, real and imagined, between a Christmas tree valve and a schrader fitting, and most, for allowing me to turn a bit of fact into fiction. My grateful heart sends you all gobs of love and Beach Boys-esque good vibrations in five-part harmony.

A note about the technology:

The idea for *Oil and Water* first surfaced after I read an article in *Discover* magazine about a machine that turned trash into oil created by a company called *Changing World Technologies* (CWT). They were working on a pilot project at the Philadelphia Naval Shipyard — a converted industrial park — developing and commercializing the technology known as thermal depolymerization, referred to by CWT as thermal conversion process.

In the book I talk about converting anything carbon-based into oil. That's what the original literature discussed. However, I'm not sure if CWT ever progressed beyond turkey offal, which is what they started out incinerating. I've had no conversations with any representatives of CWT, so my portrayal of the technology is limited to what I was able to glean from Google searches, pictures on CWT's website, and a couple in-depth articles in *Discover*. As a result, the descriptions set forth in the book of what the technology actually looks like are just my best educated guesses.

I do know that from the Philadelphia Naval Shipyard CWT moved to Carthage, Missouri, where it operated from 2004 until it went bankrupt in 2009. At the time they were using turkey remains to fuel the conversion process, but problems with a smell escaping into the nearby environs caused a backlash from the Missouri Department of Natural Resources and a lawsuit by the locals. CWT sold the Carthage plant to a Canadian firm, Ridgeline Energy Services, in February 2016. Ridgeline plans to expand the business, but in what capacity, I do not know.

So that's it. It all sounded like a terribly good idea to me when I first read about it. Imagine an *in situ* conversion unit in every new home built. Imagine last night's leftovers becoming tomorrow's fuel for your car instead of landfill fodder. After a century and a half of drilling for oil, isn't it time we gave Mama Earth a break and figured out another way to power our lives? What better way than with our trash?

Yesterday I was clever
So I wanted to change the world.
Today I am wise
So I am changing myself.

- Rumi

There's never a crowd on the leading edge.

- Esther Hicks, Channeling the Conscious
Collective Known as Abraham.

CHAPTER 1

Marty Tirabi sat on a stool aside his drafting table, an aluminum pie plate in each hand. His eyes were closed, his spine erect, his breathing slow and regular, his conscious mind sitting on the pinnacle of present awareness. At the exact moment Marty's consciousness shifted, sliding across the threshold from beta to alpha to delta like a single-base hitter stealing home, Marty's grip slackened, and the pie plates clattered to the floor. He woke with a start and stared, wide-eyed, at the back wall of the barn where *It* sat, all the while scanning his interior databases for a revelation that refused to be retrieved.

Marty rubbed his forehead. This was how Thomas Edison had done it, mining the gem-rich ground of his subconscious by bringing himself to the brink of sleep, then pulling back with a start for a third-party observer's view. The results of Edison's efforts were the light bulb and one thousand and ninety-two other patented inventions, but Marty'd be damned if he could get Edison's process to work. For him it was just there, a vision that sometimes crept, sometimes hurtled from unconscious to conscious awareness — claircognizance some called it, a simple knowing — and suddenly Marty would know how to pull it all together.

But not tonight. Frustrated, Marty spun his stool around, laid the pie plates and his overtired brain on the drafting table, and stared at his father's oil lamp, its soft, incandescent glow casting ectoplasmic shadows on the blueprints beneath his head. He started to fall — no aluminum pie plates to stop him this time — but was jarred back to wakefulness, halted again by a faint hum, a soft, deliberate noise like the whir of a refrigerator motor or the patter of a soft rain. He felt it in his feet first. It climbed up his legs as it grew in intensity, settled in his heart and then shot up to his forehead. His head vibrated. Marty rose slowly so as not to disturb the hum's cadence and strolled across the barn floor toward the back wall, convinced that a nonchalant attitude was imperative to the hum's survival. He tried not to smile, tried not to look directly at *It* until he had stopped in front of the thousands of pounds of steel assembled in six distinct units. He sniffed the air. Dozens of smells slid past the cilia in his nose and traveled along his olfactory nerve, stopping at the cerebral cortex to register: methane, plastic, burning rubber, decay, ash. Even in a closed-looped system, the vapors, like his dreams, always escaped.

And then, suspended in the air like dust motes lollygagging in a single ray of sun, the smell of oil, sweet and slightly acrid, pierced Marty's nasal cavity, shattering his equilibrium.

"Hahahahaaaaaaaaaaaaa!"

Marty clapped his hands and, because he was half-Greek, did the only dance he felt comfortable doing, a little hop/skip combo that was the back-bone of most traditional ethnic dances. He repeated the steps over and over until he came full circle. He added a little jump to his combination.

Marty stopped and laid his face against the side of the metal grate. It was cool to the touch and not at all indicative of the fire raging inside. He shook his head and started his hop, skip and jump dance all over again, this time adding an ecstatic laugh to the mix. He'd done it. Just like Dr. Frankenstein, he'd brought the beast to life: his Thermo-Depolymerization Unit, or TDU, lived! Years in the making, like nothing the world had ever seen, and until five minutes ago only a theory.

Marty had envisioned that the TDU would take garbage, comput-ers, old sneakers, last night's dinner, yard waste, old fence posts, plastic Tupperware, with or without lids, old sweatshirts, used ball point pens, broken picture frames, old love letters, paint waste, empty cardboard box-es, broken refrigerators, busted telephone poles, wrecked car parts, or the whole car for that matter, old comic books, unwanted furniture, hell, this machine could take anything carbon-based, and do something magical with it, something that, to date, no one else had figured out how to do — take trash and convert it into oil — pure, unadulterated, car-starting, engine-revving, turbo-driving, eighteen-wheeler-moving oil. Marty figured that the TDU would mimic what Mother Nature did every day hundreds of miles below the earth's surface — break down fossils into fuels. But Marty's contraption would take about three hours instead of millions of years, combusting nothing, and leaving no waste. After twenty years of toil, Marty had his share of false starts. But now the whir and hum of booster pumps and coolant fan units was evidence: modern-day alchemy. Marty had called down the vision.

Yet the world had no template for it. Like the shaman of the first American Indian tribe to come into contact with Columbus, Marty had to mold the vision into a discernible shape, give the people something palpable that they could recognize. For even as Columbus's ships approached the shores of the New World, the Native Americans couldn't see them, not until their shaman provided them with a frame of reference.

But being a shaman was at times an exhausting, aching and lonely occupation. So Marty did what any man in his place would do when faced with a discovery of unrivaled proportions. He propped himself up on the hammock in the corner of the barn and took a nap.

CHAPTER 2

Avery washed the dinner dishes while Kori sat at the table, sketching.

"The rule is, he who cooks does not clean up. That is the rule. And frankly, I'm flabbergasted to hear that you've never heard of it," Avery said. "My advice? Find a guy with plenty of money 'cause you don't know the first thing about work, sister."

Tall and sinewy with inches still to go, Avery had his mother's good looks and a healthy dose of her wavy, red hair. At sixteen, he towered above his sister, destined to be not only the tallest but most loquacious one in the family.

"Hey, jabber jaws. Easy. I'm trying to work here," Kori replied. She stood up, grabbed her eraser and dropped back into the chair, her shoulder length hair flouncing around her like the head of Medusa, dark, coppery strands writhing and whirling in all directions. Kori was older by five years, but looked younger than her brother. She stopped to admire her long, slender fingers under the pretense of inspecting her fingernails for paint residue.

"Work? That's not work. That's fun. *This* is work." Avery pointed to the mound of dishes waiting to be rinsed and placed in the dishwasher.

"Hey, we could have had pizza."

"Ingrate."

"I can't tell you how many times I cook *and* clean up," Kori said.

"For yourself, yeah. But other people live here, too."

4

"Robbie ate your food and he didn't do any cleanup."

"Robbie gets special treatment. He's taking me to see *Tom Petty* this weekend."

"*Tom Petty*? Geez, Avery. He's so *old.*"

"That doesn't mean he's not still good. It's better than that classical crap you listen to."

Kori shook her head. "You're a cheap date."

"And you're just cheap."

Avery fixed her with a *top-that* look, but it was useless. She was her father's only daughter, blessed with grace and beauty and used to entitlement. She rolled her eyes and picked at her cuticles.

Avery put the last dish in the dishwasher. "Let me just repeat – Big Fat Checking Account."

"I'm making my own money now."

"What, hawking second-rate oil paintings?" Avery said.

"They are not second-rate. What's second-rate are your attempts at dating."

"You suck." He threw a dishtowel at her and stormed out of the room, still fuming when he sat down next to Gil in the living room.

"What a b...."

"Ssshhhhh," Gil said, covering Avery's mouth. Gil rocked back and forth, his narrow shoulders bouncing off the couch at two-second intervals. At almost eleven, he still maintained the little boy looks that would soon be lost to puberty. He removed his hand from Avery's mouth and drew it very deliberately across his forehead, anchoring his bangs just below his eyebrows.

Avery huffed, crossed his legs and practiced some deep breathing exercises. After a minute, he forgot all about Kori and engrossed himself in the final scenes of *Die Hard*. He didn't notice Gil walk to the dining room table, roll up a stack of blueprints and stuff them into a cylinder. Nor did he notice Gil retrieving their shoes from the hall closet.

Gil placed Avery's shoes at his feet and sat down to put on his own. "The bad guys are coming," Gil said.

"It would appear so," Avery said, his attention focused on the television screen.

"We have to go."

"Hmmm?" Avery turned to see Gil slipping into his sneakers. "Gil, it's only a movie."

Gil picked up Avery's shoes and handed them to him before turning off the television.

"What are you doing?" Gil scooped up the cylinder and Kori's shoes and walked into the kitchen. Avery slipped on his shoes and followed.

Gil laid Kori's shoes at her feet.

"What are these for?" Kori asked.

"We have to leave," Gil said.

"Why?"

"The bad guys are coming."

"What bad guys?"

"The bad guys on TV," Avery answered for him. "C'mon, Gil. Let's watch the end of the movie."

"Yeah. Take a chill pill," Kori said.

"We have to leave NOW!"

Avery and Kori both jumped. Gil covered his own mouth. His siblings exchanged glances.

"Okay, okay," Avery said. He grabbed the car keys. "I'm driving."

Kori slipped her feet into her sandals and swiped the keys from Avery.

"I have my permit!" he protested.

"Your *learner's* permit only allows you to drive during daylight hours." She opened the door to the pitch-black night, and put a hand on her hip.

"You suck."

"That's the second time you said that tonight." Kori blew Avery a kiss, and held the door for Gil and ZiZi, the family Golden Retriever, then closed the door on her brother.

𝗔

In exchange for driving privileges, Robbie had completely rebuilt Kori's engine, supplying it with more torque than a freight train. The second child, Robbie was stocky and athletic and possessed of neither Kori's prima donna attitude nor Avery's command of the English language. Born with dyslexia, he struggled with spelling yet was mechanically inclined and could build anything from scratch. That, coupled with a keen imagination, earned him the moniker "Mr. Fix-It."

Kori stuck the key in the ignition and the car roared to life, radio blaring. Gil covered his ears and screamed. Kori jumped and turned to see ZiZi licking Gil's face where he lay huddled on the floor, his hands tightly clasped to his ears, his vocal cords exploding in wave after wave of high-pitched wailing.

"Gil, take it easy. Gil!" Kori turned off the radio, but the engine still wailed like a colicky baby. Avery climbed in the back, pulling Gil up to a sitting position, covering his ears and rocking him gently. Gil stopped screaming, but his body continued convulsing.

"Do something before he has a fit," Kori yelled to Avery. Avery's gaze swiveled, his eyes settling on the glove compartment.

"Tissues," Avery said.

Kori handed Avery a package of tissues. He folded two and rolled them between his hands, scrunched them into conical shapes and inserted one into each of Gil's ears, grabbed Gil's shoulders and took several deep breaths, indicating Gil should mimic him. Gil's chest rose and fell rhythmically, and after a minute his shaking, along with the tension in the car, subsided.

"Are you sure you want to leave?" Kori asked.

"Just go before he has another freakazoid attack," Avery said. Gil looked past Avery with wide, doe eyes and a slack mouth.

"Drive!" Avery commanded.

Kori watched Gil in the rear view mirror, rocking gently in the back seat, tissues sticking out of his ears. She stifled a laugh and pulled out of the driveway; she'd only made it a few hundred feet when Gil spoke.

"Pull in here."

"What?" Kori asked.

"Just do it, Kori," Avery said. Kori shook her head and muttered something under her breath, but pulled into Aunt Stella's driveway anyway, a scant three doors down from their own.

"Why are we parking at Aunt Stella's house?" Kori asked. "We're practically still at our house."

"Yeah, Gil," Avery added. "This doesn't bode well for concealing our whereabouts."

Kori fished through her purse for a cigarette, found the pack and pulled one out.

"You shouldn't smoke," Gil said.

"I don't, really. Just once in a while," Kori answered.

"Shut the lights and cut the engine," Gil said.

"Stop telling me what to do," Kori said, but obliged. "This is ridiculous." She found her lighter, flicked it once. It didn't take.

"No!" Gil whispered. He shoved Kori's head down across the console. Avery bent his head down next to Gil who was crouched on the floor in the back seat.

"Geez, Gil," Kori said, her chest pressed against the drive shaft. "You've been watching too many Bruce Willis movies." After a minute, she sat up. "Gil — enough!"

"Get down!" Gil said and turned to peer out the back window.

A car was creeping down the road. The driver killed the lights as it passed Aunt Stella's house. The trio huddled together, peering out the back window as the car pulled into the Tirabi driveway. A dark figure emerged, climbed the porch steps and unscrewed the light. The porch went dim. They watched the dark silhouette playing with the lock. Moments later, the figure walked in the Tirabis' front door.

"Did you lock the door?" Kori demanded of Avery.

"Ssshhhhhhhhh!" Gil said, staring wide-eyed and fascinated. The children saw a shadow pass by the window, followed by the erratic beam of a flashlight, sweeping the room. The figure emerged, carrying a long tube under its arm. In one fluid motion, the figure jumped over the railing and rolled onto the ground. The car backed out of the driveway and crawled down the street. Halfway up the block, the driver flicked on the lights and drove away.

"Let go of me," Kori jerked away and Gil released the stranglehold grip he had on her neck. Kori breathed in short bursts, trying to regain her composure.

"What just happened?" Avery asked.

"The drawings," Gil replied.

"What drawings?" Avery asked, but even as the words left his lips, an explosion on the Tirabi's porch caused their car windows to vibrate. The front door of the house blew off its hinges and several of the windows on the front porch shattered.

Kori screamed and scrambled over the console into the back seat, squishing in with her brothers. ZiZi yelped and Kori screamed again. She was wide-eyed with terror, yet put a protective arm around Gil.

"What the hell!" Avery said, staring in amazement. Several dogs began barking. The neighbor's car alarm, activated by the blast, began its cycle of warning. Porch lights flooded the darkness. A small blaze started on the porch, its flames licking delicately at the tattered Venetian blinds partially emerging from the broken windows.

"Our porch is on fire," Avery said, fumbling through Kori's purse for the cell phone. "We've gotta call the fire department." He found the phone and pushed the "on" button. Kori shook her head and grabbed the phone.

"No. We've gotta call Mom and Dad," she said. Her hands were shaking.

"Mom and Dad are in Philly. We have to call the fire department. Otherwise it's going to be more screwed up." Avery grabbed the phone out of Kori's hand. She put her hand on top of his and they sat, locked together in a game of push me, pull you.

"Avery. Stop!" Kori yanked the phone from Avery's hand. He pulled it back before she had a chance to dial the first number.

Aunt Stella's garage lights flicked on. An aunt in name only, the Tirabis watched as Stella's stout frame, adorned in robe and slippers, lumbered across the front lawn at full throttle.

"Mmmmmm, cookies," Gil mused.

Aunt Stella's pudgy, round face peered in through the back window where the kids huddled together like war orphans. She opened the door, pushed the driver's seat forward, and thrust a hand inside. Kori grabbed it, and Aunt Stella eased them out one by one.

"Are you all right? What are you doing in the car? Thank God you weren't inside!" Aunt Stella looked at Gil who still had tissues sticking out of his ears. "What happened?" she yipped. "Did an experiment go bad or something?"

All three of them started talking at once, which instigated a round of ZiZi's agitated barking. Aunt Stella waved her hands in the air, the international symbol for *enough already*, and gathered them together like a head coach at halftime.

"All right. It'll be okay. Let's go inside," she said. "I already called the fire department." As if on cue, a fire truck screamed down the road. Everyone turned to watch as the massive vehicle parked on the Tirabi lawn. A second truck could be heard off in the distance, sirens blaring. Four firemen alighted from the truck and began assembling the hoses, their yellow emergency vests glinting in the firelight.

"Mom and Dad are in Philly," Kori continued, her voice cracking from the strain.

"I know, honey. Your mother called me this morning."

Aunt Stella placed a large arm around Kori's shoulder and held fast to Gil's wrist with her other hand. Flames licked the front of the house. The double-wide porch swing, made of wood, canvass and macramé, crackled and spat and danced in the darkness, spitting bits of light in wide arcs over the railing. The fire chief shouted several commands and the firefighters trained their hoses on the light.

"Come. They'll soon have it under control. Robbie will know where to go." She steered Gil and Kori in the direction of the house without releasing them. "Let's try and call your parents."

Kori shot Avery a look and wrinkled her nose at him. They walked across the lawn, ZiZi bringing up the rear. Aunt Stella pushed a reluctant Gil into the house.

Avery stood alone on the front stoop, mesmerized. Flames darted about the porch leaving a crackling trail of blazed, scorched wood. The macramé seat on the porch swing – Avery's favorite reading chair – looked like a million writhing snakes. Avery grimaced as the acrid smell of burning memories accosted his nostrils. He stood immobilized, clutching Kori's cell phone, anguish pouring from him like water from a hose.

Aunt Stella popped out and grabbed Avery by the arm. "C'mon, baby, there's nothing to be done right now. And I don't want you having nightmares."

Avery swiped at his eyes and followed Aunt Stella inside.

Chapter 3

The fundraiser for Governor Jackson Randall was in full swing. White-gloved butlers circled the Independence Visitor Center with delicacy-laden trays. Champagne flowed. Marty exchanged his empty glass for a full one and Ruth, declining her own, took a sip of Marty's. The orchestra began a swing tune.

"Wanna dance?" Marty asked.

"Don't change the subject."

"I'm not." Marty rolled his champagne around on his tongue and puckered.

"You know I have terrible night vision," Ruth said.

"Duly noted. I will be clean and sober by the stroke of midnight. Now, please. Dance with me."

Ruth basked in Marty's adoring eyes. Resplendent in her slightly risqué gown, the vigor of her convictions adding a blush to her cheeks, she looked to be a woman ten years younger. If Ruth Eugenia Tirabi missed the earlier version of herself, she never showed it. A brilliant strategist and a great campaign manager, she was courted by many a politician, even those whose social agenda ran far afield from her own. Had she been a man, *she* could have been governor. But soon after marriage, Ruth became pregnant with Kori, and four children and twenty-four years later, was still working politics into the periphery. She was in no rush. Statistically speaking, Ruth had a fifteen to twenty-year greater life expectancy than her male counterparts; she could jump start her career at any time

Ruth kissed Marty on the lips, slipping him a bit of tongue. It wasn't lost on him.

"Let's blow this clam bake," Marty whispered. "I got something to show you." He dipped her, and rolled his eyebrows up and down, a Groucho-esque lewdness to his gesture. Ruth laughed out loud as he set her upright.

"A little while longer. C'mon. Let's dance." Ruth grabbed Marty's arm. Marty set his champagne down and twirled Ruth onto the dance floor before sidling up next to the Governor and his wife. Mrs. Randall laughed as if her husband had just said something supremely funny.

"Enjoying yourself, Mrs. Randall?" asked Marty.

"Immensely, Mr. Tirabi." She looked at Ruth. "I can't thank you enough." Mrs. Randall whirled around so the women could dance shoulder to shoulder. "You gave him back his idealism."

"Hey, Ruth. Sure I can't convince you to hit the campaign trail with us tomorrow?"

"Thanks, Governor. But I must respectfully decline," Ruth said.

"Well, aren't you going to give me a pep talk or something?" the Governor asked.

"Give the people more than they ask for."

Governor Randall gave Ruth a peck on the cheek. "Thank you. For everything."

"I'm just a phone call away if you need me," she said. Ruth squeezed the Governor's arm then looked at the watch on her gloved wrist.

"We gotta go. Not only am I dying to get these gloves off, but we need to get home and make sure the kids haven't blown up the place," said Ruth.

"Sometimes I close my eyes going down our street," Mrs. Randall said. "Our 16-year old loves to host some wild parties."

"Good luck, Governor," Marty said and escorted Ruth off the dance floor. Ruth blew the Governor and his wife a kiss before fading away.

⋏

Marty drove slowly down Market Street and took the on-ramp for I-95 South. The lights of the Walt Whitman Bridge did little to illuminate the ghostly night sky that had assumed the pallor of the thick stratus clouds, hovering close to the city. Pockets of swollen cumulonimbus clouds floated below the tight formation of stratus' looking as if they might kiss the Delaware River.

"Looks like a storm's coming," Ruth said. She leaned back against the headrest as the car glided onto the highway.

Traffic was light. Ruth watched out the passenger window long after the city, vague and foggy with the inclement weather, disappeared from view. Marty pulled his wife in closer and wrapped an arm around her shoulder, moving over to the slow lane. Three cars back, a pickup did the same.

"First rate party, Ruthie." He gave her arm a squeeze.

"It was, wasn't it?" Ruth nuzzled into Marty's shoulder.

"Remember when we were first married?" he asked. "I had that little English Ford. That thing took every bump like it was its last. Why did we get rid of it?"

"We had Kori. The car barely had room for two, let alone three," Ruth laughed. "I really loved that car."

"I wish I could have kept it for you."

"We couldn't afford it, remember?"

"Do you regret all the years you've spent with me, Ruthie? I mean you could have married someone that had more ambition, money-wise." Marty stroked his wife's hair.

"We have plenty of money. We own our house, our cars...."

"I'm talking big money. The kind that lives longer than you do."

"Marty, you've been married to me for twenty-five years and you still don't know me, do you?" Ruth squeezed Marty's thigh, sitting up to her full height. "Silly man." She kissed him on the cheek and he turned to wrangle a full-blown kiss on the lips. She unbuckled her seat belt, and shifted to wrap her arms around his neck. Just as she kissed him, the pickup rear-ended them.

"What the ... ." Marty yelped.

The impact and sudden change of trajectory sent Ruth sprawling. Marty cut the wheel hard to the left to avoid driving off the road and after a few squeals, set the car right as Ruth crawled back up onto the seat. Marty checked the rear view mirror.

"Are you all right?" he barked. Ruth nodded and rubbed the arm that had taken a beating against the dash on the way down.

"Did you hit something?" Ruth asked. Marty pulled over to the side, but before he reached the shoulder, the pickup nicked them. Ruth screamed and turned in her seat to see two giant headlights barreling toward them.

"Oh my God," Ruth yelled. The pickup made contact and Marty hit the accelerator. Ruth flew back and forward, banging her head on the dash as Marty cut the wheel.

"Get down." Marty said. He tugged at her arm, but Ruth remained steadfast, watching as the pickup dropped back and began weaving back and forth.

"It's a drunk driver!" Ruth said as the pickup began an erratic dance between the lanes.

"Marty, he's coming again!"

"You bastard," he mumbled.

"What the hell does he want?"

"Ruth, get down and hold on," Marty yelled, and pushed his wife to the floor; he veered back and forth across the lanes, trying to lose the pickup.

Ruth crawled onto the seat to look out the back window. "Marty, he must be drunk. Stop the car. Get the hell out of his way," said Ruth. Marty checked his rearview mirror, sped up.

"Ruth," Marty boomed. "Get down!" He shoved her onto the seat as the pickup sideswiped them. "This son-of-a-bitch doesn't know who he's dealing with," Marty said through gritted teeth. He slammed down on the accelerator and the pickup dropped back. Ruth peeked at the speedometer. It read ninety-two miles per hour.

"Marty, slow down. You're going to kill us."

"Better me than him."

As they rounded the curve, the pickup accelerated and rammed into the backend on the driver's side. The impact hurtled Marty's car, already approaching 100 mph, off the road and through space. The car flew at first, then hung there for a moment, suspended between the finite and the infinite, between the possible and the impossible, between life and death, and at the exact moment when it seemed that Ruth and Marty Tirabi might float away, gravity reached out and slammed them to the ground. The car landed with an ear-splitting crash, a cacophony of steel and glass and metal. A loud hiss emanated from the interior as the air bags expanded.

The pickup switched on its turn signal and pulled to the side of the road behind the Tirabis' car, but no one emerged from the wreckage. The driver opened a bottle of Mad Dog 20/20, unscrewed the cap and took a long draw on the bottle. He burped, said "excuse me" to himself, and sucked down another quarter. He rubbed the raspberry-colored liquid in his hair, poured some in his hand and flicked it with his fingers at his pants and shirt. He drained the bottle and threw the empty on the passenger's side; the last few drops, like Chinese water torture, dripped with excruciating slowness onto the seat.

The driver unbuckled his seat belt, checked himself in the rearview mirror, took a deep breath, and floored it. There followed a blood-chilling scrunch of metal as the front of the pickup crumpled upon impact with Marty's bumper. The Tirabi car lurched forward, condensing further like one last push on the accordion. The pickup's air bag sprang to life, engulfing the driver who passed out. The right taillight of the pickup blinked inexorably like a heartbeat keeping time.

CHAPTER 4

Aunt Stella busied herself at the stove making hot tea for Kori and Avery, warm chocolate milk for Gil. She waddled back and forth between the stove, the microwave and the refrigerator, pulling out milk, mugs, tea bags, and honey, and checking the clock on the microwave every thirty seconds.

"Can we call Mom and Dad again?" Kori asked.

"You already left three messages, honey." She checked the microwave clock again.

"Well, can we have them paged?" Avery asked, walking into the kitchen.

"Anything else burning?" Kori asked.

"Nope. Just the porch still," Avery said.

"You don't want your parents getting into an accident on I-95 because they're racing home to you kids, do you? You're safe here. The firemen will take care of the rest." Aunt Stella set a plate of chocolate chip cookies in the middle of the table. Gil reached over and grabbed three at once.

Kori smacked his hand. "One at a time."

"Oh, for God's sake, the boy's starving. Let me fix you a sandwich, Gilly." Aunt Stella shuffled back to the refrigerator and pulled out imported ham, Swiss and provolone cheeses, prosciutto, salami, sliced thin, a hunk of asiago and a giant loaf of bread.

Avery left the room; Kori's gaze followed him. She bit her nails.

Aunt Stella cut chunks of bread with vigor, a woman in need of a purpose. She filled a basket, set the meat and cheeses on a plate, and put it all on the table, checking the kitchen clock this time, and then the clock on the stove. She knew time hadn't stopped, not yet, but she could feel its relentless grind in that direction and the thought made her throat thick. If time were about to stop, she needed to be the first to know.

Stella sniffed the air: "I smell smoke."

Kori peered around the doorjamb and across the living room to where Avery stood on the front stoop, watching the fire. The open door allowed the smoky night air full ingress.

Like a giant luxury liner, Aunt Stella turned toward the smell. "Anything else?" she asked Avery.

"Still just the porch." Avery shut the door and returned to the kitchen.

Gil reached for the bread and Aunt Stella, happy for something to do, intercepted him and made him a sandwich. He devoured it.

"Who else is hungry?" Stella asked. Avery shook his head and Kori grimaced.

Aunt Stella sighed, letting her gaze slide across the hands of the kitchen clock. Barely two minutes had passed. She held out the plate to Avery who took a piece of cheese and placed it on the napkin in front of him. Aunt Stella rolled her eyes and set the plate in front of Kori who preferred her fingernails. Aunt Stella turned her gaze to meet the stove clock behind her.

"Well, children, the party's got to be winding down by now. Let's give your parents another holler, eh?" She padded to the phone.

"Nice slippers." Gil smiled at Aunt Stella's feet. Giant Mickey Mouse heads sat atop each one.

"I'll get you some next time I go to Disney World, Gilly," she said. She handed the phone to Avery.

"Why doesn't Kori call?" Avery said.

"Because you're the man of the house," Aunt Stella replied. "At least until Robbie gets home."

After a few rings, Ruth's voice mail picked up. "Hey, Mom. It's Avery again. Call us as soon as you get this message. We're still at Aunt Stella's." Avery hung up the phone and handed it back to Aunt Stella.

Gil took a piece of bread and made another sandwich while Stella poured him more milk. "Where the heck are they? It's almost midnight," Avery asked.

"Ah," Stella said, "now the shoe's on the other foot."

"I'm not the curfew abuser." Avery folded his arms and raised his eyebrows at Kori whose response was drowned by Robbie's entrance into the house.

"What the hell happened over there?" he barked. A wave of relief passed palpably through the room as if Robbie's mere presence alleviated all woes. Even though he was younger than Kori by two years, he was in charge when Ruth and Marty were not around. Gil ran over and threw his arms around Robbie's muscular torso before scuttling back to his seat to finish eating. Everyone but Gil started talking at once. Robbie raised his hand; his eyes settled on Kori.

She recounted the story beginning with Gil's imperative need to leave the house, but broke down soon after. Robbie wrapped an arm around Kori's shoulder and looked at Avery who finished the story with the call to Ruth's cellphone.

"Have you talked to the police yet?" Robbie asked.

"Yes. They're coming back later for a statement," Aunt Stella said.

"I give it two stars," Gil said.

"Give what two stars?" Kori asked.

"The explosion."

"Gil, somebody just blew up the porch. The windows even shattered," Kori said.

"That's why I only give it two," Gil said, taking another bite of a cookie.

"I don't get it," Robbie said. "Why would someone bother with us?"

"I know," Gil said.

Avery shrugged while Kori gnawed at her pinky nail. Robbie waited for Gil to swallow.

"They were looking for the drawings."

"What drawings?"

"Dad's waste-to-oil machine."

"What would they want with that?" Robbie asked.

"What anybody would want," Avery said. "The patent."

"Oh c'mon," Robbie said. "How did anyone even know?"

Avery made a line of defense with a group of crumbs on the table. "You know all those 55-gallon drums out behind the barn? There's gas in a lot of them. I don't know if Dad realized how much he'd refined or if he just wanted to give me an opportunity to fatten up my bank account." Avery moved the crumbs, rearranging the line formation like a general strategizing his next move. "I sold some to Cooper's Gas Station."

"How much?" Robbie asked.

"Four or five fifty-five gallon drums a week for the last couple months," Avery said.

Robbie burst out laughing. "So they blew up the porch?"

Avery looked hurt and concentrated on his crumb line. "Maybe he canceled his deliveries from Akanabi Oil and the company got pissed." Avery took a deep breath. "Maybe they found out that Marty Tirabi makes better gas then Akanabi, and he doesn't need to drill a hole to get it."

"Avery, think about it. Four fifty-five gallon drums a week is two hundred and twenty gallons. My tank holds twenty gallons and I fill it once a week. At that rate, you were giving Mr. Cooper enough to supply a whopping total of eleven people with gas for a week." Robbie raised his eyebrows; Avery blushed a fiery red.

"Look. It's not like Dad didn't tell everyone who was even remotely interested all about the TDU," Robbie said. "There was that magazine article in *Omni* a few years ago. So chill out. It wasn't your fault."

Gil sat back and placed his arms over his now-protruding belly. A big burp escaped and Gil giggled, covering his mouth. Avery laughed. Aunt Stella grimaced.

"Excuse me," Gil said.

"It was pretty damn stupid though," Robbie said.

Avery's smile faded and he returned to rearranging crumbs. Robbie squeezed his shoulder and Avery smiled half-heartedly.

Robbie sighed. "So how do we tell Dad the drawings are gone?"

"We don't," Gil said, rose and walked out the kitchen door.

"Where's he going?" Kori asked.

A minute later Gil returned with the cylinder tucked under his arm.

"The drawings?" Gil nodded and Avery hugged him so hard his face turned crimson

"Excellent!" Robbie said, spinning Gil around. "High five me." Gil smacked Robbie's hand.

"Try Mom and Dad again," Robbie said. Kori obliged, but got Ruth's voice mail.

Robbie bit the inside of his lip in concentration. "They went downtown so they'll be coming back I-95. They may have broken down. I'm going to go look for them," Robbie said with an authority belying his twenty-two years.

"I'm coming with you," Avery said.

"Me, too," Gil said.

"You stay here, Gilly." Aunt Stella squeezed his hand. Gil looked at her with imploring eyes, but her face was resolute.

"No. I have to go by myself."

"I'm the one who started this," Avery said.

Robbie shook his head. "You gotta stay here to talk to the police when they call."

"Kori can do that."

"Avery. Please." Robbie tilted his head in Kori's direction where an ash-white Kori sat, leaning against the table, hugging herself tightly.

Avery looked at Kori and sighed. "All right."

Robbie squeezed Avery's shoulder and Kori's hand and kissed Gil on top of the head. He looked at Aunt Stella who checked her watch and nodded assent.

"C'mon, kids. Help me make up the beds. You can sleep here tonight," Aunt Stella said, standing up. "I'll speak to your parents when they call."

"Thanks, Aunt Stella." Robbie said.

She touched his cheek. "Be careful, eh?"

"I'll be back with Mom and Dad before you guys are finished with the beds. After a chorus of "goodbye" and "be careful," Robbie left, the air thick and strange and still in his absence.

"Thank God you were home tonight," Kori said, hugging Aunt Stella

"Ditto," Avery said, kissing her on the cheek before heading upstairs. Gil fell in one step behind Aunt Stella, his pockets stuffed with cookies.

"Gilly, you just leave those cookies there until tomorrow," she said without turning around. "I don't want any crumbs in my beds."

Gil halted in mid-step, wide-eyed, contemplating. He stared after Aunt Stella for several seconds in disbelief, emptied his pockets onto the kitchen table and ran up the stairs after her.

Chapter 5

Dave Hartos scrambled eggs over a low flame, his broad shoulders leaning into the alchemical task as the runny, yellow liquid sizzled into tangible shape. Satisfied with its consistency, he scooped two heaping portions onto plates and flushed the pan with water, scaring the steam out of it.

Sonia found him at the sink, still holding the pan, staring out the window. She approached on silent feet, wrapping her arms around his waist, a difficult task given her considerable girth around the mid-section. Even at 5'8", her lips reached only as high as his shoulder blades so she planted a kiss between them. Hart set the pan down and scooped her up.

"Soon my fingers won't touch back here," Hart said and laughed.

Sonia smacked him and then sniffed the air. "Mmmmm. Lightly scrambled with cheese." She flopped down at the table and pulled the heaping plate to her. "Besides. You can't care that much if you're serving me portions like this." She spread blackberry preserves on toast and bit into it with unbridled delight.

Hart rubbed her belly, the size of a bowling ball, in slow, concentric circles then stopped.

"Felt that, did ya'?" She moved his hand to the side and he felt the baby kick again.

"Stronger every day." He kissed the spot and was rewarded with a light jab to the face.

"Ow."

"You're a glutton for punishment," she said, shoveling a forkful of egg into her mouth. "So. Tell me. What strange and dangerous task awaits you? Where's he sending you?" Sonia's eyes watered and she became preoccupied with her juice.

Hart took both her hands. "Iraq. I'm off to Iraq. It should only take two weeks, less if things go well, and then I swear I won't leave your side for a second until the baby's in college. Not even when you have to go to the bathroom." He managed a weak smile.

"David … I was kidding. I knew you were going away, but … " Her eyes turned hard. "Bicky's idea, I presume?"

"Desert life's tough on machinery. Some of the older rigs have problems. Akanabi volunteered to help get the equipment up to speed."

"Volunteered? Since when does a corporation *volunteer* to do anything?" She spat out the words, sat back and folded her hands over her belly. Dark circles hung beneath Sonia's hazel eyes, clutching weariness to them like a baby blanket.

Hart said, "What's good for Akanabi is good for the country. The money they make will help them build their infrastructure."

"You've been brainwashed," Sonia huffed. "Likely in response to toiling under the close tutelage of my father for the last seven years."

Hart stood and refilled his coffee. "I've got to assess the rigs and decide what needs to be torn down. I can't do it from here, Sonia. I have to see them for myself."

"And I guess Akanabi's going to do the rebuilding, right?" She wiped her mouth with a napkin, stood and stretched her back. "You know what I find so repugnant? The war had barely begun when American contractors were staking their claims to rebuilding the country. Don't you find that attitude a bit imperialistic? I mean, shouldn't the Iraqis make those kinds of decisions?"

"Sonia. Please. It's not that simple. If that country is ever going to get on its feet, it needs outside assistance."

"Assistance. Here's how we assisted. We bombed them into infancy in the first Gulf War, took out their power stations and hospitals, bombed the crap out of their water supply stations. They're barely crawling because of our *assistance*."

Hart leaned back and took a sip of his coffee. "Two weeks and I'll be back. I promise."

"Somebody else can go. Someone who's not about to have a baby." She wrapped a hand around her throat to stall the inner turmoil threatening to jump her voice.

"There is nobody else."

"David … "

"Sonia. No more."

He brushed the hair back from her long, angular face and kissed her open mouth. She pulled back to speak, but he shushed her as one does with an agitated child and kissed her again. She broke free and sat down.

"What happened to the idealist I fell in love with?" she asked.

"Baby, you fell in love with a chemical engineer. This is what we do."

"It's not all you do."

"No, but it makes way more money than most things," Hart said. "What if I couldn't afford to buy you the things you're used to? What then?"

"Money is not something we need, David. Time is." She took her plate to the counter, dumping the eggs in the sink.

"I don't want to leave you. I just don't have a choice."

"All we have are choices," she murmured, but the hostility was gone from her voice. She rinsed her plate and ran the garbage disposal. He came up behind her and massaged her neck, lightly at first, and then with more pressure. Sonia leaned against the sink and gave over to his healing hands, allowing her neck to fall to the side.

His nimble fingers poked and prodded, kneading the muscles, banishing the knots. "I promise when I get back we'll talk about this until you can't stand it anymore."

"You could be a healer, David, with hands like those. You don't have to work in oil."

Hart leaned into Sonia's hair and kissed her ear. "Friends?" She tried to say something but he had moved to her lower back, rubbing with great care. Sonia moaned.

"David, what if … "

"When I come back, we'll talk to your father. Maybe there's something else I can do. Who knows? I may have to give him another year, but we'll set a definite date. I promise." He turned her face to him and kissed her nose. "The best part of my job was always the field work, but I'm less inclined to go tearing around the world now," he said, moving his hands down to her belly.

Hart pulled Sonia over to a chair and sat her gently on his knees. She put her arm around his shoulders and rested her head in the crook of his neck, listening to the steady rhythm of his breathing. He smiled and whispered in her ear.

"I'm still the same idealist I was when you met me. I just got side-tracked is all."

CHAPTER 6

A week later, Sonia strolled into the lavish offices of Akanabi Oil.

"Hey, Jerry. How's it going?" She extended a gloved hand to Jerry who sat behind the security desk.

"Great, now." Jerry Dixon, Akanabi's head of security, had been hired by Sonia's father, Bicky Coleman, over thirty years ago because of Jerry's former life as a Navy Seal. Jerry's rugged good looks and natty dress didn't hurt either. He made an excellent first impression on anyone looking to retain Akanabi's services. Now that handsome and hard face bent to kiss Sonia's hand. "I miss you coming around."

"Jerry, I haven't been *coming around* for years."

"That's how long I've missed you."

Sonia blushed. In the early years, before Sonia's relationship with her father completely rutted out, Bicky would bring her into the office on Saturday mornings. But instead of spending some quality time with his daughter, Bicky would leave Sonia with Jerry to monitor hallways and closed circuit cameras, push phone buttons. They got on well — better than Sonia did with Bicky — as if their connection preceded their arrangement. As for Bicky, he felt his paternal duty had been fulfilled, simply because his daughter was in the same building. Sonia's mother, Kitty, had wanted Jerry to be Sonia's godfather, and Bicky found that in addition to being a sharpshooter, Jerry was an excellent babysitter.

Jerry released Sonia's hand, reached behind the counter and held his hand behind his back. Sonia smiled broadly, knowing full well what was coming next. She closed her eyes and opened her palm into which Jerry deposited a red lollipop. Sonia planted a kiss on his cheek.

"You never forget do you?" she asked.

"Can't say as I do, my dear." He wrapped an avuncular arm around her shoulder and steered her to the elevator. He looked at her belly and raised his eyebrows. "That husband of yours better get back PDQ."

"Talk to my father," she said, a catch in her voice.

"Aw, geez, I'm sorry. We'll get him back in time, don't you worry. Even if I have to fly him back myself."

"I wish Bicky were more like you," Sonia said. "You missed your calling, Jerry. You really should have had kids."

Jerry smiled, but it was a sad one, and Sonia thought she'd said something wrong.

He turned a key, calling a special elevator, and waited until it arrived. He held the door for Sonia as she got in, and turned the key in the lock once more.

"I'll call Phyllis and tell her you're on your way up," he said, all traces of melancholy gone. "Can't wait to see that little guy," he added with a huge smile. Sonia blew him a kiss as the elevator doors glided to a close.

Sonia got off the elevator at the 45th floor, the doors opening with an imperceptible swish into the reception area of Akanabi Oil's penthouse suite. As CEO, Bicky Coleman claimed the entire floor for himself, and what a floor it was, affording spectacular views over all of downtown Houston. Although Sonia despised her father's pretensions, she had to admit he had a great eye for stunning details. Bicky participated not only in the architectural reconstruction of the building, but handpicked the decor, right down to the ancient Chinese vases displayed prominently in niches and tastefully interspersed among the ceiling-to-floor French tapestries. Walking these halls gave Sonia the distinct impression that she was inside a well-endowed museum.

Phyllis was away from her desk so Sonia walked down the hall and let herself into Bicky's prodigious office. Beyond the floor-to-ceiling windows, the city glittered and glistened, all glass and mirrors, in a blaze of afternoon sun. Houston's story as an American city began in the early part of the 19th century after the founding fathers wrested control from Mexico. Although the city predated the discovery of oil, the town flourished during the boom and bust days of early oil when fortunes were made and lost on the turn of a drill bit. The first inhabitants of old Houston, the ones who built the city, combined the rugged individualism of the West with the genteel manners of the South. Walking its streets, you could almost feel the pride and bravado mixed with courtesy and goodwill that brought the city to life. But Sonia thought the newer part of Houston, where Akanabi's offices were located, lacked the charm and distinction of old Houston with its ethnic diversity, grand architecture and historic flare.

Sonia busied herself with Bicky's vintage book collection, his rare and exquisite gems, many of which had historical significance beyond anything that Bicky Coleman would ever do with his life. Maybe it was Bicky's subconscious desire to tame his own demons, but for whatever reason, his taste leaned toward the psychological and philosophical, original printings of Freud, Jung, and Nietzsche. He didn't pass up an opportunity when it was offered. It was the acquisition that drove him, the thrill of the chase. Once his, he placed the item neatly on the shelf, or under glass, where he could watch without interacting

Bicky had placed Sonia on a shelf soon after she was born, and she'd spent the better part of childhood trying to get down. By thirteen, she'd given up, and now, at thirty, she was fully resigned: The man whose offices she perused with more than a hint of disdain was too artificial to be her father. Their vibrations were at opposite ends of the light spectrum, and Sonia felt she had nothing in common with him other than the X chromosome he'd provided for her DNA to replicate itself.

Sonia sat down behind Bicky's desk and leaned into the plush leather. Nine months of pregnancy had taken a toll on her arches. She stretched her back, cat-like, and yawned as the massive grandfather clock in the corner chimed five o'clock. Exhaustion snuck up behind her and laid its head on her shoulder so she laid her own head down and would have fallen asleep, but for a piece of mail sticking into the soft, fleshy underside of her arm. She dug it out for inspection.

It was a thick brown envelope marked "Urgent and Confidential. To Be Opened By Addressee Only." The seal had already been broken and Sonia helped herself to a peek. Inside was a report with curled corners, folded pages, and a big coffee stain on the cover, all indicating heavy use. The title looked simple, and boring, enough: "World Oil Report."

Sonia skimmed the pages, looking for something of interest before settling on a page with a folded corner.

CHAPTER 3. STATE OF THE WORLD'S OIL RESERVES.

The world's oil reserves peaked in the mid-1970s. All previously undiscovered oil reserves have been marked and estimated. At the current rate of usage and barring the discovery of oil reserves on other planets, the earth's oil reserves will be depleted by the year 2025.

Sonia put the report down and stared at the cover. *Could this be true?* Her grandfather's empire, her father's world, would soon collapse? *Would they be wiped out?* Her hands shook, her breath grew shallow and she could hear her heart pumping in her ears.

"I don't care how you do it. I just want it done." Bicky's anger was distinct even through a closed door. "And don't come back to me until it's finished. Understand?"

Sonia heard a muffled assent and, without even thinking, shoved the report in her brown leather backpack, knocking a cup of water across the desk in the process.

"Damn." She grabbed a bunch of tissues and was mopping up when Bicky burst through the door.

Sonia smiled.

"Sorry. I hope it doesn't leave a mark."

Bicky stared at his daughter as if he couldn't place the face before bewilderment gave way to annoyance.

Sonia jumped to her feet. "Oh, sorry, I ... was tired. Your seat is the most comfortable." She stood, draped her backpack over her shoulder, and exchanged places with her father.

"How long have you been here?" he barked, and with a gentle touch that belied his tone, moved his mother's picture out of the water's trajectory and onto the windowsill.

"I don't know. Half an hour," Sonia said, clearing her throat. "I see you got a new Dickinson." She nodded in the direction of Bicky's rare book collection. "Nice catch."

"It came at quite a price, let me tell you." He smiled and Sonia regained her composure, relieved to be on neutral territory. Bicky took his seat behind the desk, a reigning monarch, and pressed the intercom.

"Phyllis, some paper towels please." Bicky released the intercom before Phyllis could answer, snapped open the humidor and pulled out a cigar. Sonia cleared her throat. He shut it with a muttered apology.

"So. What can I do for you, Babe?" Bicky asked, adopting an air of lightheartedness. Sonia responded by shoving clammy hands into the wide pockets of her maternity dress and wrapped them around the baby.

"It's about David. I just wanted to know … when is he coming back?" She squared her shoulders as if getting out the words freed her to stand straighter, and thrust her belly forward, marking her question with an additional exclamation point. Bicky stared at her and she held his gaze. Had it always been this emotionally draining? She remembered so little of her father's presence from childhood that it couldn't have been the case.

"I already dispatched a guy. Your husband will be on the next plane home."

"Really? Oh, Dad thanks!" She ran around the desk and threw her arms around Bicky's neck, a move instigated by relief and unbridled hormones. Bicky shifted uncomfortably in his seat and looked to Sonia like he might run.

"Sorry," Sonia said, stepping back.

"That's all right," Bicky said. He rubbed his neck gingerly, feeling for the welt.

Sonia hadn't touched her father in so long, hadn't wanted or needed to, and so had forgotten his adversity toward the simple act of it. She rarely saw her parents touch, much less kiss. It didn't bother her, but under the circumstances, she never understood how she'd been conceived. She slumped in the closest armchair with relief. "So what changed your mind?"

Bicky waved his hand "Your mother … she didn't want you to be upset."

So there it was. Kitty had trumped him. Sonia tried to summon some love for the stranger that sat across the desk sorting wet mail. Feeling none flow, she stood to leave.

"Thanks," she said, grateful no matter what the circumstances that forced her father's hand. Bicky dismissed the gesture with another wave and smiled, a cross between an impatient grin and a grimace. The phone buzzed and relief washed Bicky's face clean.

"Where are the paper towels?" he barked into the intercom.

"Try the bottom drawer of your desk," Phyllis responded, her tone syrupy sweet.

Sonia bit her lower lip. Phyllis had put up with Bicky since he came to Akanabi over thirty years ago and showed no signs of relenting. For reasons Sonia couldn't decipher, Bicky attracted and held people in his life, quality people, like flies to the spider's web.

The phone buzzed and Bicky checked the caller ID. "I gotta take this," he said. He tried another unsuccessful smile as Sonia turned to go.

"Your mother wants you to come to dinner tonight," Bicky said, reaching for the receiver. Sonia waited for any additional proclamations, but Bicky grunted and jerked his head toward the door. Sonia took this as her unmistakable cue to leave.

Sonia leaned against the smooth, polished walnut, fingering the clasp on her backpack and listening to Bicky's imperial tone through the lavish doors. She reached in and touched the edges of the envelope. She could drop it on Phyllis's desk, no questions, and walk out. *Or …*

"Hey there, girly. Where've you been?"

Sonia stumbled and Phyllis was at her side in an instant, directing her to a chair.

"I remember these days," Phyllis said. "All top heavy and off-balance. Like one of those Weeble-Wobble toys. You remember them?"

"Weebles wobble, but they don't fall down." Sonia sang.

"Isn't it amazing how you can forget your kid's birthday, but remember ads from forty years ago," Phyllis said. Phyllis was a lithe figure, still beautiful well into her sixtieth year, all grace and high cheekbones. She pushed an ottoman in front of Sonia's chair.

"Feet up," Phyllis said with the authority of a drill sergeant. She smiled and squeezed Sonia's shoulder. Bicky's personal line rang and Phyllis put him on speakerphone.

"Where the hell's my report?"

"Try looking on your desk."

Bicky ended the conversation with a dial tone. Phyllis rolled her eyes at Sonia.

"Your father," Phyllis started, "is not big on patience."

"Or much anything else unless there are dollar signs attached. Really, Phyllis. How do you stand it? You couldn't pay me enough."

"Oh, he's not so bad. He was so green when I first got him, all eager to prove himself to your grandfather. Who knew he'd grow to be the pompous ass he is today? I think a part of him died with your grandmother and it's been rotting inside him ever since. And between you and me, I feel a little sorry for him. He's just a kid who really misses his mother."

Sonia considered this a possible reason for Bicky's strong gravitational pull: memory and pity. Memory of what the man was, pity for who he'd become, and a desire to help him crawl out of the quagmire. Sonia had made the same mistake many times, thinking that her father would then include her as a relevant part of his life only to find that Bicky considered himself a single planetary solar system, a man who shared the cosmos with no one.

From the wet bar, Phyllis grabbed a bottle of chilled Evian and handed it to Sonia.

"When my son was born, my husband was in Vietnam. I thought I would lose my mind. I got through it, though. You always do." She smiled and stroked Sonia's hair. "We're tougher than they are. That's why we bear the babies." Phyllis strode across the room, grabbed something off her desk and handed it to Sonia.

"I printed out a copy of his itinerary. He'll be in about the middle of the night so don't wait up," Phyllis admonished. She smiled, revealing a lovely set of pearly white teeth.

"Thanks, Phyllis," Sonia said, standing. She gave the older woman a hug. "I'll call you as soon as something happens," she said, a hand on either side of her belly. "They have these websites now, where you can log on and see the newborns just a couple days after they're born. You won't even have to go to the hospital."

"Are you kidding? Try keeping me away." She held the door for Sonia; the phone at her desk rang again.

"Bye love," Phyllis said, throwing a kiss to the air. Sonia watched as Phyllis bounded to her desk, before turning to get on the elevator.

⋏

When the elevator opened in the lobby, Jerry stood waiting as if summoned.

"How do you always know?" Sonia teased. Jerry tapped his chest and smiled.

"My heart beats a little more quickly when you're around," he said. "You let us know the minute our baby pokes its head into this world." He smiled, dazzling her.

Sonia kissed him on the cheek and turned to leave. "I will, Uncle Jerry."

He opened the door and watched as she walked away, their usual ritual. At the moment before Sonia rounded the corner, she turned and blew him a kiss as she'd done a million times before. His turned his cheek to catch it, reeling backwards, holding one hand on his heart and the other over the newly planted kiss so as not to let it slip away. She smiled and disappeared around the corner. The smile did not leave Jerry's face.

⋏

Dave Hartos knelt inside the base of an oil rig, fiddling with a stalled pump. He whacked his wrench against the pipe and the wrench clanged to the ground. Even in the bowels of the derrick the sand writhed and swirled, infesting the machinery. With a heavy sigh, he lifted himself out of the hole and climbed the metal rungs of the ladder back up to ground level.

An open-air jeep approached, a dust bowl swirling behind. Andrew Mahajan, second-in-command to Hart, and his best friend, got out grinning.

"Good news. You've been sprung." Mahajan handed Hart a telegram. "Go home and help your wife pop that baby out." Mahajan clapped Hart on the back with one hand and handed him a box of Cuban cigars with the other. "For when the baby comes."

"Hey, I don't need to get arrested on the way home."

"Customs won't bother if you have less than a box," said Mahajan. He opened the lid and removed two cigars, clipping the ends. "Now there's less than a box." Mahajan produced a lighter from his pocket, but desert winds foiled attempts to light it. He shrugged and pulled a bottle of Jamieson and two whiskey glasses from the jeep.

"Let's celebrate." He wiped his brow with a bandana and motioned toward the trailer.

"Isn't it bad luck to toast before the baby's born?" Hart asked.

Mahajan shook his head. "Only thing bad is not taking advantage of an opportunity when it bites you in the ass. C'mon. A driver's coming for you soon."

Hart grabbed the glasses out of Mahajan's hand. "You gonna be all right here?"

"Right as rain, buddy. Right as rain." Mahajan clapped Hart on the back and pushed him toward the trailer.

CHAPTER 7

Bicky rustled through stacks of reports, shoving things around his desk in haphazard fashion. He picked up the receiver and buzzed Phyllis.

"I still can't find the yearly report," he snapped.

"Did you look on your desk?" she asked

Bicky snorted. "Would you come here and lay hands on it please?"

He was still holding the receiver when Phyllis materialized. He pushed his chair back, making room while the flurry of Phyllis's hands restored order to his finite universe.

"It's not here," she said, straightening.

"I know that. I'm thinking that eventually you'll tell me what you did with it." Phyllis raised an eyebrow in response, the equivalent of a shove.

Bicky rolled back an imperceptible inch. "Well, it didn't walk out of here by itself," he mumbled.

Phyllis shot him another arrow, which he dodged by walking to the window.

"Did you stick it in your briefcase?"

Bicky's briefcase sat perched on the mocha leather couch, the two leathers barely distinguishable. Bicky watched Phyllis peripherally, pretending to gaze out the window as she rifled through the bag.

"If I had put it in my briefcase, I wouldn't need you to look for it now, would I?" Bicky turned and met her gaze with the temerity of a spoiled child so Phyllis addressed him as one. "You can get your own report if you use that tone with me again."

He turned back to the window. From this angle, Phyllis's slate blue eyes would do less damage. She would only be able to bore holes into the back of his damn skull as opposed to his own two eyes. He watched her reflection in the window while she watched him watching her. Phyllis snorted and Bicky sighed, looking down at his feet, battle lost. After all these years, Phyllis Steinman had no trouble handling Bicky Coleman.

"Get me my calendar, at least," he half-pleaded.

Phyllis turned and walked out the door, returning moments later with the calendar.

"Who was here today?" Phyllis scanned the calendar entries.

"Every meeting you had today was either in the conference room or away from the office. Except for the one with Graighton which was here and which you were present for, I presume." She scanned the pages again nodding her head once to confirm.

"Graighton didn't take the report. He's got his own," Bicky barked. "Nobody else was in here?"

Phyllis scanned the pages again and stopped. Her face contorted slightly and she slammed the book, regaining her composure.

"What?" Bicky asked.

"Nothing."

Bicky opened the book and checked the entries. He sat mulling over the day's events then narrowed his eyes at her. "Sonia."

Phyllis shrugged.

"How long was she waiting?"

"I don't know. I was away from my desk when she got here."

"Well, find out."

"What does it matter? You know Sonia. She probably thought she'd use it as ammunition to get her husband out of Iraq."

"Her husband is out of Iraq."

"He's not home yet."

"I need that report."

"I'll order another one."

"You know I can't do that. Besides, they're $32,000 a copy."

"You just gave yourself a $4 million bonus. What'd you do? Spend it all?"

"Very funny, Phyllis."

"What would like me to do?"

He turned back from the window to face her. "I want you to get the first one back. It's dangerous for her to have it. You know that."

"Why? Because only a select few are privy? Besides, how do you know she has it?"

"Don't act stupid, Phyllis. It doesn't suit you. Sonia was the only one in here today."

"That doesn't prove anything. Maybe somebody off the street snuck in and grabbed it."

"Unless Jerry's lying dead in the lobby, I doubt it," he said. Phyllis sniggered.

Bicky sighed. "Just call her … please." He said the last word under his breath.

Phyllis shook her head.

"Forget it. This is between you and your daughter," she bristled, "and if she's got a bone to pick, it's with you, not me. She probably wants a little attention. Maybe she's trying to get you to make up for the last thirty years."

"Spare me the armchair psychology."

"It's tough to swallow so much crow." Phyllis patted his hand. "But you're a tough guy," she said, closing the door behind her. Bicky snorted as he watched her go.

CHAPTER 8

Sonia would have regretted accepting the dinner invitation had it not been for her mother's usual effervescence. They holed up in the kitchen chatting amiably about how the baby's imminent arrival would change things between Sonia and Hart, about the wisdom of getting a dog before mother and child were sleeping through the night, and, of all things, wine.

"Oh for God's sake, Sonia. The kid's not going to get snookered off half a glass. I drank one every night when I was pregnant with you. I even smoked an occasional cigarette, but they started making me sick so I quit."

"What were you thinking?" Sonia asked, horrified.

"Nobody told us anything then. I never got *loaded*. It helped me sleep."

"Yeah, but didn't you at least think it might not be good? For me, I mean."

"You're not a dimwit." Kitty squeezed Sonia's shoulder. "A half a glass of wine is not going to drop his I.Q. Not at this late date." Kitty shoved a Cabernet into her daughter's hand. Sonia set it down and rubbed her finger up and down the delicate stem of the glass.

"Actually, I'd rather have a Guinness." She laughed. "I've been craving one for weeks. You got any?"

"I don't drink the heathen brew," Kitty said, peeking in the oven. She donned double mitts and hauled the roasted pheasant out for closer inspection, her slender muscles obliging her. Kitty weighed a hundred and six pounds. The pheasant had more body fat. "Check with your father."

Sonia frowned. "Really, Mom. How have you done it all these years?"

"It's one of my greatest joys," Kitty replied.

"I'm not talking about cooking. I'm talking about living with him."

"You do it for the baby, Sonia. It's all for the babies."

Sonia raised her glass and spoke to her belly. "Here's to you, baby." She took a small sip, shuddered and poured the rest of the wine in the sink.

Kitty rolled her eyes and prodded the bird lightly with a fork. "Go tell your father dinner's ready," Kitty said.

Sonia sighed and left in search of an audience.

She blew into Bicky's sitting room like a sudden wind blasting through a broken window. A low fire crackled away in the hearth, emanating warmth that offset the chilly October air. The curtains had not yet been drawn and the last rays of the sun's daily trek left streaks across the western horizon like an early Picasso, all color and angle. The surreal light coming through the floor to ceiling windows cast odd shapes about the room. Sonia grabbed the armrest of Bicky's chair and sank to her knees, staring out at the beauty of it.

Bicky chose that exact moment to return to the sitting room and his seat. In the dusky light, Sonia's inert figure was practically invisible. Bicky tripped over his daughter and fell headlong, ending with a thud on the slate surrounding the hearth.

"Oh my God," Sonia said, and jumped up to turn on the light.

Bicky sat up, wincing, and rubbed at the red welt, already the size of a walnut, forming above his right eye. He glared at Sonia for a moment and grimaced.

"Oh, geez, Dad, I'm so sorry, I … " She snickered, then cleared her throat to cover the *faux pas* "Can I get you some ice or something?"

Bicky motioned with his head toward the wet bar.

Sonia fixed her father a Chivas and water and handed him the glass. "Mom said it's time for dinner," she said, and left.

Using a fire poker for balance, Bicky hoisted himself up, turned off the light, and sank into his armchair. His long slender fingers probed the delicate area. He could hear Sonia rummaging around in the kitchen, sense the lowered voices of mother and daughter, feel the muffled laughter like a poker in the ribs. Bicky was scowling at the fire when Sonia returned a minute later with a plastic bag full of ice wrapped in a dishtowel. He sniffed the towel before applying it to the walnut-sized lump on his forehead.

"What, you think I'd give you a used towel?" Sonia said, reading his mind.

Bicky smiled and busied himself with the ice. He didn't say thank you, just sat in silence, recalling the many non-lectures of Sonia's youth, willing the words to form on his tongue, yet unable to manage a syllable, for either a tongue-lashing or executive pardon. Before Sonia was born he had joked that if the baby were a girl he'd throw it in the river. His first glance at Sonia was rife with disappointment, and not just because of her sex. Something deeper was at work, something Bicky couldn't identify. His wife hoped that in time he'd turn a favorable eye toward his daughter, but infants do little else but sleep and eat and poop and cry, and Bicky, the mover and shaker, didn't have the time to invest in that kind of nonsense.

As a result, Kitty chose Sonia over him, pushing her sulking husband even farther away. Soon after Sonia's birth, their sex life began its precipitous decline, which probably would have been reversible, but for one unfortunate evening when Bicky came home, quite intoxicated, and when his advances were declined, slapped his wife in the face. Kitty never willingly slept in the same bed with her husband again. In Bicky's mind, the two events – the birth of his daughter and the loss of a willing, companionable wife -- were inextricably intertwined. Had he been able to see beyond the prominent, handsome nose on his face, he would have realized that in her inimitable southern style, Kitty was using sex, the only weapon she had in her arsenal at the time, in the hopes of bringing Bicky around to loving his daughter

But truth often remains hidden until one trips over it – literally – and even then it's hard to face. So Bicky sat, sullen and craggy, staring at the fire while Sonia waited patiently for a tirade that wasn't coming. What Bicky didn't know was that Sonia was in her early teens when she concluded that a parent who couldn't rouse sufficient anger to correct a guilty child was a parent who didn't give a damn.

Sonia cleared her throat and rose to go. "It's time for dinner. If you feel up to it."

The sun had set; the only light in the room came from the fireplace and Bicky could barely make out Sonia's shadowy figure walking away. "Where is it?"

"Where is what?" Sonia stopped but did not turn around.

"You know what," he hissed.

"No, I don't," she said coyly.

And so went their game, and only now did Bicky give her his undivided attention. "I'm not going to ask *why* you took it. Although I suspect it has something to do with gaining leverage to bring your husband home."

Bicky flicked on the lamp next to the armchair and stood to look at his daughter. Sonia's countenance and bearing were regal. She had her mother's high cheekbones and slender figure. Even pregnant, her face retained its sculptured look. From the back, he would have been hard pressed to say she carried the extra weight.

Sonia stood still, head facing Bicky, body facing the kitchen, refusing to turn to him

"I had hoped you and I could find some common ground," Bicky said, his business voice taking over. "With this baby and all, it might be the thing we need to get past our...differences." He strolled over, squeezed her shoulder and flashed a tight-lipped smile meant to convey warmth. She flinched. He lowered his hand and patted her arm. He felt her relax almost imperceptibly into the arms – arms which had withheld their support for most of her life – and then constrict again.

"I know you can't wash years away in an evening," he said. "But maybe we can start." Bicky's eyes were wide and sincere.

Sonia dropped her head to Bicky's shoulder as if she were trying it on for size. He stiffened, but didn't recoil. She reached up a hand to touch the knot on his forehead. He squeezed an eye shut, but allowed the invasion. She smiled, a small, tentative thing, and he squeezed her arm in response.

"Shall we dine?" he asked. Sonia nodded.

Without releasing his grip, Bicky steered his daughter into the dining room.

❁

Kitty's mother didn't know a spoon from a spatula and as a result, passed on none of the culinary arts to her daughter. Kitty's parents had a brutal and unforgiving marriage hidden behind congenial outward social appearances so Kitty believed her mother when she told her that in order to get and keep a man, Kitty needed to learn how to feed a man, her mother's own marriage as evidence of *not* feeding a man. She long ago declared the kitchen off limits to the myriad servants that kept the Coleman household running. After years of study with some of the best chefs in the world, Kitty had become a first-rate chef herself, although apparently it had no measurable effect on the quality of her marriage. Still, even Bicky couldn't deny that Kitty had perfected her art. Tonight the table was adorned by stuffed pheasant, prawns sautéed in avocado oil and Cajun seasonings, baby potatoes baked in olive oil, lemon and oregano, snap peas, lightly steamed, and a lovely arugula and mixed greens salad.

Kitty was palpably relieved to have Sonia's company at the dinner table and wondered, as she bit into a prawn, whether her daughter had fared any better in the marriage department. Sonia and Hart seemed to have a good marriage, but many who knew Kitty and Bicky would swear the same was true of them, since in public they demonstrated what appeared to be love for each other. Kitty was a vital woman, full of youthful efflorescence, not the sort that would be predisposed to abstinence, yet all the years without the companionship of her husband had taken their toll on her. She felt herself drying up on the inside, like ripe fruit left for days in the sun. Being distinctly Southern with all its foibles and genteel sensibilities, sex was something Kitty could not bring herself to talk about, not even with her intimates, which included Sonia. She was sure Bicky blamed the end of their sex life on Kitty's inability to forgive one unfortunate incident, but Kitty had seen worse growing up, and that wouldn't have kept her from Bicky's bed forever. Rather it was the lack of intimacy, or any kind of emotional connection with her husband that pushed her away. Bicky had shoved his emotions so far down they lived in his feet. The man would not recognize love if it threw up on him.

These days the Coleman's maintained separate bedrooms in opposite wings of the mansion. The move occurred sometime after Sonia shipped off to Columbia and Kitty *discovered* that Bicky had kept mistresses for the last twenty years, usually for periods of six to eighteen months, like a prison term for a misdemeanor. Sensing her own interests would be served by the revelation, Kitty made her knowledge public, the public constituting Bicky and Sonia. She chose her words carefully, paying particular attention to present tense syntax so neither one was ever really sure just how much Kitty knew and for how long she knew it.

To Bicky she simply said, "I know what you're up to. And I'm leaving. Don't try to stop me." Bicky said nothing as usual, but waited on Kitty's next move. Luckily, it was only across the foyer and down the hall.

Kitty knew that Bicky loved her to the extent he was capable. She also knew that had she even once confronted him, raised her voice, thrown a Chinese vase, shown some territorial frenzy over his nocturnal meanderings, Bicky would have ended his affairs. But recalling her mother's misery, Kitty decided the best course of action was to remain complacent and aloof and so she allowed Bicky's transgressions, knowing it was her indifference more than anything that branded Bicky's psyche and bound him to her. Kitty also knew that Bicky had come to interpret her attitude as one of intense loathing disguised by good Southern breeding, and on that point, he wasn't too far off the mark.

⅄

Dinner was delightful and Sonia couldn't remember a time when Bicky was so charming. He told jokes that left both Sonia and her mother clutching their sides in laughter. For a moment, they were a family and Sonia felt an affinity for her father that left her feeling both sated and bereft. After dinner, Bicky sat by the fire sipping cognac while Sonia stretched on the couch, her grandmother's handmade quilt, a swirling vortex of color pulled over her legs as a nascent, tentative bond was forming with her father.

"Tell me something about when you were young," Sonia said.

A handsome man in any light, the glow of the fire gave Bicky a swarthy, Roman look. Somber, he sipped the amber liquid and gazed at the crackling fire.

"I had two shirts, two pairs of pants, three pairs of socks and a pair of shoes. My mother was constantly mending things just to keep our wardrobe together. When your grandfather struck oil, we celebrated by buying a new outfit."

"Well, eventually he bought you more clothes."

"Oh yeah, but that wasn't until later. After Mason died and it was just me and him, he realized that life really wasn't waiting for anybody." Bicky's voice cracked. Sonia studied him, intrigued by the uncharacteristic show of emotion.

"He was a tight-assed bastard, your grandfather. Never spent a dime. Not on us, anyway. Why do you think you have so much money?" He swirled the cognac around the tumbler.

"I don't remember him that way," Sonia said.

Bicky grunted and grew silent. The grandfather clock chimed ten times. Sonia yawned, stood and folded the quilt. "Thanks for a great night, Dad." She smiled at her father, but Bicky said nothing. "I'm going to say goodbye to Mom," she said, and left the room.

Bicky walked Sonia out to her car while Kitty stood in the archway. Sonia blew her mother a kiss and Kitty disappeared inside.

Bicky leaned in and pecked her on the cheek, flashing his perfect teeth, a smile few could resist. He patted her arm and rested it there. "Don't forget to bring me the report tomorrow."

"Ah, the report. I hadn't planned on coming to town tomorrow. How about I mail it?"

"No!" Bicky's voice was gruff and agitated. "You're putting yourself at risk."

"Dad, I'm not even going to be home."

"Let me tell you, if word gets out that you have a copy of that report...."

"Is it me or you that would be in trouble?" she asked, finishing his sentence.

Bicky put his hands on the car door and straightened up. "You probably didn't read it so you don't understand how damaging it is."

"I read it. And I understand. That report gets out and it could mark the beginning of World War III. That's why you sent David to the Middle East. You want your best people surveying the world's largest remaining oil reservoirs."

Bicky's face turned the color of blanched almonds; he squeezed the doorframe. "Sonia...do not get messed up in this."

"I'm already messed up in it."

Bicky looked back at the house where Kitty had turned on the lights in her suite. His eyes wandered to his *side* of the house, dark and uninviting. "And he'll be back before the sun comes up," he said. "So let it go."

"I would if you'd let him stay more than ten minutes before sending him off again," she said. "Are you that desperate to have him secure your interests?"

"There are terrible people in this world, Sonia, and they do terrible things. Be happy your grandfather's money keeps you from having to deal with them on a daily basis."

"If you don't want me messed up with them, why would you allow David to be?"

"Hart's a man. And a damn good engineer." Bicky met Sonia's gaze at eye level. "Do you know what will happen when people realize we only have twenty or thirty years of oil reserves left? I mean, when they really stop to think about it? Pandemonium."

"Well if it's so precious, just charge more money and people will drive less."

"If we charged per barrel what oil was really worth, the average consumer couldn't afford a trip to the grocery store. Our whole economy is premised on the consumption of cheap fossil fuel, Sonia. Every aspect. It's not just about driving your car to the movies." He paused to let his words sink in. "Most of our products are trucked across the country. Milk and butter are cheap because oil is cheap. But higher food prices are only the beginning. The majority of our products are made from plastic, not steel, and you need oil to make it. It's not just about Baggies and milk jugs. It's about camera bodies and television sets and lawn furniture and car parts. It's actually a waste to burn oil as gas. It's too valuable. Liquid gold."

"Don't you think you're getting a little carried away?" she asked.

"I'm serious." The lawn sprinkler hissed to life and Sonia jumped.

"I'm not trying to scare you, dear," he said. "I'm trying to enlighten you." He looked from her to Kitty's window and said, half to himself: "So much like your mother." His eyes softened and Sonia thought she detected a trace of fear in his unshakable demeanor.

"If you wanted to avoid it, and by you I mean the energy industry, you could. You'd be pouring money into R&D, developing a cheap way to access solar power, or hydroelectric power, or any of the myriad *powers* that show promise. But you don't. Why? Because you can't make enough money. Once the technology's there you can't harness it for yourself and, God forbid, you don't want people to be self-sufficient. Then they wouldn't need you."

Bicky raised the corner of his mouth in a mocking smile. "Touché, my dear," he said. "Still that doesn't make your knowledge any less dangerous. And if not the danger, think of the resulting plight of all those poor out-of-work oil company employees."

Sonia laughed in spite of herself, but she was not fooled. Under Bicky's shiny veneer there lurked the soul of a survivor, one who made no pretense of not taking anyone with him.

"There's got to be a way for the rich to keep on being rich and the rest of the planet to be comfortable. Not everyone longs for world domination, you know," Sonia said.

Bicky watched the sprinkler throw tiny droplets in wide, circular arcs. The streetlight lent his face a preternatural glow. He shook his head and sighed, a deep heaving sigh to indicate that nothing that came before and certainly nothing that will ever come after carried quite as much weight.

"If I could do something, I would. But it's beyond my frail powers," Bicky said.

Sonia laughed and started the car. "Frail is not an adjective I'd use to describe you."

Bicky stood motionless, arms locked on the door, looking like an old, weary man. His fuzzy gaze fell on Sonia's belly and after a few moments the spark returned.

"Bring me the report in the morning, please. And don't say anything to your husband. A little knowledge can be life-threatening in certain situations. He doesn't need that kind of information coloring his field work." Bicky's vacant stare signaled the end of the conversation.

Sonia nodded. A tight, pinched smile graced Bicky's lips. He banged twice on the car door, dismissing her. Sonia pulled out of the driveway and didn't look back.

Chapter 9

Hart arrived home sometime before dawn. He quickly surveyed the exterior before unlocking the door. Sometime in her seventh month, Sonia developed bionic hearing; the tiniest creak of the floor boards and she bolted up in bed. Not wishing to disturb her, Hart tiptoed across the threshold and placed his bags at the foot of the stairs. As he stood, light flooded the living room.

Sonia ran down the stairs and locked him in a bear hug. "I missed you," she cooed, kissing his face. She grabbed a suitcase in each hand where they dangled like misplaced appendages.

"Sonia! Put 'em down," he commanded.

Sonia dropped the suitcases to the floor with a thud and stared wide-eyed at her husband.

"What? They were too heavy." Hart said.

"Contraction," she replied. She wagged a finger to a ready-packed bag in the corner. Hart leapfrogged over his own felled luggage as Sonia headed up the stairs.

"You call the doctor while I put some clothes on. I'll meet you in the car." She leaned over the railing and blew him a kiss before ascending.

⋏

Four hours later, they were back home, the baby still cozy and afloat in Sonia's belly.

"What are you going to do now?" Sonia poutedPlease don't go into the office."

Hart smiled and kissed her cheek. "I'm going to take you out for breakfast and a walk along the creek. Then we're going to take a little nap, you and I, because we're both way tired, and then I'm going to do right by you." He squeezed her hand, intoning his meaning. "Then an early dinner and only after I've popped a movie in and propped you up in bed will I go to the office.

"After dinner?"

"I have to go see Bicky today. He wants a debriefing. In person. But my person is going somewhere else right now. So hey, what are we waiting for? Why don't we just go?" he said. "Move that stuff." He tossed her backpack to the back seat. A large manila envelope spilled out, addressed to Bicky marked *Personal and Confidential.*

"What's that?"

"Nothing."

"It doesn't look like nothing." Hart said.

Sonia released a mini-tornado of air. "I should have never ... " She stopped and eyeballed Hart, remembering Bicky's none-too-veiled warning. "It's Bicky's. I was gonna to take it to the post office today."

"Shall I take it to him tonight?"

Sonia hesitated. "Okay. I guess." The envelope was sealed. If Hart opened the letter, Bicky would know it. And David wasn't one to pry. She shoved the envelope into her backpack. "I'm going to go in and squirt. I'll be right out."

"You never can get yourself to say the word *pee,* can you? What are you going to tell our son? C'mon, baby. Time to squirt."

"What's wrong with that?" She waddled off while Hart watched her go, a gleam in his travel-weary eyes.

⅄

They window-shopped along the streets of Houston in a haze of love, and Hart admired his wife's reflection in every storefront they passed.

When Sonia's feet were so swollen they seemed to spill out of her shoes, she finally called the game. "How about a decaf cappuccino? There's a little outdoor café a couple doors up."

Hart carried a giggling Sonia the last three hundred feet and they sat down at a corner table with an umbrella for shade. The waiter materialized, took their order, disappeared. Hart placed Sonia's feet on his lap and began to massage them. She groaned with delight.

"So what's in the envelope?"

"Nothing."

"You are the worst liar."

Sonia blushed and tried to remove her feet from Hart's lap, but he held firm.

"Why do you have to be so nosy?"

"Just trying to keep you out of trouble, is all." He tweaked a baby toe.

"Ooowww."

"Spill."

Sonia appraised her husband with narrowed eyes, the broad shoulders and chiseled arms, the blue eyes and wavy brown hair, the air of confidence that surrounded him, the gentle look he reserved only for her. With him, she was safe. She drew a breath.

"I was at Dad's office. There was a report sitting on his desk written for that coalition of oil companies. So I looked through it."

"And … ?"

"And, I borrowed it. I wanted to read the rest."

"When was that?"

"Yesterday. Bicky told me if I didn't give it back I'd be in danger. And if I told you about it, you'd be in danger, too."

Hart guffawed. "He said danger, not trouble? And you believed him?"

"It says we don't have much oil left," Sonia said in a whisper.

A light flashed in Hart's eyes and he snickered.

"What?"

"It's only dangerous for the oil companies because it's overt admission. A smoking gun. If they didn't write the report themselves they could dismiss it as rubbish. But to be caught red-handed with the information and do nothing to rectify the problem. It's a time bomb, even to a largely self-regulated industry."

"But Dad really believed … "

"Well, he may be right. But more than that, I think he senses a possible corruption of his power base and he's trying to cover his tracks. He doesn't know that you won't do something stupid like give it to the newspaper. Not just the altruistic are passionate about causes, Sonia. I'm sure Hitler believed his own hype."

"Are you comparing Bicky to Hitler?"

"No. Bicky's got a better *schtick*. But there are one or two people that can still dwarf him in the power-broker department. And he doesn't want to piss any of them off. Sonia rubbed her head as if the whole conversation were giving her a headache.

"Why didn't you just give it back to him last night?"

"I don't know. I was thinking of using it to force his hand."

"To do what?"

"To get you a job closer to home."

Hart placed Sonia's feet on the floor, leaned over and kissed her. "Well, I am home. For good."

"What do you mean, for good?" Sonia asked.

"I mean, that was it. The last job for your Dad. Time to do something for us."

Hart smiled and massaged Sonia's fingers. Sonia stared at her husband for several moments before dropping her head back to smile at the sun.

⋏

Hart roused Sonia from a half-sleep as they pulled into the driveway sometime around 7 o'clock. He had plied her with all kinds of hot sauces at dinner because he'd heard they bring on contractions. Sonia had appeased him until her mouth couldn't stand anymore. Hart laid a hand on Sonia's belly, the only part of her not sleeping, when Sonia stirred.

"I think he's doing backstroke," he whispered. "C'mon. Let's get you both inside."

"Just take me with you. I'll stay in the car."

"And what? I go inside and drink cognac with your father? How's that going to look?"

"It's going to look like you can't stand to leave me." Sonia smiled and pouted at once. "Pleeeaaaase. Take me with you."

"No. You need to rest. We've been going all day."

"I'll sleep in the car. I promise."

"What if something happens? The baby's breech now, right? What if your water breaks?"

Sonia pulled out her cell phone and jiggled it in Hart's face. "First of all, your water breaks when it breaks, and second, I'll already be in the car if it does so you can get me to the hospital that much faster."

"All right, Miss Smart-Ass. Get your butt inside."

"What if the boogey man gets me?"

"Sonia, c'mon. The longer we do this, the longer it is until I'm lying in bed with you."

Sonia gripped the dashboard.

"Have it your way." He ran around to the passenger side and hoisted his wife out of the car. She flailed and Hart buckled under the weight, which got Sonia's attention. She wrapped her arms around his neck and pantomimed the part of the damsel in distress. He staggered into the house and after several false starts because of mutual bouts of laughter, managed to navigate the stairs without mishap. He ceremoniously draped her across the bed, covered her with a hand-woven quilt and handed her the remote.

"There's nothing I can say to make you change your mind?" she asked.

"I'll be home by nine. Promise."

"Enough of your promises, David Hartos. Call me later and let me know how late you're going to be." She smiled, tight-lipped and sad, and he brushed a lock of hair back from her eyes.

"Hey," he said. "What's wrong?"

"I missed your face."

"After tonight you can look at it as much as you want. All day in fact." The corner of her mouth suggested a smile. He stroked her belly gently in response, slowly moving his hand lower. Sonia moaned, rising to his touch.

"Based on field research conducted today, I'd have to say that it's not true what they say about pregnant women."

"At least not this pregnant woman," she replied, kissing him.

"Maybe I should just tell Bicky I'll see him tomorrow."

She grabbed his hand and kissed it. "I can wait. But hurry home." He kissed her hard and turned to go, hesitating at the door to look at her.

"What?"

"It only takes seven seconds to imprint an image in the mind forever. I'm fixing you in mine."

"Who told you that?" Sonia asked, smiling.

"My high school art teacher."

"Well get going, Rembrandt. I'll have use for you later." She tossed a pillow at his head. He dodged it and headed down the hall, whistling.

Hart stood at the base of the stairs in the foyer and called up. "I'll take the envelope for Bicky," he yelled. From their bedroom on the second floor came Sonia's muffled assent.

Sonia watched from their bedroom window as Hart's car pulled out of the driveway. When he was gone, she switched off the TV and reached in between the mattress and box spring, her hands coming to rest on a manila envelope. She pried the coffee-stained report free, made herself comfortable and began to read.

$$\curlywedge$$

As Hart drove down the street, he fingered the manila envelope marked *Personal and Confidential* resting on the briefcase next to him. He slowed the car to a halt at the red light and ran a hand over Sonia's tight, neat script before turning the package over to inspect the seal. He knew what was inside, but curiosity was getting the best of him. He tested the seal. It held fast.

There was no way Bicky wouldn't notice. He tossed it back on the seat. He already knew what damaging evidence the report contained, but it would be nice to see the bastard admit something for once. Hart drummed his fingers on the dash and wondered for about the billionth time why he was still in the oil business. Then the light changed.

ᐱ

Hart walked into the Union Club – an oxymoron since union workers were the last people that this particular club would ever admit – wearing a polo shirt and a pair of Dockers and carrying his worn but stylish leather brief-case. The maître d', a tall man, about fifty, with jet black hair and eyes as warm as the inside of a root cellar, scanned Hart's periphery, a distasteful job if his twitching mouth was any indication. He asked Hart between pinched lips whether he had a jacket, perhaps in the car.

Hart shook his head. "No jacket. Bicky Coleman, please." Hart scanned the room and spotted his father-in-law holding court at the far end of the room with four expertly tailored gentlemen. It was hard to tell one tanned face and Armani suit from the next. Hart sidestepped the maître d' who protested until he saw Mr. Coleman coming toward them.

"About time," Bicky said gripping Hart's hand in a firm, as opposed to bone crushing, hand shake. "Where the hell've you been?"

"I told you I was going to spend the day with … "

"Leave your damn cell phone on next time." The corners of Bicky's mouth quivered as he attempted a smile. Hart struggled not to laugh. Bicky wrapped what might be termed an affectionate arm around Hart's shoulder and led him to a pair of leather armchairs set in a private alcove. A waiter materialized and asked if the gentlemen would prefer a cocktail. Bicky ordered Chivas, Hart a Jamieson, both with rocks. Hart noticed that some of the thick, brocade curtains were closed. Apparently, the rooms could get pretty cozy. *Maybe I could take Sonia here sometime.*

"Did your wife give you a package for me?" Bicky asked nonchalantly.

Hart opened his briefcase as the waiter set two whiskeys before them. Bicky looked at his watch and took a sip. He swirled the ice in his glass, transfixed by the beverage.

"Is this a bad time?" Hart asked. Bicky took another drink, a swig this time.

"I'm scheduled to talk to Graighton at 7:30."

"Bill Graighton?" Hart asked. "About what?" Hart followed Bicky's glance at a shadowy figure sitting alone in an alcove across the room, talking on the phone.

Bicky snapped his fingers and held out his palm. Hart's remorse for Sonia's hasty actions was replaced by a protective annoyance. Hart pulled the report from his briefcase and slapped it into Bicky's outstretched hand. Bicky gazed at his daughter's handwriting before opening the envelope. He scanned the cover and shoved it back in the envelope. Hart thought he caught a grimace on Bicky's face, but the man couldn't smile to save his life, so he wasn't sure. Bicky nodded once, an almost imperceptible nod, and the figure in the alcove rose, closing the curtain.

Bicky turned to Hart. "I shouldn't be more than half an hour. Go have a drink. Talk. It's time you started making these people your own."

Hart was about to protest, but Bicky was already standing. Hart grabbed his drink and briefcase and did the same.

"Just leave the briefcase. I'll be back in half an hour."

Hart looked at his watch. The image of crawling in bed next to Sonia was already dimming, but if the cloak and dagger stuff had something to do with the report, he'd better oblige Bicky for Sonia's sake. Hart waited until Bicky entered the alcove, and headed to the bar.

CHAPTER 10

There were few people that gave Bicky Coleman pause, but William Graighton was one of them. A large man in all respects, Graighton was also the most powerful man in the oil industry and had the last word on a host of things that the oil companies did together. If OPEC could have their little coalition, so could the giants of U.S. oil, and William Graighton was the glue that held them all together. Bicky thought he had a slightly unorthodox way of dealing with things, but Akanabi had made a ton of money since Graighton took over, leaving Bicky to assume the man was prescient. Given the state of things, having a cocktail with Graighton this evening was downright unnerving.

"Have a seat," Graighton said.

Bicky slid into the plush velvet armchair. Two drinks were already on the table. Bicky raised his glass. The ice clanked against the sides in his shaking hands. He took a sip.

"Nervous?" Graighton asked. "You think I'd poison you?"

A corner of Bicky's mouth quirked up in response. He coughed.

Graighton laughed out loud and grabbed Bicky's arm, applying pressure with a firm grip. "Lighten up. It was a joke." Graighton flashed a half-smile and took a slow slip of his whiskey. When he spoke again, it sounded gravelly and harsh, like the bottom of the barrel.

"Where's your report?"

Bicky pushed it across the table. Graighton laid his hand on it.

"Where's the original?"

Bicky coughed. "What?"

Graighton turned a gimlet eye on Bicky.

"In a safe place." Bicky tried to hold Graighton's gaze and failed.

"So says you," Graighton said, and flashed Bicky a wry smile punctuated by the beep of his cell phone. Graighton looked at the number and waved Bicky away.

"Yeah," he said into the mouthpiece, all but dwarfed by his beefy hands.

Bicky tried to gauge the substance of the call, pretending to sip his drink. He watched Graighton's large hand, resting on the envelope. *How did he know? Were the Akanabi offices bugged? Surely, Graighton couldn't have guessed.* Graighton had his back to Bicky and was speaking in hushed tones. Despite their proximity, Bicky couldn't hear what Graighton was saying. *Well, to heck with him.*

He tapped Graighton on the arm and the big man stiffened.

"Bathroom," Bicky said. Graighton pushed the report back to him, waving him away as one would a gnat. Bicky turned and headed for the front door.

He stood on the front steps of the Union Club, waiting for his car. The valet arrived and held the door open.

"Are you sure you don't want me to call your driver, Sir?"

"Yes." The response was curt and conclusive. Bicky handed the valet three $100 dollar bills. "As far as you know, I never left."

The valet nodded and shut the door as Bicky pulled away.

It was only after Bicky was out of sight that the valet looked down at the bills in his hand. He smiled and pocketed the money, turning up his collar against the cool night air, then turned and walked back into the foyer. A second car crept out of the parking lot, following Bicky's car at a safe distance. The valet never saw the second car leave.

Forty-five minutes later, Bicky was at the bar, Chivas in hand, his full attention on Hart.

"So. Tell me," Bicky said. Despite the central air conditioning, Bicky pulled out a handkerchief and wiped at the beads of sweat forming on his brow.

"Well, it's hot. And sandy. No humidity though. Which just goes to prove that those people who say it's not the heat, it's the humidity, have never been to the desert."

"What else?" Bicky arched an eyebrow and waited.

"It's state of the art stuff. Really. Those guys didn't skimp when it came to installation. The problem is all the sand. The finest equipment in the world doesn't hold up with all that stuff blowing around. And it can get windy as hell there."

"Can we make money?"

"We can always make money. You just gotta keep somebody on the job is all. But a couple hundred thousand in salaries is nothing compared to what you can pull out of the ground there. It's like a geyser."

"Like our wells used to be before we pumped the crap out of them," Bicky said with a trace of melancholy. He sipped his whiskey and stared off into the alcove across the room for so long that Hart finally turned around to see what the hell his father-in-law was looking at: empty space.

"You all right?" Hart asked.

"Yeah. Sure," Bicky said.

Hart eyed his father-in-law with mild curiosity. "We can finish this tomorrow."

Bicky looked to his watch. "Nonsense. Too early. Have a drink with me, boy. Wash that road dirt away." He motioned to the waiter to bring two more whiskeys. Hart checked his own watch. The night was about to get long.

A crowd had gathered around them. Bicky was going strong, telling tales about the early days in the oil business. Hart had made several valiant attempts to part company, but each time Bicky pulled him back into the fold, talking, joking, making introductions. Right now, Hart was sitting at the center of Houston's power base and decided it was in his best interest to humor his father-in-law. If he were going to quit as he'd promised Sonia, he'd need a new job and the people sitting around this table listening to Bicky wax prolifically were the very people who employed ninety percent of Houston's employable.

By 10 o'clock, Hart was feeling the effects of the past two days of travel and two hours of alcohol consumption. He wanted nothing more than to lay his head on the nearby rosewood table. He decided to call Sonia while he could still speak coherently and let her know of his plans: a brief respite in one of the alcoves to clear the cobwebs in his head. He'd drive home later.

Hart rose on unsteady legs and left the room. Raucous laughter followed him out, seeping into the hallway's wide-open spaces only to be absorbed by the elegant, plush carpet and thick walnut walls. A series of dimly illuminated sconces lined the hallway; overstuffed leather armchairs dotted the landscape. Hart flopped down in one and rubbed his face with both hands to revive or steel himself, he wasn't sure. He checked his watch. If only he could keep his promises. He pulled out his cell phone and dialed home.

The phone rang six times before the answering machine picked up. Hart blathered into the phone, his words tumbling out in a self-effacing rush. "Hello? Sonia? Pick up. Are you there? Are you asleep? In the shower? I know it's past 9, and I'm not home yet. Will you pick up the phone, please? All right. Well, I'm still here and I probably shouldn't drive home. I'm really tired. I'm going to take a short nap in a corner somewhere and then I'll see if I can … "

The machine ended his little speech.

Hart banged the phone shut between his hands, "Damn." He punched in the numbers again. The phone picked up after three rings this time. "Sonia. Pick — Up — The — Phone." Hart waited several seconds before continuing: "Listen, Babe, don't be mad at me. I'll be home as soon as I can. I'll wake you up when I get there." Then he added as an afterthought: "Let's sleep in all morning tomorrow." He waited a few seconds before hanging up. "Damn."

He replaced the cell phone on his hip and stood with a slight waver. Though only seconds had passed, he checked his phone to make sure Sonia hadn't returned his call. The face glowed a phosphorescent green, but did little else. "No calls," he said to no one in particular and staggered to the men's room.

Hart washed his face and stared at his intoxicated reflection in the mirror, looking for hidden clues. A sudden, unsettling thought gripped him. What if Sonia's not asleep, but on her way to the hospital about to give birth to their baby? He didn't travel half way around the world only to have his baby born while he was across town. He willed his reflection to give him an answer. His normally handsome, exuberant face peered back at him, pale and haggard. His head throbbed like he was being riven: a meat cleaver to the head, a ragged split down the middle.

Hart loved his life and was reluctant to give up the part of it that made him feel so viable, so indispensable. How many people took the physical risks he took on a daily basis without even a second thought? His occupation, not the engineering part, even Sonia could live with that, but the field work – that's what set him apart from the average guy, and Hart liked it that way. Hell, there wasn't enough money in all of Akanabi Oil for Hart to take a desk job, toiling away under the leak and glow of florescent lighting. *Damn her need to control.* Hart had noted the similarities between Sonia and Bicky long before he married her. The attributes that lurked just below the surface of genteel Southern behavior had formed more distinctly with time. Some parts had broken off or withered away, while others were polished to a smooth, impenetrable finish that only water and a million or so years would be able to alter in any appreciable way. He married her because of, and in spite of, those attributes. That, and the fact that she was beautiful, and probably the most passionate woman he had ever met.

Hart himself was from a family of academics. His father was a professor of law at the University of Pennsylvania and his mother a professor of Shakespearean minutia, one of only a handful of scholars across the country with that particular nomenclature, which put her in high demand in academic circles. His mother was constantly being wooed by competing universities desirous of her services. Sabbaticals and six-week architectural tours of Europe were the norm when Hart was growing up. He'd read more literature by the age of fourteen than most people read in a lifetime. It was no surprise then that his parents weren't exactly thrilled when Hart went to work for Akanabi Oil. They had wanted him to choose a more scholarly occupation — as if chemical engineering was for slackers — something with a professorship attached. But his parents' reticence, or perhaps inertia, was so entrenched they couldn't arouse sufficient passion to convince him otherwise, so off to Columbia he went, which is where he met Sonia. To Hart, Sonia Coleman was the antithesis of his beige upbringing. Her colorful, passionate outbursts about everything from Goethe to guacamole were something Hart had never known on any intimate level, and something he soon found he couldn't live without.

He also found that passion and the need to dominate often went hand-in-hand. Thankfully, Sonia was more like her mother than her father, and lacking Bicky's mendacious spirit, her demands on life in general and Hart in specific were guileless, prompted by a need to be loved. He pandered to her whims when he could, and when not they fought an aggressive fracas that could reach levels of inanity for which Hart had no frame of reference. Despite their different temperaments, they hung together. The battle scars did not run all that deep, not yet, and were still easily erased by the night of intimacy that inevitably followed. Hart knew this kind of behavior would eventually catch up with them, but they were young and he believed in the power of love.

He shook his head to clear the sense of foreboding that had begun creeping into his grey matter, checked his cell phone again. Nothing. *What if something really was wrong?* He closed his eyes. Sonia knew where he was and could have had him paged if he didn't answer his cell phone.

What if she couldn't get to the phone? He shuddered involuntarily, threw the towel in the trashcan and sprinted out of the bathroom intent on coaxing Bicky into handing over his car and driver. He found Bicky sitting in the place he'd left him, gesticulating with abandon.

Hart begged the pardon of the gathered crowed and pulled Bicky over to the bar.

"What?"

"Hey, thanks for the madcap evening, but, I gotta go."

"Stay. Have another drink." Bicky's tone was sharp.

"Can't. It's Sonia. I can't get her on the phone and I'm just … worried. You know, with the baby and all." His voice cracked, uttering the last bit, and Hart felt a little foolish given the way Bicky glared at him. Bicky attempted a thin-lipped smile, his head bobbing up and down mechanically, the closest thing he could manage to empathy.

"So be it. Who am I to stand between a man and his wife."

"Do you think Manuel could run me home? I'm a little tired."

"Sure. Sure." Bicky snapped his fingers once and Manuel, his driver, materialized out of the shadows. Hart started, wondering how much you had to pay someone to stand within finger- snapping distance.

"Would you see to it that Mr. Hartos arrives home safely, Manuel? And come right back. I suspect I'll be ready to leave by then." Bicky patted Hart on the back and shook his hand. "Give my regards to my daughter," Bicky said. His voice was sad, but Hart's slushy brain didn't pick up on it. Instead, he nodded thanks and followed Manuel out the door.

Chapter 11

Manuel slid the Rolls Royce into the Hart's driveway on wheels silent as death. "Here you are, Mr. Hartos." Manuel got out and opened Hart's door. Hart stepped out and shook Manuel's hand.

"Thanks, Manuel. You're a lifesaver." Manuel returned the gesture but didn't make eye contact. Apparently, Bicky Coleman never shook Manuel's hand.

"Anytime, Mr. Hartos. Give Mrs. Hartos my best." The car retreated as quietly as it came. Tired and disheveled, Hart watched Manuel leave before heading up the walk.

The front door of the house was slightly ajar. Hart stared at it, then back over the expanse of lawn. His heartbeat quickened, yet his hands were steady as they opened the door in infinitesimal increments so as not to wake, or alert, anyone inside.

Hart saw no one in the foyer as the door swung wide and his eyes adjusted to the darkness. He peered into the silent study. A single ray from the streetlight illuminated it. Nothing appeared amiss either here or across the hall in the formal sitting room, useless space they never used. The couch cushions, plush, white and fluffed to capacity were offset by the deep red, hand-stitched Moroccan pillows, an attempt to convey reckless indulgence, except they were exactly where they always were. Sonia couldn't go to bed at night until the magazines were in the rack, the recycling in its bin, and all errant glassware stashed neatly in the dishwasher, as if a careful regulation of her home before bed would afford her an ordered night's sleep. When she couldn't sleep, she sorted Tupperware.

Hart continued down the hallway past the stairs. The kitchen was dark so he turned back to the stairs and crept slowly up to the landing. The effect was comical, and he suppressed the urge to laugh. *Just who in the hell am I sneaking up on?* Sonia was probably asleep, and Hart's overtired, overactive imagination was stressed beyond endurance. The light from their bedroom spilled into the far end of the hall. Hart inhaled deeply and let out a sigh of relief as he strode toward the bedroom door, the monotonous drone of the television growing louder with each step.

"Geez, you had me so worried," he said, crossing the threshold. The bed was empty, but a light from the bathroom escaped from under the door. "Why didn't you pick up the phone?" he shouted to the door, shutting the television and crossing the room. "Sonia?"

Hart turned the handle, pushed open the bathroom door and pulled back the bathtub curtain. He found the tub filled to capacity, the water cold. Small rivulets of water cascaded over the side. "Jesus." He reached in and shut the dripping faucet. "Sonia?" He turned and ran out of the bathroom, the fear spilling out of him.

"Sonia? If this is a game, it isn't funny," he said loudly. A growing terror gripped him as he tore down the hallway and hit the stairs, taking them two at a time. "Sonia!"

He rounded the steps at the bottom and ran back into each of the rooms he had already inspected, flipping on the lights and scanning their perimeters in urgent, yet methodical fashion, opening closet doors and checking behind furniture. The rooms were as empty in the light as they were in the dark.

"SONIA!" After a brief glance outside, Hart bounded down the hallway and into the kitchen. He reached for the light and tripped over something solid and inert. He half fell, half flew headlong across it. He crashed with a loud thump, his head hitting first, and lay sprawled on the floor.

"Dammit." He rubbed his head and sat up, looking back at the source of his precipitous fall. Sonia's prone body stretched in front of the kitchen door, as if in sleep. "Sonia?"

Hart scrambled over to her and put his fingers to her neck, checking for a pulse. He recoiled in horror as his fingers touched her cooling skin. He wavered, dizzy, gulping air to keep from passing out, then shook his head to regain his dwindling presence of mind. He tried CPR, a rotation of pumping the chest followed by mouth-to-mouth resuscitation, cringing each time his warm, twitching lips touched her cool, lifeless ones. She made no move to breathe on her own. His large rough hands, the same hands that stroked her gently during their afternoon lovemaking, now shook her gently at first, and then, as realization dawned, more violently.

"Sonia! Wake UP." Gripping her by the arms, he shook her again and again, her hair, wet and sticky, flipping back and forth around her face with each surge. Her neck jerked and bobbed like a ragdoll until Hart heard a snap that brought him round, and he abruptly stopped shaking her. He looked at her face, illuminated by the night light in the corner, her eyes closed, her mouth agape. He laid her back on the floor, smoothed the hair back from her face and kissed her cool lips tenderly.

"Sonia. Please. Wake up." His voice, contorted by fear and sorrow, seemed to hover above them, alien and disengaged. His fingers reached again for her soft, white neck. There was no pulse to enliven the hardening body.

As if he just remembered something, Hart's head jerked toward her belly and his eyes grew wide. In that moment, he tasted eternity. One second, and then a million passed as he held his breath and looked, not with the detachment of an ascended master, but the calm of one in a state of shock at what should have been his son. Sonia's splayed legs, her twisted arm, the displacement and slight concavity of her stomach as a result of the partial delivery, and then ...

Hart shuddered and a chill ran the length of his body. He was back, lucid and substantial, with full awareness of the surreal snapshot lying before him. He made no move to turn on the light, perhaps to hide her visage for a moment longer from the pain that would surely color her face and stay with him for a lifetime

He inhaled raggedly and gripped his hands together to stop their shaking. Sonia's robe, her only garment, hung loosely around her body. Unwilling to look on the child just yet, he steeled himself and began an examination of his wife. He inspected her body inch by inch looking for signs of injury, using his powers of analysis, long honed in the field, all the while trying to maintain a clinical, dispassionate attitude. If he felt for a moment that this was his wife, the woman whom hours before had been alive and vibrant in his arms, he would surely crumble on the spot.

Hart noted no bruising around her neck. No large hands had held her, squeezing the tender blood vessels beneath the surface until they were pinched and bruised and dying. He took another deep breath and ran his hands through her hair starting at the face and coming around to the back where his fingers intertwined with something sticky. His heart jumped and he raised her head to find a large welt and a small cut at the base of her skull, misleading because of the amount of blood in her hair and on the floor. Head injuries bled profusely, but this bump didn't cause her death.

He continued his foray downward, slowly, haltingly, stalling the inevitable. His fingers probed her belly, still plush, although somewhat less than round now that its occupant was only partially home. He steeled himself for the final examination, letting his glance fall between her legs. Tears welled in his eyes and he turned away, his body shaken by paroxysms of vomiting.

After several minutes, he stopped, wiped his mouth and looked again at the gruesome scene. Protruding from his wife's vagina, approximately half a foot into the world laid the legs and torso of his dead baby. Hart touched the curled, little legs, clammy with the blood of childbirth, and noted the fingers of one hand protruding from Sonia's body. He tried pulling the baby the rest of the way out, but he was stuck. Rigor mortis was already starting to set in for both mother and child. Even without the rigor mortis, Hart knew from the parenting classes he and Sonia had attended that breech births were the most difficult and delicate, and that the baby was likely not coming out without assistance.

Whether it was the need to know, to see his child at least once, or to set him free in the world even if only in death, Hart couldn't say for sure, but he began pulling and prodding and adjusting until he had managed to wedge out the chest. He continued wiggling the baby back and forth until he heard a crack. He reached in and pulled out a tiny arm, broken now from all the jostling. And still he pulled until he reached the neck and only the head remained inside.

The neck was wrapped tightly with the umbilical cord, three times around, leaving no more give in the line. Hart stood and walked calmly to the counter and pulled a large pair of scissors, used for cutting meat, out of the knife rack. He took a deep breath and began cutting the cord, still slightly warm to the touch, the tendency toward life the last thing to go. He worked one piece at a time until he'd cut it thrice, then pushed it away. He pulled again and this time the baby emerged with a pop, his lackluster, unblinking eyes fixed on his father.

Hart cradled the head, a halo of blood forming beneath it. He leaned over and kissed the tiny cheeks, touching the faintest line of the small eyebrow and ran his finger over the little nose and then the whole face, the color of a midnight blue sky. He closed the baby's eyes and laid him on his wife's belly. He stared at them for several minutes, tears spilling down his cheeks, anointing their bodies like holy water. He wiped his eyes and clawed at his face, the blood and ooze of the afterbirth smearing it, a warrior preparing for battle.

The scream started as a low moan, growing in intensity and fury, building and climbing toward the crescendo, a high-pitched wail that ended when Hart was out of breath and fallen and left with his only remaining partner, Grief, who lay prostrate on the floor alongside him, a pale separating his past and future.

CHAPTER 12

Robbie, Gil, Kori and Avery piled into the late Ruth Tirabi's Honda Odyssey. Thanks to Honda, Ruth hadn't needed to substitute comfort for clean air simply because she had a large family. The *Odyssey* had accommodated her need to transport a husband, four kids, their dog and their gadgets without sacrificing low emissions, and it still got pretty good gas mileage, two things American car manufacturers had, in the past, deigned unworthy of research funds.

"Where we going?" Kori asked, starting the engine.

"What about Jersey? We could go down to Cape May Point?" Avery said, fiddling with the lid of the cardboard that contained his parents' ashes. "This way they can look at the sun rising *and* setting all the time. I'm also thinking I should drive."

"Forget it. I'm driving," Kori said.

"Cut him a break once in a while, Kor, or are you too old to remember sixteen?" Robbie said with raised eyebrows. "Soon he won't need your permission. But you're still going to need a lawyer someday."

"If you let me drive today, I promise I won't charge you," Avery added.

"I'm thinking Chickies Rock overlooking the Susquehanna. Mom and Dad loved that spot," Kori said, ignoring both her brothers. "I'm also thinking you should both shut up and just be passengers."

"Awwww, you said shut up," Gil said in a singsong voice.

"Yeah, and who you gonna tell?" Kori said. Gil turned to the window. Robbie shot Kori a sad look; Avery squeezed Gil's thigh, but said nothing.

When Ruth and Marty died, Kori installed herself as the family matriarch despite her lack of any obvious mothering instincts. She hated to cook, couldn't stand the sight of blood, and her advice in no way resembled Ruth's thoughtful and incisive rumination. If Ruth's words were like creamy hot fudge over vanilla ice cream, Kori's were more like motor oil. There was a good flavor in there somewhere, but you'd be likely to throw up before you were finished.

The boys shouldered on even though most days they wanted to tell her to just shut up. But they held their tongues out of love and a sense that Kori's assumption of Ruth's role was the only thing keeping her from fracturing into a billion jagged shards. So the three brothers exchanged glances and suppressed smiles that Kori didn't notice.

"Whatever, Kori. Let's just go," Avery said. An excellent judge of character, a skill that would serve him well throughout his life, Avery was the first to discover that going head-to-head with his sister rarely worked.

"We'll let Gil decide," Robbie suggested. All three siblings turned to Gil for a decision.

"Rock," he said, and Kori peeled out of the driveway.

"Hey, let's get there in one piece, huh?"

"Hhmmmph," was all Kori said in response.

⅄

Almost two hours later, they pulled up to the precipice at Chickies Rock, a favored spot of the remote-controlled plane geeks, a steep three-hundred foot drop straight down a rocky ledge. Four pairs of eyes looked upon the banks of the mighty Susquehanna River.

Robbie pulled Gil's remote-controlled plane from the back hatch, and Gil plopped down on the ground to fiddle with it, adjusting the tail, the landing gear, and anything else that moved. ZiZi ran over to Gil, and after a cursory sniff, licked Gil's face several times.

"Down, Zi," Robbie said.

Gil made no move to push ZiZi away while he scrounged through his toolbox, huffing and shoving the tools around. Robbie reached in and pulled out a small wrench. Gil snatched it and adjusted a few screws on the plane.

Although the weather was balmy, the force of the wind whipping up the sides of the cliff made it feel ten degrees cooler. Like an insistent child, it swiped at Kori's hair as she stood, clutching the cardboard box to her chest. She dropped to her knees, squeezing her eyes shut. Moments later, she felt the gentle pressure of Robbie's hands as he placed his baseball cap on her head and tucked her hair up underneath. She leaned against his leg in gratitude.

In private, Kori had cried every day since her parents died, her body wracked and shuddering with silent tears, her shoulders aching with the weight of grief and new responsibilities, and the one thought that kept returning to her again and again — tinny and insistent — they were orphans.

Avery joined Kori on the precipice. Gil handed Robbie the small wrench and stood back to remotely test the landing gear, driving the plane forward and back on its makeshift runway.

"Box, please," Gil said to Robbie.

"He's ready," Robbie called over his shoulder.

Avery took the box from Kori and set it next to Gil's plane, pulling out the contents: two thick plastic bags filled with charcoal grey ash and small white bits of bone.

"How are you going to keep the bags in the plane?" Robbie asked.

Gil's imperturbable face grew wide-eyed, and he looked to Avery for help.

"Don't look at me, man. I just record the stuff," Avery said.

Gil rummaged through his toolbox, picking up each tool and throwing it down again. Robbie walked to the car and returned with a role of duct tape. He made a ring, sticky side out, and stuck it to the bottom of each bag before setting them in the plane.

"Good to go," Robbie said. Avery put a hand on each bag, blinking away the water that flooded his eyelids. Kori shuffled her feet and folded her hands across her chest.

"Anyone want to say anything?" Robbie asked. Kori covered her mouth; Avery shook his head from side to side.

"I'm no good with words," Robbie said, his voice cracking. "They know how we feel."

Gil stepped forward, cleared his throat as if about to deliver an edict. "Mom, Dad, we love you very much. It sucks that you're dead."

Avery giggled, breaking the tension. Gil leaned over, his face touching the bags containing the last mortal remains of Ruth and Marty Tirabi. He opened them and whispered something to each, then stood back and started the plane's engine. It lurched forward, bucking under the additional weight, bumping over small sticks, and gradually picking up speed as it approached the end of the makeshift runway and the cliff's edge.

"It doesn't have enough speed, Gil," Robbie said. "It's gonna crash."

Gil bopped his head slowly in time to a beat the rest of them were not privy to. At the exact moment when the plane would run out of ground, and gravity was about to have its way with it, Gil flipped a switch on the remote and a turbo thrust sent it hurtling out and up, clearing both rock and trees. It hung tenuously for several seconds, but Gil hit the turbo switch again and it took off like a shot arching up and away.

Gil sent the plane soaring over the cliffs of Chickies Rock, swooping and sliding, in, out and around, but not upside down, edging closer each time to the banks of the Susquehanna. Bits of the plane's contents were occasionally swept away by an errant gust of wind, but for the most part, Ruth and Marty's ashes remained solidly ensconced inside the cockpit of the little plane.

"Mom's going to get dizzy," Kori said. They watched the plane, now far across the river. Handfuls of ash spilled out, whirling like mini-tornadoes before drifting to earth.

"Last chance. Anybody want to say anything?" Robbie said. Avery's speech sounded more akin to a whisper:

"You are in our breath and in our bones. You are in the lights of our eyes, and the shapes of our hearts. As long as we live, we will think of you and remember, and we will never be a minute without you, for it's your blood that mingles with ours, your life, the life you've given us."

Gil sent the plane hundreds of feet into the air before bringing it back down to dive-bomb the river. At the last minute he pulled out and sent it up again, this time, though, instead of climbing straight, he performed a series of spirals that sent the plane up through a spinning vortex of ash. "Bye-bye, Mommy and Daddy," he said, as ashes arced out and down to the river. When the wind scattered the last of them, Gil brought the plane in for a landing.

Robbie dried his eyes and removed the bags from the cockpit, turning them inside out; they were empty.

"What do we do with the bags?" he asked.

"Burn 'em," Kori said.

"You can't burn them," Avery said. "They're plastic."

Robbie gathered everything up, plane, plastic, remote control and placed it all in the backseat of the minivan. He pulled out an insulated backpack and a blanket and walked to a small clearing. From the backpack he procured a small feast: bread, cheese, pepperoni, olives, grapes, mangos, peanut butter, yogurt, a bottle of wine and some dog treats for ZiZi. He whistled low and ZiZi charged over, tail wagging. Robbie handed Gil, now smashed up against his brother, clutching his arms around himself as if he were cold, a yogurt and a spoon.

"Nice insulation," Avery said. "Does it work?" Robbie nodded, and wrapped an arm around Gil who relaxed. He handed a knife to Avery to cut pieces of cheese and pulled plastic glasses out of the pack along with a bottle of spring water.

"Geez, how much' ya got in there?" Kori asked.

"Gil doesn't make anything half-ass, sister," Robbie said, accepting the half glass of water from Avery. He topped it off with a sip of wine and handed it to Gil.

"You're giving him wine?" Kori glared at Robbie, then Avery. "You've done this before, haven't you?"

Gil giggled and cast his eyes downward. He sniffed the glass several times then put it under ZiZi's nose and let her sniff. The dog shook her head to remove the scent from her nasal passages.

"We're going to miss the heck out you, Mom and Dad," Robbie said, holding up his glass. They clinked plastic. Robbie and Avery threw theirs back. Kori and Gil sipped theirs.

"That was nice, what you said earlier?" Kori said.

"Thanks. Well, thank Mom for all the poetry she made me read."

"I miss Daddy's laugh," Gil said. "And Mommy's smell. Like bread and flowers." Gil devoured a small sandwich of bread, cheese and pepperoni. The corner of Kori's mouth crooked up watching him eat.

"I miss Mom's cooking. And her stories. And Dad's stupid jokes. And his crazy inventions." Kori sipped her wine. "You don't suppose that those *people* might come back, do you, looking for some of Dad's other things?"

"I hope they do." Robbie said. He downed the rest of his glass, and Gil and Avery did the same. Kori bit her thumbnail and cast a worried glance out across the river.

CHAPTER 13

Several weeks later, after all porch repairs had been completed, Gil sat in a darkened room, ZiZi at his feet, watching *Mad Max, Beyond Thunder Dome*. He held a fistful of popcorn halfway to his mouth, eyes wide with fear and excitement as the music swelled and the crowds called for a great show-down. Kori came up from the basement wearing a pair of overalls doused in paint, several brushes sticking out of the top front pocket with the paint still on them.

Gil was so engrossed in the movie he didn't hear her enter. She surveyed the scene, strolled casually to the coffee table, picked up the remote and pressed the off button. The TV went blank and Gil went ballistic. With a grunt he threw a handful of popcorn at her face with more emotion than force.

"Turn it back ON!" he shouted, reaching for the remote. Taller by a head, Kori was able to withstand this onslaught with little effort. Gil clutched and yanked and tried to knock it from her hands. "KOREEEE. TURN IT ON!"

"No." She pulled away and walked to the window, throwing back the curtains. Sunlight blasted in, temporarily blinding him. He blinked in reptilian fashion until his eyes adjusted to the glare. Kori pulled back the rest of the curtains, flooding the room with light, and pointed to the door. On her signal, Gil's accomplice moved to the front door where he stood, head erect, tail wagging, more than ready to take the punishment with his master.

"It's 11 o'clock. In the morning. It's Saturday. Go OUTSIDE."

Gil took a deep breath and blew it out in a huff before turning toward the door.

"C'mon, Zi." He grabbed a baseball cap off the coat rack, carefully pushed his bangs to the side, and held the door open for Zizi, who barked once and bounded out into the brilliant sunlight. Gil stuck his tongue out at Kori and was gone. Kori watched from the window as they played fetch the stick. She smiled and headed back to the basement.

She was halfway down the stairs when she heard Gil's high-pitched wail.

"Zi, Zi, no! Come, Zi! Now!

She took the stairs two at a time and threw open the front door. Gil sat in the middle of the street with ZiZi's head on his lap. He rubbed her ears and spoke softly to the inert figure. A boy of about eighteen hovered in the background, his car door still open, radio blaring, looking on help-lessly. Kori sprinted across the wide front yard to the road and dropped to her knees.

Gil was rubbing one hand softly over ZiZi's body while the other hand scratched instinctively at her favorite spot behind her ear. There was very little blood, but one look at her and it was clear the internal injuries were critical. She was panting, each attempt at a breath wracking her body. Kori placed her hand on ZiZi's ribs, and the dog whimpered before paroxysms of coughing began.

"Take your hands off of her," Gil said, throwing Kori's hand back at her as if it were diseased. "This is *your* fault."

Kori opened her mouth to protest; her voice caught in her throat.

"Broken," Gil said. ZiZi's body looked to be shrinking. She shiv-ered and Gil covered her with his arms. Kori touched ZiZi's nose; it was warm.

"She's broken and she can't be fixed," Gil said, rocking, his eyes locked on the dog.

Kori touched Gil's arm. It was cold, like ZiZi's body, and his face had turned a preternatural white. He scratched ZiZi's ears and murmured soft clucking noises meant to soothe. ZiZi took a deep breath and shuddered again.

"Do you have a cell phone?" Kori asked the young kid pacing behind them. The boy nodded. He looked too young to have a license. "Can you call a vet? Tell them it's an emergency." He nodded and ran to his car.

Gil continued his quiet incantations, alternating between stroking ZiZi's head and scratching her ears. They were like two lovers who know the end was imminent, but continued making plans for the future.

"After lunch, we'll go down to the creek and look for baby minnows," he whispered, his voice straining with the effort. "And maybe we'll take a nap under the Willow tree." ZiZi thumped her tail once and whimpered. She raised her face to Gil with considerable effort and licked his nose. Gil stroked her head and rubbed his face in her fur.

"What do you want for lunch, girl?" Gil asked. "How about a melted ham and cheese sandwich?" ZiZi wagged her tail twice, winced and stopped. Gil rubbed her tail. "Maybe a few chips, too, huh?" Gil rubbed his nose in the nape of her neck and she moved her head to nuzzle him.

"The vet's tech is on his way." The young driver was back, pleased with himself that he was able to make the arrangements, but his face fell after seeing ZiZi's condition.

Her breath came in short bursts and recognition lit in Gil's eyes. He'd seen this before in movies and shuddered at the thought of what was coming next. Gil had watched them all, the hurt, the hunted, the hapless, their last breaths coming in fits of fury or lackluster sighs. Gil had watched people die so often that he thought he'd become immune to it. When his Mom and Dad died, he reacted in stalwart fashion, just like the heroes on TV, dry-eyed and tight-lipped. Now he clenched his teeth, but he couldn't stop the tears that poured from the corners of his eyes.

"Please don't go, Zi," he murmured. He rested his head on ZiZi's and she raised her nose an inch to meet him then dropped to the ground, her last breath escaping in one small sigh. Gil tightened his grip, trying to hold on even as he felt her spirit go. Gil began to cry, a low, crazy moan that sounded like death itself.

"I'm so sorry," the young driver said. "She ran right out in the road. I didn't see her until she was right in front of my car." Kori nodded, but Gil had no room to hear him above the sound of everything ZiZi'd ever told him.

Chapter 14

Kori pulled salad fixings out of the refrigerator. She piled the lettuce and veggies in the crook of her arm and squinted out the window. A shadowy figure, illuminated by the barn light, moved inside.

"That's it," she said.

"What's it?" Avery walked in as Kori slammed the refrigerator door.

"I'm going to get him. He's been out there for three days with no food and probably no sleep." Clutching the vegetables to her chest, she peered into the darkness.

"You know what he's doing," Avery said.

"Actually, I don't." Kori whirled around to face him and the carrots flew from her arm. Avery grabbed the bag before it hit the floor.

"He's making something for ZiZi. Or himself. Probably not you." Avery blushed. "I'm sorry. It's just, well, he's processing it. That's how he does it. And you need to let him."

Kori dumped the armload on the kitchen counter. "Doctor Freud, I presume?"

"Hey, I'm not the one that made them go outside."

Kori snorted and turned her back on her brother. "It wasn't my fault," she murmured, but her words carried no conviction. "The point is, it's been three days and you're not even a little concerned."

"Oh, geez, Kori. Mom and Dad. Zizi. I'm having a hard time dealing with it all myself and Gil's only ten." Avery sat down. "He's doing what he always does. He'll be in when he's done."

Avery poured a glass of milk. As if on cue, the door flew open and Gil sauntered in, handing Avery the contraption in his hand in exchange for the glass of milk. Gil sat down, placed ZiZi's urn on the kitchen table, and drained the glass.

Kori snapped at Avery. "You planned that!"

"Yeah, right," Avery laughed.

Gil looked at each of them in turn and held up his empty glass. "More milk, please." Avery refilled his glass.

"You must be starving," Kori said.

"Just thirsty," Gil replied, downing the second glass. "Avery brought me breakfast, lunch and dinner. Except, it's not dinner yet, so I didn't have that today. It's just ... well you forgot the milk at lunch." Gil leveled an accusatory look at his brother.

"Life was getting a little too cushy out there, Gilliam. I thought if I put the pressure on, you'd snap to it." Avery handed a half glass of milk to Gil who drained it and pushed it forward for Avery to fill again.

"That was only half," Gil said.

"A half too much," Kori said, grabbing the glass. "We're going to eat dinner in an hour." Gil shrugged, grabbed the urn and retired to the living room. Kori torpedoed an agitated glance in Avery's direction, but humor danced on the edge of her eyes.

"Sorry," Avery said. "I couldn't help egging you on. You're so ... maternal these days. It doesn't suit you."

"I should make you do dinner for that."

"No way, Jose. I did dinner the last three nights." He raised two fingers in an imaginary salute, grabbed Gil's invention and joined his brother in the living room.

⋏

Gil took *Mad Max, Beyond Thunder Dome,* out of the DVD player and replaced it with *The Lord of the Rings, The Two Towers.* He didn't know if he could ever watch Mad Max again. Bummer, because it was one of his favorites. He sat, cross-legged on the floor, ZiZi's urn wedged between his legs.

"It's funny," Gil said to Avery as he walked in.

"What?"

"I was in this exact same place three days ago, but I was rubbing ZiZi's ears instead of holding a can of them." He tapped the urn and looked at his brother matter-of-factly. Avery grimaced and sat down. "You slept outside the barn the last two nights," Gil said, a statement not a question. "Thanks."

Avery wrapped a protective arm around his brother's shoulder and squeezed. "Do you want us to get you another dog?"

"There is no other dog." Gil said. "And no other Mom and Dad."

Gil hadn't cried when his parents died. Nor had he processed their deaths by locking himself in the barn and building something to fix it. What he had done, after the ashes were scattered, was hang a "do not disturb" sign on his bedroom door and retreat. For a few days he surfed the web, researching the topic of drunkenness, hoping to find a cure.

"It'll be something you can take and in fifteen minutes you'll be okay to drive again," was all Gil would say about his proposed brainchild. He made a pill, a spray, and a lotion, all of which he tested on Robbie one night, but whether it was due to being out of his normal environment or just out of ideas, or maybe because his heart was too broken for his head to focus, Gil gave up and resorted to sleeping, watching TV, and playing computer games. Tray upon tray of his favorite foods, placed at the bedroom door by his concerned siblings, he left on the floor, untouched. He drank only water, milk and juice.

For the first couple days the rest of the Tirabis allowed Gil's withdrawal, but by the third day Robbie began pacing the floor and threatening to break the door down. Avery alone knew that this was what Gil needed and pleaded Gil's case for him. It was through Avery's intercession that Gil was allowed to continue his self-imposed isolation. At the end, he cried. On the morning of the seventh day, the door swung wide and a gaunt and starving Gil emerged, catharsis completed, despite his failure to cure drunkenness.

Avery squeezed Gil's shoulder again before removing his arm.

"Awww, this is a good part!" Gil said. "He's gonna toss the dwarf." Avery fingered the collar-like contraption Gil had given him.

"Hey, Gil? What's this?"

"A dog collar," he responded without taking his eyes off the TV.

"But we don't have a dog anymore and you just said..." Avery turned it over and over in his hand, trying to figure out the mechanics.

"It's not for us. It's for the people who have dogs. Now their dogs won't ever get hit by a car." He looked up and sighed, taking the collar back from Avery.

"It looks like an ordinary dog collar, just with a battery pack on it. What's it do? Some kind of electric charge?"

"A zap?" Gil asked, poking Avery. "Would you like to be zapped?"

"No. And I don't suppose that dogs do, either. Pardon my insensitivity."

"That's okay." Gil reached in his pocket and pulled out a bracelet identical to the collar. "Here. Put this on your wrist."

Avery obliged. Gil adjusted the volume and held it up to Avery's ear.

"Ready?" Gil asked.

Avery nodded as strains of *Raindrops Keep Falling on My Head* poured out. "It's different, I'll give you that. But how do you expect a dog to keep this thing on its wrist?"

Gil's tongue probed the interior surface of his bottom lip, a wacky smile on his lips.

"Hey, cut it out. I'm not condemning your project. I just want to know how it works."

Gil grabbed the bracelet, his exuberance apparent, and wrapped the collar around Avery's neck.

"It's a training device. There are fifteen different songs so you can train them to do whatever you want. Here." Gil put the earphones in his own ears and pressed the remote, his head bobbing in time to music Avery couldn't hear, but could feel. His hands flew to his neck, probing the device.

"What is this?" Avery demanded.

"The music's in the collar," Gil responded. "The dogs can feel it. Every song has a different vibration."

Avery furrowed his eyebrows.

"You train them to do different things to different songs," Gil said. "You want them to come to dinner? You play *Everybody Eats at My House*. You want them to go outside and run around? You play *Who Let the Dogs Out*. You want them to do tricks? You play *Jump*. You want them to come right away when you call them and turn around and not run out into the street and get hit by a car, you play *Raindrops Keep Fallin' on My Head*. Gil's throat felt thick and it was hard to swallow. He knew boys didn't cry so he squeezed his eyes shut and forced back the tears. He slumped over the urn.

"Why, *Raindrops Keep Fallin' on My Head?*"

"Because that was Dad's favorite song, Avery."

Gil opened his eyes and looked to his brother, but Avery avoided his gaze. They sat in stoned silence, each wrestling with their internal demons, until Avery's cowed in submission and he gave Gil's arm a light punch.

"I think it's an awesome idea, Gil. I'll take it over to Roley's Hardware in the morning and see if I can talk them into buying a few."

Gil nodded, pushed his bangs to the side and swiped at the three or four tears, running down his cheeks like a spring rain.

Chapter 15

Robbie backed out of the driveway and cranked up the volume on the radio to override the noise of the engine. Ten minutes later, he pulled into a strip mall and parked in front of the Army Recruiting Center. Sweat formed on his upper lip and his knuckles bulged white from his vice grip on the steering wheel. He realized he was holding his breath and let it out. After a single, agonizing minute, Robbie grabbed the keys and his backpack and strode inside.

A young, pimply-faced young man, no more than twenty-two with a well-pressed uniform and excellent posture sat behind the reception desk. He stood as Robbie walked through the door.

"Can I help you?"

"Captain Russell, please."

"Your name?"

"Robert Tirabi."

The young man disappeared and after several moments returned. His stone face beckoned Robbie to enter.

"The Captain will see you now." The boy stood aside allowing room for Robbie to pass and closed the door behind them.

⚔

Captain Russell occupied a spacious office that overlooked the shopping center's parking lot. He knew better men who'd risen to lesser ranks and, although the Army didn't pay well, he'd enjoyed a modicum of success, first in Grenada and then in Desert Storm. More importantly, his men respected him. But his last combat mission was fifteen years ago, and he'd be the first to admit his reflexes had slowed since then. Now he was killing time until retirement.

"C'mon in, son. Sit down." He pointed to a chair. "I understand you're having second thoughts."

Robbie nodded and shifted uneasily in his chair.

"Well, how bad do you want to get out?" asked the Captain.

"Pretty bad. I told you over the phone what happened to my parents … "

"It's a damn shame, that." Captain Russell sighed. "Unfortunately, I can't help you. The army's desperate for bodies. You signed. I've got you scheduled for a six-week basic training starting end of the month. Think of it as a sixteen-week crash course. We'll teach you how to shoot. How to survive with just a pocketknife and an aspirin. That kind of stuff."

Robbie stared, wide-eyed, managing little more than, "But, I..."

"Look, I'm real sorry about your folks. You can appeal. Might be out by Christmas next, but unless you know somebody. Captain Russell leaned forward, folded his hands. "You know anybody?"

Robbie shook his head, a helpless look overtaking those few facial muscles that hadn't gone numb.

The Captain smiled. "Hey, those siblings of yours can use the money. You do get paid, you know." Robbie nodded.

"You're a car guy, right? Stuff's always breaking down in the desert. Something about the sand causes everything to go to crap ten minutes after you get there. You'll be in demand. Probably pull the beauty duties because of it." He laughed an infectious, light-hearted laugh. Robbie smiled, a half-crooked thing, in response.

Captain Russell paused, stood up, and looked out the window across the parking lot like a man surveying all he owns.

"It'll be over before you know it. I promise." Captain Russell handed Robbie his business card. "Call me if you have any other questions."

A

Gil sat on Robbie's bed asking a million questions as Robbie packed his life's essentials into two large duffle bags. After throwing in several pairs of jeans and a bunch of underwear and socks he routed through the closet, talking to himself. "How many shirts?"

"But why do you have to go?" Gil asked. While Robbie's back was turned, Gil pulled out the seven pairs of socks Robbie had just stuffed in the duffle bag and hid them under the bed.

"Because I'm doing my duty for my country," Robbie replied. "And besides, I can't get out of it. I tried."

"What's duty anyway? Duty to who?" Gil removed Robbie's underwear and placed it underneath his pillow.

"I have a duty to my country just like you had to feed ZiZi every day. We all have obligations."

"But why do you have to go so far away? Don't they have people who live there to do their own duty?" Gil removed several pairs of jeans from the duffle bag and shoved them under the nightstand. Robbie turned and tossed his shirts onto a pile on the bed. Gil leaned back nonchalantly, distancing himself from the duffle bags. Robbie began taking his shirts off their hangers and folding them neatly.

"Yeah, but sometimes people need more help."

"But we need more help. Especially because of Mom and Dad." Robbie stopped folding shirts and sat down next to Gil.

"Hey. C'mon." He held his arms out and Gil jumped into them. He cradled Gil as best as you can a five-foot two-inch baby.

"I'll be back before you know it. You'll see." Gil crinkled his nose and buried his face in Robbie's shoulder.

"Are these people more important than we are?"

"Nothing's more important than you are." Robbie rubbed Gil's back. "It's just that some people don't have the same freedoms we have and so that's why I have to go. It's about democracy." Robbie shifted Gil back to his spot on the bed.

"Isn't democracy when you get to choose for yourself?" Gil asked. Robbie nodded.

"Then maybe they've already chosen."

"Well said, little brother." Kori tossed several books on the bed and flopped down after them. "Some of my favorites. For the plane ride and après." She smiled at Robbie. "Sorry. I was eavesdropping."

"Since when did you become a philosopher?" Robbie asked.

The lock sprung open in Gil's hand and his smile spread-eagled across his face. He closed it and tried again. It pinged open and he began anew.

"Since my brother became a right-wing bonehead. What's next? White cloaks? Skinheads? Listening to Rush Limbaugh?" Kori lay down on the bed next to the books.

"Kori, weren't you an apolitical ar-teest like two minutes ago?" He pronounced the word with a mock French affectation. "What the hell happened?"

"Mom died. And someone had to take over for her. Besides, the more I think about it, the more I realize that Mom and Dad died for oil the same way you will if you go." She bit the nubby nail of her right index finger.

"Yeah, well, Mom knew what she was talking about. You haven't got a clue." Robbie walked to the hall closet, pulled his shoeshine kit out and tossed it onto the bed.

The roar of a motorcycle could be heard coming down the street. The driver stopped in the Tirabi driveway and cut the engine.

"Jack!" Gil jumped off the bed and ran downstairs.

"Great," Robbie said. "Who invited him?" Robbie glared at Kori and strode to the window. "If that mother is riding without a helmet, I'll kill him myself. Then he won't have to worry about wrecking." Robbie peered down to confirm that Jack was not wearing a helmet. He watched as Gil ran out the door and jumped into Jack's arms. "Stupid Jackass! He turned to Kori grimacing. "And I mean that in the nicest way."

"Why are you getting so bent out of shape? They passed the no-helmet law, ya' know."

"Yeah, and if you think it's safe to be riding anywhere without a helmet, you don't have two brain cells to rub together. You know why they did it, don't you? Because you're more likely to die in an accident if you're not wearing a helmet. The other way, you just run up exorbitant medical costs."

"You're so critical."

"Did you ever see a guy driving down the highway at sixty miles an hour with no helmet? His skin's plastered to his face, rippling in the wind. Even with glasses, your eyes are squinting and tearing from the pressure. Let that guy get hit with a bug, like a bee or a cicada or something, and at that speed, I'll bet you he gets a welt the size of a half dollar. And that's if he doesn't wreck first."

"Enough. I'm going out." She tossed the book she was fingering back onto the bed.

"Will you watch Gil, please?" Robbie nodded and turned back to the closet.

"Take the helmets off my bike," Robbie warned.

Kori slammed the bedroom door in reply.

"Like talking to a wall," Robbie muttered. He peeked out the window, careful not to let Jack see him. Once Robbie's best friend, the partnership had waned when Jack started dating Kori. Robbie knew the kind of guy Jack was, possessed of a wanderer's eye, but convincing Kori had been a waste of time.

Kori walked over to Jack and handed him a helmet. He shook her off, but she cocked her head, a coquettish gesture, and he obliged. Jack looked up to Robbie's window and saluted. Robbie flashed him the finger and resumed packing. The roar of the motorcycle filled the room then faded into the distance.

CHAPTER 16

A full moon glowed, casting an iridescent light over the farm-cum-landfill that loomed in the far distant corner of Kori's bedroom window. The first inkling of the sun's rays wouldn't be seen for more than an hour on this chilly late October morning. Gil tiptoed into the room, hovering above the bed where Kori and Jack lay sleeping. He pinched his fingers around Jack's nose, cutting off Jack's oxygen supply. After several moments, Jack inhaled a frantic pull of air through his mouth, and his eyes flew open to see Gil looming above him.

"What?" Jack hissed, shoving Gil's fingers away.

"Are you awake?" Gil asked.

"I am now, you little jerk," Jack said, but watching those salamander eyes hold his own, Jack smiled in spite of himself. Gil could stare, unblinking, for well over ten minutes. Jack loved Gil like a brother, and even with the little cretin's exasperating habits Jack would do anything for him.

"What time is it?" Jack asked, discouraged by the murky darkness still clinging to the curtains.

"Five o'clock." Gil said. "C'mon. I want to show you something." Intuiting that there would be no more sleep for him this morning, Jack allowed Gil to pull him to his feet.

"Hhhhmmmph. Briefs. I wear briefs, too," Gil said approvingly.

Jack scrambled into his jeans, pulled a tee shirt over his head and a sweatshirt over top. He looked over at his boots and opted for bare feet. He took one more longing look at the bed, sighed and headed toward the door.

"I gotta take a whiz," Jack announced, stopping at the bathroom. Gil tried to follow him, but Jack barred the way. Gil leaned against the closed door tapping his foot in exaggerated fashion for the minute it took Jack to emerge, disheveled and still half asleep.

"Okay, let's go." Gil led. A light clicked on in Robbie's room as they walked by, but the door didn't open. Gil put his finger to his lips and tip-toed down the stairs, Jack trailing him. Once outside, Gil took off running across the lawn to the shed. Determined not to be outdone by a ten-year old, Jack sprinted the hundred yards to the barn, but bare feet and the fact that Gil was more awake at this regrettable hour put him at a disadvantage, about fifty paces behind, he'd later estimate.

At the barn door, Gil found the lock on the ground, and the door swung wide. "Huh?" A shadowy figure rooted through the drawers, a roll of drawings under one arm.

"Hey! What are you doing?" Gil demanded.

The figure ran, knocking Gil to the ground and whacking Jack in the face with the drawings in his bolt to the woods. The impact caused stars to jump before Jack's eyes and he staggered, holding his nose.

"Hey! Come back here," Gil yelled, and before Jack could clear his head, Gil took off running after the intruder. Jack ran after Gil, grabbing his arm moments before he disappeared behind the copse.

"Whoa, man. That wouldn't be a good thing," Jack said. Gil struggled, but Jack's grip was firm.

"Jack. Let Go! He took something — some drawings." Gil pried Jack's hand off his arm and yanking free of his grip, dove to the ground. Jack grabbed his collar and pulled him back, surprised to hear his own heavy breathing. After a few deep breaths, Jack knelt down beside Gil and wrapped an arm around his waist.

"We can't go, Gil. It's too dangerous."

"But he's getting away," Gil said.

"We want him to get away. Then he won't hurt us." Jack squeezed Gil's arm gently.

"This isn't a movie, buddy. It's real life. And somebody really wanted something bad out here. Bad enough to break in." Jack searched Gil's eyes for understanding.

Gil grimaced at his besmirched barn and turned to see Robbie running toward them dressed only his underwear.

"What going on?" Robbie asked.

Jack pulled himself up to his full height. Despite their differences, at this moment they behaved as if nothing had ever come between them.

Gil darted over to Robbie and jumped in his arms, sniffling. "He took some drawings."

Robbie ran his hands up and down Gil's body, checking for injuries.

Jack shook his head, reviving the dull ache in his own head. He raised his hand to his eye and probed delicately.

"He wasn't expecting us," Jack said. He winced as he touched his nose.

Satisfied that Gil was injury free, Robbie set him down and turned to Jack. "Did he hit you?" Robbie asked.

Jack shook his head. "Only by accident. The drawings caught me in the face when he was making his getaway. You know when people say they see stars, you always think like, 'yeah, right.' Well … " Jack rubbed his nose again, then his eyes. "Little brother here's lucky he stepped aside. I think that guy was taking no prisoners."

"Did he have a gun?"

"I don't know. It's so dark out here. It's the middle of the night, for Chrissakes."

"Yeah, so what are you doing out here?" Robbie asked.

Jack smiled and tilted his head in Gil's direction. "The salamander woke me up."

Gil toed the dirt in response. Jack scanned the tree line, but the light was still too dim to see anything clearly. In the opposite direction, the sun's first rays whooped and hollered, mad streaks of reds and oranges overtaking the horizon like a five-star general.

"He's long gone by now," Jack said. Robbie nodded in agreement, folded his hands across his chest and rubbed his arms.

"Let's go inside. It's freaking cold out here," Robbie said. Jack nodded and they hoofed it back to the house, pausing once to glance back over their collective shoulders.

The light clicked on as they entered the kitchen. Kori stood in the doorway wearing a revealing nightgown and suppressing a yawn. Jack shot her an approving glance, which dissolved the camaraderie of the last few minutes when Robbie intercepted it.

"What are you doing? Don't tell me you're hunting? Why do you have Gil with you if you're hunting," she said to the room at large. "And why are you in your underwear?" she said to Robbie in particular.

"I heard a noise." Robbie brushed past her on his way to the stairs.

"Where are you going?" Kori called after him.

"To put some clothes on, Kori," he replied. "I suggest you do the same." Kori and Jack exchanged glances. Jack tightened his mouth so as not to smile in front of Gil and nodded in the direction of the stairs. Kori spun on her heel, leaving Jack and Gil alone.

"How about some breakfast, Salamander?" Jack asked, grabbing the coffee pot and filling it with water. "Sleuthing always makes me hungry."

Gil said nothing, but walked out of the kitchen and to the hallway closet. He climbed way in the back in between bulky winter jackets, past umbrellas and over hiking boots. Jack heard an occasional grunt followed by several more minutes of rooting around and Gil emerged victorious, the precious bundle in hand.

He returned to the kitchen, the bundle of drawings hooked under his arm, and took a seat at the table waiting for Jack to serve him. Although already ten, up until now he had led the life of the pampered. There was very little Gilliam William Tirabi did for himself. Jack poured a bowl full of cereal, added some milk and set it before Gil.

"So they didn't get what they were looking for?" Jack said.

Gil shook his head, set the drawings on the table and scooped up a heaping spoonful of Cheerios. His cheeks bulged and his words were drowning in milk and wheat. "After breakfast, will you and Robbie help me find someplace safe to hide them?" Gil asked.

Jack nodded. "Sure."

He pushed Gil's hair back and sat down next to him to wait for his coffee. "Better eat up. My guess is the Spanish Inquisition's comin' down the stairs any minute now."

CHAPTER 17

Robbie, Kori, Gil and Avery stood in the middle Terminal C of the Philadelphia International Airport waiting on a round of coffees from the kiosk. Robbie wore the telltale uniform of a man on his way to basic training. Sunday morning terminal traffic was tranquil and, as a result, you could hear the music emanating from the stand. Gil tapped his feet and chomped on a chocolate chip muffin, his jaws moving in a ravenous, rhythmic dance.

"How many stars, Gil?" Robbie asked.

"Three and three quarters," Gil responded.

"For a muffin?" Kori asked.

"Has he ever given anything four stars?" Robbie asked Avery.

"There was that gelato he had when Mom and Dad took us to Rome. I think he gave that four and a quarter stars. But nothing's come even remotely close since."

Robbie glanced over at Gil inhaling the remains of his muffin. "Well, I'd like a glimpse of whatever he deems worthy of five stars."

"One mocha, two hot chocolates, and a decaf latte," the coffee jock said, setting the cups on the counter.

Kori sprinkled chocolate on her latte, took a dainty sip and closed the lid. Robbie doused chocolate powder on his and took a big draw.

"Kind of redundant, don't you think?" Kori asked as she watched Gil vigorously shaking chocolate powder all over his drink. She grabbed the shaker from Gil's grasp and set it on the counter.

"Well, the whipped cream was still white," Gil whined. "And the chocolate wasn't coming out fast enough." Avery steered Gil away.

They moved like an octopus toward the metal detectors that refused entry to all non-ticketed passengers while x-raying the bags, purses, pockets and shoes of the ticketed ones.

Avery pointed to a woman standing barefoot, one foot balanced on top of the other. "Modified flamingo pose," he mused.

Robbie slung an arm around Gil's shoulder. "Listen, buddy. While I'm gone, somebody's gotta keep your sister in line. Think you can do it?" Robbie asked, poking Gil's chest. Gil grabbed Robbie's finger and pulled himself in close and tight, leaning into Robbie's broad chest, holding on to him like a lifeline.

"I don't know if I can do it alone," Kori whispered, pulling in close.

Robbie smoothed her hair back and kissed her forehead. "You can. I'm only going to be gone for four months. Then I'll be back."

"Yeah, but once basic training's over they're going to send you somewhere and they're not going to wait for world peace to do it." She lowered her voice conspiratorially. "The world needs heroes, Robbie. I just wish you weren't one of them."

Kori slumped down in one of the quaint white rocking chairs in front of the window, closed her eyes and rocked to an internal rhythm. Robbie sat beside her and waited. Gil and Avery pretended to window shop, not wishing to disturb whatever fragile truce was being forged. After several minutes, Robbie grabbed her hand in his and spoke softly to her.

"Look. I'm gonna do the basic training, and then I'm going to find a way out of the rest. I won't let you down, Kor." His eyes searched hers. She looked down at her lap, voice cracking.

"It's not just you being around. Jack can fix the plumbing if it breaks. But what about the money? We were barely making it with your paycheck?"

"Your business is taking off. Plus you can have my whole pay."

She stared at the hands in her lap, hers and Robbie's mixed. "I don't know if I can raise Gil by myself. He's ... " she raised her free hand to her mouth to hide the treason, "a handful." She began rocking again, the weight of her confession resting between their hands.

"He's work, but he's no invalid. The kid could survive for weeks without us. He might eat nothing but cereal and never take a bath, but he'd be okay." Kori gazed at Robbie, her eyes soft and moist. "It'll be fine." He squeezed her and released. "Now let's go. I've got a plane to catch."

They stood and flanked him. Gil jumped on Robbie's back and Robbie carried him until they reached the metal detectors.

"This is where you get off, Salamander." He set Gil down and hugged him, then encircled Avery's slender shoulders in a mighty bear lock.

"I'm trusting you with the finances," Robbie whispered to Avery. "Kori's a scatterbrain with numbers. You need to help her manage the books for her business, too, but without bruising her ego." He squeezed the back of Avery's neck and smiled. "I'll get you through Penn, but keep your grades up. You're going to need at least a partial scholarship."

"Hurry back," Kori said. "And write to us, would ya'?"

"You're leaving," Gil said, a statement, not a question. Robbie put one knee on the floor and knelt at eye level with his brother.

"Are you coming back? Or are you leaving like Mom and Dad?"

Robbie did not take his eyes from Gil's face. "Definitely coming back. That's a promise." A wide-mouthed smile broke across Gil's face exposing all his teeth. Gil raised his hand for a high-five and Robbie smacked it.

"I love you," he said, and before Gil could respond, he was up and through the metal detector, collecting his bags. "See you in a bit," he said, and disappeared down the corridor.

Chapter 18

The walkout basement was light and airy, one wall comprised completely of French doors, the opposite wall built into the bedrock below the house. Kori's drafting table faced out to the back yard and the bucolic setting where beyond the horizon a decomposing and noxious mountain they called a landfill hid at the edge of her tranquility, its spawn leaching exponentially into the groundwater while she worked.

Avery bounded down the stairs. "What are you doing?"

Kori was draped over the table. "A wedding invitation for Stacey Clinghoffer."

"That cow?" said Avery. "Who would marry her?" Kori stifled him with a look. "Hey, Kori?"

"What?"

"Since you're bringing home the bacon, I want to do something to contribute, other than every single menial, yet necessary, task that goes into running a household, that is."

"Why can't you talk in English? I'm not sure I even understood what you just said."

"That means, I don't mind cooking and cleaning and helping with the laundry, but you're not sticking me with all of it." Avery picked up the medicine ball and bounced it off the wall.

"I never said you had to be my personal slave. It would be nice, but ... "

"I was thinking of selling off all that gas and oil out in back of the barn. We must have more than a hundred of those fifty-five gallon drums. It would take a long time for us to use it all. We may as well make some money with it. At least until Robbie's checks start coming."

"We don't need any trouble, Avery. I just paid off the porch repair." She paused to look at her work. "As long as I keep getting jobs, you don't need to. We'll be all right. Just worry about school. You need the grades." She flashed her steel blue eyes at him.

"I have the grades."

"Yeah, well." Unlike her average self, Avery was always a straight A student. Kori thought he could simply sleep with a book under his pillow and still get an A. And although he didn't have Gil's ingenuity when it came to inventions, he could recreate either from drawings or Gil's verbal direction, anything Gil envisioned. Kori seethed at the ease with which Avery excelled, but then she discovered that art was her forte and forgave her brother his gifts.

"I was also thinking of creating a web page to sell some of Gil's contraptions on the Internet. You know, he's got that state-of-the-art juicer. And now that dog collar thingee," he said, repeatedly tossing the ball. "A couple other things kicking around in the garage. Maybe some of the local hardware stores would want something."

"Sounds like a plan." Kori looked up at the incessant noise. "Could you please stop bouncing that ball? It's hard to concentrate."

Avery nodded. "I'm going to get started on the web page right away."

"Let me know if you need help with the graphics," Kori said.

Avery stood looking at her, but said nothing.

"What?"

"I could help with the checkbook, too, if you want. Especially if I'm going to start selling stuff. I'll need access to the house account. For the deposits." Kori didn't even look at him.

"Robbie told you to do that, didn't he?" she said.

Had Kori not suddenly been swamped with the responsibility of raising her siblings, the fact that she couldn't balance a checkbook wouldn't have bothered her. She couldn't care less how much money she had as long as it was enough for art supplies. But phone, gas and electric bills, not to mention groceries, cost much more than art supplies and the need to know exactly how much money she had in her checking account took on new significance. She'd already been denied the use of her Mac card at the grocery store once and had to use a credit card to buy the weekly groceries because of bad planning. She was furious, and later determined there were insufficient funds in the account as a result of a simple arithmetic error on her part. Still she was too embarrassed to ever shop at that store again.

"Did he?"

Avery's lips formed a tight line and he nodded once. When Kori didn't answer, he went upstairs. Kori could hear him banging around in the kitchen. She wanted to jump at the offer, but to turn the checkbook over with a zero balance and not look like a moron would be tough. He'd press her to sell off that stupid oil.

"Avery!" she yelled up the stairs.

"What?"

"Let me think about it," she said. Avery walked halfway down.

"Okay. Well, do you mind if I take your car? I want to take a ride over to Cohen's Hardware and see if I can unload a couple dog collars."

Relieved to switch topics, Kori tried to sound motherly, but remembered those first days, itching to get behind the wheel. She'd go anywhere with one of her parents: the gas station, the grocery store, even the dump, just for a chance to drive. "You don't even have your license."

"I have my permit."

"For which you need a licensed driver." She gave him a look, but wanted to giggle, and turned away before she lost her composure. "Take your bike."

"Fine!" Avery stomped up the steps.

"Take Gil with you," Kori yelled after him.

CHAPTER 19

Avery and Gil saddled up with baseball caps and sunglasses, and, sporting dog collars wrapped around their wrists and calves, rode off into the clear light of day in search of fortune.

Three hours later, they headed home, exuberant with the success of unloading the entire booty. Avery had pitched their wares to the owners of three different hardware stores and left with each believing that no self-respecting dog owner could be without one.

"This calls for a celebration, Gil," Avery said. "There's a Rita's Water Ice just up the road. Gelato?" Gil nodded, irrepressible, and bobbed and weaved the whole way to Rita's. Twenty minutes later, wrapped in a buzz that comes from a good sugar dose, Gil smiled.

"You gotta wash your face and change your shirt before Kori sees you," Avery said as they parked their bikes. Ignoring Avery, Gil ran inside to find his sister.

"Kori? Where are you?" He checked the basement, but it was dark. He ran to the hallway stairs and yelled into the air above them, "Kori."

Avery joined him at the base of the hallway stairs. Gil looked perplexed.

"Robbie's car's gone. She probably finished those wedding invitations and went to deliver them. Which means ... " Avery smiled and stared at Gil, arms folded.

"What?" Gil said, eyes wide.

"She won't be home for a couple hours going over the changes." Avery rubbed his hairless chin in contemplation. "I got an idea," Avery said. "But first you need to get cleaned up."

⋏

Half an hour later, Avery climbed in behind the wheel of Ruth's minivan. Wearing his father's lightweight overcoat and hat, Gil slipped into the front passenger seat and onto the phone books Avery had stacked, enabling Gil to be higher than the dashboard. He struggled with the seat belt until Avery snapped it into place. Three fifty-five gallon drums, one oil, two gas, were loaded in the back. It had taken a makeshift ramp and their combined strength to roll the drums in, and now there was no time left for second thoughts.

"You ready?" Avery asked, hands gripping the wheel.

"Kori's going to be pissed," Gil said, rocking.

"Not if she doesn't know, she won't," Avery replied. Gil shook his head and wrung his hands together, moaning softly.

"Easy, Gil. It's no big deal. I can drive, but I need an adult with me. So sit there and try to look old. No cop's going to stop me with my dad in the car." He cocked his head and looked at Gil for emphasis. Gil nodded and stared straight ahead. Avery crawled out of the driveway and onto the street.

"Oh, no!" Gil shouted. Avery looked in the direction Gil was pointing.

"Jesus, it's Aunt Stella," Avery said, ducking down in his seat. Stella was walking back to her house, sorting through the mail, her back to the street. Gil moaned and Avery put the window up. He crawled past Aunt Stella's house then gunned the engine, disappearing over the hill before she looked up. Avery glanced in the rearview mirror long after they were out of sight; Gil turned around to see if they were being followed.

"She's not going to run after the car," Avery said. "I don't even think she saw us."

Gil mulled this over for a moment then broke into laughter so contagious that Avery violated the first rule of driving: keep your eyes on the road.

"Look out!" Gil shouted.

Avery's head snapped back so fast he could feel the air around him swirl. He cut the wheel and zigzagged right, grazing the hip of a mangy-looking dog now limping to the side of the road.

"Stop," Gil screamed. "Avery, stop!"

"Shut up!" Avery said. He cut the wheel hard to the left, and the combined weight of the drums sprang to life, bolting in the opposite direction and wreaking havoc on a suspension system already under duress. The van bucked and moaned and after much screeching of tires, Avery skidded to a halt.

Gil bolted toward the injured animal now lying on a soft patch of grass under a tree. He knelt down, shed his father's coat and pillowed it under the dog's head. He scratched its ears, hummed softly, and placed a hand on the dog's hip. The dog licked Gil's hand in thanks.

"Gil!" Avery parked at the curb, got out and ran to check the back hatch for damage. The walls of the van had been scuffed in the pandemonium, the drums dented, but the lids remained secure. Avery breathed a sigh of relief then turned to Gil and the stray.

"Gil, we can't keep him."

"We have to. He doesn't have a collar and he needs a vet. And you have to take him because you almost killed him." Gil eyes grew wide, his face resolute. Avery leaned over and scratched the dog behind the ears. He tried to examine the dog's hip, but the animal winced and pulled away so Avery withdrew his hand. He looked at Gil's pleading eyes and his own softened.

"All right. Let's take him to the vet and get him checked out. He probably needs shots, too," Avery said, wondering how he was going to pay for it. Gil smiled so big that Avery could feel the force of it.

"I guess that ramp's going to come in handy for the second time today," Avery said and trotted off to the car to retrieve it.

CHAPTER 20

When they arrived home four hours later, Kori was pacing the kitchen, mad as a wasp. She ran outside when they pulled in the driveway.

"Where the hell've you been?" she demanded of Avery. "And what the hell do you think you're doing driving Mom's car? With Gil in it, for God's sake."

Avery didn't answer. He walked to the side of the van and slid the door open to reveal the prone body of the newest Tirabi. Gil ran to Kori's side, grabbing her hand and pulling her over to the van for a closer look. Kori's face contorted when she glimpsed what was in the back seat.

"Oh, no. No way! We've got enough to take care of. She shook her head, refusing to look at the animal.

"Kori, please! Max's hurt and he's got nowhere to go," Gil begged.

"Max! You've named him already?" Kori demanded. Gil nodded. Avery looked the other away. "Who's gonna walk him? Feed him? Pick up his poop?" Kori asked.

"I will," Gil responded.

"You? You can't even take care of yourself."

"Hey, shut up! What's the matter with you?" Avery said. His eyes smoldered in Kori's direction, but she met his gaze with equal force.

"We don't need another dog. I've got more than I can handle now."

"But we do," Gil protested. "For protection and stuff."

"No. What we need is for you to get this … thing out of here. Now."

Gil stomped his foot like an angry colt and stared at his sister. "I hate you, Kori!" He ran to the house and turned, hand on the doorknob, eyes alight with a vortex of unexpressed emotions. "You killed ZiZi, and now you're going to kill Max, you, you … dog-killer!"

He stormed into the house slamming the door so hard the glass rattled in its pane. Avery snorted and shot her a look of disgust before striding into the house after Gil.

Kori stood immobile in the driveway, her breath coming in short quick bursts. Overwhelmed with the weight of her decisions and the lives that depended on them, she dropped to the ground, hung her head in her hands and cried, letting the panic of the last few months run free. Spent, she stood and braced herself, then walked over to Max who was licking his wounded hip. She sniffed the air and retreated. Max hadn't had a bath in a while. She reached out a tentative hand and touched the matted fur. He ceased his ministrations and raised a cold nose, which she grabbed reflexively.

"I can't take care of you." She tugged his nose and gave it a pat. "I'm sorry."

A low, piercing moan emitted from Max's larynx followed by one of a deeper and more menacing pitch through the living room window. Kori looked up in fear. She'd heard that sound before and it could mean only one thing.

"Oh, no." She ran inside to find Gil on the living room floor, kicking and thrashing at his invisible demons. Avery, responding to the same guttural sounds, ran down the stairs, and seeing Gil's violent explosion, sprung over the bannister and into the living room with one movement. A flailing Gil threw himself into the leg of the coffee table, banging his head with a whack. Kori stood watching, open-mouthed and helpless.

"Don't just stand there," Avery shouted. "Help me hold him." Avery straddled Gil, restraining his shoulders and turning him on his side. He talked in the soothing tones reserved for a skittish animal. "It's all right, buddy. You're all right. Just relax."

Gil was unresponsive and unwittingly tried to break free of Avery's grasp, rolling his shoulders and kicking his feet. His eyes fluttered open for a brief instant, then closed to half-mast. He rocked and bucked while Avery sat astride him like a rodeo cowboy. Kori dropped to the floor, halted by the spectacle.

"Noooooooo," Gil yelled to the room. "Nooooooo."

"Kori, dammit. Help me get him on his side," Avery shouted as Gil wrenched from his grip. "What the heck's the matter with you?" Kori snapped to life and crawled to them. Gil threw his arced arm into the air, hitting Kori in the head, and knocking her to the ground, taking her breath away. She lay there stunned. Avery wrestled with Gil and spoke to Kori without turning.

"Are you all right?" Kori did not respond. Gil was getting the upper hand in the struggle and Avery couldn't afford to stop and look at her. "Kori! Are you all right?"

"Yeah, I'm all right," she said, rising to her knees. She rubbed her head and winced.

Avery laid Gil on his side and locked Gil's arms by sheer strength. At each attempt Gil made to move, Avery clamped tighter. He turned to see Kori kneeling at Gil's feet.

"Bend his upper leg," Avery said. She looked up at him with pale, un-seeing eyes so he explained. "For circulation." She nodded, her usually sanguine complexion gone white.

"Get me a pillow," said Avery. "And a towel."

Kori threw him a couch pillow and ran to the kitchen for a dishtowel. Avery wrapped the pillow in the towel and put it under Gil's head. Gil had fallen asleep and was snoring. He choked, then coughed, interrupting the sonorous rhythm. Spittle mixed with phlegm ran out of the side of his mouth onto the dishtowel. After a few more moments of coughing and throat clearing, he lapsed back into a deep sleep.

"Go call the doctor," Avery whispered to Kori.

She didn't move. Instead watched Gil sleep while her breathing fell into a rhythm with his. Avery snapped his fingers in Kori's face, and she stood and wobbled to the kitchen holding her head as if she were the one that just had a seizure.

Avery relaxed his leg grip. Gil snored and shifted positions but did not awaken. Avery rubbed Gil's back in long, slow strokes and spoke softly to him. "It's all right, buddy. I'm here."

Kori returned after several minutes, more composed. "The doctor said if he's sleeping, just let him be and to move anything he could bang his head on in case he has another attack." Kori moved the coffee table, one end at a time, out of harm's reach. "He's sending an ambulance." She grabbed a blanket off the couch and draped it over Gil. "Maybe he'll sleep it off."

She slumped down next to Gil and rubbed his head. "Did he take his meds today?" Avery nodded, and Kori ran her hands tenderly through Gil's hair.

"I'm sorry I was so useless. I never did this before."

"What? How is that possible when you live with an epileptic?" Avery asked, staring.

"Mom or Dad was always there," she said. "They always told me to go away."

"They never did that to me," he said. "I think I was eight or nine the first time I saw him do it," Avery said, no trace of malice. He released his leg hold on Gil whose snoring had reached epic proportions, and sat, cross-legged behind his brother. He grabbed a pillow off the couch and propped it behind Gil's back, then lay down behind him.

"You can go. I'll stay with him," Avery said.

Kori shook her head. The whole episode had rattled her more than she cared to admit, but she sat down anyway. "I'll stay, too." She tucked the blanket under Gil's chin.

"Avery, what were you thinking taking Mom's car? And that ... " she nodded in the direction of Max outside.

"I took a look at the checkbook. I know it's not like you said. We need money, Kori."

Kori folded her trembling hands.

"Hey. It's not your fault," Avery said. "Just bad luck. I mean, how many kids our age have gone through half the stuff we've been through in the last two months. This stuff's not normal." He said the last bit with an air of authority that made Kori burst into giggles.

"What's so funny?"

"I don't know. Nothing. Everything." She sighed and turned her neck from side to side, working the kinks out. "You're right. We do need money. But you can't work for it. You need a scholarship."

"Stop, already. You're not telling me something I don't know. It's just that if we starve to death, I'm not going to be able to make much use of a scholarship, will I?"

"Don't be ridiculous. We're not going to starve to death."

"I know that. But we could lose our house. And maybe get split up. What would that do to Gil?" They looked in unison at their brother.

"The house is paid for. They bought it outright with money from one of Dad's inventions. We'll always have a place to live."

"Yeah, but we'll soon have taxes to pay. And then there's everything else."

"I've got some new clients. Robbie said he'd send money. And we should be getting the insurance money soon. As soon as they finish the investigation … "

"I wish they would have planned better," Avery said.

"They probably thought there was time," Kori said. "All Dad needed was one big invention … " She ran a finger up and down the carpet pile, a sad, strange look on her face.

"There's thousands of dollars sitting out back," Avery said. "It could hold us over."

Kori walked to the window. The landfill sat off in the distance shrouded by trees. Patches of corn, grown in rotation to keep the soil healthy, dotted the landscape. A dozen dairy cows walked single file along a fence playing a game of follow the leader. "We can't be sure that it's not all connected, Avery. The porch. The oil. And if it is, we'll put ourselves in danger again." She stared out the window. Choice had immobilized her.

"No, we won't. I'll limit my sales to one customer."

"No," she whispered, kneeling down next to him. Gil snorted, but did not wake.

"We'll figure something else out." Kori smiled, hoping she appeared confident. "We'll wait. Something'll come along. You'll see." She smiled and squeezed his hand.

"All right," he said. "But in the meantime, can I drive?"

Chapter 21

Things happened fast after Sonia died. Hart had slept all night on top of his wife's cold, dead body, holding the hand of the child he would never meet in life. Weaving in and out of consciousness, he recalled only fragments of dreams indistinguishable from reality. He landed in a dark, terrible place, blacker than the bottom of any ocean, a place that even the full light of day would be hard-pressed to illuminate. And there he saw Sonia and it terrified him, because she was dead. Because an ocean of space and time now rippled between them.

But like most missives from the unconscious, unless you pull them to wakefulness, they languish in fallow ground, the seeds unplanted. If the key to Sonia's death lay in Hart's dreams, he'd be damned if he could piece together their meanings, and when the cold shock of morning came and the dream proved reality, Hart looked up to see the ashen face of his father-in-law standing above him while Hart lay prostrate, still strewn across two dead bodies.

For a moment he thought he might be accused. "I don't know what happened."

"It's all right," Bicky said, his voice surprising Hart with its tenderness. He pulled Hart to his feet, handed him a glass of water and one of scotch, and sat him on the couch with his beverages and a tenuous hold on reality. Then Bicky attended to the details of clean up.

Hart asked precious few questions himself. By the time Bicky's personal physician had administered Hart a healthy injection of morphine, "for the shock," Hart was so confounded by pain and medication that he hadn't the presence of mind to ask what in God's name Bicky was doing there. He passed out just as the men in black from the funeral home carried the shroud-wrapped bodies from the house on a stretcher.

The physician's face ebbed and flowed like the tide before Hart's eyes. Hart wasn't sure how long he lay between worlds. Maybe hours, maybe days. He awoke, ravenously hungry and with a headache that wouldn't quit. Bicky's physician offered him Valium, but Hart refused, choosing a blinding headache over just being blind. Apparently he'd been out for days and having eaten no food in that time, his stomach had shrunk. After a shower and a bit of lunch, a car appeared driven by Bicky's chauffeur, Manuel. He held the door open and Hart crawled into the back seat.

"I'm very sorry, Mr. Hart," Manuel said into the rearview mirror. With over thirty years in, Manuel qualified for the list of people who spent most of their lifetime working for Bicky Coleman. Hart nodded, accepting the genuine grief Manuel offered. Manuel turned away before their eyes met as the car crawled down the road.

Kitty insisted the wake be held at the Coleman estate in the rich suburbs of Houston. Overcome with grief, she lost herself in the details. It was a major undertaking, a wake with over five hundred guests in attendance. Sonia was very active in the philanthropic community, a member of the Junior League, on several local boards, and everyone that worked for Bicky knew and loved Sonia in her own right. It seemed that all of Houston had turned out for her funeral and for that of the poor, unfortunate child.

As the day wound down, Hart sought refuge in Bicky's study. Exhausted from a day of laughing, crying, and occasionally throwing up, he sat, hands clasped, staring at his feet. A fire had been lit against the fall chill and Hart breathed the subtle whiffs of wood smoke into his lungs. A murmured conversation was taking place in the hallway. He ignored the chatter at first, but something about the strangled urgency of the words made him perk up and listen as through the doorway, mourners came into view. Bicky had

Jerry Dixon by the lapel of his expertly tailored suit. The two men were locked in a battle of wills, their voices low to maintain secrecy.

"You haven't done a damn thing to figure this all out, have you?" Bicky asked. "I should have fired you a long time ago."

"I should have quit a long time ago." Jerry looked murderous. He grabbed Bicky's wrist, forcing him to release the vice-grip he held on Jerry's collar, and tossed it aside as if it were a slug.

Hart shifted and his chair creaked, calling their attention to himself. Bicky noted Hart's figure, silhouetted before the fire, and motioned to Jerry to leave.

He entered the room without saying a word, flopped into his overstuffed armchair and stared into the flame as if he were the only person on earth. After several minutes, he turned to Hart, eyes wet with tears. Hart narrowed his eyes at his father-in-law. He hadn't formed words, or even the idea yet, but something in David's heart knew. Bicky Coleman, practiced in the art of delusion, of bending people to his will, was hiding something. Hart involuntarily braced himself for Bicky's onslaught, which in his current state he knew he couldn't defend. Bicky made a show of drying his eyes before speaking.

"I want you to go down to the Gulf of Mexico. There's a rig that's been waiting for repairs for a while now."

Hart took a deep breath. Whatever he thought Bicky was going to say, it had nothing to do with work. He searched Bicky's face, trying to divine his true motives, but as always, it was a blank sheet of paper.

"You're telling me about work now?"

"Work's the best thing for you right now," Bicky said. He cleared his throat. "EPA inspected the rig while you were out." There was a wryness in Bicky's voice that made it sound as if Hart had been on vacation as opposed to mostly unconscious. "They say we've got some uncontrolled leakage. And we need a better SPCC Plan."

Hart stared at the tongue-in-groove floor. Sonia had wanted him to lay a new one in their dining room — him, not a contractor, because of his skill with wood and intricate design. A hexagonal pattern, that's what she'd wanted.

Hart looked up to find Bicky staring at him. "Spill Pollution Control and Countermeasures Plan," he said, as if trying to remind himself. "It's mandatory for anyone dealing with oil. And water." He rubbed his hands together as if for warmth. "I'm just not sure that I'm going to go back. What with this … " he choked back the emotion and fell silent.

Bicky grunted. "Why? Because Sonia wanted you to quit?" He waved a hand in the air as if to sweep all of life's little details away and wiped his eyes with the other. "Well, that hardly matters now." He stood and walked over to the desk where a decanter and four glasses sat. Bicky's hunched shoulders and slow, careful gate were sure signs that this father-in-law was exhausted, Hart noted with satisfaction. The vivacious Bicky Coleman seemed to have aged overnight to reveal a chink in the armor of his unflappable demeanor. Bicky poured two glasses, measuring a couple jiggers in each, and tossed in some ice. The fire reflected off the dark amber liquid splashing and winking in the glass as Bicky crossed the room and handed a glass to Hart. "You have nothing left to you, my boy, but work. Join the club." Bicky drained his glass and stood staring at his son-in-law.

"If you want to take some time off, you have plenty coming to you," Bicky said.

Hart raised his glass to his lips and sniffed. He downed the whiskey in two gulps and handed it to Bicky. He swallowed the lump in his throat and swiped at his eyes.

Bicky poured two more glasses.

Hart gripped the sides of the armchair. "The last time we talked about it I told her that by this time next year I'd be done with oil. I told her I needed to work it out with you, though. Didn't want to leave you scrambling to fill positions, though." Bicky returned with another round, handed it to him, and sat down. The men sipped their drinks silently for several minutes.

"Now it really doesn't really matter what I do. I just know I can't stay in that house." Hart hunched over his glass and stared at the fire.

"She sat right there, you know. The night she died. She came over for dinner. It was the best time we'd had in years." Bicky rubbed his forehead and eyebrows, his drooping shoulders and his tight, pinched face revealing his anguish. A small moan emanated from his throat and he looked around as if startled by the noise.

"We didn't get along that well, I know. But she was my daughter." Bicky's face was half in shadow, half illuminated by dancing firelight. Any doubts that Hart had as to Bicky's true feelings were dispelled the instant he looked into Bicky's eyes and saw the profundity of his sorrow. Emotional exhaustion had set in and Hart's initial impulse was to leave, but unseen forces had him rooted to the chair. He drained his glass, the alcohol working its magic on him, and stared at his shoes.

"Why don't you stay here tonight?" Bicky asked. He grabbed the decanter and refilled both their glasses. Hart swished the whiskey around in his glass before draining it. He let his head loll against the high-backed leather chair, closed his eyes and waited for oblivion to find him.

CHAPTER 22

Streetlights struggled against a foggy, moonless night, their beams crashing to a halt against the first heavy water particles they met. Only intermittent porch lights remained aglow. The occupants of the homes on Willow Street were asleep for the night. A car crept down the road, pulled into the Tirabi driveway and killed the lights and the engine.

Upstairs, Gil flicked on the small light next to his bed, his own invention, a forearm and claw. Light emanated from the palm of the claw and down toward the base which held it in place. Kori had helped him with the design.

Gil held his breath to better hear the outside world. He threw the covers back and walked silently to the window. Despite the chilly November air, Gil slept with the window cracked. He drew back the curtain a hair's breath, allowing only enough space for one eye to peer down to the car parked in the driveway. A Pacifica, Gil thought, but his one eye couldn't confirm it.

Muffled sounds rose from the driveway, and Gil could see the car windows starting to fog. The door swung wide. Gil drew a sharp intake of breath and pulled back from the curtain. He stood in contemplation, eyes rolling back and forth as if trying to deduce further information. After several seconds, he bolted out the bedroom door and ran down the corridor, taking the steps two at a time. He grasped the doorknob with both hands and flung the door open, hitting the wall and sending a shiver through the house.

"What the heck are you doing?" a disembodied voice asked as it rounded the corner and came up the front steps. Gil let out a short yelp and jumped full on at the approaching figure, wrapping his arms around its neck and squeezing for all he was worth.

Robbie dropped his bags just in time to catch his brother, but not in time to get his balance. The pair went clattering to the ground in a confused tangle of limbs, their fall broken only by the bags at Robbie's feet. "Gil," he grunted, more of a guttural sound than a word. Gil released his death grip and Robbie wheezed, regaining his breath. He raised himself on one elbow and Gil did the same, as if lying on duffel bags on the front stoop in the middle of the night was a normal thing.

"I knew you were coming back tonight," Gil said. "Kori said not until tomorrow, but I knew it would be today."

"Well, technically Kori's right since it's after midnight, but we're not going to tell her that, right?" Robbie asked. Gil nodded and lunged for his brother again, toppling him back and onto the ground.

"It's been three months and twenty-seven days," Gil said into Robbie's neck. Robbie rubbed Gil's back in a circular motion.

"I missed you, too, buddy," Robbie said. "What do you say we get out of this fog? It's creepin' me out a little." Gil helped Robbie to his feet and grabbed his duffle bag, grunting with the strain of it. Robbie smiled, watching him crash and bang his way into the foyer. A light crept out from under Kori's door and spilled down the stairs.

"Hawk at twelve o'clock," Robbie said, and Gil looked up the stairs to see Kori's slippered feet standing at the top.

"Gil, what are doing? It's the middle of the night."

Robbie's voice was hoarse from lack of sleep. "He did the hospitable thing and came to greet me."

"Robbie!" Kori ran down the stairs and jumped into Robbie's arms, knocking him down for the second time in the last five minutes. He lay sprawled on the floor with Kori straddled on top of him. She blushed, mumbled an apology and pulled him to his feet. She held his grip and stared at him intently for a moment, a specimen under a microscope. He folded her into his arms, and in a heartbeat she returned the mantle of responsibility to her younger brother.

"That bad, huh?" She shook her head and stifled the urge to cry. He squeezed tighter. "Hey, how about a drink?"

"Yeah, hot chocolate!" Gil yelled. A moment later the hall light clicked on, and a crusty-eyed Avery stumbled out of his room and into the hallway.

"Gil?" he called downstairs. "Are you all right?"

"He is now," Robbie called back.

"Robbie!" Avery said, taking the stairs two at a time.

"When did you get home? I mean...that's a stupid question. Why didn't you tell us you were coming?"

"The element of surprise, my brother," Robbie said. "C'mon. I'm starving. What've you got to eat in this place?"

"A little salmon with lime and Wasabi sauce," Avery said. "My own creation." Robbie crinkled his nose.

"How about a little spanakopita from Aunt Stella," Avery said. "And some baklava for dessert."

Robbie's eyebrows shot up in appreciation. "God, it's good to be home." He wrapped his arm around Gil's shoulder, and they headed for their midnight raid on the refrigerator.

CHAPTER 23

Robbie's breath snaked out in steamy tendrils as he raked at the earth's palette of bronzes, golds, reds and browns. Tiny veins shot through the musculoskeletal structure, transparent in death. Leaves. There were a million of them. He gathered giant piles together, stopping on occasion to glance at the ones that glowed. He would shuttle the piles back to the woods later with the tractor. For now, he maintained a steady rhythm, grunting on occasion, but with single-mindedness, lost in deep thought.

The previous night's fog had lifted, replaced by rows of cumulus-stratus clouds broken intermittently by the brazen morning sun. Where dawn broke through the empty spaces, patches of orange and gold hurtled across the landscape and scattered the ground with a brilliant luminosity. Robbie stopped to watch the effervescent and mutable light show, evolving before his eyes. He inhaled its beauty with a peace that comes only in the small moments before returning to the task before him.

Avery stepped out on the back deck wrapped in a blanket and wearing bedroom slippers.

"What are you doing, fool?" he whispered. "It's 6:30 in the morning?"

Robbie smiled and nodded but didn't answer so Avery went back inside. Ten minutes later he returned, rake in hand and dressed for the day.

"Is this what basic training has done to you?" He thrust a coffee cup into Robbie's hand. Robbie gulped it down in four swallows.

"Didn't that hurt?" Avery asked, stunned.

"I was doing my Gil impersonation," Robbie responded. He flashed a set of picture perfect teeth. At five feet, eleven inches, Robbie would never achieve Avery's height, but an additional fifty pounds and the build of a linebacker left Avery with no advantage. Where Avery's lithe, wistful frame reminded one of a willow tree, Robbie's solid, massive build was more akin to an oak.

"You couldn't have gotten more than a few hours' sleep. Go crawl back in." Robbie rolled his coffee mug across the freshly raked ground. It halted at the nearest leaf pile.

Avery shook his head. "I'm up now. I'll hang." Avery took a sip, set his steaming cup down and threw himself into the task. They worked in silence for several minutes before Avery spoke, his eyebrows furrowed in thought.

"Robbie?"

"Hmmm?"

"Tell me about Mom and Dad."

A shadow crossed Robbie's face. "What do you want to know?" He didn't look at his brother.

"Did you talk to them before … " Avery's voice trailed off and ended in silence. "Well, I know that, I mean, you said … but, did you … ?" He coughed to clear his throat. Robbie searched Avery's face before laying down his rake.

"Go get me another cup of coffee and I'll tell you," Robbie said. Avery turned and walked inside, retrieving Robbie's mug along the way.

⅄

Avery returned with two mugs, and Robbie joined him on the step. They sipped in silence, allowing the last streaks of oranges, purples and blues to pass before Robbie spoke.

"It was pretty bad."

"I can handle it."

"I know you can handle it," Robbie said. "I just don't know if I want to plant that visual in your overactive imagination."

"That's Gil."

"It runs in the family."

"If I have nightmares, I promise I won't call you," Avery said.

"You can always call me. And you can always ask me. Anything."

"Really?" Avery said.

"What do ya' think?"

Avery cleared his throat. "Okay. What's it like to sleep with a girl?"

"Oh." Robbie ran his hands through his hair. The rhythmic *who-who, who, who* of a Great Horned Owl broke the tension. "You know how all the body parts work?"

"I'm sixteen. Give me some credit," Avery said, toeing the step with his sneaker. "I was looking for something more...subtle. You know. Maybe something I could use...." He ended his sentence with a little fake cough, covering his mouth.

"Truth be told, if you weren't a novice, I might have a thing or two to say about it. You're still pretty young."

"Well? Can you give me something useful anyway? For later?"

The corner of Robbie's mouth twisted up in a grin. "At first it's a lot like hunting, all adrenaline pumping and going in for the kill. And you'll feel half-dead afterward, like somebody gutted you, but also like you're light as a feather. After, you've done it a few times and gotten the hang of it — I say that because you never really get used to it enough to take for granted, at least not if you're doing it right — then it becomes more like fishing. You've got plenty of time. You may as well relax and enjoy the boat ride."

Avery waited, but Robbie said nothing more. "That's it?" he asked incredulously. "That's your brotherly advice?"

"What do you want from me? I can only deal with one earth-moving topic at a time. You choose."

Avery hesitated. "Mom and Dad then," he said, obviously torn. "But promise you'll tell me about the other one before you go back."

"All right," Robbie replied. The smile faded from his eyes.

"After I left, I headed to Philadelphia. I knew they'd take the I-95 home. I was looking for accidents. It was a busy night for the cops. Three accidents that night." Robbie shuddered and wrapped his hands around his coffee cup for warmth. "I stopped at every one. I had to cross I-95 on foot and hop the median to get a look since the emergency vehicles were the only thing you could see from the other side." Robbie grimaced and shook his head. "I won't tell you what the first two looked like. You wouldn't sleep for a week. I held my breath every time, praying it wasn't Mom and Dad, and every time I said a little prayer of thanks. I was feeling lucky." At that, Robbie's eyes watered and he squished his eyelids against them.

"And then, that third time, my luck was done 'cause there they were. It was so dark. It seemed like the whole world was on tilt. Maybe the street light blinking, I don't know. Everything had this hyper-kinetic feel, like flashing strobe lights." Robbie's face was a mask of calm, betraying none of the raging vortex of emotions hovering just below the surface.

"Were they conscious? Did they know you were there?" Avery asked.

Robbie shook his head. "I don't know. The paramedics had already strapped them onto Gurneys. I saw them load Mom into the ambulance. Her eyes were closed and her mouth was open. I called her, first Mom, and then by her full name. She mumbled something, but I was too far away to hear. I think I startled the hell out of the paramedics, coming from the middle of the road and all. I told the guy they were my parents, but he just kept at it. Told me to drive to the hospital." Robbie shrugged. "Bastard." He took a deep, jagged breath.

"What about Dad? Did you see him?"

Robbie's throat constricted, but he squeezed the words out. "He was already in the ambulance with a sheet pulled over his head." Robbie held his coffee cup in a death grip, his knuckles white with the strain. "I talked to the sole cop at the scene."

The boys sat shoulder-to-shoulder, so intent on their conversation that neither heard the door open behind them.

"He hadn't seen the accident," Robbie continued, "but surmised based on the positioning, that they were forced off the road by a second car."

"What second car?" Both Robbie and Avery jumped at Gil's query.

"When the heck did you get here?" Robbie asked, agitated.

"Just when you said 'forced off the road by the second car,'" Gil said.

"Yeah, well, go back inside. Avery and I are talking."

"I want to know what happened," Gil said. Robbie and Avery exchanged glances. "I'm old enough." Avery shrugged and Robbie relented.

"All right, come sit down." Gil sat down next to Robbie with Max at his feet, the brothers all in a line.

"There was a man passed out in the front seat. The air bag had exploded and the car reeked of alcohol, like a bottle spilled. I have a different theory now." Robbie cast a strange look in Avery's direction, but Avery didn't follow.

"I stuck my head in the back seat and the freaking ... " Robbie looked at Gil and blushed, "the smell of alcohol was overwhelming. Like a frat house on prom night."

"The cop came over and I asked him why the guy was still lying in the car. He said the paramedics checked him over and there was nothing wrong with him other than being drunk. They were short of ambulances so the guy was still waiting for a ride. Judging from the cop's reaction, I think he was happy to leave him there to rot."

"Did he ever wake up? Gil asked. He stared wide-eyed at Robbie as he continued with the story. Max thumped his tail twice on the wooden step when Gil spoke.

"Actually, he did."

"Did you talk to him?" Avery asked. Robbie stared off into the distance, the scene replaying before his eyes. He shook his head trying to dispel the memory.

"There was just a minute where the cop was in his squad car, talking on the radio and it was just me and this guy. He reached out his hand so I took it. He smelled awful. I almost puked."

"Was he hurt? Did you get him out?" Gil asked. Robbie drank the rest of his coffee and set the mug down at his feet.

"He didn't ask for help. He just looked at me and said he didn't want to do it."

"Didn't want to do it or didn't mean to do it?" Avery asked.

"I'm not sure," Robbie replied. Several pots with hardy mums adorned the sides of the steps. Robbie plucked the head off one, sniffed it and tossed the scentless flower to the ground. "And the weirdest thing is, I could swear the guy was faking it. I mean, he talked like a drunk, but his eyes were lucid. I had the strangest feeling like … "

"Like what?" Gil asked.

"Like he had drunk the alcohol after the accident. Drunk people stink from inside not outside. It smelled like he poured it on himself instead of down his throat," Robbie said. Gil's eyebrows shot up as he pondered this new information. Avery responded more cynically.

"That doesn't sound right. The guy's in prison now," Avery said. "Why would he do it on purpose?"

Robbie shrugged. "I can only call it like I saw it."

"But why would anyone want to hurt Mom and Dad?" Avery asked. "They didn't have any enemies."

"Well maybe they didn't, but what if someone they worked for did?"

"The Governor?" Avery asked. "You're not serious."

"I don't know. None of it makes any sense." Robbie rubbed his temples.

"Well, Dad didn't have any enemies. He was too nice a guy. All his students loved him," Avery said. He polished off the rest of his coffee, a tawny mixture of three quarters milk and one-quarter coffee, and set the mug in the crook of his arm. Gil tapped his foot.

"What about all the stuff Mom was doing, trying to get the landfill shut down. Maybe someone didn't want her meddling," Robbie said.

Gil continued tapping, his whole body following a trajectory back and forth. "Can we eat breakfast now? I'm starving." He jumped up and ran into the kitchen without waiting for a response. Avery shrugged, following.

"I'll be there in a minute," Robbie said. He sat, staring at the landfill in the distance.

"Hey, Robbie?"

"Yeah?"

"Since you're leaving and we don't know when you'll be back, I was thinking … "

"Yeah?"

"I was thinking that we should have a big backyard party. Bonfire, food, fireworks."

"Sounds like a plan," Robbie said. He rose wearily and followed Gil inside.

λ

The sun was low in the late October sky, and Robbie judged by the dwindling light that it was soon dinnertime. He turned on his flashlight and circled the perimeter of the barn, checking the foundation, the walls, the roofline, looking for any breaches in the exterior. He completed his circle and banged on the barn door.

"All tight. Not even a mouse could get in here."

"What's that?" Jack emerged from the barn, wiping his hands on a rag.

"How'd it go?" Robbie asked. Gil followed Jack out of the barn, pounding his fist in his open palm over and over again.

"All finished," Jack said. "He's safer out here than in the house." Gil walked over, still punching, and stood beside Robbie who grabbed both Gil's hands in his one, silencing them.

"We should have done this before," Robbie said. "Now I'll sleep better." Gil smiled and removed his hands from Robbie's grasp.

"Let's show him how it works." Jack went inside and the brothers followed.

"There's a couple different ways it can go. But the most important is, when the alarm goes off, it sends a signal directly to the police station. So if you're in here and you're armed, be sure you know where the call buttons are. You don't want to be sending signals to the police all the time and have them show up looking for bad guys who aren't here."

Jack cocked an eyebrow at Gil who wiggled his shoulders, his excitement growing.

"The call buttons are here, here, and here," Jack said, indicating places on the wall and side of the door. Gil sat down on the swivel stool at his drafting table and spun around once.

"As soon as you're in, you turn the key for the deadbolt," Jack closed the barn door and turned the key, "and that will automatically activate the alarm. You can override it by pressing this button here," Jack said, indicating a yellow button on the alarm panel. "That red light up there," he continued, pointing to a spot above the door, "will let you know if the alarm is working. If the light's on, you're armed."

Gil squirmed in his seat, beaming. "Gilliam William Tirabi!" Robbie said. "I cannot stress enough the significance of this item. It is not, I repeat, not, a toy. And this is not a movie." He looked at Gil for emphasis. "If you trip the alarm too many times – either by accident or on purpose," Robbie raised his eyebrows and stared intently at his brother, "the cops won't come when you do need them. Do you understand?"

A wide smile revealed most of Gil's teeth. He spun around again and nodded. "Yes."

"Good." Robbie looked at Jack for him to continue.

"If you want to bring the whole system down, you hit this button." Jack indicated another switch, this one in blue. "And finally, if you're under attack, I mean full on, no holds barred, take no prisoners, all-out assault, you hit this button." Jack pointed to a red triangular button that sat alone on the alarm panel." This one is hard-wired to call not only the local cops but the state police. And it wails, an eardrum-bleeding screech of an alarm system that will wake Kori, Avery, and every neighbor within a three-block radius. But your ears are super sensitive, so I'm tellin' you, man, don't use this one unless you really, really need it."

"Okay, okay, I get it," Gil said, unable to suppress a smile.

"All right," Robbie said, "we're done."

"Oh, one more thing," Jack said, picking up a pack of earplugs off the shelf. "If you do activate the alarm of death," he smirked and grabbed Gil's arm, "make sure you use these."

Gil opened his hand and Jack placed a pair of earplugs in it. Gil rubbed them between his fingers, scrunched them down to nothing and stuck them in his ears where they expanded.

"Okay, gentlemen," Robbie said. Jack deactivated the alarm and Robbie locked the barn up for the night, handing Gil the key.

"I'm giving Avery a spare key. He'll know how the alarm works," Robbie said to Gil.

Gil smiled. The bright green neon earplugs sticking out of his ears made him look like Dumbo.

CHAPTER 24

On the eve of Robbie's departure, the party at the Tirabi's had been seven days in the making and it showed. There were kids everywhere, the youngest, a ten-year old girl named Arianna, lived across the street and had snuck out of her bedroom window to see Gil, her secret crush. They'd been palling around all night, hanging together on the tire swing and talking about "stuff." Gil tolerated her attentions with more than the modicum of interest he reserved for family members and appeared to be enjoying himself until Arianna tried to hold his hand. Rattled, he mumbled something about forgetting to feed the fish, ran inside and locked himself in his room for the duration of the evening. Robbie checked on him around 10 o'clock, picking the lock with a dexterity possessed by burglars and jewel thieves, and found him lying on his bed, fully clothed and dead asleep. No amount of nudging would rouse him, so Robbie removed Gil's shoes and turned off the light.

For her part, Aunt Stella sat in the kitchen like a sentry on her watch, guarding the troops, restocking and rearranging the platters of food, and looking for signs of unruly visitors. When the cops came, drawn by complaining neighbors, Aunt Stella sent them packing, a meatball sandwich in one hand and a baggie full of her homemade goodies in the other. She and Avery had spent every day after school huddled together in her kitchen, churning out cookies by the dozens, along with appetizers, salads and sides, tireless kitchen warriors armed only with whisks, spatulas and carving knives. Now at 11 p.m., Aunt Stella was feeling the pull as she wearily collected the night's refuse.

Robbie burst in as if escaping. "All this talking and hugging and girls crying. I'm starving. Anything left?" He peered under the lids of the various Crockpots lining the counter, savoring the aromas in each. "I haven't eaten a thing since lunchtime," he said, spearing a meatball with a plastic fork. He popped it in his mouth and slumped against the counter, eyes closed, chewing.

"What do you want? Pork, chicken, or meatball sandwich?" Aunt Stella asked.

"One of each," he said. He grabbed her around her substantial midsection, picked her up and squeezed her.

Aunt Stella blushed, at a loss for words. "Oh my."

Robbie set her down and kissed her on both cheeks.

"You're the best, Aunt Stella. Thanks," he said, waving a hand over the mounds of food still crowding the counter. He grabbed a plate and made a sandwich. "For everything."

"What about this plasticware?" she asked, holding a dirty spoon. "Shall I wash it?"

"Nah. What for?"

"I was thinking of your mother and how it would probably be something that would happen in Ruth's kitchen," Stella answered.

Robbie's face changed but he kept chewing. "Fair enough," he said, mouth full to capacity. "In honor of Ruth." He stuck a used, heavy-duty plastic fork in the dishwasher.

Aunt Stella loaded the rest of the used plastic utensils into the dishwasher. "In honor of Ruth," she said. She closed it, turning her attention to the disarray of desserts on the table, less to restore order than to avert her watery eyes from Robbie's careful gaze. When she had regained her composure, she said, "This is your two-hour warning. At one o'clock, the entire lot of them in the backyard is going to turn into pumpkins. That means I want to see them getting in their cars and heading home. Those that can't drive can sleep down there," she said, indicating the basement.

"And if anyone thinks there's going to be any funny business, they better think again. 'Cause Aunt Stella's on patrol."

She smacked Robbie's arm and shuffled off to the living room to catch the 11 o'clock news and a catnap before her next shift began.

ᛏ

The next morning, Robbie rose at four so he could shower and collect his thoughts before his ride arrived. At six, a car horn beeped. They were all sitting in the kitchen again, drinking warm beverages to fight the chill of the coming loss. Robbie gathered his brothers and sister, enveloping them each in a bear hug before collecting his things.

He climbed in the back seat, rolled down the window and patted his heart twice while the rest of the Tirabis stood on the front porch, holding each other. Robbie watched them watching him as the view diminished and the space between them stretched out into infinity.

CHAPTER 25

Dave Hartos walked into Bicky's penthouse suite on the 45th floor of the Akanabi building. Not much of a voyeur himself, Hart had always felt uncomfortable up here. Bicky loved it though, and once remarked that from a height this great you could see into a man's soul, and in Houston that was a valuable trait to have. Phyllis sat at her desk, sorting a cart full of Bicky's mail when she saw him. Her eyes brightened and she tossed the letter opener onto the desk, embracing him warmly.

"It's you," she said, brushing her hand across his cheek as if she had no control over it. She assessed him for several moments. "You know, if there's absolutely anything you need that is within my power to procure ... " she looked at the closed door to Bicky's office, "and you know I have consider-able resources at my disposal, then you shouldn't hesitate to ask."

"I know, Phyllis. Thanks," Hart said. "We didn't get a chance to talk at the funeral."

Phyllis put a hand to her lips to stop the forthcoming apology.

"It's going to take a lot of time, my dear. And it may never get better. It's just something that you get used to ... or learn to live with." She said the last bit with assuredness.

"He's on the phone." Phyllis nodded toward the door. "You don't need to sit here watching me sort his mail. Go on in. He hates that." Her smile radiated benevolence. Hart noted the distinct lines of her face, the beauti-ful, almond-shaped green eyes, the lovely, high cheekbones, and thought that in her youth Phyllis had been a knockout. No wonder Bicky had hired her. He'd recognized her as a trophy, and Bicky liked nothing more than to collect trophies.

"Thanks." He searched for more to say, to give this moment the meaning he wanted. The words, "we should have lunch sometime," were out of his mouth before he knew he had thought them, trite and non-committal; they sounded ridiculous even to his grief-laden brain. For her part, Phyllis was gracious and, as always, in charge.

"That would be nice," she said, and squeezed his hand. Hart knew she meant it.

⅄

Bicky was on the phone, a burning cigar in the ashtray. He stood with his back to the door looking out over Houston's great expanse with an antique pair of opera glasses. He didn't turn to greet Hart when the door opened, but his shoulders stiffened, probably because he'd been caught spying.

The conversation wound down and Bicky hung up, walked around to the front of the desk and stood in front of Hart. He handed him the opera glasses, which Hart accepted for closer inspection.

"They belonged to my mother," Bicky began. "She never saw a live opera, but we had an old Victrola and some albums that she played over and over again. My dad bought the glasses for her at a flea market where he used to take the pelts he'd trapped. Came back with those glasses. They were cheap, maybe a couple bucks, but it was an extravagance we really couldn't afford. My mom pretended to be mad at him, but I used to watch her at night sometimes, listening to the swell of the music with the glasses to her eyes, looking out into the foothills, seeing what, I'm not sure."

Bicky stopped and snatched the glasses back, unaware that Hart hadn't finished his inspection. He picked up his cigar, flopped down into his chair and put his feet up on the desk.

Mr. Big. Hart smiled to himself.

"One of our oil platforms in the Gulf's got a slow leak. A little sheen on the water, no biggie. They think one of the valves in the Christmas tree's shot. I called Mahajan. I'm not sure he located a diver yet."

"When did they first see the sheen?"

"Four days ago."

"Why didn't you do something four days ago?" Hart asked, deadpan. "The feds inspect those platforms every week. And they come down hard on repeat violators." Hart watched Bicky's face, an emotionless mask. "You can't keep pushing the envelope, or you're going to have another crisis on your hands."

Half of Bicky's mouth quirked into a leer: "I'm sure that whatever happens, you'll be able to handle it."

Hart shrugged and looked away, unable to raise the contempt he should have felt in this moment.

"It's up to Mahajan, of course." Bicky took a puff of his cigar and blew out a large, round smoke ring. "But I don't think it's a rush. Inspections are way down, thanks to the Bush Administration. The guy from the U.S. Minerals Management Service shows up once a month, if that. So we've got at least three weeks to handle this, and if it's just some valve change outs like I think it is, we can handle that in three hours." Bicky took another drag on his cigar and tried to blow the second ring through the first. The smoke hovered in the air insidiously.

"What about the EPA?" Hart asked.

"Who the hell cares about EPA?

"You will when they slap you with a huge fine," Hart said. Bicky tapped the desk in metronomic fashion and watched his son-in-law; Hart obliged and looked out the window.

"Who's gonna tell them? We're two hundred miles out in the middle of the Gulf of Mexico, for Chrissakes. Not exactly a drive-by." He tapped the ash on his cigar. Hart stole a sidelong glance at his father-in-law.

"Look, I'm not blind. I know that since Sonia … "

"That event and the one before us are completely unrelated."

Bicky placed his cigar in the ashtray. "You're the best guy I've got. I'd hate to lose you but … " His sentence hung in the air alongside the cigar smoke.

Hart's emotions swirled, trapped in a rip tide: guilt, rage, horror, fear, and somewhere deep down, both loathing and respect for the man who sat across the table from him. He didn't say anything, just stared at Bicky, forcing him to address the unspoken. Vestiges of the solemn, haggard face Hart had seen the night of the funeral clouded Bicky's ready-for-business face.

"I miss her, too," he said simply. And that was all the emotion Bicky Coleman could muster for his dead child. Hart's eyes were locked on Bicky, but all he could see was the last ten years of his life, happy years spent living with Sonia and working for Akanabi Oil, incompatible bedfellows at best, he now knew.

"So what I need to know is, are you still on my team?" Bicky's voice floated like bubbles to the surface of a turbulent lake.

A lump, all fibrous and full of itself, wedged in Hart's trachea. He tried to dislodge it by clearing his throat, but the lump would not budge. His eyes watched Bicky, but his mind saw Sonia. Except she was dead and all he had left was the job, and despite his desire to honor her memory, he didn't feel up to losing that now, too. Not trusting his own voice, he nodded.

"Good." Bicky sighed, relieved. "Very good." He walked around to Hart's side of the desk. "You fly out tomorrow night, assuming that will give you sufficient time to get your act together." Bicky said the last part as if Hart had a choice. He leaned back against the desk in front of Hart. "Take a few weeks. Since you're out there, you may as well look the whole platform over. When you're done, maybe you and Mahajan can take a vacation. Some excellent fishing out there." Bicky smiled and held his hand out to Hart who raised his own to meet it without an awareness of the movement. "The trip'll do you good. Some surf and sun. Some good hard work. You'll come back a new man."

Hart nodded mechanically as Bicky showed him to the door.

Chapter 26

Two days later, Hart stood on the deck of an oil platform floating a hundred feet above the water. The cabling and mooring anchors that held the rig in place paralleled out at distances of up to half a mile and dropped at 30-degree angles to the bottom of the sea. In a storm, the crew could tighten the cables to make the rigging more secure so that in fifteen to twenty foot seas the platform wouldn't even budge. Hart hadn't felt so much as a ripple since he'd been here and would have forgotten he was on the water if there wasn't water in every direction straight out to the horizon.

With a half-dozen anchors each weighing up to twenty tons, the platform could float two hundred yards in any direction without causing a blip on the radar screen. However, once the drilling stem was attached, that flexibility was lost and the platform sat fixed on the sea, tethered by a single pipe and the anchors that held it. This particular oil platform was named *The Eva*, purportedly after the fifties movie star, Ava Gardner. At the time they named it, no one thought to check the spelling.

Here in the depths of the Gulf of Mexico, the floating platform, first used after World War II, worked best. A monolithic superstructure capable of drilling below the ocean bottom to depths of more than three thousand feet, it housed drilling and production equipment like gas turbines, compressors, revolving cranes, generators, pumps, a gas flare stack, survival craft, a helicopter pad and what Hart and everyone else on deck considered some pretty cushy living quarters, a hotel of industry-quality rating and five-star catering facilities. With nothing else to do but work, eat, and sleep, the governing philosophy behind oil platform management was that the men should be comfortably housed and well fed.

The superstructure, or topsides of the oil platform, all forty thousand tons of it, floated on a substructure comprised of a dozen clusters of six tubes per cluster. The tubes were five feet in diameter and spaced evenly across the underside of the platform. The air in these steel tubes kept the entire monstrosity afloat and the levels could be adjusted, adding air to compensate for the tenor of the sea by opening or closing a series of valves. In calm seas the tubes were about three quarters full.

Hart had supervised the inspection of these rigs hundreds of times and was still amazed at the physics governing the floatation: get it right and she'd float for decades; get it wrong and she'd sink like a boulder in a matter of hours, millions of dollars' worth of machinery and equipment, and even lives, destined to spend eternity at the bottom of the sea.

The only way on or off the rig was a three-hour helicopter ride or a ten-hour boat ride from the mainland, depending on weather. But Hart didn't think much about that. In ten years, only once had he seen a rig fail.

He'd been employed by Akanabi for only a few years and had not yet achieved his current Chief of Engineering position. Recognizing his brilliance as well as his ability to lead men, Bicky had sent Hart out to inspect what was suspected to be a corrupted platform in the North Sea off the eastern coast of Scotland. After two days, Hart concluded that the crew should be evacuated and the platform should be sunk before the approaching storm and imbalanced mixture of air and water in the hollow piping system sank it for them. Bicky stalled and doubled the pumping schedule, pushing the machinery past maximum capacity and dragging his feet to the point of crisis. Hart overrode Bicky's authority as CEO, and evacuated the platform barely an hour before it began its precipitous decline into the icy waters of the North Sea. Hart shivered thinking of the agonizing minutes spent loading three helicopters and a Coast Guard rescue boat. Rather than thanking Hart for the savvy that had spared the lives of thirty-three employees, Bicky harbored a grudge, blaming Hart for the mistreatment he received in the press. Hart, however, had emerged unscathed with a commendation from the Board of Directors of Akanabi, the loyalty of the men on board that day, and his hero mystique firmly in place.

⋏

One of the older rigs, *The Eva* took as few as fifteen and as many as thirty crew members to tend it. Known as "roughnecks," they were a stout, aggressive and resolute bunch, always seeing a problem to its logical conclusion. Hart had worked with all the members of this crew before and liked every one of them.

The *Poseidon*, a one hundred and sixty foot dive boat that serviced *The Eva*, shuttled back and forth from the mainland every two weeks with a replacement crew of roughnecks and divers, food and other supplies necessary for operation of the oil platform. The dive boat slept twenty-five, had its own captain and crew, and docked, whenever it wasn't in use, at the moorings erected half a mile from the oil platform. Right now she sat, motor running, rammed up against the side of the platform for stability as its visitors hustled around on deck, preparing for a dive.

A hard-hatted Hart stood at the bow of the dive boat watching as several handlers helped Stu, one of Akanabi's four commercial divers on the payroll, suit up. Although Akanabi employed four divers, only Stu and another guy, currently on medical leave, were full time. Then there was Hart, who served primarily in his capacity as the company's chief engineer, but in a pinch switched hats and donned a commercial diving helmet — not that tube sucking puke stuff those scuba sissies wore, but the hard core hat — thirty-five pounds of bronze and brass designed for driving stakes into the bottom of the ocean with your forehead, if necessary. Akanabi's fourth diver was Andy Mahajan, who was also running the show. Since Mahajan wore more than one hat at Akanabi, he dove only when necessary, that is, when they were short-staffed and couldn't get contract help.

Mahajan had failed to procure a second diver for this trip, so Bicky dispatched Hart for use of his expertise in handing oil spills, but also for diving backup. Although Hart outranked Mahajan in the Akanabi hierarchy, by design Mahajan had the last word on the divers. And Mahajan had yet to give Hart his blessing to dive.

⋏

Akanabi kept Stu busy by shuttling him in round-robin fashion to all of its waterborne facilities across the United States. Anything outside Akanabi contracted out since Stu had a phobia about leaving the country. Stu's diving expertise was nationally acclaimed, and because of that, Akanabi overlooked Stu's self-imposed travel restrictions. They sent him from oil platform to oil platform in two-week rotations, planned months in advance, and due to the demanding nature of the job, Stu normally followed each stint with two weeks off.

Akanabi had pulled Stu from his last two days on a job off the coast of California to come to the Gulf. Stu was less than thrilled. The Gulf trip cut into his two weeks off which meant that if they didn't correct the problem here quickly, there was a very real possibility that Stu would roll right into his next two-week rotation and miss the interim two weeks with his family.

Stu had a four-man team that traveled with him: a radio communications man, whose job was to keep in constant contact with the diver; a manifold operator who assured that the gas mixture Stu received through his umbilical, aptly named since it was a diver's main source of air and radio communication, would sustain him in depths of three hundred feet below sea level; and two tenders who helped Stu in and out of his suit, the water, and any other situations that might arise. Today, Mahajan was training two additional tenders, or greenhorns, bringing Stu's team to a total of six. Hart sat on the deck watching one of the greenhorns help Stu climb into his neoprene suit while Dan, the gas man, checked the pressure in the tank on Stu's backpack.

⋏

Hart made notes on his clipboard and occasionally barked out an order, but it was Mahajan's show. It was the beginning of fall in the Gulf of Mexico, which felt much like the summer absent the infernal heat. The sun's warmth was pleasant, allowing for short sleeves without the sweating. The water, however, was a different story since the temperature could drop anywhere from fifteen to twenty degrees from the summer to fall months, depending on storms and choppy seas. Swells of four to five feet were commonplace this time of year. Hart shuddered despite the warm breeze coming off the Gulf and realized he hadn't been warm since the night he found Sonia and his baby lying on the kitchen floor. He tried to shake off the chill.

Hart's last couple months seemed like a surreal, watery dream. He hadn't forgiven himself for leaving Sonia that night, hadn't accepted that she was really gone. The unbearable heat of guilt, like hot coals driving through his intestines, was his unpredictable bedfellow. Mahajan had found him once, curled up on the floor in the fetal position, clutching his belly. Hart refused the hospital and Bicky's personal physician. He welcomed the pain as atonement for failure to keep the family safe. At Mahajan's insistence, Hart finally did go see his family doctor, but the doctor concluded that Hart's problem wasn't physical.

"Drink more water," the doctor said and sent him home with a prescription for Percocet. Hart flushed the pills down the toilet. Pain was evidence of life.

The activity on deck was slowing. Stu stood in full dive gear, holding his helmet and waiting for a command that would send him over the front of the boat and three hundred and ten feet below the surface. Mahajan was explaining the next steps to the greenhorns. After double-checking the helmet's communication system, securing the weight belt, and checking that Stu had the requisite wrenches, screwdrivers, calipers and other tools, Robert, Stu's main tender, pronounced him dive-ready.

Stu instinctively reached for the air tank on his back and checked the valve. The tank was purposely attached upside down so the diver could reach behind his back at waist level and turn the valve to start the flow of air without contorting his body. Stu opened it slightly. It made a hissing noise as a mixture of nitrogen and helium escaped. Stu closed it quickly to conserve the precious mix.

⚓

"A mother pleaser," Mahajan said to Jason, one of the greenhorns.

"What?" Jason asked.

"A mother pleaser." Hart wrapped an avuncular arm around Jason's shoulder. "It's mixed gas in that tank," he said, pointing to Stu's, "not straight oxygen, right?"

It was Jason's first time on an oil platform assisting a dive. He stood, mouth slightly agape, looking a little disoriented. Hart waited as Jason regained his equilibrium.

"Yeah. I knew that," Jason said.

"Good. So you also know that around one hundred feet down the pressure on your eyes is so great that your retina actually changes shape and you start getting tunnel vision."

Jason nodded, gaining momentum. "If you're just breathing air that far down, you feel like you're drunk, right? You can't even do simple things like change a light bulb."

Hart nodded. "Exactly. And the mixed gas does something to your brain which compensates for its lack of oxygen." Hart walked over to Stu and patted the tank on his back. "This thing'll buy a diver twenty to thirty minutes depending on his depth and how fast he takes the air in. It's time enough for them to tell you what the problem is and get some help on the way."

"And since it looks good and it keeps the insurance companies happy, they call it a mother pleaser," Stu said, picking up the thread of the conversation. "But the gas mixture in that tank won't get a deep water diver anywhere near the surface. Because if you don't decompress in a way that lets your body catch up, you can get dissolved gasses that turn into free floating bubbles in your body - joint pain, rashes, death even. They call it the bends."

"Yep." Hart continued. "Once you get down around two hundred and eighty feet you have to come up slow, about a foot per second. Then when you get to about forty feet, you need a decompression stop. It gives your body a chance to assimilate regular air again. If you do that, you won't get the bends."

"So you just hang around the down line for an hour?" Jason asked.

"No. You sit on a T-Bar hooked to the towline. And when you get back up you hit the decompression chamber for half an hour. Didn't they teach you anything at school?" Stu asked.

"I didn't go yet. My dad knows the head of Akanabi. That's how I got this job."

Stu grimaced and turned away, shaking his head.

Hart and Stu had dived together on many occasions, spending weeks of twelve to sixteen hour days out in the middle of a sea. Over the course of that working relationship, they'd developed a friendship that transcended their aquatic office. Even when he was out in the middle of the ocean, Stu had called Hart every day since Sonia's death to check on Hart's mental health. Hart was grateful for that, but if Stu harbored a few doubts about Hart's readiness to dive today, he kept them to himself. Hart's banter with Jason was more for Stu's benefit than the greenhorn's, calculated to put Stu at ease.

Stu made some adjustments to his hose, fiddled with the regulator on his helmet, and moved his weight belt farther up his back. He wiped the sweat from his brow and leaned against the railing. Sensing Stu's impatience, Hart looked around for Mahajan and spotted him in the Captain's quarters on the phone. He nodded sympathetically at Stu before grabbing Stu's umbilical and continuing with his tutorial.

"This is where the real stuff comes from," Hart said to Jason. "And this is your job for the duration of the dive." He held up the diving hose as if it were a rope of gold. "Feed it to him as much as he needs, like a fish on your pole, but don't hamper his progress. You should be able to feel him moving around. Not too much slack, though. You don't want him getting caught on the bottom. There are all kinds of discarded cabling from the old crane lines that have been dumped there for the last forty years. Nasty old rusty stuff that could slice through this in a second." He held out the dive rig to Jason who grabbed it eagerly. Hart smiled, but his tone was serious. "So pay attention and stay alert." Jason nodded. Mahajan walked up, smacked Jason on the back and smiled.

"You ready?" Mahajan asked.

"You bet," Jason replied.

Mahajan nodded to Hart and they walked to the stern of the boat. The diesel engines churned noisily, making it impossible to hear, so they moved off to the side.

"Do you still want to do this?" Mahajan said. "It's been a while since you suited up and ... ." His voice dwindled, mixing with the sound of the groaning compressors, leaving behind only a look of concern on his broad, tan face. Mahajan studied Hart's face. It showed none of the intensity of the last few months.

"I didn't think you'd deem me worthy. My gear's still up in the room," Hart said.

Mahajan looked over at Stu who stood wilting in the mid-morning heat under the crush of neoprene. "Stu's gonna melt if he waits another minute. How much time do you need to grab it?"

Hart looked up at the oil platform looming a hundred and ten feet above them where his gear waited in his room. "Twenty-five minutes," Hart replied.

Mahajan scowled. "Fifteen," Mahajan replied. "I'll cover Stu 'til you get back. He clapped Hart on the back before pulling a walkie-talkie from his belt and radioing the crane operator to send a basket down for Hart. Mahajan signaled for Robert, the other greenhorn, who came running over.

"Get me a harness with a tank on it. Have Dan check the gas-mix levels to make sure everything's in working order." Robert looked from Hart to Mahajan.

"Are you going down, Boss?" Robert said to Mahajan. "Shall I get your suit?" The jeans and t-shirt clad Mahajan shook his head.

"The harness is all I need. The water's not that cold yet," Mahajan said, looking at Stu who spread his arms, palms up in query. Mahajan jerked his head in the direction of the supply room and Robert left.

A moment later, the crane lowered a basket within reach. Hart clambered in and disappeared into the mid-morning sun. Mahajan joined Stu at the railing. Robert helped Mahajan strap on his harness.

"Time to rock, Stuey. Get your helmet on; I'll cover you 'til Hart gets back," Mahajan said. "He's good to go." Mahajan and Stu exchanged a meaningful look.

The radio communications gear crackled to life, as Stu lowered his helmet into place.

"You got a good signal?" Ted, the communications guy asked.

"Loud and clear," Stu said and flashed the thumbs up.

"Tell him he can take off whenever he's ready," Mahajan said to Ted.

Ted radioed the message into Stu's helmet, and Stu jumped over the railing, disappearing beneath the surface, trailing bubbles and his umbilical in his wake.

"Remember what Hart told you. Not too much slack, but room to move," Mahajan said to Jason before moving off to talk with the other handlers.

CHAPTER 27

The crane dropped Hart on deck sixteen minutes later, lugging his diving gear, a smile splashed across his chiseled features.

"What the hell happened to you?" Mahajan asked.

"Nothing," Hart replied

"You look like the Cheshire cat," Mahajan said.

Hart stared at a pile of dive rigs wound meticulously in concentric circles, a diver's lifeline in deep waters. "I didn't think you ... never mind. It's good to be back."

Mahajan clapped Hart on the back. "All right. Let's do it." Mahajan walked to the bow of the boat with Hart right behind him.

⚓

"What are you looking for, Boss?" said Smith, Hart's radioman.

Hart stood in the middle of the boat in his underwear, looking over his shoulder. "Believe it or not, I was looking for a woman." A ripple ran through the men surrounding him.

"So do we, just about every night," said Tom, a tender, holding Hart's diving helmet.

"Were you looking for a particular woman?" Ian asked. At twenty-one, Ian was the youngest guy on board and painfully shy, a fact the rest of the handlers noticed.

"Oh, I think anyone would do," Tom said, to the amusement of the handlers.

"Well, the nearest one's a ten-hour boat ride from here," said Nelson. "Unless you're thinking about flying one out. It'll only cost you a few hundred bucks and your job. Well, probably not you, Boss."

"Never mind. I forgot where I was for a minute," Hart said, whipping off his briefs. He twirled them overhead, like a stripper, and tossed them on deck.

"Better watch, Boss," Tom said. "Nelson sleepwalks. Might mistake you for a chickie some night he's walking the decks." Peals of laughter rolled out in all directions.

Mahajan appeared suddenly by Hart's side, and the laughter rippled into silence.

"All right, gentlemen. Let's get serious. No matter how many times you've done this, things can always go wrong. This guy's gonna be three hundred feet below sea level and not a one of you wants to be responsible if his gear's not singing a happy tune when he goes under. Snap to it. I want everything checked and double-checked and checked again."

As if preparing for battle, a naked Hart allowed the handlers to dress him. Had there been a woman within fifty miles of the platform it wouldn't have mattered. On deck, modesty went out the window. Tom held Hart's neoprene diving suit open and Hart slid in a leg at a time feeling the cool second skin as the surreal fabric sprung into action. The neoprene fit snugly without strangling the occupant, making underwear a redundancy. A thrill shot through Hart's solar plexus as he zipped the suit up the front. In very cold waters, the tenders would pump warm water through a second umbilical attached directly to the suit, eliminating the risk of hypothermia. In the Gulf in October, though, the waters were still relatively warm. Still, at three hundred feet down where the sun didn't shine and the currents were strong, it was better to be prepared. At three hundred feet, speed and efficiency were paramount.

Tom wrapped a sixty-pound weight belt around Hart's waist, adjusted the harness holding his mixed-gas tank and pronounced Hart dive-ready.

Lastly, Hart put his helmet on, all thirty-five pounds of it, and snapped it into place. He adjusted the regulator and the umbilical and tightened the valves on the helmet. He donned his gloves and stood, arms akimbo, looking at Mahajan and the rest of his handlers and smiling. He said something into his helmet that no one but Smith, his radio guy, could hear.

"What did he say?" Mahajan asked.

"He said, 'Ask Mahajan how I look?'" Smith said, smiling.

"Like Superman," Mahajan replied. "Tell him whenever he's ready." He took off his own harness and handed it to Ian, the greenhorn.

"Mahajan says to fly whenever you're ready, Superman," Smith radioed into Hart's helmet.

Hart flashed the thumbs up, stepped to the front of the railing and in one graceful movement he was over the side and beneath the surface of the sea.

The first ten minutes in the water were always the worst. Water cascaded with an agonizing slowness down Hart's back as it thoroughly soaked his dry wet suit. Hart swam, lazy at first, enjoying the feel of buoyancy despite the heavy gear. He made his way toward the small buoy that tethered a fifty-pound weight at the bottom of the three hundred foot line. He found the rope and used it to guide himself to the bottom. The first hundred feet were a cakewalk, but when Hart hit the one hundred and twenty foot mark, his vision started to crowd in on itself and for a minute he felt nauseated. Hart's pride – and perhaps more than a bit of the arrogance indigenous to the commercial diving profession – kept him from asking Smith to switch over to mixed gas.

"Hey, Boss?" Smith barked into Hart's helmet.

"Yo," Hart replied.

"You're cooing like a morning dove. You're not going to pass out on me, are you?"

"Nah, I'm fine. I could go another fifty or sixty feet."

"Well, just the same. A couple hundred bucks is not going to make Akanabi's stock prices fall much. I'm switching you over. Hit your free flow valve and purge the umbilical. Let me know when you feel the gas."

Despite the dark waters, Hart instinctively grabbed the valve. Images of Sonia and the baby floated in his mind's eye, on the periphery, just slightly out of reach. Hart tried to focus on them, but they eluded him: chimeras in the dark. He cranked the valve hard. Cool air immediately washed over his face and out the exhaust ports under his chin and at his left cheek. Hart tried to mentally count, thirty, twenty-nine, twenty-eight, twenty-seven, but soon lost the thread and settled for mindless waiting. About twenty-five seconds later, the sound of incoming air shifted to a soft, higher-pitched squeal, indicating the change to mixed gas. Hart shut down the free flow valve and made a minor adjustment to his regulator, the dial-a-breath, or "dial-a-death" as the more cynical divers called it.

The mixed gas worked like a wonder drug and the cobwebs that had short-circuited his synapses floated farther away with each breath. His eyesight returned to normal. He saw Sonia's smiling face float by his left eye before she disappeared.

"Boss. I don't hear you," Smith said in singsong fashion. "D'ya find it okay?" Hart's fingers made a final adjustment to his regulator.

"Yeah," he said, and cleared his throat. "I'm good."

"I knew you would be," Smith's replied.

Hart's hands grasped the line loosely as he allowed the sixty-pound weight belt around his waist to pull him languorously to the bottom. By about a hundred and fifty feet there was no sunlight left to speak of, Hart's headlamp being the only source of illumination in the murky, churning water.

"Pretty thick down here, Smithsteen," Hart noted. "You can't see past your ass."

"Yeah, well, write when you get work. Meanwhile, I'm up here sweatin' my balls off."

"I don't know if I'd consider chatting me up on the radio to be working, Smithy," Hart said. Thoroughly suffused with mixed gas, he continued his descent.

λ

Two hundred feet down, Stu fumbled with a change-out on a battered Christmas tree valve. A small amount of oil trickled from the barnacle-covered steel and Stu could faintly make out the area underneath where a valve on the back-flow preventer had worn thin, eroded over time by rust, saltwater and marine growth. He pulled a screwdriver from his harness and scraped at the barnacles and rust chunks, brushing them away with a gloved hand as he wrenched the tenacious little buggers free. He grabbed his water blaster and blasted the crap out of them, removing maybe half. Oil squirted out in a steady, thin rivulet, momentarily suspended in time before it rose up and eloped with the current.

"I found it," Stu said to Ted, his comms guy. "I got the leak. Valve on the back-flow preventer's shot. I need to clean it off before I can change it out." Stu scraped at the rust and barnacles revealing a number of cylindrical shapes above the offending valve. He counted them then advised Ted. "Of course, it's the last damn valve on a series of four. And they all look like remnants of the Titanic."

Stu frowned and scraped diligently at the marine growth and other aquatic debris covering the valves like a point guard. After twenty minutes, he'd only progressed halfway and the frustration level was rising. He pulled out a wrench to loosen the first valves, but they were stuck fast so he gave them a few quick whacks. The pounding didn't have the same force and effect as it would on dry land, but it made Stu feel better.

"Whoever put the cathode protection on this unit didn't do such a good job," he muttered, more to himself than Ted. The seeping oil floated up to his headlamp, obstructing his vision. Irritated, he swished his hand in front of his headlamp, but only a foggy illumination returned.

"Damn it!"

"Now what?" Ted crackled through the umbilical into Stu's helmet.

"My damn faceplate's all fogged up." Stu opened the free flow valve on his helmet and a rush of air flowed through the exhaust port flaps, clearing Stu's faceplate.

"Stu, you sound a little agitated this morning. Anything I can do?" Ted replied.

"Unless you can get me out of here by tonight, the answer to that would be Goddamn no!" Stu said with more emphasis than Ted had expected.

"What's the problem, Boss? Too long away from the wife?" Ted asked, joking. The reverberation shot through the umbilical as Stu pounded on the recalcitrant valve.

"Tomorrow's my daughter's first birthday, and I'm stuck on the ocean floor fixing a freakin' backflow protector that should have had a shelf life of five to ten years, but because of some jerkoff's shoddy workmanship has rusted out in twelve months."

"Oh," was all Ted could manage.

In contrast to the sheer blackness of the ocean bottom, on deck the sky was wide and bright with patches of cumulus clouds interspersed for good measure. Mahajan stood next to Ted making notes on a clipboard. He had heard their exchange, and cracked a half-smile, without looking up from his work.

"Tell him, he fixes the leak and I chopper him out tonight," Mahajan said.

"What about the rest of the inspection?"

"Hart and I'll do it."

"You supposed to be getting wet?" Ted asked. "Who's gonna hold down the fort?"

"I don't know yet. You maybe. I got another comms guy on board maybe can take your place at the radio." He looked at Ted who smiled wide. "Hart said I'm too long out a' water. That my reflexes are slooow. I need to make sure he's not right." He jerked his head in the direction of the communications system, and Ted returned to the task at hand.

"Yo, Stu. Boss says you fix the leak and you'll be home in time to help her blow out the candles," Ted relayed.

"Wit-woo!" Stu said, and Ted heard the pounding and banging efforts redouble.

Ten minutes later, Stu had the top two valves off and was working on removing the flow regulator, scraping at the bigger rust chunks and other aquatic debris with a screwdriver. He tried loosening it with his wrench, but it wouldn't budge. He shot it with the water blaster. Barnacles, rust and other debris swirled in a million directions. Stu waited until the water cleared, then, low on patience, he drew his arm back and hit the free flow with as much force as he could muster. The second before the wrench hit the valve Stu knew it was the wrong thing to do. The shock severed the gas line, which split wide open, spewing natural gas straight at him with the force of an oncoming freight train. Stu was propelled through sheer blackness some seventy-five feet from the Christmas tree. He landed with a thud in a pile of discarded metal cabling long since left to rust on the bottom.

⋏

"What's happening down there, man? Sounds like a demolition derby," Jason said, peering over the railing. Stu's umbilical dangled languidly from his hand.

"The valves are stuck," Ted said eyeballing Jason. "Stu's trying to beat them into submission." He watched Jason staring wistfully out to sea.

"How long do you think it'll be until I get down there?" Jason asked.

"A pretty damn long time, especially if you don't keep your eye on that umbilical," Ted replied.

Jason glanced down. The line had spiraled out and now looked like a slalom course on the surface of the sea. He pulled it in, dropping it onto the deck in concentric circles as he did, but couldn't find the drag. He dropped the umbilical the moment it ripped through his hands.

"Oh crap," he said, looking down. His hands were red.

Mahajan sprung to life. He looked over the side, but the line had gone slack again. He snapped his fingers at Ted who immediately radioed Stu while Mahajan pulled in the line. Mahajan had twenty-two years' experience as a diver, five of them as the chief overseer of diving operations, and he'd seen just about everything: clogged umbilicals, hypothermia, faulty radio gear, a shark bite, even emotional breakdowns, generally brought on by a sudden paranoid fear of being isolated several hundred feet below sea level. It had all reinforced his belief in the need to act purposefully and remain calm even in the dire situations. There were myriad reasons why the signal might be lost. And an experienced diver like Stu should be able to fix the problem and be back on line for as long as he could hold his breath, which in Stu's case was about two minutes.

"He's offline," Ted said. "Stu, do you copy? What the heck's going on?" Ted's voice quavered a little before he yelled into the radio. Mahajan checked his watch. "Stu! Stu!" Ted looked wide-eyed at Mahajan who snapped his fingers in Smith's direction.

"Tell Hart we got a problem," Mahajan said to Smith. But before Smith could open his mouth, Ted's radio crackled to life.

Stu lay there for several moments in utter darkness, stunned. He drew a deep breath and reached for his headlamp. Duct-taped to his helmet for hands-free operating, it had been knocked loose in the blast and now dangled from his helmet, secured by only the barest remnant of the sticky stuff. He fumbled for the switch that had been turned off, but how, Stu wasn't exactly sure.

He flicked on the light and it illuminated the immediate area, sending out beams at a forty-five degree angle. Sight restored, Stu moved his arms, then his legs. Both appeared to be in working order. He raised himself on one elbow. Piles of metal coils, old cabling line, he presumed, lay beneath him covered with spiny oysters. The air in his helmet felt a little thick, and he took a long pull trying to get a full breath.

"What the ... " Stu maneuvered into a sitting position and rotated his shoulders and his neck. His body parts all seemed to be in working order, but he felt as though he'd been catapulted from a large slingshot and hurtled against a solid brick wall. He checked his harness. Still secure. He reached back and touched his mother pleaser. Thank God.

A voice crackled into his helmet, barely audible through the static.

"Stu! Stu! What's going on? Do you copy? Over." Stu could make out Ted's voice, rife with static, a million light years away.

"I'm here … just lounging around," Stu said, his breath coming in jagged bursts.

"What the hell happened?"

"The gas pipe blew. Farther than I'd care to guesstimate." Stu groped in the dark, pulling at the umbilical that floated freely away from him, trying to rein it in. The radio snapped and popped as he did so.

"What the hell are you doing," Ted shouted. "You're killin' me."

"I'm pullin' in my umbilical. It's all over the place." Stu pulled the umbilical slowly through his gloved hand until the line went taut. He took another jagged breath, ripped his flashlight from his helmet and swam along the line, pulling as he went until he got to the problem. The line had snagged in the same pile of cabling where Stu had landed. There was a small gash in the spot where it stuck. "Damn." He took another raspy breath.

"What," Ted replied.

"The umbilical's severed. That's why you sound like you're transmitting from Venus." He took a deep, unsatisfying breath and cranked his dial-a-breath out to keep up with the diminishing pressure. And why I'm having trouble breathing?

"There's no way I'm gettin' to the top with this line," Stu said.

"Any idea where you are?"

"No. There's a bunch of old cable line on the floor, is all."

"All right, sit tight. We're gonna raise Hart and get you another line. Try not to move that one too much. I don't want to lose radio contact," Ted said.

"How long, do you think?"

There was a pause before Ted's voice crackled through. "Twenty, maybe twenty-five minutes."

Stu took a labored breath and this time water seeped in through the free flow.

"Your tank's full if you need it, right?" Ted asked. Stu didn't respond. "Right?" Ted persisted.

The water level in Stu's helmet was already to his Adams apple. "I got water seeping into my helmet."

There was a long pause on the other end before Ted's voice came through, tinny and strange as if from outer space.

"Mahajan wants to know if you got any duct tape from your flashlight." Stu reached up and yanked free the last remaining piece of duct tape.

"Not much," he replied.

"Well wrap what you got around the leak and see if you can slow it down. We gotta keep your radio on as long as possible." Stu wrapped the duct tape around the hose. It slowed the leak, but not enough to give him comfort.

"All right. But I'm still sucking pretty hard," Stu said. "And it's still spittin' in here."

"Hold on a minute." Ted went offline and Stu was left feeling like he was the only man on earth. The crackling in his helmet signaled Ted's return.

"You got the air in your tank. Hold out for as long as you can before you cut the cord just to buy an extra minute or two then switch over. And Stu, I need to know the exact time you cut it so I can time it."

Time how long I have left, you mean. Stu listened patiently as the water drip-dropped into his helmet, now just below his mouthpiece. He could feel the headliner getting soaked. Soon he would lose all communication with the outside world. Then the water would be up to his mouth and the amount of air in his helmet might be insufficient to support him. He'd have to turn his bottle on and blow the water out.

"You know that adage about not taking your helmet off underwater or it'll be the last thing you do? Well, I'm gonna have to if I don't cut this umbilical right now," Stu said calmly as the water trickled in. He heard Ted sigh and go offline again. Stu's head felt light as the available air in his helmet shrunk.

"Okay. Mahajan says switch over to your tank, but do not, I repeat, *do not* let the umbilical go. After ten minutes, start climbing your line.

Remember to time it, only one foot per second. And if you can manage, roll your flashlight up and back like a searchlight. Hart'll meet you with a new umbilical." Stu was feeling lightheaded from the lack of air. He nodded but did not respond, prompting Ted to yell.

"Stu!" The noise roused Stu from his reverie.

"Yeah," he said, snapping to alertness. "Okay. I'm gonna cut it now."

"Really, man. Don't let go of the umbilical and swim straight up. You only got twenty guaranteed minutes!"

"Don't worry, man. I'm not into playin' hero today," Stu replied. It was the last thing he said before radio communication went dead.

"Shoot," Smith said.

"What is it?" Hart's reply came through the radio.

Up on the deck of the *Poseidon*, chaos loomed, threatening a coup, but Mahajan's cool exterior and the combined experience of the handlers kept it safely off the bow — for the moment. Mahajan stood waiting patiently next to Smith as he radioed Hart his instructions. He looked at his watch as the second hand flew around the dial. A minute and a half had already elapsed.

We got a problem," Smith barked into the phone. "Quit your descent and hold the position. I'll be back in twenty seconds."

Nelson and Tom materialized at Mahajan's side with a backup umbilical.

"Tell him to come back up pronto," Mahajan said to Smith. "Follow the tow line. Somebody'll meet him at the surface with a new umbilical for Stu." Mahajan stared after the umbilical. Smith pressed the button and called Hart.

"Wait," Mahajan said. Cancel that last part. Tell him I'll meet him at fifty feet with the umbilical," Mahajan said. Smith's eyebrows shot up, and Mahajan responded to his unspoken query. "It'll only take me a few minutes to meet him part way. Stu may need those minutes."

"You gonna suit up?" Smith asked. Mahajan shook his head.

"Get me some goggles, fast" he said to Ian. "There's some in the supply room."

"Boss, are you sure? It's only an extra couple minutes to the surface from fifty feet," Smith said.

"Yeah, but Hart'll pay for it later with the bends even if he's only up here for a few minutes."

Mahajan removed his shoes, adjusted his harness and walked over to Sam who stood calibrating the three-cylinder diesel backup compressor system to which he had just hooked the new umbilical. A second backup compressor sat next to it.

"I thought it would be cleaner than disengaging Stu's original hose," Sam said by way of explanation.

Mahajan glanced at the two nine-tank cascade systems which currently serviced Hart's working hose and Stu's severed one. Each had its own control valves that ultimately tied into a single manifold operation. Both systems had three rows of three tanks encased in a special frame. The tanks weighed over a hundred pounds each — with the frame, one system approached a thousand pounds — and were so heavy they could only be set on deck by crane or helicopter. The combined weight of the two cascade systems and the back-up compressors, which sat now, gleaming in the sun, was more than all of the handlers put together.

"If something happens, switch over to the cascade system servicing Stu's severed hose, not the backup compressor."

"Okay, Boss," Sam replied.

Mahajan turned his back to Sam. "Check my tank one more time, would you?"

Sam checked the pressure gauge and opened the valve. A brief spurt of air whistled out before he closed it. "Good to go," Sam said.

Ian ran up and handed Mahajan a pair of goggles, which he took and adjusted to his face.

"Hart knows what's going on?" he asked Smith.

Smith nodded. "He's on his way up. He'll meet you at the T-Bar."

"All right, gentlemen, Smith's in charge. You're on your own until I return. Make me proud," he said, a wry, half-smile on his face. And clothed in nothing but Levi's and a T-shirt, Andrew Mahajan stuck his umbilical in his mouth and jumped over the side of the bow, an emergency umbilical trailing behind him.

⋏

Radio communication died abruptly and, as promised, remained out for the next sixty-three seconds. In the sensory deprived world of underwater diving, even ten seconds ticked on into eternity. Sonia's smiling face floated in front of Hart's retinas again, but this time he pushed her away. Not now, he whispered to her. He squeezed his gloved hands into balls and concentrated on his grip, squeezing and releasing while waiting for his instructions. When they came, Hart was focused and ready.

"Yo, Boss," Smith's voice was steady and in control.

"Smithsteen," Hart replied. "I was beginning to think I'd been replaced on your dance card," Hart said.

Smith chuckled. "Stu's hose's severed. There was a pipeline break and he went for a ride. He's offline. Mahajan's meeting you at the T-Bar with a spare hose."

"Why's he doing that?"

"Worried about the bends. And Stu's not sure where he is so you gotta follow his umbilical down. Mahajan'll have the new one at the T-Bar."

"All right," Hart said.

"Check your watch," Smith said. Hart set his second hand. "In about seven minutes, Stu's going to start climbing his hose. With some luck he'll be meeting you halfway. Over."

Hart immediately started his ascent. "Sonia used to say something about luck."

"What's that?"

"That next to love, it was the second most powerful force in the universe." Hart pulled himself up the rope hand over hand, using the umbilical. "Do you know me to be a lucky man, Smith?" Hart asked.

"Looking back on your history, I'd have to say yes, Boss. I know you to be a very lucky man." He paused before continuing. "It's the people around you that aren't always so lucky." Hart sniggered, but said nothing.

"One more thing, Boss. You realize you gotta do the changeover in free float 'cause by then Stu should be a hundred or more feet off the bottom," Smith continued. "You can handle that, right?"

"Smithy, who you talkin' to?" Hart joked. He took a deep breath and soldiered on toward the T-Bar.

"Tell Mahajan I'll see him at the bar."

"I would if he had a comms system on," Smith said.

The air must be getting pretty thick up there, too. Hart gripped the towline hard and pulled for all he was worth.

⋏

When Hart arrived, Mahajan was lounging on the T-Bar at the marker buoy like a passenger on a cruise ship waiting on cocktails. He sat up when he saw Hart and spread his palms wide as if to say, what took you so long. Hart flipped him the bird, tough to do with such large gloves, and took both the spare and severed hose from Mahajan. Mahajan grabbed the spare hose back and attached it to the snap shackle on Hart's harness so he wouldn't have to hold it.

Mahajan pointed to his watch and held up five fingers and a fist.

Five minutes left in Stu's tank.

Mahajan removed his mouthpiece and mouthed the words "you all right?" Hart nodded. Mahajan gave him the thumbs up and pushed him in the direction of the deep.

Hart moved off the T-Bar and gave Stu's severed rope a little tug, but the rope was slack, suggesting the end floated unencumbered. Hart hoped that wasn't the case as he dropped through the blackness, pulled down by the sixty-pound weight belt around his waist, trying not to pull too hard on the severed umbilical lest he wrench it from Stu's unsuspecting grip.

Other than his own breathing, Hart heard nothing. Occasionally he'd spot a fish, sleek and shimmery, its bulging eyes turning away to avoid the harsh headlight.

"Got anything yet?" Smith's voice crackled to life in Hart's helmet.

"Not unless you count a school of mackerel," Hart replied.

"Stu's gonna be rockin' his light back and forth. Just in case he lost the … ." Smith's voice trailed off into oblivion.

"I'm on it, Smithy. Don't worry about it."

Hart checked his watch. Two minutes and fifty-five seconds elapsed. He redoubled his efforts, pulling harder on the rope, and this time the rope went taut with a slight tug from the other end. Hart stopped and gave the rope three jerks, a signal he and Stu had used on previous dives. The rope jerked back three times. Stu was at the other end.

"I got tension on the line," Hart relayed to Smith. Hart gave another tug at the rope to let Stu know he was coming and lurched forward at full throttle.

"I can see a glow," Hart said into his mouthpiece. The beam from Stu's headlamp moved back and forth like a searchlight. "Almost there."

The two men, both proficient swimmers, moved toward each other in a graceful, underwater ballet of brass, belts and tubing. Each pulled on the umbilical and kicked, moving closer together until their gloved hands grasped and they were intertwined. Hart held Stu in an awkward bear hug, as Stu collapsed against Hart in relief. They began to spin then sink with the combined weight of their belts and gear. Hart let go of Stu and disengaged the new umbilical from his harness. The severed umbilical floated free.

"I got him," Hart radioed to Smith. "You can pull the old dive rig in." Almost immediately, the severed umbilical began rising to the surface.

"I'll hold my congratulations, Boss. You don't have much time for the change out," Smith said.

Hart looked at his watch as Stu swam over to join him on the rope. *A minute and fifty seconds.* Hart pulled Stu closer and looked inside his helmet. The water had risen to just below Stu's chin, but no further. Hart placed the forehead of his own helmet against Stu's, locked his hands on the sides and looked into Stu's eyes as if they were a pair of reunited lovers. Hart spoke loudly, the combination of voice and vibration making it possible for the men to hear each other through their helmets.

"How much air you got left in your bailout bottle?" Hart asked.

"About a thousand pounds," Stu replied, confirming what Smith had said.

"You know there's no way for us to share air, right?" Hart asked. The words reverberated through their helmets, all choppy and tinny. Stu nodded. "Let me know when you're getting down to the wire. Maybe there's something else we can do," Hart said.

Stu's eyebrows shot up. "I'm not taking my helmet off," Stu said emphatically.

Hart nodded. Stu could take his helmet off and suck air from Hart's exhaust port all the way up, but chances were, if Stu took his helmet off he wouldn't make it to the top.

"Can you still hold your breath for two minutes?" Hart asked. A broad smile lit Stu's face.

"You bet your ass," Stu said.

"We gotta change you out right here," he said, indicating Stu's new umbilical. "Wrap your legs around my waist and hold tight to my harness."

Stu complied. Hart grabbed the new umbilical back from Stu and wrapped it around both of them, tied a slipknot and clipped it to the quick release on his harness. They looked like underwater koala bears. Hart touched his helmet back to Stu's.

"Keep one hand on the umbilical. We'll probably spin a lot since we're not anchored. Just keep your legs locked on me and we'll get through this, okay?"

"Okay, Boss," Stu said.

Hart patted Stu's helmet. To Smith, Hart said, "I'm gonna loosen the compression fitting on the cut hose first. The tricky part'll be getting the new one in." He touched his helmet to Stu's: "Hold on." He checked his watch before setting to work. *One minute and twenty seconds.*

Hart loosened the fitting holding the remnants of the severed umbilical, gave the hose a tug and set it free. It traveled past his faceplate then beyond his periphery vision. He removed the stub of the Schrader fitting – the check valve was the only thing keeping the water out – and inserted a new fitting. The movement caused them to spin like kids on a tire swing and the uncontrolled motion made Hart queasy. *Fifty-nine seconds.* He touched his helmet to Stu's.

"You all right?"

"A little dazed. Getting tough to breathe."

For the first time Hart noticed Stu's labored breaths. The pressure gauge on Stu's tank read zero. "I'm gonna hook the hose in now. Hold tight to my harness."

Smith's voice crackled to life in Hart's helmet and Hart lifted his head. "What's happening down there?"

"Hold on. I'm doing the new umbilical," Hart said to Smith. He checked his watch. *Forty-three seconds.* He touched his helmet to Stu's.

"Take the biggest breath you can now. Dial your regulator all the way out and suck all the air out of that thing. Don't leave a drop. And let's hope you weren't lying about that two minutes." Hart smiled ruefully. "I'm moving as fast as I can."

Stu shook his head and Hart could see the fear on his face.

"Go," Hart said. He set his watch for two minutes as Stu sucked all the remaining air out of the tank and secured that few pounds of pressure in his lungs, the only thing standing between him and the rest of his life.

Hart's fingers shook as he inserted the new umbilical into the Schrader fitting. They started to spin, and Stu locked his legs so tightly around Hart's mid-section that Hart winced and dropped the wrench. Stu's eyes flew open in horror. Holding tightly to the umbilical, Hart reached back and grabbed another wrench from his harness, but the umbilical, not yet fitted, popped out. The movement jarred them and they dangled like fish at the end of a taut line, the weight of their belts pulling them down. *Thirty-five seconds.* Hart glanced at Stu. His eyes were closed and his lips were moving, but Hart couldn't hear what he was saying through his helmet.

"Slack off the extra line," Hart barked to Smith. "Just a little. Don't pull in until I tell you." In moments, the line went slack and Hart pulled it down and fitted it snugly into the empty space. He fumbled with tightening the connection until in frustration he pulled his gloves off and cast them aside.

They floated away intertwined, hands without a body, and then down to the bottom of the sea. *Thirteen seconds.*

Hands free, Hart worked fast now, tightening the Schrader fitting on the umbilical. He could see Stu's face straining with the lack of oxygen, crimson even by the light of Hart's single bulb. He checked the connection once more and satisfied, threw open the free flow valve.

"She's in. Tell 'em to hit Stu's gas." In seconds, there was a squeal and a hiss as the life giving mixture of helium and nitrogen and the few remnants of water flooded Stu's umbilical. Hart watched Stu's face; he could almost feel the breeze as Stu opened his eyes in disbelief. Clearly he had made his peace with whatever divinity he worshiped and was shocked to realize it wasn't his time after all. Recognition lit his face like a hundred-watt bulb and he winked at Hart.

Hart radioed Smith. "Ask Chewey Stuey if he's got any dinner plans, would ya'?" Smith relayed the message to Ted who radioed Stu in a voice that Hart thought must sound like a choir of angels about now. Stu laughed and spoke into his mouthpiece. In a moment, Hart's radio crackled to life.

"He said whatever Hart wants. As long as there's a bottle of Dom to wash it down," Smith said. "Hey, Boss," Smith said. "I think Stu just asked you out on a date."

Hart guffawed and gave Stu the underwater version of a high-five. "Tell him I accept."

⋏

Forty minutes later and still a little shaky from his ordeal, Stu climbed the rope ladder and hopped onto the deck of the *Poseidon.* Hart did a lazy back-stroke waiting his turn while crew members tended to Stu, clapping him on the back, removing his gear and ascertaining his general condition en route to the decompression chamber.

Anxious to redeem himself, Jason yanked Hart in before his leg had a chance to clear the railing, and Hart went sprawling, helmet first, a thunderous entrance onto the deck. The landing would have blind-sided a lesser man, but after a few moments Hart sat up, hurting, but lucid.

"Geez, oh my God, I'm so sorry," Jason apologized.

Hart and Stu had just spent the last thirty minutes on the T-Bar, decompressing at forty feet, and both of them still looked a little green. Mahajan put Hart's laughter down to the fact that the oxygen levels in his body had not reached equilibrium. Hart sat up, wobbling.

"How about some help here," Mahajan said. The tenders assisted Hart, removing his helmet, belt and harness.

"That's quite a noggin you got," Mahajan said, inspecting the damage. He looked at Jason who stood nearby and waved him over.

"Get this guy some ice. And for the next twenty-four hours, he says jump, you say how high. He asks for anything, you're on it. You understand. Anything." Jason nodded and left.

Mahajan held out a hand and pulled Hart to his feet. "Nice work." He flashed Hart a smile before continuing. "Did you have a backup plan?" Hart smiled back, nodding. "D'ya mind telling me what it was? 'Cause you know, air expands. He probably had enough to exhale all the way to the T-Bar."

Hart held his hand up, silencing Mahajan. "We wouldn't have made it."

Mahajan nodded, accepting Hart's assessment of the situation and checked his watch. "Jesus, we gotta get you in. You only have five minutes and four are gone." Mahajan pushed Hart toward the door of the decompression chamber.

Jason came running over with a cell phone, holding it out to Hart, but he tripped over Hart's discarded equipment and went hurtling through space. Acceleration halted when he contacted Hart's inert mass and together they clattered to the ground, Jason still holding out the cell phone. Hart pushed Jason off and sat up, rubbing his head for the second time before accepting the phone.

"This is Hart."

And that was the state Hart was in when Bicky Coleman summoned him with all due haste back to Akanabi's corporate headquarters.

Chapter 28

Kori sat at the kitchen table going over accounts receivable for the umpteenth time. She wrote numbers on a yellow legal pad, arrayed neatly in columns, punched them into a calculator and wrote them down below previous groups of numbers. The paper was covered with at least a dozen such reckonings, all with lines through them. Upon transferring the final tally, she scribbled over the column and dropped her head.

"Aaaaaaah!" She banged her head on the table several times.

Avery walked in, took one look at Kori and walked out. A couple of minutes later he peered around the corner. Kori's head was still on the table, but she'd stopped banging it.

"Just shoot me now," she said without raising her head.

"You talking to me?"

"You see anybody else here?"

Avery looked behind him and then back at his sister. "No."

"Then I'm talking to you, but it doesn't matter," Kori said. "I could be talking to the Queen of England. It wouldn't matter," she said, sitting up.

Avery sat down and assessed the mass of paperwork spread before her. "Are you going to tell me what the problem is or just go on in high drama?"

Kori raised her head and slacked her hand on the table again. "The problem? The problem is we don't have enough money. That's the problem."

"I thought you just got a check from Robbie?"

"I did," Kori said, "and I used it to buy groceries, and clothes for Gil since all his pants were like three inches too short, and pay the insurance and the electric bill so they don't shut us off, and the overdue cable bill … "

"We should be dropping cable. It's an expense we don't need," Avery said.

"Oh yeah? You gonna listen to him whine all day about how there's nothing to watch. Some expenses are necessary — for sanity's sake." Avery dismissed the argument with a wave of his hand.

"And just today I got a $3,700 tax bill and you know what I have left in the checking account? Two hundred and thirteen dollars. Enough to buy groceries for the next two weeks which is two weeks short of when Robbie's next paycheck will be here."

"What about the insurance money?"

"They're still investigating cause of death," Kori shook her head. "Bastards."

"Well, what about your clients? Don't they pay you?"

"Just sent out the bills."

"For work you did in the summer? Kori, you really have to stay on top of that stuff."

"Don't you think I know that, Avery?" Kori's voice trailed off. Avery followed her gaze out the small portal window flanking the kitchen. "Even if everyone pays right away, it's not enough to cover the tax bill." Kori dropped her head to the table again. "I can't do this."

Avery studied a handful of papers. He pulled the checkbook from Kori's slack fingers and perused its contents.

"I can make this work."

"I'm scared," she said, and squeezed his forearm so hard he winced.

Avery saw all the pain and sorrow of the last months in his sister's face and felt his stomach lurch. He rubbed her back. "I'll take care of it. It'll be all right. I promise." He took a deep breath before proceeding. "I'll limit it to a few gas stations. And I won't supply them more than a week at a time so their standing orders won't be off by too much. Last thing we need is an oil company rep nosing around." He looked at Kori who, Avery noted, was not protesting. "I'll keep selling until I unload it all. Then we'll be officially out of the oil business."

Kori shook her head, a vehement toss that petered out as she covered her eyes with her hand. When she looked up, Avery noted a new emotion there — despair.

"What about Gil? He works out in the barn still. Sometimes for days at a time."

"It's armed," Avery said. "Anything happens, the cops show up."

"Avery, I could never in a million years forgive myself." She squeezed his hand. "I know you're trying to do what's best for us. And I couldn't do this, any of this," Kori's hand arced out, taking in the expanse of the house, "without you. It's just … it's too risky."

"But, Kori … "

"Something good's gonna happen for us, A. I know it will. It's got to."

As if on cue, Aunt Stella rapped at the back door, a squat, red-cloaked figure, peering in, hands clasping her cloak together at the throat, eyebrows raised in greeting. Avery got up to open the door, and Aunt Stella, looking like a plus-sized Red Riding Hood, blew in, followed by a cold November gale. She set her basket on the table and began the meticulous process of removing layers of clothing: a woolen hat hidden under the cloak hood, woolen scarf and mittens, and a fine woven cloak, all red.

Kori gave Aunt Stella a peck on the cheek and pulled out a chair for her. Aunt Stella was sweating lightly above the brow, a result of so many layers of clothing for what amounted to a two-hundred-yard dash, but she rubbed her hands to warm them as she accepted the proffered seat.

"Oh dear. My goodness, it's cold out. No need to go to the freezer section to get a turkey this year. They'll be frozen in the bush," Aunt Stella said. "It's uncannily cold for November."

"It's global warming, Aunt Stella," Avery said. "And the ultimate demise of the human race, I suspect." Kori rolled her eyes while Avery resumed.

"Let's see, twenty or thirty more years of wrenching million-year old fossil fuels from the earth's core so I can drive my brand new Hummer, or another few centuries of life on this planet as we know it, rolling brooks filled with trout, mountains that rise into infinity, not the kind that have their tops blown off so they can get to the coal seams beneath, but the majestic kind whose crowns are still intact. Hmmm. I'll take the oil for twenty, Bob."

"See what you did?" Kori looked at Aunt Stella, clearly perturbed.

"All I said was, 'It's cold out.'"

Kori filled the coffee pot with water, a sibilant phfphfph, escaping clenched lips.

A confused Aunt Stella looked to Avery for clarification, but he waived a dismissive arm at his sister, punctuating her rudeness. He mouthed the words *don't worry about it*, and Aunt Stella waved her own arm at Kori's back, ending the matter.

Aunt Stella pulled off the layers of cloth covering the basket and the most glorious of smells escaped, ensuring Gil's materialization at Aunt Stella's side with Max close on his heels.

"There's blueberry-walnut with brown sugar topping and apple-currant with pecans," she said proudly, letting her own olfactory system get a whiff of those divine vapors rising straight up to heaven where God could have a sniff. "My daughter sent me the recipe. She's taking a cooking class."

Gil pulled up a seat next to Aunt Stella and, without waiting to be asked, popped a chunk in his mouth and gave a bite-sized piece to Max, careful to first remove the almonds. Curiosity piqued — generally Max's palate wasn't quite so discriminating — Aunt Stella couldn't refrain from asking.

"Gilly, why are you taking the nuts out? Are you afraid the dog will choke?" Gil shook his head, his chipmunk cheeks bulging with blueberry muffin. Kori set a glass of milk before him, and he gulped some down.

"No," he said, his mouth full. "It's because he loves them so much. I save them until the end."

"And how do you know this, Gilly?"

"He told me. He's not stupid. He knows what he likes." Gil blinked his large eyes once at Aunt Stella before shoving his face into the basket. He took a long, slow draw, gathering every available scent, and after a few seconds he emerged, a muffin between his teeth. Aunt Stella's eyebrows rose up, and she pinched her lips together to suppress her smile.

"Gil," Kori snapped, yanking the basket out of his reach.

Aunt Stella covered her mouth to stanch the ensuing giggle. "Oh my, I almost forgot." She waddled over to her cloak, rummaged through the pockets and pulled out a letter. "The postman left it at my house by mistake." She handed it to Kori.

"Robbie!" Kori ripped open the letter without a moment's hesitation. "It's been almost two weeks," she said. "Why doesn't he just use the internet?" She started reading to herself, but Avery grabbed it.

"Wow, it's a big one," he said.

"Read!" Kori demanded.

Avery glared at her before beginning.

Hi guys,

"He means you, too," Gil said, opening his hand to Max. Max swallowed the almonds in two bites. Gil grabbed him by the snout and kissed him.

Avery cleared his throat and began to read.

Sorry I haven't written, but so much has happened. I guess in order to do it justice, I have to start from the beginning, so bear with me while I recount it, plus all that I've left out over the last few months. Maybe then you'll understand the decision I'm about to make. "

"Uh-oh," Kori said. "Here it comes."

Life in hell continues. It's so hot (average 120 degrees Fahrenheit) that we have to wear gloves to hold our guns or even a screwdriver. We have to wear masks on our faces because the sand never stops and eat hovering over the food because the flies are so bad. At night it's mosquitos. We went to Karbala today, a holy site of the Shiites and former wetland (before Saddam drained it), to test the water. We left behind a portable water tester so the people could use it. Water is really scarce here, and more important than oil.

And I met a girl. She's pretty amazing.

"See. Told ya'."

"Shhh," Gil gave Kori the hairy eyeball. Avery continued:

Her name is Amara Mir Ahmad. She lives in Baghdad now, and was educated at Oxford, England. Her dad and three uncles are all college educated. Well, were, but I'm getting ahead of myself. Amara's paternal grandfather comes from people known as the Ma'adan. They've gone through a lot, believe me.

The Ma'adan are also called the Marsh Arabs. They live on the water in the middle of the desert. Their home is what the bible refers to as the Garden of Eden. Nobody knows for sure if it's Eden, but they do know that it used to be the largest wetland ecosystem in the world, measuring 20,000 kilometers, which is about 7,500 square miles. But that was before Saddam Hussein dried it all up.

Kori, you may remember studying about Mesopotamia and the Cradle of Civilization in art history? It's the area between the Tigris and Euphrates Rivers. On today's map, it's between Baghdad in the north and Basra in the south. The Sumerians lived there. They were the first people to build dams and irrigate crops. The Marsh Arabs can trace their roots back to those people and have been living the same way for the last five thousand years. They harvest reeds, grow date palms, rice, millet, fish, and raise water buffalo. They build their houses on artificial islands by fencing off some of the marsh and building it up so it stays clear of the tide of the marsh waters. Then they layer mud, woven mats and these giant reeds that grow everywhere in the marshes. Their houses sit on top of all this stuff and they add layers every year to compensate for settling and to make sure their floor stays dry.

Can you imagine? Living on water like that? To go to your next-door neighbor's you need to paddle over in your mashuf, a small canoe. Some of the villagers have larger boats, but everyone has at least a mashuf. People travel everywhere like this. There are no sidewalks. You can't drive. They make the boats from qasab, these humongous reeds that grow in the marshes and which they also use to build houses. Everything revolves around the water, the fishing, the water buffalo, the rice and millet, even getting goods to market. When the water started drying up, fishermen, reed makers and the other tradesmen were wading through hip-deep mud carrying their goods to market on their backs.

"Wow, that's terrible," Gil said.

"Enough of the history lesson," Kori said. "Get to the point."

"Just shut and listen, please," Avery said. Kori grunted, but said nothing further.

Amara's grandfather, Ajrim Mir Ahmad, left his home long before any of Saddam's draining campaign, but the rest of his family stayed behind.

"How many more pages are there to that letter?" Kori asked. "'Cause I can come back when he gets to the decision part." Avery shot her a nasty look. She rolled her eyes and bit at a hangnail.

His family didn't want him to go. They'd lived in the marshes for centuries. They were a tight-knit community. People didn't leave. But he felt the call so he moved his wife and their young family to Khan Bani Saad, a market town northeast of Baghdad and became a fish merchant, selling the wares harvested from the marshes by his own people. He became wealthy by Marsh Arab standards, enough so that he could afford to send his four sons to the University of Baghdad. His family grew up educated, which is not a luxury that was afforded the Marsh Arabs until the last thirty years. The sons took wives and got jobs in the city.

Amara's father, the youngest son, became a civil engineer working for the state. He was well respected until he refused to work on the dam building projects that Saddam started in 1991 — the ones that would eventually drain his ancestral home. He was arrested under the pretense of supporting members of the Shiite uprising, something the Marsh Arabs have a history of doing. Saddam's soldiers came in the middle of the night. Amara was 12 at the time. She hid in the shadows clutching her younger brother and holding his mouth shut to keep him from crying as the soldiers questioned, then beat her father and mother. They took her father that night and she never saw him again.

The next week, Saddam's soldiers came and took Amara's grandfather away. The charge was suspicious behavior and crimes against the state. Her mother supported the family with a state-sanctioned job. She taught English lessons to members of Saddam's army. Amara believes that had her mother not been of some use to Saddam, they would be living with other Iraqis in a refugee camp in Iran. Because of her mother and her education, Amara speaks English beautifully which is lucky for me since I haven't yet picked up much of the local dialect. I tell you all this, not to make you feel sorry for her, but so you will understand where she comes from. She's a brilliant woman. She speaks three languages, her native language, English, and believe it or not, Italian, and has learned everything her mother has been able to pass on to her. It was because of her mother that she was educated at Oxford. They're incredibly strong-willed people. She's made up her mind to do this thing and I've decided to do it with her. It seems more like my calling then enlisting in the army ever did. Mom was right. It's not about democracy. It's about what it's always about — money. So in the true spirit of democracy, I'm voting with my feet."

"Oh my God, that is soooo like him. Always playing the hero. So what, he walks her down the aisle and saves her from a life of oppression?"

"Kori! Mind your mouth," Aunt Stella said, cupping her hands over Gil's ears. "Anyway, who's talking about marriage?"

"Robbie is. Don't you get it? He's going to marry her. All this cloak and dagger talk about making a decision."

"Well, I have no idea how you gathered that from his letter. I'm actually not sure what he's made a decision about," Aunt Stella said. "Read on, Avery."

Avery scanned the rest of the letter before continuing.

There's so much more I want to tell you about Amara, about my life here, about the people. But I want to get this to post and the guy's leaving right now with the mail. Let me just say that the people here, they really want a democracy, but they've been duped. That's not going to be enough for you to understand, but maybe enough to buy me some grace until I'm home to explain in full. Take care of yourselves, as I am not there to take care of you. I know you'll be fine. Kori, if things get to be too much, lean on Avery. He can handle it. Give Aunt Stella a kiss and Gil an especially big hug for me. Love, Robbie.

"I'm confused." Aunt Stella said. "Do you think he's really going to marry her?"

"Of course, he's going to marry her," Kori said. "That moron. He has no business getting married yet. He's freaking twenty-two, for God sakes."

Everyone turned to look at Kori whose face was shot red with anger. She stood, tipping her chair over in her haste, and strode to the sink. She washed her hands with a fury and threw water on her face before covering it with her hand. Tears cascaded down her face, pooling on the porcelain. No one spoke while Kori stood there, fighting back her fear for the brother she knew was no longer miles away, but light years.

CHAPTER 29

Kori rummaged through her purse, searching for spare change. Frustrated, she dumped the contents onto the bed. She picked two crumpled dollar bills and a few coins from the debris, turned to her nightstand drawer and found four more coins inside.

She ran down to the basement and threw open the swinging doors to the little room where the washer and dryer sat. Perched above the machinery were two rows of six-foot long shelves, which, in another incarnation, served as bleacher seats for the local high school football stadium. Marty had rescued them from the trash heap when the township had built a bigger stadium, whitewashed them and bolted them to the wall. Instead of high school derrieres, they now housed laundry detergents, dryer sheets and stain removing products, used sparingly since Ruth's death.

Stepping over the mound of dirty clothes, Kori pulled a small box from the shelf, about the size of two decks of cards, and rifled through its contents. Three dozen coins, several buttons, a Sharpie magic marker, and a single ear plug that had survived the dryer, hapless travelers in an unplanned foray through the cotton cycle. She dumped the contents of the box into her hand and weeded out everything but the coins. She counted the money: $5.76. That plus the money she got from ravaging the rest of the house and she had about $13. Enough to buy a gallon of milk, some bread, peanut butter and jelly for Gil, a pack of hot dogs and buns, a head of lettuce, and a few other miscellaneous items.

But what about tomorrow? They were out of fresh fruits and vegetables. The only thing left was canned goods: tuna, beans, corn and the like. She could live on the cans for a couple days, maybe even three or four, but after a while her body would revolt. She clenched her teeth and threw the money to the floor, scattering change to the four directions. Filled with regret, she slumped down after it, falling in a dejected heap on the floor. She screamed for several moments, the crescendo a high-pitched wail, and then, silence. She rolled over and lay on the floor, her breathing shallow, her eyes dazed and unseeing.

After several minutes she walked to her work area, flipped on the computer. Beyond the screen, the French doors of the walkout basement beckoned her eyes to the east, that place of peace and spiritual renewal, of new beginnings. Kori breathed in the pastoral setting, allowing the spiritual rejuvenation it afforded to settle in her bones. She took a deep breath and pulled up some client billing information.

The bill was sent two days ago. Her hand hovered above the keyboard a moment, and then she began. She added a few hours to the labor, a few dollars to supplies, tweaking it here and there, enough to increase it by almost $200. Then she composed a letter of explanation.

Dear Sir or Madame,

It has come to our attention that the bill you received on 11/14 was in error. Enclosed please find a more accurate accounting of work performed on your behalf. We apologize for any inconvenience this may have caused.

Also, the billing cycle has been shortened. Please remit payment to the undersigned within the twenty (20) days of the date of this letter. Please be advised that failure to pay in a timely fashion will result in incurring late charges, which will begin to accrue immediately at the close of the grace period. Prompt payment is therefore, requested.

Thank you for your attention to this matter.

Very truly yours,

"Whatcha' doing?"

Kori jumped so high she banged her thighs on the bottom of the computer table and sent the mouse flying. She turned to glare at the interloper.

"Geez, Gil. Don't sneak up on a person like that."

"I didn't sneak. I walked right down the stairs. It's not my fault if you didn't hear me." Gil peered over Kori's shoulder to read what was on the computer screen. Embarrassed, Kori closed the screen before Gil had the chance to figure out what she was up to. In an attempt to change the subject, Kori focused on Gil's attire: pants that were two inches up from the ground and shirt sleeves that didn't come anywhere near his wrists.

"Gil, what the heck are you wearing?"

"Clothes."

"Very funny. I meant, why are you wearing clothes that are too small for you?"

"Because I can't find anything else." Kori glanced over toward the alcove that housed the washer and dryer. Even from here she could see several mounds of clothes behind the swinging doors, overtaking the little room. Kori sighed.

"You mean you only have a week's worth of clothes?"

"Of clothes that fit." Gil looked out the window transfixed.

"Kori. If you keep working on the computer, can we buy that farm?" Gil asked, looking out at the broad expanse of now slumbering fields.

"The farm?" Kori shook her head and laughed. "Well, if you want to buy the farm I suggest you get busy and invent something big because that farm's gonna cost a lot more than I've got in the bank.

"I'm hungry," Gil said. "And there's no bread. Also almost no peanut butter."

"All right," she said, shutting the computer. "Help me pick up the money that's all over the floor. Then we'll go to the grocery store."

⚔

Kori stood at the kitchen table unpacking the groceries when Avery walked in the door, bundled against the wind, backpack flung over his shoulder.

He dropped his pack on the table, shed his hat and coat and flopped down in a chair. His cheeks looked red and chapped.

"How was school?" Kori asked.

"Fine." He sighed without looking and absent-mindedly poked at the loaf of bread. "I need $75 to go on the field trip to D.C. To the holocaust museum." Kori removed the bread from his grasp before he did further damage. "If I don't go, I'll have to spend the day hanging out with the kids in detention. Not that I'd be in detention, *per se*. It's just that there wouldn't be any other place to put me." He did look at her now, and his resignation threatened to split Kori's heart.

"Okay," she said.

"Okay, what?"

She sat down beside Avery and took a deep breath. "Go ahead and sell it."

Avery's eyes grew wide.

"I can't stand this hand-to-mouth living anymore. And I can't for the life of me figure out what else to do."

Avery smiled, and Kori noted his eyes had shifted and taken on a translucent quality.

"It'll be okay, Kori," Avery said. "I promise."

Chapter 30

Avery pulled Ruth's van into Cooper's gas station. Kori sat in the passenger seat; Gil and Max were in the back reading comic books. Kori slunk down in her seat, pulled her hoodie up and bit her nails.

"You guys wait here, okay?" Avery said.

"All right, already. Just hurry up," Kori snipped.

Avery blew out of the car as if he'd been sandblasted, rolling down to the pavement and out of sight before Kori had a chance to change her mind. Max's ears pricked up, but Gil made no move to indicate he was even listening.

⚐

Avery walked with swagger across the parking lot, a walk he'd been practicing for weeks in anticipation of this meeting. He could see Mr. Cooper's bald head through the window, bent in concentration over a stack of papers. When he got to the door, though, Avery wavered, and rather than boldly stepping into his future, he knocked lightly, the little bell over the door tinkling as he entered. Mr. Cooper didn't look up but continued reviewing the stack of papers before him, initialing them one at a time as he placed them into the "completed" pile.

"Lazy bastards," Mr. Cooper said, not quite under his breath.

"Excuse me," Avery said, half-turning to leave. Not the welcome he expected.

Mr. Cooper's head, gleaming like a cue ball in the florescent light, popped up to greet him. "Oh for Chrissakes. Avery Tirabi. I thought you were one of my employees in here for another cup of coffee." He stood and offered his hand, recently washed, but still bearing the grimy remnants of what looked to be a mid-morning oil change. Avery gave him a firm handshake and Mr. Cooper's round belly, stretched over the limit of his size forty-two pants, jiggled in greeting.

"Sit down. Have a cup of coffee." Mr. Cooper motioned toward the "Mr. Coffee," formerly white plastic, now oil-stained from years of dirty, greasy hands. A few stacks of Styrofoam cups and a shaker of sugar sat next to the pot. Avery looked at the whole ensemble and grimaced.

"Oh, no thanks, Mr. Cooper. I don't drink coffee," he lied. When he did, Avery needed tons of sugar and milk, the latter of which was nowhere in sight. Instead, there was a powdery plastic known as "non-dairy creamer" on the table. Avery never understood the American penchant for creating fake substitutes when the real thing was so readily available.

"So what's up? Did you come to sell me more of that lovely gas and oil?"

Avery brightened. Mr. Cooper was interested before he'd even opened his mouth. "Actually, I did. I've got a few fifty-five gallon drums outside."

Mr. Cooper raised an eyebrow. "How'd you get them in the car? They're monsters."

Avery shrugged his shoulders. "I rigged a ramp." Avery waved a hand in dismissal as if the feat were no big deal. "Car was dragging a bit on the way over, though. Hell on the suspension." Avery felt like an adult, using the word "hell" without coming off like someone who regularly used vulgarity. Mr. Cooper tried to suppress a smile, but Avery caught it. *Right where I want him.* "So, Mr. Cooper, you said before you'd take all the gas and oil I could deliver. Are you still thinking that way?"

"Absolutely. Finest product I've come across in all my thirty years of running a service station. Your father made a fine product." A shadow crept across Mr. Cooper's face. "Tragedy," he said, shaking his head. "Terrible tragedy."

Mr. Cooper shot Avery a half-smile, half-grimace, walked over and clapped him on the back. "What are we waiting for, my boy? Let's go unload. Same price as before, I presume?"

"Actually, Mr. Cooper, I need to raise the price about 10%," Avery said. "Overhead."

Mr. Cooper assessed Avery for a few moments. "Anything I can do to help old Marty. Cold as he may be personally, his legacy lives on." He squeezed Avery's shoulder. "Your father'd be proud of you, boy. Well. Why am I saying, boy? You're not a boy. You're a man. And a fine one, too." Mr. Cooper opened the door and held it for Avery who was still seated.

"Mr. Cooper. There's one more thing."

Mr. Cooper closed the door and stood, hand on the doorknob.

"No one can know where you got this stuff."

Mr. Cooper raised himself to his full height of five feet, nine inches and sidled up close to Avery, whispering. "What's happened? Something else?"

Avery shook his head. "No. It's just my sister's still freaked out about the porch. She thinks it's all tied together. So if anybody comes around … "

"I'll just tell them that I've started buying from a competitor who wishes to remain anonymous."

"You think that'll do it?"

Mr. Cooper rubbed the stubble of his unshaven face, deep in thought. "Don't worry about it. I'll handle them. Haven't been in business for thirty years without some savvy of my own, eh?"

"Thanks, Mr. Cooper." Avery stood and they shook hands.

"Okay, let's walk. We'll talk on the way."

Avery stepped into the garage, abuzz with the whir of motors and power tools, and thought of Robbie's penchant for mechanics. He should be home running a place like this. *Maybe if I sold enough oil …*

They walked out into the parking lot where the noise level dropped substantially. Mr. Cooper's step was quick and light for a man with so much girth, and Avery had to walk fast to keep up with him.

"So how much more of this you got, and more importantly, can you make some more?" Avery was about to answer, but Mr. Cooper continued.

"Frankly, I'd be happy to tell all these oil guys to go to hell. They've been gouging me for years. Government's no help. Lets 'em get away with murdering, thieving and stealing from the American public. They say they're a unified front to help with the foreign competition, but I call it price-fixing." He poked Avery in the ribs. "You know what I predict? I predict it'll come back to bite 'em in the ass someday. I just hope I'm around to see it." He chuckled then laughed full out, exposing a mouthful of metal. Now standing at the back of Ruth's minivan, Mr. Cooper lifted the hatch without waiting for a signal from Avery.

Mad Max greeted him exactly the way Cerberus would have if someone had tried to breach the gates of hell, brown eyes ablaze and barking for all he was worth. His single head moved so fast that he very well could have had three. Mr. Cooper jumped back as if stung.

"Gil! Get him under control!" Avery shouted.

Gil's eyes peered out, an iridescent green gleaming between the barrels. He grabbed Max by the collar and pulled him down to sit. "It's okay, boy," he said sweetly, rubbing Max's ears. Max settled his head onto Gil's lap, calmer, but still growling, the sound rolling around in his massive jowls. Mr. Cooper could hear it a hundred feet away.

"It's all right. Gil's got him."

"I hate dogs," Mr. Cooper said. "Scared to death of 'em."

Max barked once as if to say you should be, but Gil tugged at his collar and he relaxed again. Mr. Cooper signaled for one of his employees to bring the handcart. Gil gave Max an ear rub so thorough that he could do little more than roll over when Mr. Cooper's guys unloaded the van.

CHAPTER 31

Kori, Avery and Gil poured out of Ruth's minivan and staggered toward the house, drunk with the success of their mission to Cooper's Service Station. Kori hung back watching while Avery lectured Gil about the finer points of backwards butt-kicking.

"No, it's like this," Avery said. "You walk next to the person and then you take your outside leg, the leg that's farthest from them, and you swing it around and up and you kick 'em in the butt without even breaking stride. If you can help it, you don't even look at them, but it's really hard not to laugh." Avery demonstrated, giving Gil a good swift one. Gil pitched forward, catching himself before he fell and laughing at his own clumsiness.

"My turn," Gil said. "Just pretend you don't know I'm going to do it," he said. Together he and Avery walked up the few steps to the back door and once on the landing, Gil swung his leg around and kicked Avery so hard he sent him hurtling head first into the back door. Avery caught himself, grimacing.

"How'd I do," Gil asked, beaming. Avery narrowed his eyes.

"Remind me not to teach you anything anymore," he hissed, holding the door for them.

Avery sat down at the kitchen table and began counting the bills. "Two hundred and eighty-six dollars. That should hold us for a while, Kor."

"Well, it won't pay the taxes, but it'll buy groceries for a couple weeks." She walked to the counter and retrieved two glasses and then to the fridge for the milk. "Although the way you guys eat, it probably won't even last that long." She handed glasses to Avery and Gil and snatched the money out of Avery's hands while he was in mid-gulp. She stuffed the bulk of the money in a jar in the cabinet, put a few bills in her wallet and handed Avery $90.

"For the field trip. And some walking-around money." She smiled and looked at him in earnest. "I'm still a little worried, but … "

"But nothing," Avery shrugged, and polished off the rest of the milk. "We're hot-wired right into the police station, remember. As long as Einstein over here doesn't hit the alarm by accident, we're A-Okay." Gil ignored them, drained his glass and left the room. They heard the TV click on and soon the soundtrack to *Holes* was coming through the surround sound.

Avery leafed through the mail haphazardly separating bills, advertisements and solicitations from anything that looked like real mail. One piece caught his eye because of the address label. He shoved it across the table at Kori, who turned it over again and again, considering it with reverence as if it were a holy icon. Finally she opened her hands and let it drop to the table, staring after it as if it might open itself.

"Maybe we should write 'return to sender' on it, or 'no longer at this address,'" Kori suggested. Avery reached over and picked it up, studying the return address.

"United States Environmental Protection Agency," he said. "It's official." He handed the letter back to Kori, but she didn't reach for it. "Open it."

"It's Mom's."

"Kori. I hardly think that matters now," Avery said, raising his eyebrows at her. She still wouldn't take it.

Avery tore open the letter. "It's Notice of a Public Meeting." Avery's eyes scanned the page. "Hey, there's also a Federal Register notice soliciting public comment on EPA's Record of Decision for the Stahl's landfill." He flipped back to the notice in the local paper, scanned it quickly and slid both across the table to Kori. "Looks like EPA's going to have a town meeting about the farm."

"The Stahl's property?"

"Yeah." Avery pulled the papers back and read something again. "It says they just completed the Record of Decision, the ROD, and they want to inform the public about the remedy they've chosen and give us a chance to ask questions."

"What do you mean — us?"

"Well, I'm going. It's only over at the high school. It's close."

"How you gonna get there?"

"Kori! We need to be interested in this stuff. It's in our backyard."

Kori shrugged in response. "That was Mom's thing, not mine."

Avery rubbed hard at his temples. "It's everyone-in-this-house's thing. It's the whole planet's thing." Avery grabbed the envelope. The return address said U.S. EPA, but there was no name associated with the organization. "I wonder who in EPA sent this," he said, and tossed the envelope on the table. "You know, Mom was the chairman of the citizen's group that followed this stuff."

"Mom was the head of every group that followed anything like this," Kori said. Her face wore a blasé expression.

"We gotta call somebody and tell them," Avery said.

"Oh, no. You just turn that optimistic gaze in another direction, brother."

"Somebody's gotta get copies made, buy envelopes and stamps and mail this notice out to the neighbors. That's what Mom used to do. The EPA obviously doesn't know she's dead."

"How would they?" Kori snapped.

"Look, my point is, if these notices don't go out, how's anyone going to know about the meeting?"

"Maybe they read the paper."

"And what if they don't?"

"So send them out."

"You gotta help me. I can't do it alone."

"No way. I don't have the time or the inclination. And I don't want to get involved."

"But you are involved." Avery waved toward the window and beyond. "We're all involved. Our aquifer's contaminated. Do you realize that if Dad hadn't built a water purification system for our well, odds are one in four of getting cancer? And that's after drinking the water for only five years. That's how bad the contamination is. We've been using that aquifer for twenty-five!" Avery opened his hands as if Kori were stupid not to see his point. "One in four, Kori. One in four people in the Hickory Hills development has contracted cancer. Which one of us do you think it would have been?" Kori mumbled something under her breath, but Avery continued.

"You know what we'd be drinking right now, if our water came straight through from the well? The components that make up gasoline, for starters. Same stuff that's in those barrels out back." Avery jerked a thumb in the direction of the shed. "That aquifer will take decades to fix even if it ever clears up. And until everyone wakes up and realizes that we all live downstream … "

Kori laughed out loud, walked to the fridge and poured herself a glass of water.

"You sound like an ad for the EPA. Wasn't that one of their television spots?"

"They don't do TV spots. They're a part of the U.S. Federal Government. They can't advertise. Pity, too," Avery said, as if struck by a thought. He rubbed his hairless chin in contemplation. "Advertising," he said mostly to himself.

Kori took a drink and stood staring out the window. She leaned against the sink and sighed. "I've got paper and envelopes. Use whatever you want. I even have labels downstairs, and I'm pretty sure I know where to find Mom's mailing list on the computer. But just keep me out of it, okay?"

"Kor, just … "

"No, Avery. I can't. Don't you see?" She folded her arms across her chest, more of a hugging motion than an acrimonious gesture. "It'll bring her so close, but without breaking the surface. It won't bring her back. Nothing can."

Kori hadn't told Avery about the terrible nightmares she'd had following Ruth and Marty's death. Visions of her blood-spattered parents being chased by a monster with hell in his eyes and arms that shot fire from their fingertips. They wrenched her from sleep, leaving her gasping for air, shaking and sweating, so unnerved she didn't dare roll over. Kori's chest tightened at the thought.

"Why don't you call the lawyer? What's that guy's name? Bill Gallighan? His law office would probably do all of this for you. He's an advisor to the citizens' group. You could at least get him to pay for postage."

Avery shook his head and ran a hand through his hair. "He does this pro bono. His law office doesn't give him a dime. Plus he's gotta maintain two hundred and twenty billable hours a month or they won't let him work on the case anymore. They're real bastards. The firm gets all this credit and name recognition, and Bill's the one doing all the work." Avery folded his hands and crossed his legs as if in consultation with himself.

"Well, he has more money than we do. He can pay for stamps. Maybe even copies."

"Actually, the law firm will pay for copies. And envelopes. Not stamps though."

"What's the difference between paper and stamps? It all costs money."

"They want the stuff to go out on their letterhead because it's free advertising and then everyone thinks they're nice guys. But they don't want to be out of pocket for the postage."

"How do you know that?"

"Mom told me," Avery said. He picked up the letter again and stared at it for several moments as if he could conjure Ruth simply by holding it. "She did so much." Avery's voice was wistful. "Stuff we'll never even find out about."

"She didn't tell me much about that."

"You had to ask her." Avery sighed and ran his hands over his face. The conversation had brought him down.

"Why don't you go watch TV," Kori offered.

Avery nodded and left the room.

Kori stared at mounds of mail but made no move toward it. Outside, the rain clouds gathered.

CHAPTER 32

Weeks after Avery's visit, a shiny silver oil tanker sat positioned to fill the underground holding tank at Cooper's Service Station. Water droplets ran in impromptu lines down the windshield. The driver grabbed his clipboard, jumped down from the vehicle, and, throwing his hood over his head, strode to the office through the misty fog. He burst through the door into the office, a futile move since he could see through the glass that no one was in there. He scanned the garage floor, his eyes settling on the closest mechanic, Tom Johnson, only three days on the job. The driver approached with long, unhurried steps that belied his impatience.

He wasted no time with niceties. "Cooper here?"

"He stepped out for a sandwich."

"Business off or something?"

"No. I don't think," said Johnson.

"What d'ya' mean, you don't think? I ain't been here for two weeks. You should be bone dry, but you still got a lot left."

"Got some yesterday," Johnson said.

The driver furrowed his brows, annoyance creeping across his face. "Dammit. How many times I have to tell that guy? Listen, you. This is the third time I've been out here and the third time … ." The driver doffed his hood. A pair of menacing eyes remained.

"Who is it? Exxon? Texaco?" He rubbed his hand over two days of stubble. "Chevron?"

"I have no idea what you're talking about."

The driver took a step forward. "I got better things to do than come here every week for no reason," he said, looking like he might throttle Johnson, clipboard and all.

Johnson took a step back. He was suddenly and acutely aware of the sheer volume of sound at his back, the whir and hiss and clink of the body shop, all stations in use, Mr. Cooper's half-dozen motor heads fully engaged in their work. This guy could pummel him to a bloody pulp and no one would notice or hear a thing until they stepped over him to get to the free coffee.

"Look, I just started three days ago." Johnson turned to the room at large looking for support, but every last man had his head in or under a hood, engine, or wheelbase.

"Sunoco? Getty? Who is it? I at least have a right to know?"

"I don't know his name." The driver stepped so close that Johnson could smell the man's coffee breath.

"I'll ask it slow so you're little pea-brain can register it. What is the name of the company that delivered here this week?"

"There was no company. It was a guy. And I told you, I don't know."

"Then who's he work for?"

The driver's eyes narrowed and he moved even closer. In addition to coffee, Johnson now identified the distinct smells of petrol and body odor. Johnson flinched, cleared his throat.

"He doesn't work for anybody. He's just a kid makes oil is all." His voice cracked. The driver was too close. Johnson caught a movement on the periphery of his vision and turned to see Jim Snyder, the Assistant Manager, speed walking toward them.

"Can I help you?" Snyder asked the driver.

"You tell Cooper he'll be hearing from Akanabi." The driver turned on his heel and stomped out the door into the rain.

"What the heck was that about?" Snyder asked. Johnson demurred, shaken.

"You have no idea?"

"The kid that brings the gas and oil, who is he?" Johnson asked.

"No one for you to worry about." Snyder walked to the office and looked over the papers on the desk, shifting them around. He walked back onto the floor, empty-handed.

"Where's the invoice?" Johnson said nothing.

"Did he even fill the tanks today?" Snyder asked, more harshly then Johnson thought appropriate.

Johnson nodded. "Yeah, but I guess not much."

"Do you know why?"

"He said they didn't take much."

"What did you tell him?"

"Nothing. Just that some kid brings some gas and oil sometimes."

Snyder's face bulged and he sputtered, "You told him about Avery?"

Tirabi. That was it. Johnson coughed. "What was I supposed to say?"

Snyder eyed him up. "All right," Snyder said, as Mr. Cooper crossed the threshold to the shop. "Get back to work. I'll take care of it."

⋏

Johnson returned to his station, trying to look busy — he was almost done retrofitting some new brake pads — but his eyes kept drifting to the scene in the office with Cooper and Snyder, the men alternating between grimaces and head nods. At last, Mr. Cooper appeared more resigned than indignant. Perhaps he'd keep his job after all. The thought was quickly replaced by the next thing Johnson saw.

Avery Tirabi was pulling into the parking lot just as the giant tanker was pulling out. The driver didn't seem to care that Avery had the right-of-way and pulled out across two lanes of traffic right in front of Ruth's minivan. Both Avery and the driver slammed on their brakes, a near miss, and proceeded to yell and lean on their respective horns. Finally, the driver put it in reverse giving Avery enough room to squeeze into the parking lot. The driver flipped Avery the bird as he drove by and Avery responded in kind.

With the diligence of a worker bee, Johnson buried his head and shoulders beneath the wheelbase, too nervous to even peek.

⚶

"Hey, Mr. Cooper," Avery said. The door rattled shut with a bang and a jingle.

"Avery!" Mr. Cooper looked up with a start. He hadn't seen Avery coming, engrossed as he was in Snyder's story. He cleared his throat and ran a hand over his eyebrows, hoping to hide his embarrassment.

"You okay?" Avery asked. Cooper nodded and smiled.

"Fine. Fine. Bit of a headache is all. Glad you're here, son," he said, motioning to a chair. "Sit down." Avery obliged, first extending a hand to Snyder in a show of both manners and adultness.

"Look, Avery, I'm gonna be honest with you. We may have a problem." Mr. Cooper stopped, weighed his words, wondering if the kid's self-possession could withstand this potential pitfall. "That Akanabi Oil guy that just left? He was pretty P.O.'d."

"Why?"

"Not much of a delivery. He wanted to know who the new supplier was." Mr. Cooper walked over and poured a cup of coffee, which he handed to Avery. Avery shook his head at the tar-like substance so Cooper drank it himself.

"Did you tell him?" Avery's voice quivered slightly.

"No. He talked to one of the guys on the floor. Snyder and I are the only ones with that information." Cooper sighed and sat down. "Likely the driver's gonna call dispatch and tell them it's the third week in a row we had a substandard delivery. He'll recommend canceling us because we got another supplier."

"Do you?"

"No."

"Well, we're almost out," Avery said.

Mr. Cooper stared out the window. The rain had stopped and the sky was clearing. A slow smile spread across his face. He looked blankly at

Avery, took a sip of his coffee and cleared his throat. "Terrible," he said to himself, and sat down at his desk.

"Avery?" Cooper said, smiling again. "What if you supplied me?"

"Me? I can't. I told you, we're almost out."

"Well, how about making some more? I'd take all you had. I'm not the biggest station in town, but we're busy enough." Mr. Cooper looked out the window: six pumps out front, all with cars in front of them at the moment, one in back, just for shop use. He grabbed a sheet of paper and pencil, did some quick calculations and pushed the paper at Avery.

"This is how much you'd gross if you could supply me weekly. I don't know what you're overhead is or how much the raw materials cost, but even so, it's a pretty number, eh?" Avery bent his head to look at the paper and his eyes grew wide. Mr. Cooper smiled. Apparently, Avery thought the number very pretty as well.

"I don't know, Mr. Cooper, I … "

"Look. I'll take all of what you got left. And in the meantime, think about my offer."

"But Akanabi … "

"Akanabi doesn't know anything. They're probably dropping us even as we speak."

"But what if someone finds out we're not a real company?"

"No one's gonna find out. We can arrange pickup at night, after hours, whatever you want."

Avery wrinkled his eyebrows. "Well, I don't know … "

Mr. Cooper continued. "Don't worry. The guy that left here today thinks we got a new supplier, not some sixteen-year old kid who invented some damn machine turns trash into gold. He's not gonna come lookin' for you, I'm tellin' ya'."

"But somebody came looking for us. And they know where we live."

"Avery. Your father's been working on that machine for over twenty years. And he told a lot of people. Hell, I even knew about it."

Avery took a deep breath and folded his hands on his lap.

"Just think about it. If the answer's no, I can get a new supplier in a couple hours."

"I'll see what I can do," Avery said. He shook Mr. Cooper's hand before leaving.

Cooper and Snyder watched him walk to the car.

"Do you think it'll be okay?" Snyder asked.

"I hope to God, so," Mr. Cooper said, as Ruth's minivan pulled out of the parking lot and onto the road.

Chapter 33

A very stood at Marty's drafting table, pouring over drawings of the TDU, matching up the drawings with the real thing. At ground level, the outside of the TDU's receiving station looked like a gigantic child's play chest. Sliding metal doors opened and disappeared within the grated metal exterior framework — the classic European pocket door — to reveal a cavernous opening that funneled trash to the giant cylindrical tank housed below ground. With this design, Marty had been able to back his tractor right into the barn and, utilizing the trailer's hydraulic lift, pour the trash directly into the yawning mouth of the cylinder.

Marty's TDU was a democratic machine, treating all trash equally as long as it was carbon based. Once inside, the trash was mixed with water to create a slurry, an insoluble, goopy mess. The slurry passed through a pipeline to a holding tank where it was heated under pressure until it reached a reaction temperature. Another pipeline, a third unit, also cylindrical — Marty Tirabi was fond of circles — ferried the slurry along to where it finished its initial reaction and was flashed again. Here the gaseous products were spun off, the pressure lowered, the liquids separated from the volatile chemicals. Marty built a series of interconnected pipelines placed one on top of the other, some at 90 degree angles to each other, a steel matrix to house the myriad and varied reactions. Step five was another series of thinner cylinders, three in a row, tall and demure, sitting side-by-side like young girls at their first dance, waiting to be asked. But size was no indication of their strength. In these cylinders Marty heated the mixture, separating water from gas from light oils which led to the final stage, two large, squat holding tanks where Marty intended to store the gas and light oils. Even staggering the six stages of equipment at forty-five degree angles to each other, the prototype was huge and encompassed the entire back wall of the barn.

Avery sighed and flopped down at the drafting table. Marty had said there was a problem with water. Was it too much or too little? Avery couldn't remember. Gil knew, but damn it, he wouldn't help. Avery was on his own. And with at least two-dozen blueprints, this was going to take a while. Maybe a little meditation was in order.

Avery practiced meditation in fits and starts. When he did, a wonderful clarity always ensued, infused with an acute awareness of being in the present. And the help always came with it, fecund and unbidden. From where it came, he really couldn't say: probably the universal mind, the brain trust, as he referred to it. From ions, or static or electricity. From nowhere and everywhere. He knew at times he'd tapped into the morphogenic field where ideas were traded like stocks on the NASDAQ, the theory being that if a monkey in Costa Rica learned to drive a car, a monkey on the Rock of Gibraltar could do the same without even meeting the Costa Rican monkey. Or perhaps he'd tapped into the Zero Point Field, that eerie, brave new world where discoveries were deposited in the cosmic bank account, waiting to be withdrawn by anyone holding a debit card. He'd read plenty on comparative religion and had a few surreal experiences in his lifetime, enough to recognize the signs of a downloading from the *One Mind* when he felt it, which he rarely did. But Gil made regular withdrawals, engaged in constant conversation, slept with it under his pillow. For Gil, change and enlightenment were the same, immediate and visceral, played out physically each time he had a fit or an idea.

For the rest of the world struggling to catch up, the only acceptable change was a gradual climb up a low-grade mountain, the steps laborious and slow. And morphogenic field or not, it still took time for all the other monkeys to accept their new knowledge. Even if they could do it, did they want to do it? Even if he could fix this invention — something he didn't have a whole lot of faith in at the present moment — Marty had said it would make the world stand on its head. Was the world ready for such a precarious position? Come to think of it, was he?

Avery needed Gil's fertile mind where you could plant the seed and days or weeks later the answer sprung forth like Athena from Zeus's head, in full warrior regalia, engaged and ready for battle. Gil's epilepsy fueled his creativity; the disease forced him into the Zone where he was working out some serious past-life crap. Avery felt helpless at these times but appeased himself with the thought that you can't work someone's karma out for them, a fact that at the tender age of ten, Gil completely understood.

"Gil." Avery walked to the living room and shouted for his brother. "Gil!"

A muffled, "he's in his room" wafted up from Kori's corner of the basement. Avery nodded a thanks that Kori couldn't see and went upstairs to find Gil.

He rapped on the door and stepped into the room. Unless Gil was hiding under the bed, he wasn't here. Avery checked the closet then under the bed. He sat down on the bed to wait. Minutes later, he was asleep.

$$\lambda$$

The wind whipped across barren fields where only rolled bales of hay remained. The oak trees swayed and heaved in fits of laughter as the wind rose up, intertwined with their naked branches and whispered secrets only the oaks could understand. Avery took inventory. All healthy, thank God. A couple dozen were in striking distance of both the barn and house. He'd hate to see the damage one rotten tree could cause in a windstorm like this.

He touched the bear totem pole rooted to the ground, facing the barn. It was six feet high, a hundred feet from the barn's entrance; its eyes saw all who moved through those doors. Marty had carved it out of a tree gone rotten at the base after Gil had noticed it swaying in a windstorm much like this one.

Marty relayed the information to Ruth who, noticing the swing set was in the probable trajectory of the tree should it fall, called a tree service. The tree service couldn't come for two days. Ruth told Marty to leave the tree alone, that if it hadn't fallen by now, it wasn't going to fall in the next two days, and left on an errand.

But Marty couldn't leave anything alone, especially a rogue tree, threatening him through his barn window. Ruth's tire tracks weren't even cooled before Marty got out the ropes and chain saw. The whir of power tools called the kids to the backyard, but Marty banished them to the deck, more than a safe distance away, until he was done with the felling. After that, it was all fun and games. The kids played happily on the fallen log while Marty used his chain saw on the part of the tree still in the ground and routed out the finer stuff. When he'd finished, Marty had transformed his enemy into a vigilant friend, the coolest totem pole the kids had ever seen. One paw rested on the bear's stomach as if he'd just eaten lunch. His mouth was open, exposing healthy, yet deadly incisors. His eyes were wide as if he'd just spotted something. Marty let Kori paint the eyes and claws and big scary teeth all white, and when it was dry, he let the kids crawl all over it, something they still did years later whenever they hung out in the backyard. Avery smiled and rubbed his hand inside the bear's mouth. For luck.

Avery tapped lightly on the barn window. Gil threw the deadbolt and waved him in. Avery dropped the roll of Marty's drawings on the table and removed his coat while Gil closed and locked the door behind him.

"Toasty in here," Avery said. Gil had the space heater cranked up and it felt like a billion degrees in the barn. "Why don't you wear a sweater like most people do in cold weather, and then you won't need the heat to be so high?"

"Cause I wanted to wear my lizard shirt." Gil looked down at his black t-shirt with the lizard face on it and smiled.

"What'cha got going on here?" Avery asked.

"Building something," Gil said.

"I see that. But what is it?" To Avery, it looked like a souped-up go-cart. He walked over and surveyed the frame and held a tentative hand out to touch it. The frame proved incredibly durable. "May I?"

Gil nodded, and Avery stepped up on the floorboard, testing the weight load by jumping up and down on it.

"Come here. I'll show you." Gil pushed Avery's own drawings aside and peered over a stack already open on the drafting table.

Avery sifted through them, his excitement growing. "It's a hybrid engine? Are you using technology that's out there or is this something … ?"

"New. Dad says you can't talk about something until you finish or you lose the Muse. So I can't talk about it."

"You have a Muse? Who is it?"

"You know. A pretty lady. Sometimes she sings."

"What's her name?"

"She never said."

"Is she real or you made her up?

"Real."

"How do you know?"

"Because I just know. She comes at night. Sometimes she whispers ideas in my ear or if I'm stuck on something, she helps me solve it." Gil looked down at his hands and turned them over, inspecting them. "Sometimes she just holds my hands. She says they're soft." Gil smiled sheepishly. Avery snickered, but turned away before Gil caught him.

"She helped me with that," he said pointing to the ATV. "It'll be more energy efficient than the others. Less fuel, less charging time and the batteries will be smaller."

"Hmmph," Avery said, pondering the blueprints. "How long until you think you'll be done?" Gil shrugged and spun around on his stool. "Well, just let me know and I'll get busy on the patent." Avery flipped through the drawings. "Is there anything I can start on now?"

Gil unclamped the vice grips holding the drawings in place and rolled them up, a dismissal. Apparently, the conversation was, for the present, concluded. Gil unrolled Avery's drawings flat and used the vice-grip to clip the topsides to the edge of the drafting table. He reviewed them carefully for several minutes, unclamped the vice grip, rolled the drawings back up and handed them to Avery. Then he walked over to the hammock where Max reclined.

"How'd you get him up there?" Avery asked. Gil shrugged like it was no big deal and lay down next to Max who, startled from sleep, emitted a small yelp.

"I need your help," Avery said. Gil nestled in close, warming himself against Max's monstrous shape. The hammock moved in a rhythmic, rocking motion. He shook his head and buried it in Max's face.

"Why not?"

Gil buried his face deeper into Max's fur.

"Gil. Why the hell not?"

"I just don't want to do it alone." Avery detected a tremor in Gil's voice and mistook it for fear.

"You won't have to do it alone. I'll help you." Gil shook his head vehemently and Avery dropped his voice, low and soothing.

"Are you afraid? Don't be afraid. The barn's alarmed. And I swear I'll keep you safe."

"I'm not afraid," Gil spat out. "I just … I can't do it without Dad. It was his. Not mine. I can only do it if he says I can."

"But, Gil. Dad's dead."

"I know that, Avery!" Avery didn't notice the tears gathering in Gil's eyes and continued.

"Well, he's not going to be saying anything again."

"How do you know?" Gil shouted.

It was the first time Gil had shown such emotion and made Avery realize how unbearable was the angst Gil had been carrying since his father died. A sudden queasy feeling gripped Avery; it couldn't have been worse if he'd been sucker punched.

"You don't know anything." Gil jumped off the hammock and ran for the door. Max tried to follow, but his foot got stuck in between the knots. He sat there whimpering, trying to disengage his paw. Gil unlocked the dead bolt and ran out, failing to deactivate the silent alarm. Avery watched Gil run across the yard, unaware that downtown at the police station, another alarm screamed out a warning.

Max yelped in frustration. Avery untangled his foot and lifted him out of the hammock. Max took off after Gil through the open door. Avery sat back on the hammock and rocked, listening to the howling of the wind.

"Now what?" Avery said to himself. He really didn't expect an answer.

"Stuff envelopes," a voice said. Avery landed on his hands and knees and scanned the space around him. The queasy feeling was back. He sucked at the ambient air.

"Mom?" He stood up and looked uneasily around the barn. As much as he would love to sit down and have a heart-to-heart conversation with his mother, the shock might be enough to kill him. He took several tentative steps, swiped the drawings off the drafting table and high-stepped it out of the barn, slamming the door behind him. He didn't stop to lock it.

Two minutes later, he threw off his coat and sat down at the kitchen table. Stacks of paper and envelopes crowded the kitchen's surface areas. He scanned the room. The project would take all day. Avery shivered and with a single glance back toward the barn, folded one of the sheets of paper in three and stuffed the first envelope. He looked again before stuffing another. Nothing was amiss. He began folding and stuffing in earnest and after several minutes, the repetitive motion of his task took the chill out of his spine.

CHAPTER 34

The change was gradual as most changes are. Not a sweeping, life-altering moment, like *satori*, that mystical state of enlightenment where all is revealed. That only happened to people in the movies whose lives fit snugly into a three-act structure. That was more Gil's thing. Gil's was a real life movie.

No, this change began with the industrial revolution, and it was slow and steady and specious and that's why no one noticed. Avery knew the statistics. Over two thousand species of plants and animals, making their homes in various rainforests, became extinct every day. Tillable land took precedence over foraging the fertile soils for raw materials that would become medicines. Old growth forests were becoming tables and chairs and bookcases. The trees, which acted as the earth's lungs taking in carbon dioxide and returning oxygen, were being methodically clear-cut, leaving a system that ran on partial capacity, like a cancer patient who's had a lung removed. Fertile soils, the hallmark of America, capable of producing vast quantities of food, were being systematically stripped of all nutrients thanks to agribusinesses' overuse of pesticides and lack of diversification in farming, or worse, paved over for housing developments. The hole in the ozone layer continued to grow yet the U.S. walked away from Kyoto, citing shoddy science and uncertainty, allowing corporations to line their pockets a little deeper against the coming winter, the winter that may soon never go away. What will we do when floods and famine become the norm?

Avery really never understood it all. He knew it was bad, but what time he devoted was more for Ruth than the planet. He sighed, folded another group of flyers and stared out the window, looking for answers in the grey winter sky.

"Hey." Avery jumped, sending a stack of flyers sailing to the ground.

"Jesus, Kori. You scared the heck out of me."

"What are you thinking about?"

"Mom," Avery said. Kori sat down next to her brother.

"Me, too. How can I help?" She extended her hand. Avery put a stack of flyers in it.

"Really?"

"Really."

"Labels. I need some … " A loud rap at the door sent more papers scattering to the floor. Avery turned to see two policemen peering into the kitchen.

"What's going on?" she asked, and jumped up to answer the door just as Gil miraculously appeared.

"They're cops," he said and sat down at the table, his knee bouncing up and down.

"No kidding, Sherlock," Kori said, walking to the door. "Why are they here?"

"Cause I set off the alarm."

"You little jerk," Avery said. "Why didn't you tell me?"

"Cause I didn't know until just now," Gil said.

Kori opened the door and greeted the visitors. "Hi. Can I help you?"

"Yes, Ma'am. I'm officer Matheson. We're investigating a call into headquarters at 14:42 hours. Report indicates the alarm in the barn was tripped. Have you been home, Ma'am?" Avery walked over and stood behind his sister.

"All afternoon, officer."

"Have you noticed any suspicious behavior in the vicinity of your back-yard, Ma'am?"

"Not suspicious, but I can tell you … ." Avery pinched Kori in the back, hard. "Oowww." She turned to glare at her brother.

He smiled sweetly, a warning in his eyes. "Nothing suspicious, Officer," Avery said.

"Okay. Mind if we take a look?"

Avery and Kori both shook their heads.

"We'll let you know if we find anything."

The cops walked across the lawn, and Kori closed the door behind them. Avery and Gil exchanged glances.

"All right-y, then. Somebody better tell me what's going on."

$$\blacktriangle$$

The wind picked up as Officers Matheson and Traecy crossed the backyard. They arrived at the barn to find the door banging in the wind. Matheson checked the perimeter while Traecy investigated the interior. After several minutes they stood at the door.

"Just a false alarm. Probably forgot that it was on," Matheson said. "This wind's not helpin'." He turned his collar up against a fresh onslaught and closed the barn door.

"Kids," Matheson said. Traecy nodded in agreement.

Chapter 35

Kori sat at the computer feeding labels to the printer. Gil ran down the stairs, Max fast on his heels, parting the air with their testosterone-laden, electro-energy. Gil bounded over to Kori and peered over her shoulder.

"Whatcha' doing?

"Making address labels."

"It looks like the letters are marrying."

"What do you know about marriage?"

"Mom and Dad were married." Kori reached out and grabbed Gil around his waist, pulling him in close for a hug.

"I'm bored," Gil said.

"Why don't you guys go outside and play?"

Gil sighed and Max yawned, exposing a full and threatening set of teeth.

"Guess not," Kori said. "I know. Why don't you invent something?"

Gil looked to Max for approval. Max sprawled, legs out behind him, on the carpet. Gil shook his head at Kori, dismissing the plan. "What else?"

Kori scrunched her nose in contemplation. "Why don't you go outside and help Jack," she said, smiling to herself. Gil looked at Max who wagged his tail at the mention of Jack's name, but made no sign to go.

"Okay," Gil said, and Kori released him. "C'mon, boy." Gil snapped his fingers and the pair ran up the stairs, disappearing over the top stair.

Jack lay on a creeper under Kori's car, his feet sticking out the side. At least under here the infernal wind wasn't so bad. He'd already replaced the rotor cups and pads and was moving on to an oil change, a simple enough job, but for the below freezing temperatures. He rubbed his hands together to warm them before loosening the nut on the oil pan.

"Hey, Jack. Whatcha' doin'?

Startled, Jack clunked his head on the oil pan. He rolled out to find Gil, squatting at the front tire. Dressed in a down parka and wearing a hat with little jingly bells hanging from three triangular flaps, Gil looked like an elf. Max sat beside him wearing a pair of reindeer antlers.

"Don't you know not to sneak up on people like that?" Jack rubbed his head where metal had hit flesh.

"I wasn't sneaking. Sneaking is when you tiptoe and go *shhhhh*," Gil said, putting a finger to his lips. "Kori told me to come out and help you."

"If Kori wants her car finished this century, you better do something else."

Jack pursed his lips in irritation and rolled back under the car. Gil squinted after Jack's dark form, still pleading his case.

"But you said I could try it," he whined. "You said the next time you worked on the car I could go under with you."

"In a minute, Gil. Just let me get this — oh, man." Wheels on macadam followed a sloshing sound and the *glug, glug, glug* of oil being loosed. Moments later the oil pan clanked to the ground. Jack emerged, sliding past a still squatting Gil.

Gil giggled and covered his mouth.

"Shut up. If you say one word I swear to God ... "

Gil handed Jack a rag lying on top of Jack's toolbox. Jack grabbed it out of his hands and began to swab at least a cup of oil out of his now gleaming hair. He laughed despite himself.

"Did you know that a single quart of oil is enough to cause a two-acre sized oil slick on the surface of the water?" Gil asked. "Do you know how big an acre is? A little more than 43,000 square feet. So that would be

86,000 square feet worth of oil slick." Jack listened with half an ear while he rubbed, trying to absorb the clingy liquid.

"And, as you are currently demonstrating, oil is not easily removed from hair, let alone, say, cormorant feathers or seal fur. And not only that. It kills the aquatic organisms that the fish live on. You know how? It chokes 'em. Binds up the oxygen and then they can't breathe."

"If you're referring to the oil I just spilled, let me assure you of two things. One — most of the spilled oil is in my hair. The rest is safely in the oil pan. And two — I don't think there are any cormorants or seals for some miles from here."

"But it's not just that. Did you know that a single gallon of oil is enough to poison a million gallons of freshwater? Do you know what a million gallons of freshwater is? It's a supply big enough for fifty people to drink and bathe and cook with for a whole year."

Jack grimaced and poked a corner of the rag in his ear, soaking up drips of oil.

"And even though much of the earth is covered with water, only one percent of it's potable. You know what potable means, right?" Gil said.

Jack nodded and rolled his eyes. The oil in his ear was slick and evasive, covering him like tightly sealed plastic wrap.

"And even though we only need to drink about two to two and a half quarts of water a day, we each use about a hundred and twenty-five to a hundred and fifty gallons a day for all the other stuff. Very wasteful. About forty percent more than necessary, I think." Gil stared at him, wide-eyed. "I'd be willing to give up baths to save water, you know."

Jack rubbed the oil-stained rag roughly over his head and gave up. "What are you, an encyclopedia?" He threw the towel to the ground and sighed. "Let's take a break. Get a drink while we're waiting for the last of it to drain. So we can be quite certain I'm not further contaminating our precious water supply."

"Yeah, because fragments of those little spilled oil spots on driveways and roads can also end up in our water supply. When it rains it gets washed into the storm drains, and when it rains really hard, into the combined sewer outfalls which empty into the river. You know what that means, right? Sewer and rainwater together. That's really gross."

"Are you done now?"

Gil stood up, extending his hand to Jack. Jack grabbed it and allowed himself to be pulled to his feet. He rubbed his grease-stained hands on his pants and together they walked inside.

CHAPTER 36

Change was a magical thing. Avery and Kori sat at the kitchen table, folding the notices announcing the public meeting. Avery hoped that between the two of them they could account for the dynamo that was once Ruth Tirabi. He knew it was a long shot, but time would be the judge.

Kori folded a single flyer and stuffed a single envelope. Avery's system was to fold ten letters and stuff ten envelopes, faster at a rate of two to Kori's one.

"So, except for some of the stuff that wasn't blended, I got rid of the rest of it," Avery said. "Maybe we should invest the money. We could double our profits."

"Or lose it all. That money provides the cushion we need until my business is more routinely in the black." She folded neatly with an artist's eye for perfection, which also accounted for her lack of speed. "Let's not mess with a good thing, huh?"

Avery nodded and stuffed an envelope.

"I'm going to miss the extra money, though. It was nice not having to count laundry change," Kori said.

"We don't have to miss it. If we could get Gil interested, the TDU would be up and running. We'd never have to worry about money again. And Mr. Cooper said … "

Kori shot him a look of empathy. "I think for you it's a little more about getting your name on a patent than it is about the money, isn't it?"

A wry smile crossed Avery's lips. Kori was right. Avery was desperate for a patent. His father had half a dozen by this age, and Gil already had several.

"But the machine itself, Kori. Just imagine what it could do for the environment. It takes millions of years under extreme pressure to create the fossil fuels we now burn as oil. This machine cuts that creation time down to hours. Just think of the greenhouse gasses it eliminates. We could keep what's left of the ozone layer intact. Not to mention the money we could make if we held the patent on it."

Kori nodded, but he could tell she was no longer paying attention. Avery decided not to mention Mr. Cooper's offer just now.

"Hey, Kor?"

"Yeah?"

"Thanks for helping with this stuff," he said, indicating the mounds of papers across the table. "Mom would've been happy."

"You mean happy to see me finally take an interest in something other than my own trivial little dramas."

"That's not what I meant."

Kori reached over and gave Avery's hand a squeeze. "I know. It's what I meant."

Gil, Max and Jack burst into the kitchen. Gil shed his coat and sat next to Avery.

"First day changing the oil?" Kori asked Jack. "Geez, Gil could stay cleaner than that."

"Shut up," Jack said and kissed her full on the lips, smearing her mouth with oil.

"Uck!" Kori rinsed her mouth at the sink while Gil made a paper airplane out of one of the flyers.

"Ooohh, you said shut up. We're not allowed to say that in this house."

"Yeah and who's going to stop me?" Jack said.

"I will," Gil said, his tone serious. He drew himself up tall in his seat, thrust out his chest and threw his airplane at Jack.

"You and what army, Gilliam?" Jack asked, reaching over to tousle Gil's hair. "That's a stupid rule anyway." Jack walked to the fridge, pulled out a beer.

"Aaaahh, you said stupid." Gil looked at Avery for assistance, but before Avery could say anything, Jack continued. "That makes you … " Gil thrust his chin forward as if tossing the word at him, but would not say it.

Jack sat down, twisted the top off his beer and took a swig. "The only stupid things are those rules," Jack said.

Gil looked wounded. He grabbed his coat and ran out the door, Max on his heels. Avery shot Jack a dirty look and went after Gil.

"What'd I do?" Jack asked.

Kori didn't stop stuffing envelopes to look at him. "You called my mother stupid," she said, a sad smile on her face.

"I didn't say a thing about your mother," Jack said.

"Those were her rules," Kori said, without looking up. "Now who's stupid?"

⅄

Avery caught up to Gil just as he slammed the barn door and threw the dead bolt, activating the alarm. Avery knocked.

"Gil. Let me in, man." Avery knocked a bit harder. "Gil!"

"Go away."

"Why are you taking it out on me? I didn't say anything."

"Exactly."

"Gil, you ran out before I had a chance to." Gil came around to the window of the barn, peeked out at his brother then retreated to the inner recesses of the barn. "C'mon, Gil. You love Jack. He just said a silly thing."

"Robbie would have flattened him." Avery tried not to laugh. Ever since Robbie left, Avery noticed he'd been growing taller every day in Gil's eyes. Avery pondered his most beneficial course of action before responding.

"Yeah, well, Robbie is older than I am and knows a lot more than I do." He paused for emphasis, pressing his ear against the door to better hear what was going on inside. "Sorry." Avery could practically here Gil smiling on the other side of the door, his vindication pouring out through the crack under the door. "You gonna let me in now?"

Avery heard Gil's soft footsteps approach and then a soft thud. He waited for the sound of Gil messing with the dead bolt but heard nothing else.

"Gil. I said I was sorry, now open the door." Avery heard Max's low wail and ran over to the window. A table blocked Avery's direct view so he stood on one of the remaining drums. He saw Gil lying on the floor, writhing in the beginnings of an epileptic fit.

"Oh, no!" The area around Gil was relatively uncluttered, but his twisting and turning took him in proximity to table legs and the myriad tools and appliances on top of them, any one of which could end up on his head.

"Damn!" Avery rushed to the door and using his shoulder as a battering ram, ran at it full throttle. He winced. The door was sturdy and deadbolted from the inside. It didn't budge. Avery looked around wildly, his hands settling on a log from the nearby woodpile. He smashed the window in, immediately setting off the alarm inside the barn, the house, and, he knew, the police station. A shockwave of sound ran through his body, and Avery clapped his hands to his ears. The whole world can probably hear this right now.

Avery pulled his shirtsleeve up and balled the end into his hand. He poked and smashed at the remaining bits of glass still clinging to the panes and cleared an area large enough to crawl through. He dove through feet first, sending a measuring tape, calipers, and a screwdriver clattering to the floor. The last thing he saw as he dropped into the barn was Kori and Jack running out the back door toward him.

He fell to the ground, taking a beaker with him. Shards of broken glass flew everywhere. He swept what was too close to Gil aside with his feet, but that was too slow, so he used his hands, embedding a shard in the flesh at the side. He gritted his teeth and removed a substantial piece of glass before dropping to his knees next to his brother. Blood oozed from his palm.

He mounted Gil and, in moments, had him pinned by both shoulders, his injured hand spraying blood across the collar of Gil's shirt. Gil moaned and Max licked his face. Gil seemed to sense Max's presence because he lifted his face toward him. Avery loosened his grip, but did not get up. Kori and Jack appeared at the window and when Kori saw the blood, she screamed, a higher-pitched wail than the alarm. Avery's hair stood up on the back of his neck.

"He's bleeding!" Kori screamed.

Avery shuddered. "Stop. Stop screaming. It's my blood," he yelled over his shoulder. "Somebody's got to get in here and shut that goddamn alarm off."

Jack jumped through the window with the grace of a panther and moments later the alarm went silent. Gil seemed to relax and Avery moved off and sat next to him without letting go of his shoulders. Jack unbolted the door and Kori ran in, dropping to the floor next to Gil.

"Call the police," Avery said to Kori. "Tell them it was a false alarm." She rose reluctantly and ran into the kitchen.

"We gotta get a phone out here, man," Jack said to Avery. Avery nodded, watching his brother. Gil fell into a deep sleep and began to snore.

"This is probably a good time to move him," Avery said. "Let's get him inside where it's warm."

They carried him in, Jack at his feet and Avery at his head with Max leading the way.

Chapter 37

That night, Kori and Jack sat huddled together on one corner of the couch and Avery at the other end. Gil and Max sat in rocking chairs, one behind the other, watching Santa Claus 2. A pizza box lay open on the coffee table with one slice left.

Gil held a toy with small tube-like arms sticking out from a colorful base. At the end of each of the four tubes was a little plastic disc that lit up in different colors. At the push of a button, the arms spiraled around and around like a propeller.

"By rights, it's mine," Kori said. "You guys all had two pieces."

"What is that thing?" Jack asked, ignoring her.

"A whirligig, I think," Avery said. "Or if not, it should be."

"Don't change the subject," Kori said, pinching Jack's side. "Technically, it's mine."

"Yeah, but I worked this morning. And I changed the oil in your car today and replaced your rotor cups, all in freezing cold weather. I think I should have it." He leaned in and kissed her, but she wasn't budging.

"Where'd you work?"

"Something went wrong with the home brain at the Callahan's. The lights on the deck were flicking on and off and they couldn't regulate the temperature in the hot tub. I rewired one of the circuit boards which fixed the problem, but I'm still not sure what happened." He scrunched his eyebrows in thought.

Kori raised her own eyebrows like she wasn't impressed.

"What?" Jack said. "You wanted me to tell them to wait until Monday?"

"It's your business," Kori said. "You could have."

"Not if I want to stay in business."

"I'm still hungry," Gil whined. Kori looked at Jack and laughed.

"Here, Gil," she said, offering him the last slice. "Guess you lose," she whispered to Jack. Meticulously, Gil gnawed the edges of his slice, then up and down each side, all the while rocking and whirligigging. Not a spot remained untouched. He ripped a piece from the crust and tossed it to Max who caught and consumed it in one motion.

"Guess we need two pizzas next time," Jack said, pulling Kori back toward him.

"Yooooohooooo," Aunt Stella's voice along with the smell of pastries wafted from the back door straight to Gil's nose in the living room. He sniffed the air and tossed the rest of the slice of pizza to Max. When Aunt Stella walked into the living room, Gil jumped up, allowed her to kiss him then took his seat while he waited for her to remove her coat and scarf.

She grabbed Gil's chin and pulled it up so she could look in his eyes. "No worse for the wear," she said, and tousled his hair. "You're a tough one." She held the basket out to him. "Go ahead then. A little bit of sweet is the answer to all life's ailments, I say." Aunt Stella's belly shook as she laughed; she took her own advice.

Gil didn't wait for further prompting, but dug out two pieces of baklava, a square of banana-pecan coffee cake, and a napkin to catch it all. Max, still in his chair, waited for his share of the booty. Gil's toy whirled and lighted as he chomped on his banana cake.

"What, pray tell, are you doing, Gilly?" Aunt Stella said.

Gil's mouth was full, so Kori explained for him. "They're playing airplane. Gil's the pilot. We're not sure if Max is a member of the crew or all of the passengers." Gil nodded and gave no further comment. Max circled the seat of his chair adroitly, still trying to find a position of comfort, but the chair was too small for all seventy pounds of him. He gave up and sat down, hind legs squarely on the seat, front paws on the floor.

"He looks like he has motion sickness. I wonder if they're experiencing some turbulence," Kori said.

"How the hell does he get that dog to do that?" Jack said.

Avery got up, making room for Aunt Stella on the couch. She closed the pizza box with a "tsk-tsk," muttering to herself about poor nutrition, and put the basket on top.

"Dessert," she announced, as if it were necessary.

"Thanks, Aunt Stella," Avery said, grabbing a piece of baklava and a seat on the floor. Jack wiggled his eyebrows at Kori, and she passed the basket to him just as the doorbell rang. Kori looked at her watch. It was almost eight. Max barked, jumped off his chair and ran to stand in front of the door.

"Now if we could just teach him to open it," Jack said with a full mouth.

"If that's one of your lame friends here to collect you so you can go out drinking … "

Jack raised his hands, palms up, as if to say "no contest."

No one moved, but everyone looked at Avery who was propping himself up on pillows at his spot on the floor.

"No way. I just sat down. It's Gil's turn."

Gil tried to ignore them, but the pressure was too great. With a sigh, he got up to answer the door.

⅄

Captain Russell turned his collar up against the inexorable wind and waited. He smashed his hat down more firmly on his head and looked out over the neighboring farm fields illuminated by the light of the full moon. Frost reflected the light back, giving the appearance of a dusting of snow. Captain Russell shivered. He'd been dreading this visit since he got the call two nights ago. Army Protocol dictates that the family should have been told immediately, but he had waited, hoping the ongoing investigation would yield some evidence that the officers had at first failed to uncover. Unfortunately, the most damning evidence arrived by courier earlier this evening, and he couldn't put it off any longer.

Russell left his office around eight and went to the Japanese restaurant in the strip mall purportedly for a quick dinner. He left his plate of sushi untouched but had several shots of sake. Now the courage gained from his liquid dinner was dissipating, leaving behind a smoldering hole you could drive an army jeep through. He fingered the contents of his pocket again and swallowed the rising bile. It had been a long time since he had to do this, and he wished to God he was standing elsewhere. His stomach gurgled. It was a bad idea not to eat.

⚓

Gil opened the door a crack, more to keep out the wind than the man standing on the other side of it, but once he got a look, he knew something was wrong. The man was dressed respectably in an overcoat and hat, but he looked sad. *Bad news.*

"Evening. Is this the Tirabi residence?" Gil nodded, but he made no move to open the door. Max stood next to him, wagging his tail and trying to poke his snout through the narrow opening.

Captain Russell extended his hand. "Captain Jack Russell. May I come in? It's very cold out here."

Gil threw open the door, and Max began barking. Captain Russell stood on the front step, rubbing his hands together, his lips welded together in a thin tight line.

Kori ran over and grabbed Max's collar. "Take Max, please. To the living room." Gil and Max retreated and Kori opened the door.

"Can I help you?"

"Captain Jack Russell. I'm at the recruiting station down at the Park Plaza Shopping Mall. I signed up your brother, Robbie."

Kori stiffened. Aunt Stella appeared in the foyer behind her.

"Well, child, let the man in. He's not going to steal your television." Aunt Stella smiled. "Come in, come in. Give me your coat and hat."

Captain Russell stepped into the foyer for the second time that evening. "If you don't mind, I'll keep them. Give me a chance to warm up."

"It's warm inside," Aunt Stella said. She steered him from the foyer to the living room where everyone appeared to be watching television; the only indication that they were not was the undercurrent of motion traveling across the room. Gil rocked obsessively in his chair, Avery fluffed his pillows unable to get comfortable, and Kori kept looking at Jack as if she thought he might vanish into thin air at any minute. Captain Russell cleared his throat, and Kori grabbed Jack's hand.

"How about a nice cup of coffee or tea?" Aunt Stella asked.

"No thank you, Ma'am. I'm really sorry to intrude this evening and wouldn't have come if it wasn't of the utmost … "

A low wail broke from Gil's throat, and Max walked over and put his face in Gil's lap. Avery got up and checked his brother's eyes. Kori jumped up and did the same. She looked at Avery for confirmation.

"Couldn't happen twice in one day, could it?"

"I guess anything's possible." Avery checked Gil's pulse. "You feelin' all right, Gil?" Gil nodded. Avery let go of his wrist, less than satisfied.

"Is there anything I can do?" Captain Russell asked. Kori shook her head.

"You can tell us why you came," Avery said, shutting off the television.

Captain Russell nodded, reached in his pocket and pulled out a set of dog tags, which he placed on the table in front of them.

"Tell me that's not what I think it is," Kori said. She squeezed Jack's hand so tightly his bones crackled.

"It's my duty and my pain to tell you that we presume your brother, Robert James Tirabi, aged twenty-three, to be dead." Kori gasped and buried her head in Jack's shoulder. Aunt Stella coughed and put a hand to her throat. Avery fingered the dog tags, and Gil rocked furiously, eyes fixed on the blank television screen.

"Surely you're joking," Aunt Stella said. "We just got a letter from him yesterday."

"That letter could have been written more than two weeks ago. The mail takes time."

"But ... how?" Kori's voice quivered.

"Suicide car bomber. Robbie was in Khan Bani Saad. It's a market town not far from Baghdad. A man drove a car loaded with explosives directly into an open-air market. Twenty-three people were killed."

"Where's the body?" Avery asked.

"We haven't been able to identify it. We believe he might have been standing near the car when the bomb detonated. We found those," Russell said, pointing to the dog tags.

"Well, how do you know he's dead?" Avery asked. "Maybe he was just wounded."

"The wounded were all treated at the hospital. Your brother was not among them."

"Well, how did his dog tags come off?" Kori asked.

"It wasn't your typical explosive. It had amazing incendiary capabilities. Most things within a twenty-five yard radius were ashes when it was all done."

"That doesn't make any sense." Avery said. "You're still looking, right?" Captain Russell shook his head.

"So that's it. You come here and you give us these lousy ... things," Kori picked up the dog tags as if they were used Kleenex, "and you tell us he's gone and you walk out the door. You don't even know my brother." Kori's voice caught, and Jack pulled her to his chest.

"What about his personal stuff?" Jack asked.

"It's being shipped. You should be getting it within the week."

"Liar!" Gil jumped up from his seat, grabbed the dog tags, put them around his neck and ran from the room. He stomped up the stairs and slammed the door to his room.

"I'll go," Aunt Stella said, but Avery put a hand on her arm to stop her.

"If there's anything else I can do ... " Captain Russell's sincere, but ineffectual offer froze in mid-air.

After several more moments of silence, Captain Russell stood to leave. "Feel free to call me if you have any questions or if you need anything at all." He handed Aunt Stella his card. "I'm truly sorry for your loss." Aunt Stella rose to show him to the door.

"It's okay," Russell said. "I can find my way out."

They heard the door close behind him, heard his car engine engage, heard him pull out of the driveway, and then nothing more but their own moist breathing and the ticking of the clock. Avery traced a finger around the empty space where the dog tags had lain.

"Shall I go up after him?" he asked. The question hung in the air like mist.

Part Two

*T*he Delaware River, *the longest undammed and only remaining major free-flowing river east of the Mississippi, also lays claim to the largest freshwater port in the world. The river flows three hundred and thirty miles from Hancock, New York, and makes a pit stop in the Delaware Bay before spilling into the Atlantic Ocean. It serves as the dividing line between Pennsylvania and New Jersey and services twenty million residents of the New York, New Jersey and the Philadelphia area with drinking water. Washington's famous Christmas Eve ping ponging across the river began and ended on the banks of the Delaware at Trenton, New Jersey. But the river's abundance isn't limited to battles, boundary lines and the provision of potable water. It's a dichotomy in uses: heavy industry draws on her for its needs as do bald eagles and world-class trout fisheries. As evidence of the latter, about one hundred and fifty miles of this magnificent river has been included in the U.S. National Wild and Scenic Rivers System.*

In the late 1800s, approximately one million Philadelphians lived within the boundaries of America's third largest city, which boasted the second largest port in the country located in the Delaware Bay. The U.S. Army Corps of Engineers, the entity charged with assuring the river's safety, dipped its long, federally-funded fingers into a bevy of construction, flood control, and navigational projects designed to improve, among other things, the river's navigability. In 1878, before Philadelphia had electricity or the telephone, sixteen hundred foreign trade vessels arrived each year, and six thousand coastal trade vessels docked in the river's port. Trade vessels have given way to supertankers: seventy million tons of cargo arrive in the river's waters each year. From sails, to steam, to the supertankers, the Delaware River and its Bay have lent their banks and waters to the growth of the interstate and international commerce of not only Philadelphia, but also the nation.

At its deepest point, the Delaware is only forty feet, which means the river can't abide a thousand foot supertanker between her banks. Roughly the size of three and a half football fields and bearing three million gallons of oil or other cargo, a ship that size has forty foot drafts, and sits forty feet below the water line, as deep as the river's most navigable channel. Low tide causes the water levels in the tidally influenced channel from the Delaware Bay to Philadelphia to drop as much as eight feet which would leave a thousand foot ship incapacitated, floundering like a beached whale.

When the Corps of Engineers began its first deepening project in 1855, the depth of the Delaware stood at eighteen feet. The Corps dredged down to the current depth of forty feet during World War II and maintained this depth by periodic dredging and removal of silt buildup in the channel to the tune of about 3.4 million cubic yards a year. Since 1983, the Corps has studied the feasibility of dredging the Delaware's main shipping channel down to forty-five feet to better accommodate the world commodities market by making the hundred-and-two mile shipping route from the Delaware Bay to Camden, New Jersey, more accessible.

To do so, the Corps would need to remove about twenty-six million cubic yards of silt and sediment from the river bottom and continue removing another 862,000 cubic yards every year thereafter at a cost of approximately $311 million dollars. Cost notwithstanding, the Corps would need a place to put all that sand, clay, silt and bedrock. While federally owned sites have been identified, environmentalists contend that the detrimental effects to drinking water, aquatic and bird life, and the potential contamination from the disposal of dredged material outweigh the benefits. That story — small town need vs. corporate greed; environmental stewardship vs. environmental recklessness; the rights of the few vs. the rights of society — has existed since the dawn of creation, and, because of constraints of space and time, is a story best saved for another day.

CHAPTER 38

The *Ryujin* dropped anchor at Big Stone Anchorage at Slaughter Beach, Delaware, in the mouth of the Delaware Bay. The "parking lot" in the Bay was crowded this morning with a dozen supertankers waiting to offload their cargo onto barges that would take the goods upriver to Marcus Hook or Philadelphia Harbor or Becket Street Terminal in Camden, New Jersey. Once offloaded, the supertankers were light enough to make the trip upriver. Some had been waiting as much as a week while tugs and taxis cruised back and forth, bringing food and supplies to the waiting supertankers, crisscrossing the Bay like a checkerboard and leaving white caps in their wake. The great ships were parked far enough apart to allow them to spin on their anchors, a necessity when considering the vagaries of the weather. From the air it looked like a mechanical ballet: dozens of ships turning and gliding on their axes, a synchronized dance brought to life by the formidable forces of wind and tide.

The *Ryujin* traveled from the Arabian Gulf and had been parked in the Delaware Bay for the last week, awaiting the offloading of a million gallons of its crude oil onto a barge which would make it light enough to navigate the Delaware's forty foot channel upriver to the Akanabi refinery in Marcus Hook. While waiting, the *Ryujin* took on skid loads of food, supplies and mechanical parts sufficient to tide her over until arrival at the next port. And since the suppliers were not interested in receiving credit for these transactions, the *Ryujin* carried vast quantities of cash to pay for those stores as well as armed guards to protect it. The ship's superstructure housed a three-story engine room, a machine shop, steam turbine and diesel engines, a mess hall, living facilities for her Captain and crew, and a single cat who relished the job of keeping the mouse population down. Where the mice came from was anyone's guess given that the ship had spent the last three weeks at sea.

Beside the *Ryujin* sat the *Sea Witch*, an engineless barge a third the size of the *Ryujin*, but with considerably less girth. Motored by *The Grape Ape*, a seventy-five foot, single-screw, diesel-powered tugboat, the *Sea Witch* sat, waiting to remove a million gallons of elemental crude oil from the *Ryujin* and shuttle it up the Delaware River channel for her. Afloat on a tidally influenced body of water, both boats were subject to the fickle, yet predictable, moods of the moon.

Named for the Dragon King of the sea, an important Japanese deity said to have the power to control the ebb and flow of the tides with his large mouth, the *Ryujin* wasn't living up to its name today. It seemed that the ocean, the Bay, the moon and the tides were all in cahoots, as the *Ryujin* spun on its anchor at the wind's ferocious insistence, and the *Sea Witch* tried to make amends.

The process of lightering was a tricky one. The tanks needed to be drained one at a time in a specific order, or the Captain would have an imbalanced ship with the bow rising higher into the air as each tank was emptied, a disaster in the making. Therefore, the Captain took great pains to ensure that the oil was skimmed off the top of each of the tanks in a controlled fashion, draining some from one tank, moving on to the next, and back and forth until the process was completed.

After several hours, Captain Heston Reed was barking out orders like a man possessed. There was nothing he could do until the barge, the *Sea Witch,* had tied on, an event that, despite tidal fluctuations, was close to completion. The fendering bumpers, which consisted of a large piping structure encapsulated by dozens and dozens of tires, and worked like a ball bearing in between the two vessels, were lowered into place, the black scrape marks from previous lightering operations still visible on both ships. With the fendering bumpers properly lined up, Captain Reed gave the command and the *Sea Witch's* crew tied on to the *Ryujin*. The giant mooring ropes creaked and groaned as the crew cranked down on the winches, pulling them tightly into position. Satisfied that the ships had no visible gaps between them, Captain Reed signaled the operator of the *Sea Witch* and gave the go ahead to his own crew. The crew began the arduous process of lowering a dozen twelve-inch round, rigid rubber pipes down some twenty-five feet onto the deck of the *Sea Witch*. The pipes were attached by cables to small cranes. The cranes swung them into place, enabling the deckhands to make the mechanical connection to a screw coupling which was part of a larger manifold system on the deck of the *Sea Witch* and which fed into the barge's holding tanks. The deck hands inserted the pipes and, using a special wrench and the sheer torque of their body weight, screwed the couplings fast. The rubber pipes originated from a similar manifold system on the deck of the *Ryujin*, and once Captain Reed and the *Sea Witch's* operator were satisfied that all mechanical connections were secured, the transferring, or lightering process, could begin. Captain Reed personally checked each of the connections. The individual pipes were hooked to another, larger pipe so the ship and barge operators could control, via computer, which tank would give and which tank would receive the oil.

Captain Reed gave the signal and the *Ryujin* began offloading its crude, the oil flowing from its holding tanks through the manifold system and into the pipes that would carry it down to the *Sea Witch's* manifold system. The rigid rubber pipes lurched forward as the sudden thrust of oil was released. Frank Charlton, the manifold operator, sat in the control house on the barge electronically directing the distribution of oil into the various holding tanks and taking great pains to keep the ship balanced.

"All right?" Captain Reed stepped into the computer room to ascertain for himself the integrity of the operation. There'd be hell to pay if someone made an error on his ship. Charlton nodded and turned briefly to acknowledge his superior officer. Captain Reed took a deep breath and the corner of his mouth twitched, but he did not smile.

"Let me know when it's done then. I'm going to see about the pilot."

"Yes sir, Captain," Charlton replied without taking his eyes off the computer screen.

CHAPTER 39

Three hours later, the *Sea Witch's* belly had gone from four to fifteen feet below the water line as a result of its recently acquired load, while the *Ryujin* sat that much higher. The deck hands fastening the fendering back to her side looked to Captain Reed to be no bigger than children. The *Sea Witch* was off, already moving upriver, while Captain Reed paced the deck waiting impatiently for the arrival of the river pilot who would steer the *Ryujin* up the Delaware to the Marcus Hook refinery. The pilot was late, and lateness was something Reed could not tolerate.

"Company, sir," the first mate called.

A small water taxi, likely bearing the river pilot, was arriving. Captain Reed didn't think much of river pilots on the whole, thought them a lazy lot, their navigational skills gone slack from disuse as a result of gliding back and forth on the same body of water – the epitome of big fish in a little pond – but the law said that only the river pilots could take a ship upriver. The company that serviced the Delaware was owned by an old codger named Lars Andersen. He was smooth and weathered like driftwood when Reed met him fifteen years ago, and despite his prejudices, Reed had come to like the man over time.

Captain Reed ceased his pacing to watch the water taxi's approach. It pulled up close and tight to the *Ryujin,* and a young man of about twenty-five reached for the rope ladder hanging down her side. Reed frowned and moved in to get a closer look.

⋏

The water taxi bobbed on the water while Pilot Christian Anderson stood watching the swell of the waves, looking for an opportunity. The *Ryujin* rocked and jumped with the swell of the rising tide. The taxi was at optimal height and Anderson had a split second to decide: he grabbed for a middle rung of the rope ladder, and pulled hard. He threw one leg around the outside rope and hooked his foot inside a square. He grabbed another rung with his free hand just as the sea tossed the water taxi and the deck fell away. Anderson held on with ease, suspended along the side of the *Ryujin*, his strong, well-tuned muscles tensing and flexing under his own weight as he climbed the thirty-odd feet to the top. He swung over the side of the supertanker, dropping effortlessly onto the deck, and looked into the face of mocking disapproval.

"Who are you?" Captain Reed barked.

"Pilot Christian Anderson. At your service, sir." He bowed his head slightly.

"Christian Anderson? Where's Lars?"

"Dead," Anderson said, watching Reed's face. The eyes changed, but the face did not. No way of telling whether the Captain was friend or foe of his father since the man had equal amounts of both — one either loved or hated him — or whether he knew Lars even had a son. "Any other questions?" Anderson asked. Reed took a step back to better appraise Anderson.

Christian Anderson had been a pilot for about thirty-three seconds. Actually it had been three years, but only three weeks since his father died and he took over the family business. So far, he hadn't been able to lose that sick feeling in his stomach that sometimes came with the weight of being in charge. He'd played the prodigal son for so long that he couldn't get used to this new appellation. Still, that wasn't information he was about to be offering up, especially not to this dick bag standing in front of him looking all smug and holier than thou. He'd had a hard enough time convincing the other half a dozen pilots his father employed that he was up to the task of running the business, *and not into the ground*, as he had heard them prognosticate under their collective breaths. This business would flourish in ways his father never had the foresight to allow. They'd see. They'd all see. Then he'd have something to flaunt. He gave Reed his own forthright appraisal, looking him over like a prized heifer. Reed's icy glare forced Anderson to turn his own face away as if stung.

Anderson pulled out a small brown leather case and flashed his pilot's badge, then shoved it back in his pocket; Reed put a hand on his arm to stop him. Anderson narrowed his eyes at the Captain, but pulled it out again, handing it to Reed for examination. Reed examined the license then the man himself before handing it back.

"He was your father then?"

Anderson searched Reed's eyes for some glint of emotion, and finding none, figured it was simple curiosity that asked the question. Anderson nodded.

"When did he die?"

"Three weeks ago."

Captain Reed made a small gesture, a slight nod of the head, turned on his heel and walked away. Whether it was meant as an offer of sympathy Anderson couldn't tell. He stared after Reed in mute astonishment, his delicate, Swedish features turning momentarily to granite. And as the Captain turned the corner, Anderson decided it prudent to follow and sprinted after Reed.

⋏

Hours later, the moon rose above the horizon at what might be considered warp speed in moon terms, bulging and engorged, a result of the last rays of the sun's refracted light. As she climbed, she lost that overstuffed pancake look, shrunk down to normal size and simply became the moon once again, a giant, floating orb of light and beauty that possessed the mystical ability to control tides and sway men's hearts.

Anderson, his hands set tightly on the joystick, cast a glance up at the sky and relaxed his grip. To his right and behind stood Captain Reed, so close to Anderson's shoulder that he could hear the man breathing, although to Anderson it sounded more like a wheeze. The noise and the man's sheer proximity were unnerving.

"You know, you should have that looked at," Anderson said.

"Pardon me?"

"Your lungs. It sounds like you're breathing underwater."

"I'd thank you to mind your own *business.*" Reed emphasized the word business and Anderson's shoulders tightened. He couldn't stop thinking about the messy state his father had left it in.

"I'm going down on deck for a few minutes. Try not to hit anything," Reed said and left.

"Dick bag," Anderson muttered. It was only a hundred and two-mile stretch of river from the Bay to the Marcus Hook refinery, but already Anderson knew it was going to be the longest hundred miles he'd ever traveled. And by night, no less. The thought sent a shiver up his spine.

Had he been given his way, the *Ryujin* would have waited until morning to depart, but the tide had reached high water mark and was on the way down, and the *Sea Witch* had already taken off upriver. Reed had wanted the *Ryujin* to follow as soon as the Coast Guard would allow it to take advantage of the extra draft room that the high tide would provide. He was pissed that the bastard Anderson hadn't taken off right away, but Anderson was adamant about inspecting the ship, acquainting himself with all her innermost workings. With so few solo trips under his belt and a business on the line, he couldn't afford a screwup. Mostly so he wouldn't appear lackadaisical and just to shut Reed up, he agreed to leave when his inspection was complete. Unfortunately, by that time it was twilight.

Anderson came from a long line of sailors and sea captains, a nepotistic bunch of Swedish brothers, uncles, and cousins who were all active in the business Anderson's father had inherited from his own father. During early childhood, he spent many nights curled up in a sleeping bag at his father's feet as his Dad piloted a ship upriver, listening to the low rumbling vibration of the boat, the last lines of his father's bedtime story resonating in his ears. Those stories were much worse than the usual macabre of the Brothers Grimm or Hans Christian Anderson. His father's stories were of sailors lost at sea; of sea monsters with terrible fangs and breath like fire; of mermaids that grabbed unsuspecting sailors off their ships and bore them

down to their watery graves; of the sirens, lovely creatures that lured men too near the rocks with their songs and laughed as the waves bashed their ships, leaving the hapless sailors to drown in the melee. The stories had delighted and enchanted him, and Anderson would look up to catch a last glimpse of his father standing behind the wheel, smiling at him as his eyes became heavy with sleep.

Anderson's head bobbed, touching his chest. He opened his eyes and for an instant he was a boy again. He came to full consciousness, shocked with the realization that he had fallen asleep at the helm. There was no telling if it had been seconds or minutes. He blinked and rubbed his eyes, then shook himself like a dog shakes off water. It had been three weeks since he'd had a good night's sleep, haunted as he was by visions of the giant of a man he'd loved so in life.

He felt a hand on his arm and turned, half-expecting to see his father. He saw Captain Reed instead. Reed said nothing; the scoundrel just stood off to the side staring out into the blackness in front of him, his hands clasped behind his back, the picture of urbanity. Anderson cleared his throat to break the silence and cast a glance back at Reed, the asinine bastard. He saw the Captain's face out of the corner of his eye, baleful and unwelcoming. He glanced at the radar screen. The next three channel markers were well lit.

"So how long have you been a Captain?" Anderson asked. *Safe ground.*

"Longer than you've been alive," Reed retorted.

Anderson rolled his eyes and puckered his lips, blowing air out slow and silent. The air in the control deck felt thick and clogged in sharp contrast to the breezy conditions on the river. Anderson moved his head from side to side, stretching the muscles in his neck. As the silent minutes ticked by, his mind drifted to his father's last months when the Alzheimer's had him fully in its grasp. How time must have blended together for him, yet he stubbornly refused to retire, even in his lucid moments. Was time really not linear, as the physicists said, and even more absurd, all happening at once? *That would wreak havoc on the history books!*

Reed spoke, but Anderson missed what he said so Reed cleared his throat.

"Excuse me?" Anderson said.

"I said how long? Until we drop our load. How long?"

"What, you got a date?" Reed gave Anderson a stultifying glare.

Anderson harrumphed. "A few hours give or take. It's slower going at night."

"I notice you don't use the radar much," Reed said.

"I use it as backup."

Reed's eyebrows shot up in query.

Anderson gave Reed a half-smile. "I've been traveling this river since I was a boy. I can tell you where every rock and shoal lies."

Reed made a small grunting noise that originated in the back of his throat, and strode over to the radar screen. A light blipped on and off signaling the presence of something buried well below the surface out of the path of the *Ryujin*. He grabbed the Weems plotter, a fat ruler with wheels, placed it on a line and rolled it down making a compass angle.

Anderson laughed.

"You think using a chart is funny?"

"Just laughing at the hardware."

Reed raised his eyebrows, scanned the desk chart and then at the blinking radar screen.

What do you think that is?"

"Nothing to be alarmed about?"

"How do you know?"

"The GPS says we're right where we need to be," Anderson said. "There's nothing at that particular juncture big enough to cause injury to his boat."

Reed snorted. His voice was so sedate that a small shiver ran up Anderson's spine. "When was the last time you were on this river?"

"Three weeks ago." Three weeks ago, Anderson's father had died suddenly while at the wheel of a ship very similar to this, leaving his son to sort through the mess.

"If you know anything about rivers," Reed said curtly, "you'll know the last thing they are is static. Things change. How do you know that a

boulder hasn't rolled, or wasn't just missed in the plotting, or a school bus didn't drive off the side of the road and is now parked in our path, waiting to tear a large, gaping hole into the hull?"

Anderson sighed. "I don't. But regardless of that nice little speech you just gave, river bottoms don't change all that drastically. Besides, the Army Corps is always dredging this part of the river to keep the silt down so the channel stays open."

Reed eyed Anderson, a wry smile forming in the corner of his mouth and turned back to the chart. "Under the Coast Guard regs, you might be temporarily in charge of this ship, but remember this, *son*," Reed said. "I'm the Captain. Before and long after you're gone." Reed eyed the blinking radar screen. "What's that?"

Andersen checked the screen and scanned the dark horizon. He saw nothing. "A small speed boat, maybe? Or a fisherman still out on the water." Thanks to Reed, he was growing a little nervous himself. The blip on the radar screen moved erratically, not a stagnant boulder half-buried in the sea bottom, that was for damn sure, but something, and admitting it to this truculent son-of-a-bitch made him queasy.

"There's been nothing reported in the last week," Anderson said, trying to maintain an air of calm about him. "As far as the Coast Guard and the Corps are concerned, we've got ten feet of water between us and the bottom of the river. We're riding anything but light. But we've still got the residual benefit of the flood tide even though it's turned." He glanced out the window at the bank of the Delaware and gave silent thanks for the red buoys. *Red right returning.* As long as the buoys were on the right, they were safely in the channel. He shook his head, trying to cast off the vibes of impending doom, and stole a glance at the imperial jackass as he moved the Weems plotter over the nautical charts, its wheels squeaking like baby mice.

"Man, would you knock it off? You're creeping me out."

Reed gasped. Anderson turned in time to see Reed lunge at him. Reed tossed Anderson aside and wrenched the joystick from his grip, and with it, the direction of the ship, slowly altering its course by forty-five degrees. But before Anderson could react, they heard it. The sound started out low, like

a hum, and grew in volume until it became identifiable. A small watercraft. The speedboat raced by and they both looked out the window in time to see the stern of the motorboat disappearing from view, the laughter of its occupants left behind, floating on the breeze.

"Damn kids," Reed said.

A feeling of *dejá vu* overtook Anderson and he entered a place where time was no longer linear. He knew more than a few seconds had passed because the sound of laughter, mingled with the small boat's engine, had receded into silence, yet he couldn't say how long that took or what had transpired in the interim. He regained his presence of mind and looked to the river for reorientation. *The buoys were on the left!*

"Son of a bitch." By instinct Anderson grabbed the joystick, shoving Reed aside, and cut it hard, aiming the ship back into the channel. She turned slowly on her axis, a planet caught in the gravitational pull of her own sun, then resumed her forward motion, course righted. Anderson breathed a sigh as they passed the buoys on their way back into the channel. But relief was short-lived.

It was no more than a slight jolt, what one might feel when riding on a train whose tracks needed tamping.

"What the hell was that?" Reed demanded.

Anderson looked out at the river as they were clearing the buoys, then to the radar screen. Something was blinking and he had just run over it, or through it, depending on what it was. He rubbed his eyes, but the blip was still there. The two men eyeballed each other. Anderson cleared his throat.

"Why don't you go check the water off the stern and see if we're dragging anything," he said. "The moon's almost full. Should help you to see."

"What the hell would we be dragging?" Reed sneered, his voice rising. "You hit something."

"You mean *we*, don't you?" The palms of Anderson's hands were beginning to sweat on the wheel, but he retained his outward demeanor.

"No, I mean you. You're the pilot of this ship and ... "

"And if you hadn't thrown us out of the channel ... "

"If I hadn't *steered* us out of the channel, we would have had a head-on collision with a motor boat," Reed bellowed, spitting as he did. His face had taken on a crimson hue and his eyes were bulging, giving him a toad-like appearance. "And somebody would have probably died you stupid, idiotic … ."

"That boat," Anderson said, "was playing chicken with us, and you know it. A bunch of kids out joyriding. They knew enough not to take on a thousand foot ship. Trust me. They would've blinked." Anderson was sweating now from the rush of adrenaline and sheer nerves.

"Go check the stern, dammit," he barked at Reed.

Reed hesitated momentarily before scrambling out the door, giving Anderson time to collect his thoughts. He reviewed the charts and saw what he was dreading. There, just outside the channel, was the topside protrusion of a large boulder that had likely been in that exact same position since the dawn of time, the kind that originated somewhere around the core of the earth and kept twisting and rising until it reached the top with just its tip peeking out. The sneaky kind. The kind that caught you unawares and ripped the crap out of your hull.

A shiver of fear ran down Anderson's spine. *It's nothing. A small jolt is all. We bounced right off her.* He gripped the joystick tightly and clenched his teeth. He knew what a small "jolt" meant to a ship of this size and the kind of damage a boulder could do to a single-hulled vessel. The *Ryujin* was well past her prime, and, although she paid lip service to the Coast Guard regulations, her body had been worked and reworked a dozen times trying to keep her up to the current safety standards; she stayed afloat not because of strict compliance with the law, but because of some damn grandfather clause. It was the lawmakers' fault. A single-hulled ship had no business carrying millions of gallons of oil, yet it was done all the time because, the ship owners said, the cost to retire her and build a new doubled-hulled ship outweighed any potential environmental damage that a spill would cause. And the law said that until 2015, ship owners could continue to sail single-hulled ships no matter how many dead fish floated to the surface covered in oil.

Captain Reed appeared half an hour later, looking flushed from exertion, but otherwise in good spirits, his normal dour countenance having momentarily shed its pinched expression. Anderson took this as a good sign.

"What d'ya find out?"

"Nothing," Reed said. The briefest of smiles crossed his lips. "There is no damage to this ship."

"You're sure?" Anderson watched the man's face carefully. After all, he didn't know Reed from Adam, and now Reed held Anderson's career between his two damn fingers.

Reed nodded. "Engines are all in working order, we're not dragging anything, and we're not leaking anything."

"No sheen on the water? You looked?" Anderson asked. Reed nodded again. "How many times?"

"Three," Reed replied. "Once at the beginning of my inspection and once at the end. And once in between. The oil is safely in the hold."

Anderson nodded, uncertain. Whatever Reed may be, it was obvious he was a Captain foremost. He would not take kindly to any untoward incidents on the *Ryujin* while under his command, although Anderson dimly suspected that Reed might be more concerned with the integrity of his ship than that of the Delaware River. Still, Reed's environmental ethic was not Anderson's concern right now. He sighed and looked out over the bow and beyond to the horizon hidden by night. Nothing much he could do but take the man's word for it.

"All right. Let's get this baby to bed before she suffers another nightmare," Anderson said and bent to the task.

⅄

The full moon was all but eclipsed by the stratus clouds that stretched out in full battle regalia across a winter sky. An occasional break in their ranks gave the casual observer the tiniest peek at the moon's frothy demeanor, but the blaze of light she heretofore sent streaming down river before the clouds moved into the neighborhood was gone, gone, gone. Too bad, too, for the fish, birds, flora, fauna, and various species of plankton that thrived in the river because they were about to get a rude awakening. Thirty feet below sea level, a ten-inch gash ripped through the hull of the *Ryujin* by an errant boulder had begun to widen, resulting in the unfortunate release of the contents of the ship's hold into the river. The seemingly small quantity of oil leaking out at any given moment would, hours later, add up to one of the worst environmental disasters ever experienced on the Delaware.

On deck, the crew, captain and pilot of the *Ryujin* were oblivious to the danger. As they headed north, the oil headed south, and without the moon to light her stern-side, the crew would not see so much as a flicker of a sheen on the black night waters.

Of course, the clouds did not move into town alone. They brought with them the North Wind and it, coupled with the outbound tide, pushed that pure Arabian crude down, down, down toward the Bay, catching the whole hundred-mile stretch of that beautiful river unaware.

CHAPTER 40

"**What?**" An incredulous Hart stared at his father-in-law across the broad expanse of Bicky's mahogany desk. "How the hell did you let that happen, Bicky? Every regulatory agency within a hundred mile radius is gonna be on this. Not to mention the citizens' groups. The lawyers are probably running to the courthouse now." Hart stood, arms akimbo.

"Oh, would you cut the dramatics," Bicky said.

"Negative. Positive. Attention's attention. You must like it regardless."

"Of course I don't like it. Who wants to get sued?"

Hart paced the floor and ran his hands through his wavy black hair, puzzling out the next move. Bicky grabbed a cigar from the humidor, put his feet up on the desk and lit up.

"Did you get the leak in the Gulf under control?"

Hart interrupted his pacing to stare at his father-in-law.

"Well, did you at least tell them it was fixed? Or that we were working on it? They might not come inspect if you tell them that."

Hart struggled to control the myriad profanities readying themselves for dispatch. "You know, the thought just occurred to me that I have no idea how I've managed to work for you this long."

Bicky chortled, set his feet on the floor and shuffled through the newspapers covering his desk, a cigar wedged between his teeth, his right eye closed against the smoke. "My, my. Somebody needs a nap."

"You know what? You might prefer to pay the paltry fines rather than fix the problem, but I'm the guy they come looking for. And I'm not playing cover-up for you or your sorry-assed company."

Bicky leaned back in his chair and smiled. "Are you job-hunting?"

Hart waved him off. "And yes, as a matter-of-fact, the leak is fixed. Mahajan and Stu finished the job." Hart sat down opposite Bicky and glared at him. "I suppose you heard what happened to Stu on this trip?"

"Yes. Most unfortunate. But you managed to save the day once again." Bicky smiled, baring his picture perfect, ultra-white teeth. It was a malicious smile and Hart shuddered. "Sonia always said you were her hero."

The blow was calculated and intended, hitting its mark with precision. Hart blanched. He felt better, more in control since the dive with Stu, but it was tentative and fragile and he knew it. A wave of nausea surfaced and he swallowed the telltale saliva pouring into his mouth along with the urge to vomit. Hart grimaced and walked around to Bicky's side of the desk. He stood at the window behind him, a breach of etiquette, perhaps a threat. Bicky sat motionless, refusing to turn around.

"You better give the man some time off unless you want to lose your best diver."

"I've already sent a memo. He'll be receiving a substantial bonus in his next paycheck."

"It's not about the money, Bicky."

"It's always about the money, David." Bicky opened *The Philadelphia Inquirer* with care as if it were a sacred parchment. The front-page news covered the oil spill in the Delaware River and continued on A-3 with a full two-page layout.

"Not for Stu. You can't keep giving him six-week rotations with no time off to see his family. He's got a baby. And plenty of money saved, I might add." *Game, point and match.* Hart glanced down at the street below where the people scurried along. He knew why Bicky liked his window. From here, the world outside was a show, sterile and inaccessible as most things behind glass were. From here, both the minutia and the momentous in life fell the same way, like raindrops swept into the storm drain en route to the river. The river where all would be washed clean. The problem was what to do when the river needed a bath.

Hart caught a slight twitch in Bicky's shoulders as he rounded the corner and he smiled to himself. Although he would never intentionally harm his father-in-law, there was no telling what he might do in a fit of rage. And there was something about Bicky that could bring a man to a boil. More than once lately, Hart found himself wanting to throttle the stink out of him.

"Duly noted. I'll make sure he gets the next three weeks off." Bicky sighed and turned to the *Daily News*. "Happy?"

"As a clam. Although I'd sleep better if I knew you did it because you understood why." Hart knew that everything Bicky did sprang from an ulterior motive as opposed to a stab of conscience, but still he held out hopes for redemption.

"I never understood that clam reference," Bicky said. "Is it because they look like they're smiling or because they harbor expensive jewelry and think only they know about it." Hart shook his head but didn't respond.

"Sit down already. You're grating on my nerves."

Hart flopped down in a chair. Although the dark circles under his eyes looked permanent, physical exhaustion was remediable. Emotional exhaustion, however, had etched a wider swath in his soul, leaving scars so deep that even a truckload of vitamin E couldn't erase them. Sonia used to put an eye pillow filled with lavender on Hart's fatigued eyes when he hadn't slept. Then she'd massage his feet until he did. The body repaired itself in sleep, she said. The healing occurred while the mind was dreaming. She said it wasn't sleep that healed, but dreams. Whatever it was, Hart was deprived. He rubbed his eyes too hard and sparks of light shot across his closed eyelids. He finally stopped and looked bleary-eyed at his father-in-law.

"So what do you want me to do?"

"Oversee the cleanup for starters. I got guys down there now, but frankly, some of them couldn't find their asses with both hands. And I mean that in the nicest of ways."

Hart studied Bicky's face. That smooth, tan, imperturbable face. He couldn't remember if Bicky ever had plastic surgery, but if he hadn't, he was some freak of nature. At sixty years old, Bicky had barely a crow's foot. Maybe that's what a clear conscience got you.

"Get you out in the field, man. Meet some people. Life goes on. So must you." Bicky said the last bit summarily, but Hart pressed him.

"And by that you mean?"

"It means what it means. What do *you* think it means?"

"Coyness isn't one of your best attributes," Hart said rising.

"I've got a driver downstairs waiting to take you home. Call Phyllis an hour before you're ready to leave for the airport. She'll arrange for my private jet to take you to Philly. You gotta give them an hour to get ready, though, if you don't want to wait." Bicky smiled, his trademark pained expression.

Hart sighed. The job did have its perks.

"Call me with the details as soon as you have them," he said, returning to his paper.

Hart left without saying goodbye.

⅄

Mrs. Banes greeted Hart at the door. He tried to engage her in small talk, an activity toward which he knew she was favorably disposed, but she was tight-lipped and unflappable, a sure sign that something was up at the Coleman estate. He was not surprised, therefore, when she led him to the drawing room where he found Kitty holding court with Jerry Dixon. Hart saw Jerry stiffen, but his facial expression didn't change.

"Hey, Jerry," Hart said, extending a hand. "Good to see you, man."

"Good to see you, too, Hart." Jerry shook Hart's hand, warmth replacing wariness.

When Hart kissed his mother-in-law hello, she took his hands and held him to her, studying his eyes. He flushed, but did not pull away from the bony, arthritic pressure of hands that had aged overnight. He dared not look at them and was relieved when Kitty released him.

"Have a seat, David. Mrs. Banes will bring us some tea." She turned to Mrs. Banes, but the housekeeper was already out the door.

"I'm going to make a few phone calls," Jerry said.

Hart caught their exchanged glances and used the few moments it afforded to study Kitty's unguarded face. It had lost that luminescent quality that pointed to eternal youth. Where all her high society friends had plastic surgeons on the payroll, buying face lifts and tummy tucks like magazine subscriptions, Kitty came by her beauty naturally and could have passed for a woman in her forties rather than one in her sixties. Not now, though. Sonia's death had knocked those good looks right off her face. The former smattering of lines around her eyes and mouth were now deep and embedded.

"I'll be back in a minute," Jerry said, solely for her benefit.

Kitty nodded, rubbed her gnarled hands together and grimaced in pain. Tossing protocol aside, Hart knelt down and took one of her hands, and, rubbing in circular fashion, started with the knuckles then worked his way toward Kitty's palm.

"It's like it happened overnight," she said in answer to his unasked question. She lifted her free hand, studying it abstractly as if it were not her own. "Rheumatoid arthritis runs in my family. My mother's hands looked very much like mine do right now for as long as I can remember. Although that never slowed her down much." She curled her free hand into a fist, testing its suppleness.

"I thought I had it beat. I mean, there was some stiffness in my joints in the morning, and at odd moments when I stopped to pay attention, but I exercised and I ate right. I didn't abuse my body." She smiled and put her free hand up to Hart's face, tracing the jaw line over a faint line of stubble while he continued massaging her other hand.

"They aren't kidding when they say stress can kill you. It almost got me," Kitty said. "Almost."

Hart squeezed the sides of each finger and pulled them gently from their sockets, releasing the air that had gathered in the joints with a slight popping sound. Hart rubbed the other hand, massaging the stiffness out of the joints, the wrists, the knuckles. Kitty's face looked serene and, for a moment, pain free.

"I know it's not like the pain you have, but it's my own and I don't think I can come to terms with it. Children are meant to bury their parents, not the other way around." Her voice caught and she said nothing further.

Hart hugged her gently, afraid that her frail body would crumble in his arms. He felt the warm tears land on his shirt in rapid succession. He rubbed her back until she pulled away and wiped her eyes. His heart, cleaved into two useless and ineffective pieces on the night his wife died, split even farther apart. He held both of Kitty's hands in his, rubbing her knuckles with his thumbs the way he used to do for Sonia when her hands throbbed, the signs of the rheumatoid arthritis already apparent despite her youth.

"A paraffin bath would help this," Hart said. "Sonia's got a machine that melts the wax. You dip your hands in a bunch of times, put on plastic gloves and then a cloth mitt to keep them warm. I could bring it over."

Kitty smiled. "It's not paraffin I need, David."

Mrs. Banes entered with a pot of tea and a platter of cakes. She poured the tea, added cream and extended the cup to Kitty. Hart let go of Kitty's hands and took the teapot from Mrs. Banes before she could pour him a cup.

"Thank you," he said, and set the pot down next to Kitty. Mrs. Banes nodded and left.

Hart glanced at his watch. "I gotta go, Mom. I told Bicky's pilot I'd be there by three."

Kitty nodded and sighed. She handed him the teacup, which he set down. She lifted her arms to him, and he pulled her to her feet. They stood facing each other, Hart still holding her arms.

"David?" she said. He lowered his head to better hear her. "May I ask something of you?"

"Of course, Mom. Anything."

"Get out of the oil business. Before it ruins you."

The smell of jasmine tea wafted up to him, and Hart inhaled deeply, searching Kitty's inscrutable face for clues.

"It may be sooner than you think, Mom." He looked at his watch again. "But right now I'm still on the payroll, so … I'll call you when I get back." He kissed her on the cheek and released her.

"Be careful then," she said, touching his cheek before she eased herself into her chair. Not without difficulty, Hart thought, and left the room.

⋏

Jerry was walking the length of the driveway when Hart came out of the house.

"Pretty big mess you got up there in Philadelphia, eh?" Jerry said.

"Worst part of my job," Hart replied. Hart had his keys in hand, but Jerry stood rooted to the spot in front of the driver's door and Hart couldn't get in the car.

Hart always had an affinity for the man Sonia called uncle, joking and laughing with him whenever they had occasion to be together. But in the months since Sonia's death, Jerry had become remote and uncommunicative, and they found themselves with little to say to each other. More than once, Hart's mind wandered back to the snippets of conversation he'd overheard while sitting in Bicky's study, when his mind was reeling from the effects of his drug-induced state. Hart's inability to recall those few days had left him with an uneasy feeling, like Bicky and his chief of security had been involved in some sort of conspiracy which Hart was not privy to, but at the heart of which was Sonia. Unable to recall more than fragments of what transpired, he'd put his suspicions aside, but the wariness revived itself at times, on its own and without warning. What Jerry wanted now, Hart could only guess, but something was bothering the man.

"What's up, Jerry?"

Jerry bent his head like a bird trying to get a better view and looked at Hart as if he'd just spoken to him in Aramaic. "Ummm."

Hart eyed his colleague with a scrutiny generally reserved for problematic oil derricks. The once erect figure sagged a bit, the squared shoulders hunched, the closely cropped, military-style haircut had grown unkempt. Hart thought about his own appearance of late and cringed. *How could one woman affect so many people?* Their eyes locked, and Jerry stiffened as if preparing for a blow.

"I ... I blame myself. If I'd been there, I'm sure there was something I could have done. I had this feeling ... ." Jerry shook his head and stamped his foot like a bull ready to charge. "She'd be alive today."

Hart stared at Jerry, mouth agape. He wasn't sure what he'd expected the ex-marine to say, but it wasn't that. "Hey, Jer. How could you have possibly known?"

Jerry cringed and stepped back as if Hart had delivered a physical blow.

"Jerry," Hart said. "I could say the same thing. If anyone's to blame it's me." Hart had never spoken the words out loud, although he'd thought them a million times, and they came out now, slow and deliberate. He was at fault, and the guilt he stored in his gut could power a small city. The words hung in the air between them like wood smoke until they both looked away, blinking their eyes with the sting of it.

"I gotta go," Hart said. Jerry moved away as if commanded. Hart climbed in, put the car in reverse, and didn't look back.

CHAPTER 41

It was Frank Charlton, the manifold operator, who had first seen it, and what he saw made his stomach tuck and roll like a Hollywood stunt man. The sun had poked a ray or two over the horizon, visible through the few breaks that existed in the rack of cumulo-stratus clouds now marching in formation across the sky. They were just getting ready to dock at the Akanabi refinery at Marcus Hook. Charlton had come out for a breath of crisp January air in the hopes it would rouse him, but he caught a whiff of something thick and pungent instead, something that made him want to puke. He stuck a head over the side of the ship then ran to the stern with full knowledge of what was happening but a need to see it firsthand.

He peered down into the churning, black water below. The diffused light from the overcast sky laid a grey pallor over the water but didn't hide what Frank had feared: a thick trailing line of oil stretching from the stern of the *Ryujin* to as far south as the eye could see. Stumbling over his own feet, he ran to the Captain's quarters, knocking loudly.

"Captain. Beg your pardon, sir, but we have a problem."

The door flew open and there was Captain Reed. His face looked as if he'd been up all night, but his clothes were freshly starched and pressed.

"What is it?"

"The *Ryujin* is leaking oil, sir. Off the stern."

Reed's eyes grew large. He pushed past Charlton and raced to the stern with Charlton on his heels. Sure enough, a gnarled, unctuous trail of oil stretched from the stern and out across the water into infinity.

"What in God's name?" Reed ran to the front of the ship, looking occasionally over the side as he ran, but saw nothing. He ran back to the stern and looked again, just to be sure. He rubbed his face with his hands.

"But last night ... . Oh, my God. Where the hell did it come from?" Reed stopped and stared out over the black waters at the even blacker oil shimmering in the pale morning light.

"Radio the Coast Guard. No, I'll do it," Reed said.

Charlton nodded. "Shall I inform Pilot Anderson, sir?"

"Yes. I mean no. I'll do that as well. Make sure the crew's ready for landing. We're here. We may as well dock. Get some divers down there and see what's going on." Reed shook his head at the river, as if *she* had something to do with it, raised his fist and slammed it hard on the railing. Charlton flinched, knowing that it had hurt, but Reed's face did not change.

"Go," Reed said to Charlton. Charlton scampered off to relay orders and spread the news. Reed gripped the railing with both hands and stared at the growing menace.

⅄

Reed went back to his cabin, pulled out the maritime safety manual and placed it on his desk. He didn't need to look at it. He knew what it said. He'd read it a dozen or more times just in case but had never needed to use it. In the event of a maritime spill from a vessel, the vessel officer was to notify the National Response Center, which is staffed by the Coast Guard. NRC would adopt an incident as opposed to unified command system, and the Coast Guard would assign an On-Scene Coordinator, or OSC, who would be charged with overall responsibility for the incident as well as notifying the Environmental Protection Agency, the Pennsylvania Department of Environmental Protection, the state and local fire hazmats, and the County Emergency Management Association. That, times three, he thought, because the spill occurred in a tri-state area and certainly Delaware and New

Jersey would want to have a say in what goes. Not to mention the various and sundry agencies with interest: U.S. Fish and Wildlife Service; the PA Game Commission; the PA Boat Commission; the National Oceanic and Atmospheric Administration. At least only one person would be in charge and that person, the OSC, would come from the Coast Guard.

Reed rubbed his forehead in contemplation and swallowed the thick feeling that was creeping into his throat. He, too, originally came from the Coast Guard. That might help. Might. For the first time in his adult life, he felt like he might cry. In hours, the place would be crawling with personnel from dozens of agencies, and he'd be squarely in the center of it all. Damn that Anderson. For a moment he felt a stab of regret for his hasty actions the previous night and wished he wouldn't have been so quick to intervene. After all, Anderson was probably right. The small craft was playing chicken with them and was not on a suicide mission. Still, the public and the media would want a scapegoat, and if Reed had anything to say about it, it wasn't going to be him. He stood and brushed the imaginary wrinkles from his heavily starched uniform. He strode purposefully to the door, maritime safety regulations in hand. Time to radio the Coast Guard. Let the games begin.

$$\Lambda$$

Within hours roughly three dozen personnel from various agencies were swarming the banks of the Delaware like bees to the hive, loading skimmers onto pollution control vessels; unloading trucks carrying oil containment booms, spill containment berms, sonic bonded sorbent pads, emulsifiers, trash bags, over-pack drums and containers for waste disposal, Tyvek suits, black sturdy rubber gloves, yellow rubber boots and shoe coverings, safety glasses and goggles, disposable earplugs and all manner of oil spill paraphernalia. A vacuum truck sat idly by, its engine running, waiting for its first big drink of the brown, oily stuff.

Federal On-Scene Coordinator and Marine Safety Officer, Frank Zenone, stood in the center of the command post, a trailer set up along the banks of the Delaware, scratching his head in sheer bliss. Once he banished the itch, he ran his long spindly fingers through his hair, smoothing it back into place before replacing his hat. Zenone had been up long before he got the call at 5 a.m., responding to a small oil spill upriver at the New York/New Jersey border. It had turned out to be a false alarm. He'd arrived at Marcus Hook by boat, which took him substantially longer than it would have by car. Although the sun had been up for more than a few hours, the day was as bleak as any night with a cloud cover that threatened to choke the light out of it. That coupled with a threatening wind chiming in from the north, and Zenone knew it was going to be a long day. He looked out the window and sighed.

The weather complicated matters, adding its weight to a job the tide had already begun. When the oil spill occurred, the waters of the Delaware River were doing their damned best to get back to the sea, taking with them roughly 350,000 gallons of oil that had managed to escape from the confines of the Ryujin's holding tanks. Stupid bastards. Hard to blame them for not catching the trail of oil on the water with less than a flicker of moonlight to do it by. Still, they should've been checking every hour, Christ every half hour, after scraping bottom like that. Maybe they would've seen the oily sheen. And then with the depth gauge being broken. What rotten luck. He rubbed his hands up and down his face to rouse himself. He could blame them, but he wouldn't. That wasn't his job. His job was to get this damn mess under control before the tide and coming storms did more damage.

Zenone sat down at the drafting table and turned his attention to the SPCC Plan he had taken from the Captain of the Ryujin, a bound report, about an inch thick with a nice bond cover and spiral binding. The cover page read *Spill Prevention Control and Countermeasures Plan for the Ryujin* dated January 2004. So, they'd either created the plan or updated it just before sailing. Well, that was promising. He turned the page and was shocked at what he saw next: nothing. Now he could blame them. Bastards didn't even have a plan in case of a spill. He laughed ruefully to himself and sat looking out the window, lost in thought. He watched as another two-dozen workers disembarked from a large, converted school bus, joining the cleanup operation on the beach, decidedly lacking direction. He huffed, rose, and walked out of the trailer, but a ringing phone dragged him back.

"Zenone."

"Yeah, Frank. It's Lapsley. Charlton's almost done." Victor Lapsley, an OSC for the Environmental Protection Agency, had been the first responder on site, almost an hour ahead of Zenone since he had come by car. As a result, Lapsley had been the Incident Commander on the scene for a brief stint, but was showing no signs of wanting his old job back.

"Who's Charlton?"

"The manifold operator. I just talked to him. He's almost finished pumping off the last of what was in the holding tanks."

"Already? Damn."

"What? I thought you'd take that as good news since the hull's still leaking."

"Yeah, yeah, that's good. But that operation takes the better part of the day. So if he's almost done, we got more oil in the water than we originally thought."

"Nah. Akanabi got the lead out," Lapsley said, and immediately chuckled to himself. "Hey, I think there's a pun in there."

Zenone rolled his eyes, a gesture Lapsley apparently could feel rather than hear through the phone because he cleared his throat and continued.

"Anyway, last I saw, Akanabi had the Ryujin docked and hooked up to every available hose. They wanted the stuff out as fast as possible.

"So how much is in the water?" Zenone asked.

"Well, I think our original estimates are right. About 350,000 gallons, give or take."

"You talk to the Captain?" Zenone coughed. The winds were picking up and the smell of oil seemed much stronger now as it meandered through his olfactory system. He could feel it inching up his nostrils into his nasal cavity and twitched his nose to eradicate the sensation. It didn't work. He sneezed. Oil vapors went flying.

"Bless you," Lapsley said. "Yeah. Reed. And to Akanabi's Chief Engineer. Guy named Hart. Captain seemed a little jumpy."

"What did he say?"

"Some story about a motor boat soon after they left the Bay and the river pilot overreacting. Pilot swung out of the channel. Wasn't using his radar. I don't know … somethin's weird. I'm sure the pilot will have another story."

Zenone coughed. "All right, whatever. When you're done, come on down. I'm heading out now to give two dozen cleanup workers my safety spiel."

"See you in an hour." Lapsley hung up.

Zenone held the phone, listening to the dial tone. Out of the channel, huh? He put the phone in its cradle, sneezed and headed out to greet the cleanup crew.

◢

Half an hour later, after a quick synopsis of how to use the cleanup equipment followed by an even quicker recitation of the safety hazards associated with oil spill cleanups, including references to slips, trips, falls, poisonous snakes and poison ivy, Akanabi's muckers, the untrained labor hired by the company to don Tyvek suits, rubber boots, safety goggles and gloves and do hand-to-hand combat with the enemy, were mired ankle-deep in a miasma of pure crude. They hung together in groups of twos and threes, working at the shore line, shoveling clumps of oil into buckets and bags and disposing of it into the dozens of over-pack waste disposal drums standing by. The larger clumps were fairly easy to retrieve, but as they got down to the finer stuff it became more elusive, like trying to catch a minnow with your bare hands, and with the pre-formed plastic gloves, such minutia was impossible to be gathered. What couldn't be bagged was raked into the gravelly sand to be dealt with later by Mother Nature herself, either through erosion, weather or eventual degradation. Within half an hour, each of the muckers was covered, literally, from head to toe in oil. The Tyvek helped, keeping them from getting soaked through to the skin, as did the gloves and boots, but working as they were, surrounded by thick blobs of oil, and sometimes standing in ankle-deep water, the ubiquitous crude seeped into their eyes and ears and up their noses. And that was the worst part because they couldn't get away from the smell, not even by holding their breath. Some of the more industrious muckers waded out into waist-deep water in pairs, stretching a five hundred foot sorbent boom across the surface and corralling the oil back to shore to a central location where the vacuum truck could suck it out with a hose. The boom was made of oleophilic, or oil loving material, a high quality polypropylene with great absorbent qualities and generally used for the last stages of a cleanup. The problem with using the absorbent booms for large doses of oil was that saturation ultimately rendered them ineffective. As a result, the muckers were going through booms like kids through candy, disposing of them after a single use and keeping the vacuum truck busy.

The vacuum sucked up oil as well as water, but by a technological miracle, the truck only disposed of the oil, allowing the water to settle out in the bottom of a holding tank and sending it back, sans its oily compounds, to the river where it belonged. Of course, it couldn't all be removed. Oil was as persistent as it was pervasive and, although over time the chemical compounds would break down and disperse, inevitably some portion of the oily substance would remain, infused into the water column, or in pockets on the beach, or on the underside of rocks, forever changing the face of that which it touched.

CHAPTER 42

Zenone stood outside the command post, watching oil move down river, contemplating the next move. He nodded at the cleanup crew's progress, temporarily satisfied with the speed at which the raking and shoveling at the shoreline was making a difference. He could actually see the beach in some spots, whereas hours ago there was nothing to see but brown crude. As cleanup crews went, this was a savvy bunch. They got to work immediately after receiving the basic safety instructions and didn't appear inclined to loaf. Perhaps there was hope for recovery of this shoreline. Zenone had been with the Coast Guard for twenty-two years, fourteen of which he'd been specializing in oil spill removal. In his experience, it would take years for a spill of this magnitude to lose its effect on the ecosystem and likely decades before all the oil was gone from the shorelines, if ever. But right here it wasn't so bad. On a sensitivity scale of one to ten, the mixed sand and gravel beaches were about a five. This beach, and likely most of the beaches along the Delaware from Marcus Hook to just north of Slaughter Beach, Delaware — roughly eighty-five miles of shoreline — would recover with time using the cleanup strategies he was employing. What may not recover, however, was Tinicum Marsh.

Zenone pushed the thought back and coughed. He sucked in the persistent post-nasal drip that the foul smell of too much oil in the ambient air caused him and spit on the ground. He cleared his throat and swallowed.

His saliva felt viscous and unnatural. He coughed and spat again. His cell phone rang and he grabbed it off the belt at his hip, still coughing.

"Zenone." He looked in the direction of the vacuum boat idling on the water, a small barge about twenty-five feet long that could carry four to five people. It was powered by a single-diesel engine, had a storage tank below deck and an oil skimmer above and was capable of removing thirty tons of heavy oil per hour if it could catch it. Zenone could see the Captain of the tug standing at the stern, cell phone to his ear, waiting for the signal. "Go ahead," Zenone said into the phone, snapped it shut and replaced it on his hip.

The Captain flashed a thumbs-up and the vacuum boat circumvented a thick mass of the slick, trailing a boom. The plan was to circle out and encapsulate as much of the oil as possible in the boom, like outstretched arms slowly pulling together, then swing back in, leaving the boom on the water in a V-formation. The booms were made of tough, non-corrosive plastic, rectangular shaped with a bulbous center mounted to a rubber skirt that rose above and below the boom and which entrained the oil, working as a dam to stop it from rushing over or under the barrier. This worked effectively enough in calm waters, but when the winds got rough and the waves picked up, increasing the water's velocity, there was not a boom made that could stop the oil. When the boom was in place, the vacuum boat turned around and set the skimmers on the oil, munching, crunching and sucking it up using two, hydraulic-driven pumps. The pressurized system funneled the oil through a tube and then to a gravity separator. Once decanted, the remaining water was pumped off and dumped back into the river. The oil was disposed of in a two thousand gallon holding tank to be dealt with later, either by pumping it off back on shore, or to a small portable hundred foot barge that would intercept it and take it to shore so the vacuum boat could keep skimming.

Zenone checked his watch and then the sky, hoping the weather would hold. He had another ten vacuum boats working the entire stretch of the river, some provided by the Coast Guard, some by EPA, and some by Akanabi Oil. If he could get another ten ... .

His attention was drawn by the grunting and puffing of two muckers trying to stuff an oil-laden absorbent boom into a disposal bag. The third man grabbed a fresh boom off one of the trucks and headed toward the water. Zenone decided to take back what he said about them being savvy — absorbent booms weren't to be used until the final stages of the cleanup since other methods, like vacuum extractions, worked better on large quantities of oil — until he looked at the flatbed. The hard, non-corrosive plastic booms were suspiciously absent, and in their place were the sorbent ones. Damn Akanabi Oil. More like Psycho Oil. He barked at the nearest mucker.

"Where the hell are the large plastic booms?" Zenone barked.

"I don't know. This is all they sent us," the man replied then scampered off to join his comrades, leaving Zenone staring after him.

"Hey, Jim. Bring more diapers," called a young, college-age woman to her colleague walking toward the supply truck. The man nodded and grabbed another bale. She got down on her hands and knees and pressed absorbent pads — cloth diapers on steroids — into the sand. The pads soaked up small bits of oil, a time consuming process. She reminded Zenone of his own daughter and smiled at her fastidiousness: her little section of the beach was virtually spotless.

Zenone cast an appraising glance upward. The clouds looked more threatening than they had at daybreak, and so thick as to appear seamless. He knew a storm was coming, barely hours away. He felt it in the right wrist, the one he'd broken as a kid. It was the best weather detector he'd encountered to date. He flipped his cell phone open and dialed the number for NOAA anyway. After two rings, someone answered the phone.

"Yeah, who's this?" Zenone asked. "Hey. It's Zenone. I need a weather report for the whole tri-state area. Call me back the minute you got it, all right?" He flipped the phone shut.

A horn beeped and Zenone turned to see Lapsley pull up to the command post with a passenger. Zenone met them halfway.

"Hey, Chief. This is David Hartos," Lapsley said. "Akanabi's head engineer. He's your contact."

"Good to meet you," Hart said. "Whatever Akanabi can do, please let me know."

Hart reached out a hand, and Zenone gave him a death grip that made him flinch. Zenone smiled but covered it with a hand to his mouth and a little fake cough. He liked to put them in their place right off, so there wouldn't be any difficulties with chain-of-command later.

"How about you check on those booms. They sent absorbent instead of plastic. And maybe find some more vacuum boats. If we could get 'em out before the storm comes we might get somewhere. But if you really want to help, you can tell them to retire all their single-hulled ships. They're a menace." Zenone grimaced and turned to Lapsley. "Where's my helicopter?"

"Coming."

"So's spring."

"Really, you'll learn to love this guy," Lapsley said, turning to Hart. "He's got a tough exterior but a heart like gold." Lapsley turned back to Zenone, eyes glistening with humor. Zenone smiled mechanically, but his eyes reflected a hidden mirth.

"NOAA's sending one," Lapsley said. Everything the Coast Guard's got was already deployed. Apparently there's a big storm brewing down off the coast of North Carolina, heading this way, and bringing some high winds with it. Came up really fast. A few fishing boats needed to be rescued." Zenone sighed and nodded his head absently.

"Did you notify all the local water intakes?"

"Yes."

"Cause you know, if they don't shut 'em down, they're gonna be local oil intakes."

"Yes," Lapsley said again. "It was the first thing I did this morning. Now would you chill? You're giving me the shakes." Lapsley smiled and Hart snickered. Zenone huffed and glanced up at the impending storm clouds, hovering like doom on the horizon.

"All right, let's go in." Zenone turned to Hart. "I want to show you something that perhaps you can explain to me."

Hart nodded and followed Zenone into the command post.

⋏

Zenone poured a cup of coffee, a thick, viscous substance that looked itself like petroleum, handed it to Lapsley, then turned to Hart to see if he wanted a cup. Hart shook his head no. He'd had more than enough cups of bad coffee today.

"What? D'you pull this from the river?" Lapsley said, and took a sip anyway.

Zenone walked to the drafting table and handed Hart Akanabi's SPCC Plan.

Hart scanned the cover and raised his eyebrows. "Is it deficient?"

"You bet it is."

Hart opened it. Blank pages. He flipped through a couple pages at a time, but the blankness remained.

"Did you prepare that plan?" Zenone asked.

"No. And I'm not sure who did, or rather, who was supposed to," Hart said. "Did you get this from the ship's Captain?"

Zenone nodded. Hart huffed and rubbed his forehead.

"You know there's a fine. Up to $32,500 for failure to have a spill plan. And another one for failure to implement it. Not to mention the fines for all the oil in the water. They accrue daily."

"Yeah. I know."

"Just so we're straight."

"We're straight." Hart stood and offered Zenone his hand.

Zenone took it, but this time Hart was ready for him. He squeezed back with equal force, forcing a smile out of Zenone.

"It's been a pleasure, but I've got a dive to get ready for."

Lapsley rose. "I'll drive you back."

"Inspection?" Zenone asked.

"The Ryujin," Hart replied. I'll let you know what I find. And for what it matters, I wholeheartedly agree with you about the single hulls." This time Zenone smiled for real.

CHAPTER 43

Hart descended into the murky realms of the Delaware River, enjoying the cocoon-like warmth of his wet suit. He had opted for it over the dry suit even though the water was on its way to below freezing. The dry suit would keep him dry, but not warm enough, not in these arctic-like conditions. Ah, but the wet suit, that was something else. It sported an insulated neoprene hose which tied onto the outside of the umbilical, ran down the side of his body and attached at the spider, a three-way valve at the waist of his suit. The hose was fed by a hot water machine that had an oil-fired burner and a digital thermostat to control the temperature. Under usual circumstances, water to feed the hose would be drawn from the water body the diver found himself in, but given the petrol load the Delaware was carrying, Hart directed the hot water machine be fed with water from a local fire hydrant and transported via garden hose. The hose was threaded around the interior of Hart's wet suit and one hundred degree water escaped through the little holes poked in it, entering in myriad locations and keeping his whole body warm. The hose could even blow warm water through the cuff and into Hart's smaller gloves making the large, bulky, but warmer three-finger gloves unnecessary. Hart closed his eyes, allowing himself to bask for a few moments in the warmth before proceeding down the ladder into the water.

The Delaware River, a murky water with low visibility on a good day, was even worse today because of the impending storm. Hart reached a level that he assumed would be the bottom of the ship's hull, but without touching it he couldn't distinguish metal from water. He dropped another few feet, holding fast to the traveling line, but the scenery didn't change.

"Great. Now what?"

"What's up, Boss?" Smith's voice crackled, flooding Hart's helmet with sound.

"I can't see a damn thing. What are they puttin' in this water anyway?"

"Lots of industry around here. Ships going up and down the channel churnin' up the bottom. The Army Corps always dredging it to keep the depth right. Then there's the farming," Smith mused. "I'd say you got some sediment, some debris … "

"It was a rhetorical question, Smithy."

"and, I'll leave it at that. You don't want to be thinking too hard about what you're swimming in unless you want to puke in your helmet." Smith cracked up at that, and Hart joined him, his body quivering with silent laughter.

"Smithy. Help me here. I can't see the ship. It's nowhere in sight, far as I can tell." Hart flicked his headlamp on and off, looking to bounce the light off of something. He wrapped the tow rope around his leg before reaching his hands out in front of him, groping vainly in the darkness. "I got nothin'."

"The traveling rope should be about three feet in front of the Ryujin. So if you're facing in the right direction, you could jump … "

Before Smith could finish his sentence, Hart jumped, using the traveling rope for leverage, and after a forward propulsion in slow motion, his helmet came to rest against the hull of the Ryujin with a resounding thump.

"What was that?" Smith asked.

"My brains getting rattled." Hart moved his hands along, feeling for the bilge keel, the fin-like projections from either side of the hull that helped stabilize a ship in rough seas. He cast his light directly on the hull and found he could see somewhat better. Hart's thin gloves allowed for greater movement, but they also meant he'd be more prone to cuts and scrapes against jagged metal. He proceeded with caution, moving down and around the bottom of the hull, alert for sharp metallic pieces of the ship's frame.

After several minutes of dimness, Hart's glove snagged on a sharp object. He trained the light in its direction and found a hole, about fifteen inches wide and half as long. He reached his hand in, feeling the emptiness of the space where the oil used to be and shuddered. The boulder, or whatever it was, had ripped a hole right on a seam of the hull, a faulty one at that. Hart's eye followed the rip in the hull until it dissolved into blackness. He pulled out an underwater tape measure, and after ascertaining the width, proceeded down the length of the hull looking for the end of the rainbow. Eight and a half feet later, the gaping stopped. Now it made sense. Hart had been wondering how in the hell so much oil had come out of what he was thinking probably looked like a small gash in the bottom, given both the pilot and captain's descriptions of impact. With a small hole and entrainment, most of the oil would have stayed put while the ship was moving. But this was no small hole. The impact had given way to a split seam on the hull. With a hole this size, no matter how fast the ship had been going, the oil was coming out. Zenone was right: time to retire the single-hulled vessels. The expense to the company was nothing compared to what it was doing to this river. He'd talk to Bicky about it as soon as he got back. Bicky would have other ideas, but he'd never been on site for a major oil spill either.

"Hey, Boss." Smith's voice interrupted his thoughts. "Time to come home. Coast Guard just issued a squall warning. They want all ships and other non-necessary personnel out of the water, pronto."

"I can't see a damn thing anyway, I got so much oil on my face-plate," Hart said. "I'm on my way up."

CHAPTER 44

It was a wind like only January could send down, brutal and unforgiving. Zenone cursed under his breath and stumbled back inside the command post trailer; the wind slammed the door shut for him. It continued to beat against the trailer's sides, rocking it inexorably, and he wondered if he and the command post might not end up in Kansas with Dorothy and Toto. In sharp contrast to the chaos whipping white caps across the river, the snow clouds cast a calm, eeric light across the sky, beautiful and surreal like the color of Mars. By mid-afternoon, the increasing pain in his wrist told him the weather had all but arrived. With that ample warning, he had the foresight to shut down all beach cleanup operations for the day and radio in all seafaring vessels, allowing them sufficient time to dock. So far, nine out of ten of the boats had radioed in, safely ensconced at various locations up and down the Delaware.

Zenone felt it his duty to stay put until the last boat was in and all personnel were present and accounted for, but what he really wanted was a beer. It had been a long day, eighteen hours if you counted the two hours he put in before he arrived at the command post. He knew if he drank a beer right now he'd be sleeping in the trailer, but he checked the small fridge anyway, hoping for a bit of a miracle. It was empty except for a pint of half-drunk chocolate milk and a jug of orange juice. He turned his nose up at the juice. The acid would rake his stomach and he didn't need a full-blown case of heartburn. He grabbed the chocolate milk, opened the carton and sniffed the contents, recoiling at the smell that emanated from within.

"Aachhh!"

He set the milk down on the desk and made a mental note to stop at a store on his way home, that is, if he didn't fall asleep at the wheel. He was bone weary and his stomach rumbled, adding to the mix. A cheesesteak would be good right now.

The wind howled and the trailer bucked, driving all thoughts of food from Zenone's head. He took a stool at the drafting table and ran his hands through his hair. Outside, snow started to fall. Zenone stared at the phone, willing it to ring. The silence crept into his inner ear and made its bunk up for the night. The storm would go a ways toward breaking up the oil, but there was still too much in the water. If it could have just waited until tomorrow when they had recovered more. Then Mother Nature could get to work. He scanned the computer-generated simulation Lapsley had brought him. The Coast Guard had sent a helicopter up on an over-flight mission to map the extent of contamination — an aerial view of the spill was helpful in these circumstances — but it was only partially successful due to the weather. The heavy cloud cover made it hard to distinguish the slick, while the clouds' shadows cast what looked like dark stains, easily mistaken for oil, upon the water. After ascertaining the imperfection of purely visual analysis, the over-flight team notified Akanabi who had sent up their environmental consultant. He snapped a bunch of photos with infrared light cameras, which produced a much clearer picture of the spill, then fed the reconnaissance data into a computer. The program crunched the spill data, mixed in environmental conditions such as wind and weather, and simulated the spill's course and dispersion rate. The conclusion was that the oil was heading toward the Delaware Bay where it would likely be contained and, as a result, wouldn't reach the Atlantic Ocean. Although in open ocean waters computer modeling could be helpful in determining the direction of a spill, in this case, the Delaware only went two ways and the odds were staggering that the oil would return to the Bay with the outgoing tide.

"I'd say they got ripped off," Zenone said. He tossed the aerial map aside and rested his head on his closed fist.

Zenone's guys had managed to sufficiently confine the oil just short of the Bay before having to abort the mission. At that time, and by some good will of the gods, only the Pennsylvania side of the shoreline had been affected. But the way the wind was bandying the oil about now, the shores on both sides of the Delaware and likely the Bay would be gummed up by morning.

He grabbed the shoreline cleanup manual off the desk and thumbed through the various cleanup methods, looking for something he might have missed: removal, steam cleaning, high-pressure washing, chemical and hydraulic dispersion. Chemical and hydraulic dispersion. The eight-foot waves would take care of the hydraulic part. He would have preferred a good surface washing, lying down some riprap and hosing off the beaches. Then they could collect the oil off the riprap and dispose of it properly. But now the waves were going to wash the oil back into the river where it would sink to the bottom. Chemical dispersants would break it up, but ... .

Zenone removed his hat and scratched his head, then ran his fingers through his hair. He hadn't thought about chemical dispersants because the Delaware was a fresh water body and chemicals had a certain degree of toxicity. What if the dispersants could be placed before the storm came, an emulsifier that would break the oil down into smaller pieces and drive it into the water column where it would more easily biodegrade? That mixed with the oncoming wind and large waves would break the oil up fast. But what about the chemicals? The heavy oils were less toxic and tended to sit on the surface of things rather than penetrate them, but they were tough to remove — like picking up gravel with tweezers — and tended to smother the smaller organisms that lived on the shore. He flipped through the manual looking for guidance. The Coast Guard had some pre-approved areas where emulsifiers could be used — he wasn't sure without looking where they were — but how the hell were they going to get the stuff in the river before the storm, especially now since he'd recalled all seafaring vessels. He could go out himself maybe.

"Oh my God, I'm losing it." He closed the book and pushed it aside, wishing again that he had a beer. He checked the cell phone. No new calls. He grabbed the trailer phone and lay down on the small couch. *Just until I get the call.* He closed his eyes and because of his exhaustion, rapid eye movement began almost at the outset.

Zenone stood on the shore watching large waves crash against it and taking with them, back to the river, the blackness that covered the land. He smiled. The oil was dissipating. Once again, Mother Nature prevailed. The snow clouds cast an eerie orange light, enough for him to see. It was all going great until the waves started dropping things on the beach: a loud thump, followed by a scattering of black, rounded clumps of solid mass.

He walked over to investigate. A large, oiled bird lay on the ground, half-dead and shivering from hypothermia. Zenone touched the animal as it opened its eyes, blinking back the oil, trying to clear its vision. He felt his own eyes sting with tears. Zenone wiped the bird's eyes with his fingers, then his hands, removing what oil he could, but the task was impossible, like removing water from a well with a slotted spoon. He was so engrossed he didn't notice the wall of water behind him. The wave crashed on the shoreline, knocking Zenone to the ground and taking the bird with it. He climbed to his feet and staggered down the beach. Another crashing wave, another thump, followed by another, and another. Zenone looked up to see birds lying everywhere, landing on the beach with each successive wave. He dropped to his knees and crawled to the nearest bird. A glob of oil was stuck in the bird's esophagus. He reached in and tried to dislodge it. The bird fought him, flapping against both the intrusion and the lack of oxygen. It clamped down hard on Zenone's fingers, and he yelped in surprise and pain.

⚓

"Rise and shine," Lapsley said, squeezing the fingers of Zenone's hand. Zenone shrieked and Lapsley jumped back, almost dropping the pair of coffees he carried. He set the carrier down, removed his gloves and handed Zenone a cup of the steaming brew.

"What time is it?" Zenone croaked.

"Five forty-five. That would be a.m.," Lapsley said. "You look like hell." Lapsley noted the dark circles under Zenone's eyes but said nothing more.

"You're no prince charming, yourself," Zenone grumbled. He accepted the coffee and took a big swig. "Goddamn, that's good." He took another swig, walked to the table and pulled at the bag Lapsley brought, extracting a whole-wheat bagel with cream cheese.

"Hungry?" Lapsley asked.

Zenone nodded and consumed half the bagel in a bite. "Never got dinner."

Outside, the water looked choppy, but calmer than the night before.

"Looks like chocolate mousse out there," Lapsley said.

There was a loud bang at the door and Zenone jumped, spilling coffee on the table. "Damn," he said and grabbed the bag for some napkins. He spoke through a mouth full of bagel. "Come."

Hart entered carrying several cups of coffee and a box of donuts, which he set on the table. Zenone smiled at the offering.

"If you bring food, you're always welcome," Zenone said, shoving a bagel in his mouth. He nodded to a seat, which Hart took.

"Lap and I were just talking about chocolate mousse."

Hart raised an eyebrow. "All I brought were Munchkins."

"And that'll do." Zenone routed through the box and popped one in his mouth. "You know, when oil becomes aerated, generally after the second or third day, it starts to look like chocolate mousse."

"He's head of engineering for Akanabi Oil. He probably knows that," Lapsley said.

"You never know," Zenone replied. "It's a hell of a state. All whipped."

"Like you before you got divorced," Lapsley said. Zenone ignored the slur.

"In the summer, the oil turns into tarry clumps and ends up on the beach," Hart said.

"Asphaltine," Lapsley added. Hart nodded and Lapsley smiled. "Sorry. We're used to dealing with the public."

"Do you know if any of it has sunk yet?" Hart asked. "The Arabian crude is pretty heavy. It's probably just a matter of time."

"We'll find out today," Lapsley replied. "Once the water has a chance to settle."

"I got a helicopter on standby equipped with sonar. If there are glob-ules on the bottom, large or small, we can track it," Hart said.

"Hey, remember that one spill?" Lapsley asked Zenone. "These big globs of oil were up and down the river like bouncy balls, back and forth with the tide."

"Damn." Zenone jumped up, spilling the donuts, and grabbed his cell phone off the table. The command post phone was also blinking.

"It came in around eleven," Lapsley said, intuiting the source of Zenone's concern.

"How do you know?"

"Because they called me when you didn't answer your phone."

Zenone nodded and sat down, visibly relieved.

"You don't need me this morning, do you?" Lapsley asked.

"Whaddya got goin' on?"

"We're going to take a ride to Chesapeake to the wildlife sanctuary. See how they're doing with the birds. Want to go?"

A shiver ran down Zenone's spine, and he stared off into space for a moment, looking at something Hart and Lapsley couldn't see. "Nah, go ahead." He waved a hand to dismiss them.

"I'll check in at Tinicum Marsh on my way back. I haven't heard from anybody yet. Hopefully the booms held."

Zenone drew a deep breath. Lapsley cocked his head at Hart, and they rose to leave.

CHAPTER 45

The Wildlife Rescue Center in northeastern Maryland, a one-stop emergency room for oiled birds and other mammals, was brimming to capacity. Trained staff and volunteers littered the aisles like road debris, working as quickly as possible to address the backlog. The temperature was set to a balmy seventy-five degrees to keep the birds warm, a temperature which worked quite well outside, especially with a nice crosswind, but not inside a building packed with so many CO_2 breathing mammals. People were sweating profusely; a few of the workers looked like they just took a dip in the river.

The Wildlife Rescue Center was a coalition of the local SPCA, the Friends of Waterfowl, a local, well-known bird conservancy, as well as federal, state and local government partners. The building itself was huge, about fourteen thousand square feet in the shape of an open rectangle, cordoned off with moveable walls to accommodate the varying resource needs. The largest area was set aside, as the trauma center. The building sat idle, yet prepared to be used only in the event of an oil spill. It was the coalition's greatest hope that the money they'd invested in this building would go to waste and that the facility and its equipment would sit and collect dust. Unfortunately, today that hope was not realized, as dozens of veterinarians and trained volunteers worked side-by-side, attempting to undo what might not be capable of being undone.

Doctor Alyssa Morgan, a veterinarian and Director of the Wildlife Rescue Center, was on the phone in a small walled office at the back of the room, gesticulating animatedly. Lapsley and Hart walked into the middle of the trauma center and looked around like lost children waiting for direction. Dr. Morgan caught sight of Lapsley through her office window and waved, the scowl on her face softening. Lapsley took that as a good sign.

By the time they reached the door, she hung up the phone and ushered them into the office, a mere eight-by-twelve foot space, harboring a desk with a phone, a couch, which at present was a catch-all for a billion miscellaneous reports and papers, and a credenza with a coffee pot. Two more people could fit, but only if they took turns breathing. Realizing rather belatedly the ridiculousness of this arrangement, she hustled them out.

"Vic," Dr. Morgan said, extending a hand. "Long time."

"Hey, Alyssa." Lapsley took her hand, holding it a few seconds longer than necessary. Dr. Morgan blushed.

"This is David Hartos. Chief of Engineering for Akanabi Oil." Hart extended a hand, which Dr. Morgan accepted, but the bloom faded from her face, replaced with a cold hard stare.

"Lyss, he didn't go out and dump the oil himself," Lapsley said. One side of his mouth quirked in a wry smile. The joke worked.

"So what's going on?" Lapsley asked.

"You're looking at it," Dr. Morgan said, extending an arm in a wide arc.

"You look like hell, "Lapsley said, his gaze fixed on her face.

"Thanks. You look pretty lousy yourself."

"You know what I mean," Lapsley said.

Dr. Morgan nodded. "I was up most of the night cleaning oiled birds. They're still coming in. And it's not just the Rescue Team. Fishermen are bringing them in now. It doesn't look like it's going to slow down anytime soon." She gazed around the room and back to Lapsley. "We need backup."

A lock of hair fell into her eyes. Lapsley resisted the urge to brush it back.

"Why don't you just put out a couple radio ads? Akanabi'll pay for it." Lapsley looked at Hart to make sure this was, in fact, true. Hart confirmed.

"I'm sure plenty of people would be willing to volunteer," Hart said.

"First time at a Rescue Center, Mr. Hart?" Dr. Morgan asked. Lapsley detected the note of satisfaction in her voice and suppressed the urge to smile.

"Actually, I usually repair the leak before it gets to this stage, so this is a bit out of my range, I'll admit," Hart said. "But I'd be happy to help."

"You can't. You're not trained. All our volunteers have had a two-day intensive training. To allow you to work on these birds without the proper training would rise to the level of malpractice."

"There's got to be something we can do," Lapsley said.

Dr. Morgan scanned the room. About fifteen de-oiling stations had been set up, all but one presently occupied.

"Check each of the stations and make sure they have sufficient quantities of Dawn dishwashing detergent, rags and trash bags," Dr. Morgan said.

"I guess that means you want us to hang for a while?" Lapsley asked.

"For a while. You mind?"

Lapsley shook his head and smiled at her.

"When did you last take the training?" Dr. Morgan asked Lapsley.

"Probably ten years ago," he replied. She sighed.

"All right, you better stick close to me." Lapsley looked at Hart and winked. He could think of nothing better he'd like to do this morning.

Chapter 46

The day dawned bright and balmy in Houston. Bicky Coleman sat behind his antique mahogany desk, smoking a cigar and reading *The Philadelphia Inquirer*. Akanabi was taking less of a beating in the newspapers now that Hart was on the scene, commissioning over flights and vacuum boats, throwing all kinds of money at the situation. Maybe it would help them later when the feds and everyone else sued Akanabi out the wazoo for penalties the company didn't deserve. After all, it had been an accident.

When Hart had called last night, he babbled on and on about retiring all of Akanabi's single-hulled ships. Bicky had humored him but knew that suggestion would end up in the circular file.

"You want me to retire all the single-hulled ships?" Bicky had asked Hart.

"At least let's phase them out. Fifteen to twenty percent a year."

"Hart, my son, are you sure hypothermia hasn't set in and affected that brain of yours?"

"It's gonna hit you where it hurts, Bicky, but it's the right thing to do. The river's black like you've never seen. Just avoiding the devastation to wildlife should be cause enough."

"Give me a memo. We'll talk about it when you get back."

Bicky had said that to shut Hart up; he had absolutely no intention of following through. Building new ships was an expensive proposition. More than half of Akanabi's supertanker fleet was single-hulled ships, purchased in the heyday of oil drilling. To replace them all at once, even over a period of five years would cost hundreds of billions of dollars. And Bicky was loath to spend that kind of money.

The intercom buzzed and Phyllis's voice jarred him to awareness.

"Jerry's here."

"Send him in."

⚓

Jerry Dixon walked in, looking grim but impeccable. Bicky's nose was stuck in the paper so Jerry just stood there waiting. Since Bicky had several personalities that didn't always talk to each other, Jerry thought it best to wait and see which one was in residence.

He looked up from his paper and smirked. "How many of those suits do you have?"

"I don't know. How many do you have?" Jerry said, indicating Bicky's Armani.

"You know what I mean. Do you spend the whole day ironing, or change suits every ten minutes? Cause you know I'm paying you good money to keep things secure around here, so if you're ironing ... " Bicky's smirk turned to a smile.

Jerry relaxed and sat down. "How's Hart doing with the spill?"

Bicky studied his buffed fingernails. "Apparently, something a little better than damage control. Seems he's making friends."

"What are the odds on the cleanup?"

"The river will survive. It's rebounded before, as have countless of her brethren. It will do so again," said Bicky, sounding like a Sunday morning TV evangelist.

Jerry scowled, a reflex. Akanabi could dump ten million gallons of oil in the river, and Bicky would insist it was nothing.

"You have no faith," Bicky continued. "I'm don't even think there's a limit to how far we can push Mother Nature. She's infinitely capable of recreating herself."

Jerry rolled his eyes. "Yeah, well, she's not doing such a good job with the ozone layer. I got a spot on my nose here that the doc says is pre-cancerous. Too many hours spent outside in an ozone-lite environment," he said, rubbing his proboscis. "I'm getting it removed tomorrow."

Bicky rubbed his own nose absently. His face bore a healthy, radiant glow that smacked of hours spent on a tanning bed. Jerry knew he kept one in an office down the hall. Some people used makeup. Bicky used processed UV light. Jerry wondered just how many of those "freckles" on Bicky's face had their own story to tell, and when they'd decide to start talking.

"Spare me the details," Bicky said. He stood and stared out the window. "You don't have any information yet, do you?"

Jerry shook his head, watched his boss, looking for clues.

"No. I've made discreet inquiries. But no one saw anything. At least not that they're admitting to." Bicky flashed Jerry an angry look.

"The coroner says it was an accident, Bicky. Why won't you believe that?"

"Graighton's the only other one who knew Sonia had the report and he was at the Union Club that night."

"You're saying Graighton left the Union Club, killed Sonia and returned without the report?' Jerry asked.

"Of course not. Graighton didn't go himself. One of his lackeys did. You remember where we found the report? Whoever killed Sonia didn't find what he was looking for. Maybe that's what angered him in the first place."

"But what would Graigthon gain by killing Sonia and stealing a report he already had a copy of?"

"Trying to get to me. Put me in my place. Send me a message or something." Bicky sighed. "Even that doesn't make sense." He flopped down in his chair. "Just keep looking."

"Yeah, sure," Jerry said, resigned.

"One more thing," Bicky reached into the top drawer. "I want you in Philadelphia."

"For?"

"I got another tip." He handed Jerry a piece of paper. "Recognize the address?" Jerry's eyebrows shot up, but he said nothing.

"Don't botch it this time. No commando missions. Nothing getting blown up. No one dying. Just bring me back the technology. You got it?"

Jerry nodded, a face set in stone.

"You're sure you found out nothing else...about Sonia?" Bicky asked.

"You think I'm not doing my job, old man?" Jerry's face remained cool and impassive.

"I think that you're too quick to accept the opinion of other's. What's that jackass coroner know?"

"She had an accident. She died. Accidents happen."

"Accidents don't just happen. Not to us. You should know that better than anyone, Mr. Chief of Security."

"You're wrong. They do. Something goes before, yeah. A miscalculation, a lack of perception, an error in judgment, a misstep, and then — an accident. But what precipitated that? That's the question. Perhaps she was slightly depressed that day. Worried about her husband. She's flustered. Or maybe something spooked her. Or someone ... " Jerry placed his hands on the front of Bicky's desk and leaned into it, "came around hassling her for something she wasn't inclined to give. She spills her drink. The floor's wet. She takes a step. She slips. She falls. A body in motion stays in motion. She can't stop herself from falling. She bangs her head and is out like a light. And if the baby didn't decide to come out at that moment, if he didn't decide to come out upside down, what do they call it, breech? Maybe she'd be alive today. The fact is, unless you were there," Jerry looked Bicky directly in the eye with malicious intent, "you're never going to know."

Bicky shuddered. After several seconds, Jerry stood up and backed away from the desk. He massaged his eyes and forehead with one hand, trying to squeeze the images out of them.

"I loved Sonia like she was my own kid. That she's dead pains me — like you can't even believe," Jerry said. He turned and was gone, an exit as quick and silent as death.

Bicky let out the breath he'd been holding and pulled a silk handkerchief from his breast pocket. He wiped his face and dabbed at the moisture forming in the corner of his eyes.

So far, it had been a hell of an afternoon. He walked to the wet bar, poured himself a scotch and soda and stood at the window sipping it. The world below soothed him. He could control it simply by pulling the blind. When he finally turned away, he pulled out the bottom desk drawer. Below a stack of papers, tucked in the bottom drawer, lay the coffee-stained report. Satisfied, Bicky closed the drawer and thumbed through a stack of mail in his in-box. Phyllis had opened everything, laying it in a pile for his review, except for one letter, marked personal and confidential. He ripped the envelope open and pulled out a small stack of papers.

It was a letter from Kitty's lawyer, a Complaint for Divorce and a Postnuptial Agreement with which she proposed to divest herself of everything just to be rid of the marriage. Bicky sipped his scotch for five minutes before pulling a yellow sticky pad out of a side drawer. He placed one on top of the lawyer's letter, wrote *Forget It!* in bold, black ink, and stuffed the papers back into the envelope. Then he buzzed Phyllis.

"Is Jerry still here?"

"He just went down."

"Catch him, will you, and tell him to come back up. I want him to deliver something for me. To my wife."

CHAPTER 47

"**She's equally hard** on everybody, regulators and regulated alike. She holds the world to this impossibly high standard," Lapsley said. "As a result, few people ever meet her expectations." Lapsley and Hart stood in the receiving room where dozens of birds sat in blanket-lined crates and boxes, awaiting initial evaluation.

"Including you?" Hart asked. Lapsley pivoted to face Hart, eyes wide. "Did she tell you?"

Hart grunted. "I don't think Dr. Morgan's going to confide in me anytime soon. But it's not hard to see there's a history there."

Lapsley smiled proprietorially. Dr. Morgan motioned to them, and they crossed the room to join her. She was monitoring several dozen oiled birds whose body heat was being supplemented with overhead heat lamps. Hart had never examined an oil-covered bird at close range and did so now, stopping to peer into a box housing a crusty mallard. Its eyes were filled with black muck; the duck blinked with fervor and shook its head to clear them. It gave up, stuck a determined beak beneath its wing and began preening itself. Hart's stomach lurched and he snatched the duck up, holding it over the box, not knowing what to do next. The mallard squawked in protest setting off a slew of answering calls, all quacking in syncopated sympathy. In moments, Dr. Morgan stood at Hart's side.

"What are you doing," she snapped.

"Oil's toxic. If he keeps eating it, he'll die!" Hart turned to Dr. Morgan, a desperate look on his face. "We've got to do something."

"We are doing something, Mr. Hart. We're evaluating them, and if they're stable, we clean them. First we give them a temporary I.D. band." Dr. Morgan reached into her pocket and pulled one out, tagging the mallard. "If they make it, they get a permanent I.D. band from the U.S. Fish and Wildlife Service. That way we can track their progress in the wild." She smoothed a hand over the duck's head removing the excess oil, then moved the bird to a weight scale and noted the findings on an intake sheet. "Then we check their weight and body temperature." She stuck a thermostat under the duck's wing until it beeped, recorded her findings. "It has to be greater than one hundred degrees for us to get to work." Dr. Morgan opened its beak and stuck her finger inside, feeling for obstructions. The mallard let out a strangled noise and tried to bite her finger, but she held firm. She continued her inspection, checking between the feathers and under the wings, noting the extent of oiling on the intake sheet. She wiped down the duck's back, legs and wings with her hand and wiped the excess oil on a towel before depositing the mallard back in his box.

"Some are too sick to clean," Dr. Morgan said and looked back at a Canadian goose. "Euthanasia is the only option. It's inhumane to let them suffer." She stared after the bird for a moment before turning back to Hart. "Now that you've seen what can happen, make use of your position. You can prevent this." She forced a smile and grabbed a blanket from a nearby supply cart. "Here, take this and cover him. If he's contained, he may stop preening."

Dr. Morgan handed Hart a blanket and turned her attention back to the goose lying weakly before her. Her mouth formed a hard line, and she motioned to a volunteer standing nearby. She spoke softly, something Hart couldn't hear over the intermittent quacks of the frightened mallard, and rested her hand on the goose's head. The goose tried to raise its beak, but it fell back on the blanket. Dr. Morgan nodded and the volunteer toted the bird away.

Dr. Morgan returned, her knitted brow relaxing. "This one's got a good chance," she said, tucking an arm underneath Hart's duck. "Help me get him over to the table." They transported the bird to an open, portable lab equipped with a table, a heat lamp, a small generator for heating water, and several large buckets. Lapsley was standing by.

"Why don't you get started filling the tubs," she said to Lapsley. "And make sure you keep that blanket on him," she said to Hart.

Hart tucked the blanket more firmly under the squat body, but a moment later the blanket jiggled as the mallard tucked its head beneath its wing. Dr. Morgan gently pulled the duck's beak out from under its wing and rubbed its head. The duck relaxed.

"What next?" Hart asked.

"First we flush his gastrointestinal tract to pull out what oil we can. They can digest some, but too much wreaks havoc. The oil ulcerates the GI tract and causes liver, kidney, and pancreas dysfunction so they lose the ability to digest and absorb food. They either hemorrhage to death or die of starvation." She looked at Hart for emphasis. "Then we'll flush his eyes with saline solution so he can see without a brown film over them. And then we're going to remove all this sticky stuff using gallons and gallons of warm soapy water. The trick is to do it all before he either starts to freak out or dies. This bird's in pretty good shape." She rubbed its head with her thumb. "He must not have been in the slick too long." She reached in her lab coat and retrieved an ophthalmoscope. "You can watch, but you can't help."

"I can follow instructions if you just tell me what to … "

Alyssa Morgan shook her head. Hart shuffled his feet. The duck seemed to have given up on clearing his eyes, allowing the hazy film to remain, opting for preening instead.

"Why's he doing that?"

"Instinct. To them the oil's a foreign substance they need to get rid of. They also do it because they're nervous. They're not used to people." Dr. Morgan took a stethoscope and listened to the bird's heart. She turned to Lapsley.

"How's the tub coming?"

"Good. I'll be ready in five." Dr. Morgan sighed and turned to Hart.

"Look. This is totally against protocol, but we're shorthanded." She stepped aside, making way for Hart. Stay here and hold our friend while I go get some help. Nothing else, okay?" Hart nodded, and Dr. Morgan turned back to Lapsley.

"A one-to-fifteen percent solution seems to be working. Why don't you try that in the first tub for starters? Go down from there." Dr. Morgan left Hart, Lapsley and the erstwhile river-faring mallard while she went off in search of a couple extra pairs of hands.

"She doesn't trust you either, huh?" Hart asked.

"You need at least four people to clean one bird. Three to do the work and one to troubleshoot, get supplies, that kind of stuff," Lapsley said.

Hart whistled. "Resource intensive." He looked around the room and noted four people hovering about each of the workstations, about sixty people in all, yet an eerie quiet had settled on the place — the only sound the occasional squawk of one of the birds — as if there were no words to spare, all the energy of the volunteers pouring into saving the lives of their patients, the lucky ones that had made it as far as the workstations.

"It's so quiet in here," Hart said. Lapsley shook his head but did not respond; he, too, was caught up in a sort of reverence for the task at hand.

Lapsley moved around the table to the three galvanized tubs sitting on the floor, checked the temperature of the first tub, then began filling the second tub with eight gallons of what he hoped was a hundred and six-degree water, leaving room for the addition of two more gallons for temperature adjustments. He stuck a thermostat in the tub and turned up the heat on the water tank. Hart noted each of the workstations had similar tubs and generators.

"Why three tubs?" Hart asked.

"It takes that much water to lift the oil off the birds. Each tub has to be a hundred and four degrees. We fill the second and third tubs with a hundred and six-degree water, so by the time we're ready to transfer the bird, the tub is at a hundred and four degrees," Lapsley said. "Oil messes with their insulating abilities by disrupting this intricate webbing system. That's also what enables them to float. You gotta remember, these birds live outside all year round, even in winter. That's only possible because of their insulation. The oil breaks it all down, though, and then they can die from hypothermia, or drown, or they can't fly, which makes them easy prey. Then they preen themselves to death. It's nasty." Lapsley reached under the portable cart and pulled out a bottle of Dawn dishwashing detergent.

"You're gonna wash my duck with dish soap?"

"This stuff rules. It works better than anything else."

Hart watched as Lapsley measured out several tablespoons and poured them into the first tub. He pulled up his sleeve and stuck his hand in, stirring the soap around with his arm. He did the same to the second and third tubs, putting a little less soap in each tub. He topped off the first tub with two more gallons of water, bringing the total to ten.

"I'd say we're ready," Lapsley said and turned to see a stone-faced Dr. Morgan returning, trailing a young woman with her. The mallard poked his head out to see what was happening, saw two more humans approaching, and hid his head under the blanket.

"This is Cheryl," Dr. Morgan said. "I couldn't get another volunteer, so, Mr. Hart," Dr. Morgan turned to him, "you will be permitted to help as a floater, which means you don't touch anything unless told to. Understand?"

"Perfectly," Hart said.

"The washing time should take no more than thirty minutes, but let's get it closer to twenty. It reduces the stress on the bird. When it comes time to move him, Vic, you use a body hold to get him in the tub. Then I'll hold him underneath the bill and wash his head and neck. We'll clear the debris from his nostrils and flush his eyes with more saline rinse." Dr. Morgan grabbed a toothbrush from the cart and stuck in it her pocket. "Cheryl, you ladle water over his head, wings and back." Dr. Morgan turned to Cheryl, demonstrating. "Rub his belly lightly and rub beneath the wings, always in the direction of the feathers. Brush off as much oil as you can."

She turned back to the group in general. "Then we'll move him to the next tub and start the process again. Mr. Hart, you'll empty the first tub and wash it to get the residue out. The sink's over there, "Dr. Morgan said, pointing to a large wash sink in the corner.

"After the mallard's cleared the tubs, we'll do a deep spray rinsing in the sink over there." Dr. Morgan pointed to another set of sinks with hand-held shower massagers, "and we'll repeat the rinsing."

"How do you know when he's clean?" Hart asked.

"When the water runs off his back. It's called beading. The feathers will look dry. It's absolutely essential we get to this stage. If we don't, that means there's still detergent on him and he won't be waterproof. A non-waterproof bird will die once he's back out in the wild."

She touched the mallard's wing and spread it. "See it? Every single feather is comprised of tiny strands bound together by these little barbules. They're hooks, woven so tightly together that water can't get in. Underneath, are the soft, downy feathers that also insulate him, along with his body fat, of course." Dr. Morgan stroked the mallard's wing gently. "They're constantly readjusting the hooks, lining them back up, making sure the insulation's tight. But oil breaks down this armor. The bird preens and preens, trying to rid his feathers of the oil, and, at the same time, he's using up his reserve stores of body fat trying to stay warm. When the fat's gone, he uses up muscle reserves. Many of these birds die from hypothermia before they die of toxic shock from oil ingestion." She cleared a thin film of oil from the mallard's eyes with her fingers and cleared her throat.

"When we're done, we wrap him in a fresh towel and take him over there," she pointed to a set of drying tables near the sink, "and he's blotted and squeezed dry. I'll flush the eyes again and then he goes to rehab where he's placed under a heat lamp. Rehab is back there," Dr. Morgan pointed to a door, "and it's imperative that we limit human interference at that point, so I'll take him back and you guys can fill out the reports, restock the cart and check if there are any birds waiting to be washed."

Dr. Morgan nodded to Hart. "Ready?"

Hart nodded. Lapsley picked up the mallard and placed him in the tub.

⅄

Half an hour later, Hart and Lapsley were in the break room awaiting word on their patient. The team had washed, dried and wrapped the mallard in a dry towel in under twenty minutes, a Rescue Center record. Dr. Morgan was so pleased she actually smiled before whisking the mallard off the drying table to more suitable accommodations, the cozy confines of a holding pen in the "No Humans" zone of the facility, equipped with a tubing solution for rehydration.

"How long did you date her, anyway?" Hart asked.

"Couple years," Lapsley replied.

"A couple years?" Hart was shocked.

"Sshhhh," Lapsley shot back, lowering his voice to a whisper. "What?"

"In the whole time you dated her, did she ever smile?"

"Oh, she smiled," Lapsley said, following Hart's gaze. Dr. Morgan was approaching. "She's got a great smile," he said as Dr. Morgan slid into the seat beside him, a steaming cup of black coffee in her hand.

"Who's got a great smile?" she asked.

"The Mona Lisa," Lapsley replied.

"How's the duck?" Hart asked, changing the subject.

"I think he's going to make it." Dr. Morgan let loose a full-blown smile, big enough to power the mallard's heat lamp. But the brightness was short-lived.

"So, Mr. Hart. I haven't had a chance to read the paper lately. Exactly how many gallons of oil are in the river, choking the life out of my birds and the aquatic life they feed upon?"

Hart had not expected a direct attack, especially after his stellar duck work, and looked befuddled.

Dr. Morgan continued: "You know the oil mixes with the water to form these emulsions that sink below the surface, right? It smothers everything. Fish and crustaceans alike. And it destroys the birds' natural food source in addition to reducing their foraging ability." Dr. Morgan took a sip of her coffee and eyeballed him. "You like lobster, Mr. Hart?"

Apparently, it was Dr. Morgan who had not only the bull's horns, but its hindquarters as well, and she was spinning the animal over her head in tight, concentric circles. Hart had a vague feeling of vertigo, the sense that he was about to fall from a great height and could do nothing to save himself but brace for the fall.

"Ten years ago, two back-to-back spills released approximately a quarter of a million gallons of oil into the Delaware River," Dr. Morgan said. "They say it killed ten thousand birds. I was on staff here then, and I think the number was more likely twice that many. But we'll never really know, will we?"

Hart took a deep breath, conceding. "I'll do what I can to eliminate Akanabi's single-hulled ships, Doctor. I give you my word on it."

"I'll hold you to that, Mr. Hart."

Hart reached a hand across the table and Dr. Morgan shook it, smiling stiffly.

"So, what happens next?" he asked.

"You mean generally?"

"Generally, I'd assume you have another few days of this resource intense provision of medical services," Hart said, "but for the present, I was more interested in the duck."

"Well, he'll hang around in his cozy pen for a day until he's hydrated and eating normally. Feeding will be a challenge since these guys are used to getting it live. From the drying area he'll go to the puddle pen where he'll get to swim in a nice little duckie pool for a while. If he goes anywhere from fifteen to fifty minutes without getting wet, we'll know the washing was successful. If not, it's back to the showers."

"Do you have many that go back to the showers?" Hart asked.

Dr. Morgan shook her head.

"That's why they're so adamant about the training," Lapsley said. "You gotta avoid re-washing. A bird can die from the stress."

"Once their waterproofing's restored, we expose them to ambient air – temperatures comparable to what's outside today. Then Fish and Wildlife bands them, and they're good to go. We release them early in the day into a proper, non-oily habitat, which means we may have to take them some distance from where we found them."

Hart listened, attentive to her tutelage until his cellphone rang. He checked the number and turned to Lapsley.

"I gotta go. Do you mind?"

"Nah. Zenone's gonna be looking for me soon," Lapsley said. He and Dr. Morgan exchanged glances, which Hart deciphered as pent-up longing.

Alyssa turned to Hart and again offered him her hand. "Thanks for all your help this morning." This time, her smile was genuine.

⋏

"Where to?" Lapsley crawled out of the Rescue Center's parking lot, fighting against the pull of some invisible tether. He looked up and down the street, checked his phone then looked both ways again. Hart smiled and glanced at his side mirror. Dr. Morgan was standing outside the building, arms folded against the cold, watching them leave.

"She's still there," Hart said. "You could wave. Beep the horn."

Lapsley's face reddened at the suggestions. He checked the road a third time then peeled out like the high schoolers do, beeping only after he was in the roadway and turning to look only after he was out of Dr. Morgan's sight.

Lapsley drove for several miles, likely trying to outrun his desire, before speaking again. Hart smiled and turned his face to the window, but his own thoughts soon caught up with him. "It's a depressing thing, that job."

"Such a low mortality rate," Lapsley agreed. "Even if the birds survive treatment, they're different after. Like they're on too much caffeine. They eat more, preen more, wash more, everything's more, more, more."

"I thought that was the definition of an American," Hart said, but his delivery was so flat-lined that Lapsley didn't even laugh.

"They don't survive long in the wild long after they've been cleaned. Could just be the handling was enough to cause the change," Lapsley said. "Our mallard's gonna make it, though. I know it."

They drove in silence for several more miles until Lapsley's cell phone rang. He flipped it open one-handed and stuck it in the crook of his neck.

"Lapsley." He listened attentively for half a minute. "All right," he said, before hanging up.

"Tinicum Marsh's clean. You know, the National Wildlife Refuge?" Hart shook his head so Lapsley continued. "Twelve hundred acres of pristine marshland. Home to some endangered species, a bunch of other wildlife. That would have been a nightmare. Getting oil out of a marsh like that. It's the least successful removal of all. So there's some good news." Lapsley drummed the steering wheel. "I heartily embrace good news."

"How do you stay so upbeat? I mean, doing this every day?"

"Glamour." Lapsley grinned. "That's what this life's all about. We OSCs are the paladins of the cleanup world. I sneeze and five people ask me if I need a hankie. Soon it's gonna be impossible to find a hard hat to fit my head. I mean, come on, the best food, accommodations. Who wouldn't like that life?"

"Accommodations?" Hart laughed. "Like that piece of crap command post?"

"Don't be dissin' our digs. It's all in the perception, man. It's all up here." Lapsley tapped his temple lightly three times and smiled.

Hart shook his head, went back to window gazing. "What do I do with all this now?" he asked, as they passed another oil refinery, a black, acrid smoke spewing from its stack.

"Just keep doing your job, man."

"Sucking oil out of the river is not exactly what I was hired to do."

"So go with the flow, if you'll pardon the pun. That's what you're on the planet for. Adaptation. It's what we're all here for. Think of it as one great big evolutionary exercise. First guy to master transmogrification with ease wins. Kind of like reaching nirvana, only with something to do."

"Man, that woman put some kind of spell on you," Hart said.

Lapsley feigned hurt. "Look, you're not going to be able to recover much after last night's storm, so focus on what you got. You're gonna have to landfill it, or do some in situ burning. Or you could mechanically recover what's come out of the river already. Just keeping it out of a landfill is a bonus." Lapsley drummed the steering wheel in time to a song Hart couldn't hear. "Then, after a week or two, when the law of diminishing returns takes effect, we'll close down the operation. In a year or two, you hire some local fishermen to catch you some Delaware River fish. You test 'em and if they're okay, which they likely will be by then given the storms, and old Mama Nature's propensity for recycling, then you present the evidence to the state and ask them to lift the fish ban after which you have a big ol' fish fry, invite all the neighbors and you eat the first fish sandwich yourself. That's assuming you like fish."

"You think this water will be cleared up by then?" Hart asked.

Lapsley equivocated with a shrug. "I hope so. That's all I got, really. Hope. That's all we all got."

CHAPTER 48

*H*art and Sonia *sat in the kitchen of a large, turn of the century farmhouse. Sonia had lost all the "baby weight," those amorphous extra pounds that settle around the hips and lower abdomen and stayed on like an unwanted houseguest. Hart hadn't minded. On Sonia, everything looked good. Seeing her now, though, in her tight, short-sleeved pullover and Levis, he felt the pull of desire and wanted to do something about it. He squeezed her hand and smiled, but she scowled at something across the room. He followed her gaze.*

Bicky. What the hell's he doing here? Bicky smiled complacently at his daughter. On the table was a small turtle, the kind children put inside a terrarium with a little pond, some dirt, gravel, and a few ferns. Hart watched the turtle walk back and forth between his open hands.

"You can't let him do this, David. Don't you see what he's up to?"

Hart strained to listen but didn't understand. Nor did he want to confess his ignorance. If she found out he didn't know what the hell she was talking about, would she leave again? He searched her face for meaning and finding none, returned his attention to the turtle.

"David, he won't stop here. Don't you see? He doesn't care. Not about anyone or anything. Do something. Please."

Do something about what? Hart's brain cast about, attempting to divine meaning, but the more he let loose the lure, the more tangled the lines became. So he just sat there while Sonia scowled, and Bicky smiled like a Jesus wanna-be. He squeezed Sonia's hand again, as if he could intuit her meaning through touch. Tears sprung to her eyes, but the scowl remained intact.

Without warning, Bicky reached across the table and plucked the turtle from Hart's fingerless hold. He jumped up and headed toward the stove. A large pot bubbled away; a gas flame licked the underside of its metal belly and steam wafted up to the ceiling's wooden beams.

"No!" Sonia shouted, pouncing on her father. He whirled away and held the turtle above her head, dangling it there like a schoolyard bully.

"David, please. He kills everything he touches. You've got to stop him." But before Hart could move, Sonia was at Bicky again, pushing and kicking and punching. Annoyed now, the older Coleman shoved his daughter and she crashed into the kitchen door. The rickety latch gave easily; the door flew open and Sonia out with it.

"Nooo!" Hart screamed and jumped over the table reaching the door just as it banged shut. He flung it open and instead of finding his wife lying prostrate on the front stoop, he found a large, fast-moving river. He stared after the river's course dumbfounded, but there was no trace of Sonia.

Hart turned and leaped at Bicky, snatching the turtle from Bicky's hand and replacing it on the table. He put his hands on either side to guard it and watched his father-in-law through narrowed eyes. Bicky pressed forward, but Hart deflected him, his arms forming a barricade. He was desperate to go after Sonia, but Bicky's menacing presence loomed large and Hart knew that if he left, the turtle was soup. Bicky mocked him, trying to break him with derision, but Hart wouldn't blink. Finally, he just stared at the turtle, wide-eyed, babbling something crazy. At first, Hart thought it was a trick, but curiosity beat him down. He looked. The turtle had tripled in size and was still growing.

Bicky ran a tongue over his lips. "Ah, it's going to be even better now."

Hart braced himself for another Bicky attack. He hunkered down and shielded the turtle with his body. There was no assault, just the beep, beep of numbers being punched into a cell phone. He looked up, expecting a trick, but Bicky was, in fact, calling someone.

"What are you doing?" Hart asked.

"What else?" Bicky said. "Calling my lawyer."

The phone pealed and Hart shot upright, looked around the room, disoriented. Bicky was gone and so was the turtle. "Sonia." A lament. The phone rang again, jarring him to the present. He reached over and loosed it from its cradle.

"This is Hart."

"It's … Kitty." Bicky's voice was thick and choked sounding.

"Bicky?" Hart's own voice sounded strangled; trepidation lingered in the ambient air.

"Kitty had an aneurysm. It blew. She's dead." Hart felt the sickening feeling return.

"Come back to Houston … please?"

"I'll be there by late afternoon," Hart said. He hung up the phone, got out of bed and began to pack.

CHAPTER 49

Snow blanketed the fields, which were barren but for the odd bale of rolled hay. The wind whisked through the leafless branches, leaving them creaking and moaning with its passing. With only a week until the winter solstice, the mornings rose dark and still and laden with the musings of Morpheus, still lost in the labyrinth of the dreamy night. Today, the lingering full moon cast just enough light on the earth for a trail to be visible. A lone cross-country skier glided across the top of the hill at the horizon, dipped down below on the opposite side, then resurfaced, crossing the field at odd angles, leaving zigzags in his wake.

Avery stood at the open back door watching Gil ski up and across the top, disappearing intermittently over the other side, a small, barely distinguishable figure in the shadowy dawn. Gil wore Marty's headlight, and Avery watched the light shine and recede, shine and recede.

Avery wore his ski pants and an unzipped jacket. His gloves dangled at his side, his ski boots propped in the corner. His stocking feet curled at the sudden gust of wind that shot through the door.

"Either in or out, huh?" Kori shuffled in, still crusty from sleep, and clutched her robe tightly to her chest, an impenetrable shield against the wintry gust. She headed straight for the coffee pot. She had a long crease down her right cheek where the side of her face had lain, smashed into a rumpled pillow for too long. She started the coffee, grabbed a banana and sat down. Avery closed the door but continue to watch Gil out the window.

"How'd you sleep," Kori asked, her own eyes red and swollen.

"I don't think I did." He turned his haggard face to her. "Or if I did, I don't remember."

"How long's he been out there?"

"Since about four this morning."

"Are you going out?" she asked. Avery shrugged but didn't answer.

"I thought you hated cross-country skiing?" Kori stood and grabbed a mug from the cabinet. "I mean, it's pretty hard core to go out into below freezing weather at 6:30 in the morning just to get an hour of skiing in."

"Gil's out there."

"But if he's been out there since 4 o'clock, it's not exactly like he needs you, is it?" She sat down at the table and fiddled with a stray napkin, rolling it up and unwinding it again and again. "Why'd you let him go out so early? It's so dark."

Avery watched the horizon where his brother had just reappeared on the surface of the world. "It's not like I have complete control over him, Kor. He went out before I got up. I heard him clanging around in the garage trying to get the skis down is all." He turned back to her. "He left mine on the deck." Avery sighed, zipped up his jacket and grabbed his boots. "Did you know we were supposed to get snow?"

Kori yawned and covered her mouth, nodding her head. "School's canceled. I saw it on the news."

Avery laced up his boots and stood. "Bonus." He drew a deep breath before asking his next question. "Do you think it's true?" Concern had etched lines in his face that weren't there the day before, but that was nothing compared to what Despair would do should she get hold of him. Kori picked up the dog tags that were lying in the middle of the kitchen table, pulled the chain out to its full length and rested her fingers upon them. She closed her eyes as if divination could be had by mere touch. She shook her head, slowly at first, and then with more vehemence.

"Me either," Avery said. "I just have this feeling. I hope I'm not making it up." He put on his gloves, pulled his hat down over his ears and eyebrows and opened the door.

Avery?" Kori walked over and stood behind her brother.

"Did Gil have any dreams?" She shrunk an inch into herself as if bracing for a blow.

Avery touched Kori's shoulder and smiled. "I guess I'll find out now," he said, and disappeared into the cold dark of morning.

Kori closed the door behind him, watching until he vanished over the hill.

⅄

The moon, low in the sky and paling more with each creeping minute of dawn, looked like a magnificent deity bestowing blessings upon all who gazed at her. The last of her beneficence left a light touch, a shimmering wake across the snow-covered fields. Even the landfill looked beautiful: a white, proud mountain of refuse. Avery caught up to Gil as he approached the backside of it. They skied together in silence for the last hundred yards until Gil stopped at the foot of the landfill's fence, flicked off his headlamp and jammed his poles into the ground. He stared at the mound of trash, deftly hidden beneath a cloud of white, and began to hum. Only Gil could hum while looking at garbage, Avery thought.

"What are you thinking?" Avery stuck his own poles in the ground and watched the trash pile intently, waiting for something to shatter the tranquility.

"About Daddy," Gil said.

Avery turned to face Gil, the shock of this pronouncement clear on his face. "Really? About Dad? Not about Robbie?"

Gil shook his head, slow and deliberate, back and forth like a metronome.

"Well, what about Dad?" Gil turned Marty's headlamp on again and focused it on a specific spot in the center of a frozen mound.

Avery followed the light and thought he could see a computer monitor, but he was only guessing. He looked at Gil's nose, dripping profusely. Gil didn't seem to notice. Avery grabbed a clean, but crumpled tissue from his coat pocket and pushed it toward his brother who ignored the gesture. Avery held the tissue up to Gil's nose and Gil blew, producing two tissues worth. Avery fumbled for another tissue while still holding the first to Gil's nose. He produced a second, slightly used tissue and brought it to the aid of the first. He wiped Gil's nose and, grimacing slightly, jammed the soggy remnants back into his own pocket.

"Anything else I can do for you?" he asked wryly, one side of his mouth raised in query.

"He wouldn't answer me when I asked about Robbie. I kept asking, 'Daddy, where's Robbie? Is he okay?' and he just kept smiling at me. Then he took me into the barn and showed me the TDU. He fiddled around and made a few adjustments." Gil continued watching the trash pile, still showing no signs of movement. "I think he wants me to finish the machine."

Avery's eyebrows shot up. "Did he say that?"

"He didn't say anything. But I just thought that was what he wanted." Gil pulled a single pole out of the snow then drove it back into the ground. "Do you think maybe Dad doesn't know about Robbie? Like maybe, if Robbie's alive that he can't see him very well or something?" Gil looked at his brother. "Or maybe Robbie doesn't want to be seen. Like maybe he's hiding."

Avery had contemplated this same theory himself but had not voiced it. His brother was canny, knew how to live in the woods off nuts and berries and roots and other queer stuff, knew how to build a fire from two little sticks, a veritable boy scout geekazoid. He would be a great guy to have around in an apocalyptic, end-of-the-world kind of event. But disappearing without a trace from a crowded market in the middle of a suicide bombing attempt, leaving nothing behind but a set of completely unscathed dog tags, well, things seemed a little convoluted, even for Robbie. Still it was a relief to hear someone else voice the opinion. Especially Gil.

"I don't know. I was thinking the same thing myself. We can only hope that if he is still alive, he'll be in touch soon."

Gil nodded. "Will you help me?"

"Absolutely. With what?"

"With the TDU?"

"I thought you didn't want to work on that anymore?"

"Well, I don't because of Dad, you know. But I think … "

Gil's words tumbled out in a flurry, jumbled, yet coherent. "I really don't, but what if that's what he wants, Dad, I mean, and if I didn't do it well then he might be mad at me and maybe he wouldn't visit me anymore so I really should do it but it really gives me the creeps I mean what if those creepy bad guys come back so I need some backup which is why I'm asking if I did would you help me? I'd need, you know, to get the TDU up and running and help get the feedstock from the landfill and, I guess, well maybe it's okay, cause I think Dad wanted it but actually, I don't know what he wanted since he wouldn't use his words, but it seemed like he really — he kept showing me the drawings, over and over, the drawings, and some newer ones that he'd worked on for the refining part. I don't know what he was saying since I never really looked at the refining drawings I was more interested in the TDU so we didn't talk much about it, but … why do you think he just didn't come out and say what he wanted?" Gil said finally, frustrating himself.

Gil's nose was running again and this time he ran his gloved hand underneath it catching most of the watery mucus. Avery grimaced and made a mental note to wash Gil's gloves. He stamped his ski-shod feet on the ground to tamp down the cold creeping up his legs, cold to which Gil seemed impervious.

"I don't know. It's near Christmastime. Maybe he was trying to be the ghost of Christmas future."

"The one with George C. Scott?" Gil smiled. "That one was my favorite."

"C'mon. Let's get moving before my legs freeze off."

"Let's go this way," Gil said, turning toward the woods, the long way home.

Chapter 50

A fairly starved Gil started right in on the plate of eggs, sausages, Tater Tots with ketchup, and toast with butter and raspberry jam that appeared like magic before him. He didn't care whether anyone else would be joining him. He would not be participating in conversation. He could not spare a single brain cell for anything other than the food in front of him and the inner workings of his own mind, occupied as it was, with gears, gaskets and temperature adjustments.

He could see the TDU clearly, behind the eye, all gleaming steel and aluminum, its curves and junctures, the placement of each nut and bolt. He'd studied the drawings for hours, had known since the time his father had asked what needed to be done how to correct the problems, but it was only now, with his father's blessing, that he allowed himself the luxury of dwelling on the actual mechanics of its completion. Still, maybe fixing it was not at all what Marty was trying to tell him.

Gil missed his father terribly and wondered why his belly hurt now, months later, and whether those two things were connected. Maybe it was his Dad's refusal to speak last night that reminded him of the truth of things. Since his death, Marty had so often visited Gil on the astral plane, that magic place where dreams intersect reality, that Gil had tricked himself into believing his father was still alive. But last night, Marty wouldn't talk to him, no matter how much Gil pleaded. And now with Robbie … .

A lump formed in his throat, a sensation he wasn't used to, and he gulped down a mouthful of milk to wash it away.

He wiped his plate clean with the last bite of toast, downed the rest of his milk and belched. Max raised his head, wagged his tail and went back to sleep.

"Gil!" Kori's voice shook him from his reverie and he giggled. Avery stifled a laugh and took a bite of his eggs.

Kori was looking at him weirdly, like his mother used to. The resemblance was amazing, and when Kori stood and gave him a hug, he felt for a moment his mother's arms around him, shuddered as her spirit passed over his bones. She'd want him to sleep, they both would, because his eyes were red and his nose still runny from being outside for so long, and she wouldn't want him to get a cold. Still, he wasn't tired but wired with an unending series of thoughts and fractions of them. He didn't want to sleep; he also didn't want to think anymore, just wanted his mind to wait a little. And he sure as heck didn't want to fight with Kori. Better go upstairs. Pretend to do what she wanted.

"May I be excused?" he asked.

Kori nodded acquiescence. "What are you going to do now? Watch a movie?"

"I'm going to go take a nap," Gil announced.

"Oh, really." Kori raised her eyebrows in disbelief, clearly smelling a rat, but asked nothing further. He smiled at her, mustering the most innocent of facial expressions.

"Bring your plate to the counter then."

Gil obeyed, placing his plate and cup in the sink. "Good night," he said and turned on his heel. He smiled to himself as he left, pleased with the deception. Max jumped up with alacrity and followed Gil out the door.

"I need to run some errands this morning," Kori called after him. "Avery will be here if you need anything, but you probably won't because you'll be sleeping." Gil turned and from the corner of his eye saw Kori and Avery exchange a glance; he feigned obliviousness.

"Okay," Gil said. Mother instinct. They must be born with it. Plans foiled, the smile left Gil's face as he and Max rounded the stairs to his room.

⅄

Gil waited forever while Avery ran the snow blower up and down their winding driveway, and Kori shoveled out the walks. He was waiting for his chance to escape to the barn. He needed to decide whether to fix the TDU and maybe looking at it would help him. He paced the floor, indulging his impatience then sat down on the floor, closed-eyed and cross-legged, concentrating on his breathing like Avery had taught him, but neither helped. After forever and ten minutes, he threw himself on the bed, pulled a blanket up to his chin, and stared at the ceiling. Visions of valves and pistons danced in the part of his cerebral cortex where dreams come to light. Gil heard Kori's engine rev, heard her back out the long driveway and then it got quiet. Gil sighed and drew a deep breath. Patience was not his forte.

"You almost need an oil company," Marty said. "Otherwise, how do you think we'll get the oil to the dealers? UPS?"

Gil laughed. *My father, the card.*

The back door slammed, and Gil knew Avery had come inside. He sat up and looked around, rubbed his eyes. The room was empty.

"Rats." The clock said he'd given the last three hours to Morpheus.

Gil listened at the top of the stairs and heard Avery banging around in the kitchen. He sniffed the ambient air with a deer-like adeptness and his stomach rumbled in response. Heavenly smells wafted toward him, threatening to derail his plans. Melted ham and cheese. Impulse and hunger almost threw him over the railing.

Gil found Avery bent over the toaster oven, fiddling with the sandwich makings inside. He looked at the table set for two and a satisfied smile crossed his face. He snuck up behind his brother and peered over his shoulder.

"Whatcha' doin'?" Gil asked.

Avery jerked, slamming the door to the toaster oven as he did so. "You have got to stop doing that!" he said, turning to his brother in slow motion.

Gil shrugged, smiled. "What's for lunch?"

"Ham and cheese."

"Chips?"

"You know where they are."

"When's Kori coming home?"

"She went to Jack's. It's anybody's guess."

Gil retrieved the chips then watched as Avery pulled the melted deliciousness from the toaster oven. His mouth watered at the sight of his second favorite food in the entire world, his first being roasted pork cooked with loads of garlic, rosemary and sage, and a heaping pile of mashies on the side. Despite his culinary dispositions, Gil hadn't thought much about how indebted he was to the pig. He opened the bag of chips, laying a handful on each plate, rooted around the bag, found and stuffed the biggest chip in his mouth, and sat down.

Avery set a glass of milk in front of him and they ate in silence while Gil did a little happy dance in his chair. He finished his sandwich, downed the milk and raised his plate.

"More sandwich."

Avery raised his eyebrows and looked at Gil point-blank.

"Please," Gil said.

Avery retrieved a second round of sandwiches from the little oven, placing one on each of their plates. Gil leaned in close and sniffed in a lung full of ham and cheese. He held it a moment, before taking a whopper of a bite.

"Avery?"

"Hmmm?"

"Did Robbie really go to Iraq for oil?"

Avery dropped the hot pad on the counter and took his seat. "I don't know. Sometimes I think maybe there were humanitarian reasons, some factors other than economic, but then I think about what the real legacy of the current administration will be and I wake up."

Gil stared at his brother, perplexed. "What are you talking about?"

"Never mind."

Gil rinsed his food down with some milk. "Kori thinks it was for oil."

"Kori's a cynic. But she's probably right." Avery looked over at Gil's crumby, milk-kissed mouth and handed him a napkin. "Does that upset you? I mean, would it upset you more?"

"You mean if he died for oil instead of something else important?"

"Yeah."

Gil nodded, gazing out the window. "Uh-huh. Especially if I can make oil out back."

"Do you think he did?" Avery asked. "Died, I mean."

Gil shrugged. He'd been unable to formulate a coherent opinion on the subject, and all sources of help he might have received, divine or otherwise, weren't talking. They finished their sandwiches in silence.

"You gonna do what Dad said?" Avery asked. "Fix the TDU?"

"I'm not sure yet." Gil shoved a few chips in his mouth but didn't respond.

"If you decide to, I can get a few startup loads of trash."

Gil finished his milk and took his plate to the counter, wiped his mouth with a washcloth and grabbed his coat.

"Hey, Gil?" Gil stopped. Avery stood behind him and put a hand on his shoulder. "I don't think Robbie's … I don't think he's dead."

Gil turned to face Avery who knelt down to eye level. "There's no way to tell for sure. Not until he contacts us. But regardless, the world still needs Dad's contraption. Even if you don't have a reason to build it." Gil gave Avery the briefest of hugs, rounded on his heel and ran out the door.

Chapter 51

Gil lay fast asleep on the hammock in the barn, his face pillowed against Max's smooth, thick coat. The lights were off, and in the late-afternoon dusky, winter light, the figures entwined on the hammock looked like some monstrous, hibernating snow beast. Someone had turned the heat off, most likely by accident; the heat thermostat and the alarm system were side-by-side on the same wall. Gil's breath, that is, the breath that escaped the confines of Max's coat, rose in wispy tendrils mingling with the cold ambient air before dispersing its atoms at random. Gil breathed strong and steady and with purpose; the area of Max's coat surrounding his nose and mouth was heavy with droplets of condensation. It was the breath of one knee-deep in REM sleep, working through the day's problems with the help of divine guidance. Gil's face bore an intense look, which supplanted his usual innocent countenance and his eyebrows furrowed in concentration. He twitched as if throwing off some distasteful thought and buried his hands and face deeper in the folds of Max's warmth. Max had grown considerably in the months since they'd rescued each other: Max from life as a vagabond, and Gil from loneliness and despair. Max's extra pounds gave Gil all the more surface area to burrow beneath. Gil tossed his head vigorously from side-to-side, his dream angels must have been working overtime; what they revealed must have sat squarely on his chest, for he groped and clawed at it as if to eradicate some pain. The behemoth beside him did not jump, simply looked back at his master to see if all was in order, yawned, then laid his head down again. He returned to doggy dreamland just as Gil opened his eyes to see his brother staring at him.

"I didn't hear you come in," Gil said.

"That's 'cause you don't pay attention," Robbie said. Max lifted his head and barked. He and Robbie cast appraising glances at each other. Gil patted Max's hindquarters and, satisfied there was no threat, Max went back to sleep.

"Where were you?"

"Inside. Doin' stuff." Robbie inclined his head toward the house.

Gil stared at Robbie as if he were a mirage. He blinked his eyes hard and watched as Robbie strolled over to Marty's drawings on the table. He thumbed through, studying them with intense curiosity before turning his attention back to Gil. "It's a few days' worth of work, you know."

"I know."

"Then why don't you finish it?"

Gil shrugged. "It's not that."

"What, then?"

Gil sat up and studied his brother's face. He looked thinner than Gil remembered and his uniform hung limply on his frame.

"Was it hard?"

Robbie nodded, a grave look momentarily alighted on his handsome face.

"Are you home for good now?"

Robbie shook his head, barely perceptible. "I still have some things to do."

Robbie sat down on Marty's swivel chair and pushed off hard. The chair spun. Robbie pulled his legs in close and coasted to a halt. Since they were children, the Tirabi kids played this game, seeing who could spin the most times around with one push. Being the smallest, and the lightest, Gil got the most out of his spin and held the all-time record at just under four complete revolutions. Robbie pushed off again and made it two revolutions.

Gil watched him as happy and sad duked it out in his belly. "Do you still love us?"

Robbie abruptly placed both feet on the ground and focused on his brother. "I've never loved anything more in my life."

They eyed each other a moment and then Gil smiled, his lips set in a tight thin line. He thought he might cry.

"Get to work, little brother," Robbie said and pushed off as hard as he could. He tucked his knees in and was spinning around once, twice, three times, when the door opened and a cold blast of arctic air preceded Avery into the barn.

Avery stood, dressed for skiing, his nose dripping. He reached for the box of tissues on the table by the door and blew profusely. Gil bolted upright and, flush with excitement, barked at his brother.

"I can't believe you're blowing your nose at a time like this." Gil pointed to the chair and stared at Avery incredulously.

"You have a better time?" Avery responded, following Gil's finger pointing to the empty chair. "Maybe I should wait until it drips down the front of my coat and then do it."

Gil looked at the empty chair, already slowed to a halt, before lying back down on the hammock. He blinked and stared at the ceiling drawing quick, raw breaths.

"Hey, what's the matter?" Avery was at his side in a flash.

Water ran from Gil's eyes, cascaded down to form small pools in his ears. Gil plunged a finger in each side to stop the deluge. Avery sat down on the edge of the hammock, upsetting the equilibrium. Max groaned but shifted his weight.

"Did you see something when you walked in?" Gil asked.

Avery looked around the room then shook his head.

"You didn't notice anything strange?"

"No." He felt the edge in Gil's voice and a chill ran up his spine. He looked around uncomfortably, his breath billowing out in balls of white mist.

"I do notice the heat's off," Avery said. Gil shivered involuntarily and huddled closer to Max for warmth. "Are you going to tell me what happened?"

Gil looked at his brother for a moment and buried his head in Max's fur.

"I'm not sure." The voice emanating from the fur was timid and full of uncertainty.

Minutes passed and Avery was beginning to wonder whether Gil had fallen asleep, huddled beneath a blanket of fur, when without warning, Gil bounded from the hammock, dropping Avery to the floor and leaving Max to swing in the breeze.

"Stay, Max." Max whined, but Gil stifled him with a look. The dog put his head down on his paws and watched as his master zipped up his coat and donned his gloves and hat, the one with the jingle bells on it.

"Let's go skiing," Gil said. And before Avery could answer, he was out the door.

⅄

The tractor ran at a cruising rate of seven miles per hour through the woods. Gil and Avery arrived at the backside of the landfill in ten minutes. The Stahls had never put a fence around this side of the fill, a trash picker's mecca, precisely because there was no one here interested in picking trash. Until Marty.

Avery cut the engine, set the brake and hopped off. He grabbed a shovel and handed Gil one. Avery groaned. The thought of digging through trash made his stomach queasy. For some strange reason, it had relaxed his father.

Avery pulled a pair of leatherwork gloves from his back pocket and dug a few test holes, looking for buried treasure. Some worthy items lay scattered on top: a computer monitor, a box of clothes, a pair of sneakers. This was the newer part of the landfill that Jim Stahl, Jr. had worked toward the end of his reign — before EPA shut him down last year — and much of the trash still retained its original shape. In some of the older parts the refuse had already turned to sludge. Gil said the TDU could handle the sloppy mess, but Avery wasn't sure if his nose was up to the task, so he stuck to things that looked like earlier versions of themselves.

He adjusted the night light on his head and began loading trash with speed and dexterity, musing over the potential the TDU had to eliminate landfilling in his lifetime and thinking about Jim Stahl, Jr., their neighbor, and the son of the man unwittingly responsible for providing them with this bonanza of refuse.

Like a miniature volcano, the landfill burped releasing a pocket of foul-smelling methane gas into the ambient air. Avery jumped, coughed and covered his nose. Gil giggled.

Gil could feel rather than see the aquifer, bubbling as it flowed beneath the landfill, a toxic soup thick with carcinogens as unpronounceable as they were hazardous to the health. He stood up, stretching the last hour's hard labor from his chicken wings that passed for shoulders. He planted the shovel in the ground and gave the area another cursory view. The trailer was already heaping, but Gil spied a box of recyclables, plastic bottles and aluminum cans, and couldn't leave without them. Made from petroleum, recyclable plastics were the TDU's gold bullion. They yielded the highest quantity and best grade of oil. And Marty's oil, already of superior quality, bumped up a notch each time the TDU ate a batch of recyclables. He tossed the shovel in the trailer, grabbed the box, and took a seat, hesitating a moment before setting it on his lap, the only free space left.

"What a waste of time," Gil said.

"What's a waste of time?" Avery asked tossing his shovel in the trailer.

"People spend hours every week recycling. And it ends up in a landfill."

"That's 'cause there's no market. We need a law. A federal law. And mandatory labeling. Then a milk container could be a milk container again. And a cat litter container could be a cat litter container again," Avery said, getting behind the wheel of the tractor. "Right now they don't know what's what. You can't make food grade plastic out of lesser grades. That's just the science of it. Besides," he said, starting the engine, "it would be political suicide to declare recycling a failure. It makes people feel like they're doing their part."

"So even if your SUV only gets eleven miles to the gallon, you can still feel good?"

"Right." Avery grimaced at the slime now on Gil's pants. "Hey, now when I call you a slimeball, I won't be lying."

Avery turned the tractor around and headed for home.

⅄

Kori sat at the kitchen table, cordless phone in hand, rifling through Ruth's telephone book. Up to the F's, she thumbed down the list, then dialed. Avery and Gil walked in, the twenty degree air preceding them. They stamped their feet, flinging snow off their boots and leaving it to puddle on the kitchen rug. Kori scowled at both the intrusion and the mess, throwing a dishtowel at Avery's head. Avery wiped up the floor while Kori turned her attention back to her task.

"Mrs. Friedler? Hi. This is Kori Tirabi. I'm calling to remind you about the public meeting tonight at the high school. Are you going?"

"Hey, Gil," Avery said. "You want some hot chocolate?"

Kori waved Avery away, shooting him a look that said take your conversation elsewhere. Avery asked Gil the question again but silently as he pantomimed liquid being poured into a cup and someone stirring. Gil responded in kind, rubbing his belly with huge circular motions and Kori giggled.

"Oh no, I wasn't laughing at you, Mrs. Friedler. I know hemorrhoids can be dreadfully indisposing, well actually, I don't have firsthand knowledge, but my brother Avery suffers from them periodically."

Avery's eyes shot up and he threw the soggy dishtowel back at her. She ducked and it missed. Avery bowed low, making a sweeping motion with his arm indicative of a good loser.

"C'mon, Gil. Let's see what's on TV. We'll deal with her later." He grabbed Gil by the shoulder and steered him in the direction of the living room.

"Well, that's great. We'll see you tonight," Kori said. She hung up and flipped Ruth's directory to the G's.

Chapter 52

Twenty-five years ago, when Ruth and Marty Tirabi purchased their ten-acre plot with money from one of Marty's inventions, they thought they'd landed in heaven. Unfortunately, the realtor who sold them the property neglected to tell them that beyond the tranquil, bucolic edge of their horizon, a toxic stew was brewing beneath the landfill. At that time, no one thought much about the environmental hazards associated with home buying. But then the intermittent smell wafted in, the one hundred and fifty-seven single family dwellings in the Hickory Hills development next door rose up like a tsunami, and carloads of benzene, toluene, and perchloroethane joined truckloads of mercury, lead, nickel, perchloroethate, and a whole host of other hazardous substances with equally unpronounceable names, forming carpools and marching in formation to the aquifer below. The caravan traveled slowly, inch by careful inch, undiscovered until a quarter century later.

And water being what it is — ubiquitous by any standard — the contamination leaching into the groundwater from the landfill did not confine itself to any legal borders, but spread throughout the entire aquifer, a massive thing that provided water to the Stahls, the Tirabis and their neighbors in the new Hickory Hills development. Hickory Hills attracted wealthy city dwellers that pined for pristine country air and didn't know most farmers' propensity not only to sell what they grew, but also, to rent what they owned to cover the spread. The Senior Jim Stahl had covered his spread by renting a portion of his property to the county to be used as a landfill. And since there were few, if any, instances where one person's actions failed to affect the lives of others, Jim's contaminated water spread to his neighbors' homes and discreetly took up residence there, finding permanent quarters in the kitchens and bathrooms of all one hundred and fifty-seven single family dwellings.

Lawyers advised clients in hushed, confidential tones to get a blood test, and a wave of pandemonium spread through the development as test after test came back positive for cancer. Children with their developing immune systems were hit especially hard. The local newspapers did their part to raise the level of hysteria. Gossip spread rumors, and rumors spread like middle-aged waistlines, forcing the EPA to mount a public awareness campaign. EPA went door-to-door, offering all the neighbors of Hickory Hills bottled water until the in-house filtration systems could be installed. But in many instances, it was too late.

Jim Stahl, Sr. had started landfilling in 1975. At the time, rivers were catching on fire, and leaded gas was creating a smoke screen out on the U.S. highways, leaving more to worry about than a few hundred thousand pounds of unprotected trash. But if the Senior Stahl had complied with even the most primitive dumping laws in effect at the time he had started landfilling, the Hickory Hills development might not be on the Superfund list today, and Jim Stahl, Jr. would not be mired in the muck that his father's landfill had become. The National Priorities List was a list of the nation's most contaminated Superfund Sites. Making that list was not something to write home about.

Over the years, corrective measures were put into place — a bit of cover here, some plastic to act as leachate collection there — but no one anticipated the rapid growth of the surrounding communities or looked at the scheme of the landfill in its entirety. Jim's father retired, passing the whole problem on to his son, and Jim took to greeting government inspectors at the door with a shotgun.

Several months and meetings later, EPA dispatched an On-Scene Coordinator, an OSC, who directed two dozen people dressed in hazmat suits, moon suits as Vera, Jim's wife, called them, to construct a temporary cap over the landfill. The cap was like a big Rubbermaid mat comprised of heavy-duty geosynthetic material. For three weeks, backhoes, track hoes, bobcats, bulldozers and cranes dotted the landscape. When the temporary cap was complete, the contractors fenced the front half in, packed up and drove away, leaving the seething menace to percolate below and promising to send the culpable parties along to finish the job soon. Two years later, the temporary cap, held in place by used tires strung together with rope, had begun to show its age and the responsible parties had yet to come clean up their mess.

Chapter 53

Kori and Jack lay huddled together, partially clothed, a single throw covering them. A soft click preceded the quiet, familiar musings of NPR's Terry Gross. They had failed to draw the curtains before retiring for an hour or so of love and sleep, and Jack cracked one eye open and peered out the window into the expectant night air. Snow flurries added to the soft blanket already on the ground, and he groaned at the menacing, orange-grey sky. He rolled over and checked the alarm.

"Kor. Wake up." He nudged her gently, but she didn't respond. "Kori. It's time to go." He bit her shoulder gently and her eyes flew open.

"Huh. What?" Kori sat up on one elbow and blinked, trying to orient herself.

"What day is it?" Kori stared wide-eyed out the window, her unseeing eyes darting back and forth across the night sky. Jack grinned.

"It's Thursday. You have to bake an apple pie."

"Apple pie?" Kori turned to look at him but darkness hid his features.

"Two of them." This time he laughed, and Kori woke up. She checked the alarm and fell back down on the pillow.

"Oh, the public meeting." She rubbed a hand over her eyes and coughed. "I really didn't know where I was for a minute."

"I could tell." Jack lay back down and pulled her in close. "And you said you'd bake me two apple pies." He kissed her then rose to pull on his jeans. In their earlier haste, they had removed only part of their clothing.

"Where you goin'?"

"To work." He buckled his belt then sat down to put on his boots.

"I thought you were done for the day?"

"Installing home brains, yeah." Jack nodded toward the window. "But now it's snowing. People will need me to plow them out."

"It's barely a flurry."

"They're calling for another four to six inches."

"By tomorrow. Not in the next two hours."

"Hey. I gotta make money, right?"

"Jack! It's a side business, for God's sake. You said you were only going to do it until your other business got off the ground. Well, it's off the ground. You can stop now."

"Not tonight, I can't."

"You're just doing this to get out of coming to the public meeting!"

Jack laced up his boots, leaned over and kissed her on the head.

"I'll be back after I'm through."

"Don't bother." She kicked at him, pushing the blanket off in the process, and stomped past him, retrieving her clothes as she headed for the door.

"Kori, come on."

"Bastard," she said, and slammed the door behind her.

⋀

The public meeting wasn't scheduled to start until seven, but the controversy surrounding the landfill and the effectiveness of the citizens' group, helped along by the flurry of Kori's afternoon calls, brought the crowd out early and in droves, snowy weather notwithstanding.

The high school auditorium had seating capacity for two hundred people. Kori, Avery and Gil stood at the back, scanning the room for seats together, a commodity in short supply.

"Can't I just go home?" Gil asked.

"Gil, what's the big deal? It's a couple hours of your life," Kori said. She turned to face Avery in an appeal for assistance. He shrugged.

"He wants to watch Star Trek," Avery said, feeling more inclined toward Gil's preference himself.

"Star Trek is on fifty times a week on seventeen different channels," Kori said. She bent down, coming face-to-face with her brother. "But this ... this is a chance to make a difference ... this only happens once or twice, and it's really, really important. So come on." She dug in her pocket and pulled out a handful of Tootsie Roll Midgees. Gil smiled and reached for the proffered sweet, but Kori snapped her fingers shut.

"I was saving these for later, but I guess we need them now. If you take them, you have to stay and not whine and complain about wanting to leave. Okay?"

Gil nodded and she opened her hand. He grabbed every last one, accepting her gift as a compromise. Avery held out his hand, and Gil reluctantly handed over a single Tootsie Roll. Buoyed by chocolate, they followed Kori down the aisle in search of seats.

They found them near the front. Aunt Stella's coat, scarf and brilliant red hat lay draped in varying states of repose across four seats where Aunt Stella sat as border guard. She waved madly when she saw them, her knitted brow relaxing. Kori glanced around, scanning the auditorium again, looking for something a little farther back – in the event Gil started acting up, she wanted to be able to make an unobtrusive getaway – but the place was packed to overflowing with groups of people lining the walls. She turned to say something to Avery, but the boys had already made their way into the aisle and she had no choice but to follow. Gil took the seat next to Aunt Stella, who always traveled with treats in her pockets.

Kori leaned over and gave her a kiss. "Thanks for saving seats."

Aunt Stella waved it off as if it were no big deal, but given the general mood in the room, Kori knew it was a feat almost Herculean in nature.

"Where's Jack?" Aunt Stella asked.

Kori shrugged and grimaced; Aunt Stella's next question was interrupted.

"Excuse me? Is this seat taken?" Kori jerked around to see a handsome young man standing there. She frowned and smiled at the same time.

"Ah, no. Decidedly not," she replied.

"You don't remember me, do you?"

"Should I?" Kori asked. The young man smiled and held out his hand.

"Chris Kane. We went to high school together."

"Oh my God." Kori gave him the once over as surreptitiously as possible. Whatever resemblance this guy had to the Christopher "D-for- Dork" Kane that she knew in high school had long since passed. "You look … "

"Different?" He nodded. "That's what everyone says. Late bloomer, I guess. Plus I started working out."

"I'll say. What are you doing now?"

"I'm a correspondent for *The Philadelphia Inquirer*," he smiled, holding up the notebook in his hand.

"Hmmm," Kori managed, nodding in acknowledgment. She turned to find Aunt Stella smiling at her with all the wisdom of a crone and felt the blush rise in her cheeks. Gil and Avery were too engrossed in the taffy Aunt Stella had given them to pay her any mind. She glanced at her watch and turned back to Chris Kane, a bright, full smile on her face.

⚔

Kori spent the next thirty minutes engrossed. Chris proved engaging, and as expected given his occupation, a good listener, something Jack was not. Jack always nodded politely, interjecting when he thought appropriate based on Kori's non-verbal cues, but this guy consumed her words. He even took notes. Kori felt a thrill run through her abdomen. She stole a glance at her brothers. Gil was working a Gameboy while Avery and Aunt Stella, their heads bowed together, spoke in conspiratorial tones.

"So. What's your take on all this?" Chris asked.

"Do you really want to know?" Kori responded.

"Of course."

There was so much she wanted to tell him, stuff Ruth had weaned them on, always talking to them like they were smaller versions of the adults they would become. Since Kori could talk, her mother had held nothing back. Discussions ranging from the world's political machinations to the nature of life and death were commonplace. Ruth was no artist, but it was her love of it that set Kori on her chosen path. In that instant, Kori was no longer sure where Ruth left off and she began and suddenly realized that was the way of it. We either become our parents, their prides and prejudices, or we run far and fast in the opposite direction. And right now, Kori, like Ruth, was finding it hard to keep her mouth shut.

Apparently everything Kori told Chris Kane was fascinating because he'd recorded all of it in his notebook. She talked about everything from the birth of the landfill and the spread of the deadly plume of noxious chemicals to her own personal tragedies, including the mysterious death of her parents and her current position as matron of the house. She concluded with the tragic, but as yet unverified, death of her brother.

Chris wrote at a furious clip. "Whew. All right, give me a chance to catch up."

Kori waited for him to pause and when he did, he looked at her with new eyes, ones that said they wanted to stuff her in his pocket and keep her safe.

"Okay," he said. "Go ahead."

"It's these corporations that are the problem. And the government's in bed with them. They make it cheaper to buy virgin products by giving no incentive to buy used, like we're never going to run out of the new stuff. It's a pain to separate the wheat from the chaff of recyclables, I know that, but it could be a lucrative pain with the right incentives. And what about the trees? They recycle all our carbon dioxide. The fewer trees we have, the harder it is to breathe. Is it any wonder asthma in children is at an all-time high?" She bounced her knee up and down involuntarily. "People act like the environment is negotiable. Just wait. Freak weather is only the tippy-top of the iceberg. Floods, droughts, lack of food supply. Talk about end of days." She snorted self-righteously, her mother's blood rushing through her body, and folded her hands in her lap, concluding her tirade.

"But the science is contradictory. Maybe they just don't know," Chris opined, smiling.

"Bull. If the government really wanted to change the way the world did business, rather than continue to let the few loot the common resources of the many, it could give tax breaks to the high-minded companies, the ones that did business with sustainable development in mind. Don't even get me started on public lands. The government is selling our public resources at pennies on the dollar to the corporations that curry the most favor, i.e., that donate the most election dollars. Those are our lands, our children's lands. And they shouldn't be for sale."

She felt the truth of her own words and believed them with a force she'd never experienced before this moment. And whether it was this force or the fact that Kori felt woefully inadequate to carrying on Ruth's legacy, she closed her mouth, because if she said one more word, she would break down and cry.

Lucky for her, the public meeting began as a speaker from EPA stepped to the podium. "Good evening, ladies and gentlemen. If we could have your attention." The EPA representative, Stefanie Pierson, stood at the podium as everyone took their seats. The murmuring of the crowd died out like ripples spreading across a pond. A half-dozen agency officials sat on stage with Stefanie, each with a microphone. She smiled before continuing. "We're from the government and we're here to help." A brief spurt of laughter, some mixed with derision, had the intended ice-breaking effect.

"They've obviously done this before," Chris said, turning to smile at Kori, giving her a glimpse of his brilliant green eyes.

"As you know, we're here tonight to lay out our findings with regard to the Stahl landfill and to draw you a road map as to what you can expect in the future. You, as the public, have a right to be part of these decisions, and we would also like to encourage you to exercise that right by expressing your comments either here or in writing."

"What about our right to clean drinking water?" Andrew Dodd shouted. He was a first cousin to Jim Stahl. He sat way in the back, but his voice carried far and away over the din of the crowd. A general murmur of agreement swept the room like a wave.

Stefanie Pierson didn't flinch. "You absolutely have every right to clean drinking water, clean air, clean soil, a clean environment. That's the law. But you've got to help us help you."

"How the hell you gonna help us? That damn aquifer's so polluted even the fish can't live in it." The crowd rumbled in agreement, the din in the auditorium growing louder.

"Sir. First of all, an aquifer is below ground and fish don't live in it. Microbes, yes. But not fish. I do take your meaning, however. And if you could just give us a minute to run through the chosen alternatives that came out of the Record of Decision ... "

"A minute?! A minute!" Jim Stahl burst into the room pushing a wheelchair, amidst a cacophony of bottles and tubing. Gasps shot through the room when the audience got a look at what had become of the once healthy and vital Vera Stahl.

"I'll give you a damn stinkin' minute. But who's going to give that minute back to my wife, huh? Is it you? Or you?" Jim pointed an accusatory finger at each of the government representatives. "How about you?" He was only halfway down the aisle, his progress hampered by the many bottles hanging from the wheelchair: salines, antibiotics, and, from the looks of Vera Stahl, morphine. Vera looked one step away from needing a hospice nurse and clearly didn't know where she was, which is probably why Jim got away with displaying her in such a vulgar and obtrusive fashion like some circus freak.

It was at this point in the proceedings that all hell broke loose.

⅄

The public meeting broke up sometime after 11:00 p.m. with both hosts and participants showing signs of exhaustion. Jim Stahl's tactic of putting his wife on display worked well initially, getting the crowd riled to a fever pitch, but the blame worked its way around again when neighbors suggested that if Jim's father would have complied with any one of the missives sent from Pennsylvania Department of Environmental Protection then the Hickory Hills development might not be sitting atop a despoiled aquifer. Kori was grateful the evening hadn't been reduced to fisticuffs. In fact, real progress had been made as the EPA and DEP outlined their plan. The water in the aquifer would be pumped out of the ground, run through a carbon filter and returned, clean, to the aquifer, the same theory Marty had used on the family's in-house filtration system. The downside was that the treatment would likely bring the cost of the remedy up to the forty million dollar range and could take as long as twenty-five years to complete.

EPA told the residents of Hickory Hills to continue drinking and cooking with bottled water while their well water was to be used for the rest. Kori wondered about the wisdom of this – daily bathing would mean daily absorption of contaminants through the skin – and was about to raise the issue when Vera Stahl began coughing so violently that those in attendance thought that she might just be hacking her last breath. When she regained her composure, Jim gave over to the evil glares and took her home.

Gil had fallen asleep during the meeting, a deep REM sleep, which followed his inhalation of a handful of Tootsie Rolls, taffy, and half a dozen mini Reese's Peanut Butter Cups, courtesy of Aunt Stella. Aunt Stella had not plied Gil with that much chocolate. He'd found the mother lode while she was chatting and worked it until her coat pockets sagged, depleted. Aunt Stella turned after a long discussion with a neighbor to see a pile of wrappers in Gil's lap and him out cold. She flashed Kori a guilty look, collected the trash and covered Gil with her coat.

Gil was in the car with Avery now, wide-awake and fidgety. He'd have trouble falling asleep tonight, but Kori would worry about that when she got home. Chris Kane had followed her out to the parking lot and waited while she started the car. They stood in front of Ruth's minivan, awkward and antsy, trying to say goodbye. Gil honked the horn and Kori jumped. He was showing signs of driving away himself so she turned to Chris Kane.

"It was great seeing you again, Chris. I hope you do our meeting justice."

"Which meeting would that be?" Chris asked.

Kori blushed and turned away, embarrassed.

"Would you mind . . . I mean, I was thinking that a story on your brother and his, what did you call it? A TDU? That a story on his machine would make good copy for the business section. What do you think?"

"I'm not sure." Kori looked back at Gil, jumping around in the back seat more like a monkey than the young man who held keys to the world's better future. "I told you someone set our porch on fire. We don't know if those two things are related. I don't want anything else to happen." For the third or fourth time tonight, Kori intuited that Chris Kane might want to lean over and kiss her, but maybe that was just wishful thinking.

"If you're worried about it, the best thing you can do is get it out in the open. The more people who know about it, the better chance you have of staying safe."

"Can I think about it?" Kori asked.

Chris nodded. "I'll call you in a couple days then."

"Okay," Kori said, looking over her shoulder "I gotta go now."

"Sure," Chris replied. Kori offered her hand, but instead of shaking it he kissed it.

Chapter 54

Three nights later, the doorbell rang and Gil and Max ran to answer it. Chris Kane stood at the door with a bouquet of flowers in one hand and a small bag of gourmet dog treats in the other. Gil turned toward the stairs and yelled, "Kori! Time to go." He turned back to Chris, hand on the knob, body blocking the doorway. He did not invite him in, just stared at him while Max sniffed the bag.

"Oh, yeah," Chris said. "These are for Max."

Gil opened the bag and, without taking his eyes off Chris, tossed a biscuit in a high arc. Max made a mad dash across the room, snatching it from the air. One corner of Gil's mouth quirked up when Max took the first crunching bite, but his gaze didn't waver.

Kori appeared and Chris sighed from relief and appreciation. Kori smiled, waved and disappeared into the kitchen. After a few more moments, Gil took the flowers and went to join his sister, but when Chris took a step to follow, Max ceased his crunching and growled.

"Oh, they're beautiful," Chris heard her say from the kitchen. "Do me a favor and put these in water?" He heard the smacking of lips as cheeks were kissed.

"Avery should be home by ten. Gil needs to go to sleep by then."

"Awww, Kori," Gil whined.

"All right. Ten thirty." Apparently that pleased Gil because Chris heard no argument.

"You be careful now."

An older female voice, one Chris couldn't identify.

"I will." Another kiss. "Thanks, Aunt Stella." Ah, yes. The neighbor.

"Well, whether you're early or late, you know where you'll find me."

"Asleep on the couch and pretending not to be." More laughter and then she was standing before him, smiling.

"What are you doing in the doorway?" Kori asked, the smile brightening.

"Waiting for you. What else?" A hundred watt smile graced his face.

Kori laughed and grabbed his arm and he led her away.

⅄

"The more you delve into this stuff, the more that comes up," Aunt Stella said. She and Gil sat at the kitchen table amidst the remnants of glasses of milk and cookie crumbs. Aunt Stella shuffled a deck of Tarot cards, tapped them tight and placed them in front of Gil. "That's why people keep all their little secrets and don't want to bother with them. It's just too much for some to think about." She smiled at Gil. "You're still young, though. How many secrets could you possibly have?"

"Now what do I do?" Gil asked, impatient.

"Cut the cards three times to the left and then stack them up again on the pile to the right." Gil did as instructed and waited on Aunt Stella's next move. "We're just going to do a short past, present, future reading right now rather than go through the whole song and dance of a lifetime reading. Although … " She placed a hand under her chin and played with an errant whisker, something her eyebrow tweezers had missed. She furrowed her brows, further accentuating the small, almost scar-like indentation that had formed over the years in the center of her eyebrows as a result of this exact facial expression. "Nah, let's just do this." Waving a pudgy hand to erase all contrary thoughts, she placed it on top of the cards, fanning them across the table before Gil. Although Aunt Stella had several Tarot decks at home, she preferred Aleister Crowley's Thoth Tarot Deck as it conveyed more of a feeling of beneficence on the reader than say, the Egyptian Tarot that to her mind was overly preoccupied with the twin themes of death and destruction.

"Pick three cards and place them right to left facing down."

Gil acquiesced and looked up, doe-eyed at Aunt Stella, waiting for the next instruction. She pushed the remainder of the deck together in a pile and set it aside. Had any of the clergy members, all males, of the Greek Orthodox Church to which Aunt Stella belonged been here to witness such adroit familiarity with the work of Satan, they would have blushed crimson and then blue for lack of oxygen. But despite the ecclesiastical indoctrinations of the church, it could not, for all its gumption, usurp such traditions, steeped in mysticism and superstition that had survived among Greek women since the seers and high priestesses of the temple brought to light the oracles at Delphi.

"You know, my mother had the Sight. She could tell you who was on the phone the minute it rang."

"Wow. Really?" Gil asked. "I wish I could do that."

"You can. You just need focus. And some training." Aunt Stella tapped the first of the three cards Gil had turned over. "My sister inherited my mother's gift. She can read the cards just by looking at them. Not me, though. I need the book." She flipped through *The Tarot Book*, by Angeles Arrien, its pages worn and rounded from overuse. She placed her hand reverently on the cover and closed her eyes. "My second bible," she said, opening her eyes. "Shall we start?"

Aunt Stella picked up Gil's first card. "This is your recent past."

"Why didn't you get your Mom's gift?"

"It only goes to one woman in the family, usually the first born, but that varies. The others get some things, sympathetic leanings at the least, but usually only one gets the whole enchilada."

The enchilada reference triggered a visceral reaction, and Gil's stomach grumbled loudly. Aunt Stella pushed her basket of treats his way and looked up the first card in the Angeles book. Gil pulled out a white-chocolate chip and macadamia nut cookie, so loaded with nuts that there was barely enough dough to hold the cookie together.

"What happens if there are no girls?"

"Sometimes it skips a generation. Although boys can get it, too, if that's what you're asking. And sometimes it does run through the male line. Your father's told me more than once about your grandmother. Apparently she had it. I think he was always a little disappointed that he didn't have a full-fledged dose of it, although he was very intuitive, especially for a man. Still, he didn't rise to your level." Aunt Stella reached across the table and squeezed Gil's hand. "He was so proud of you."

Gil pulled out another cookie.

"That's enough now. You're not going to be able to sleep."

"Yes I will." He bit into it while Aunt Stella read Gil's first card.

"The Six of Swords. Excellent. And not surprising, actually. The Six of Swords represents science." She showed Gil the page in the book depicting the card as if that were sufficient to prove its meaning. "Objective communication is represented by the planet Mercury. See it there at the top. Then there's Aquarius at the bottom, and it's associated with 'originality, innovation and pioneering work.'" She squeezed Gil's arm and smiled. "This is good, Gilly. It symbolizes the creative mind that pulls ideas from unexplainable sources of inspiration and communicates them in a way people can understand without feeling threatened."

"It's the TDU! You see the TDU in the cards!"

"Right there in a full-color spectrum of light," Aunt Stella said. Gil allowed himself a moment's smile but replaced it with a stern countenance.

"Does it say how it'll do?" He bounced the heel of his foot up and down, the ball of his foot stationary on the floor, a habit born of nervousness.

"Hhmmmm. I'm surprised." Aunt Stella raised her eyebrows at him. "You usually don't care about those things."

Aunt Stella locked eyes with him, a penetrating gaze; he looked down and studied the lines on his hands. She moved over to his side of the table, turned his face to hers.

"You're not your father. You can only do what you can. I know you feel the burden of trying to save the world for him. And your mother. You can't help but get that from your parents. But Gilly, you're only ten, honey, and practically still a baby." She squeezed Gil then released him so she could look in his eyes. "He'll be proud of you no matter what you do." Aunt Stella placed Gil's head on her massive chest, and he shed a few tears.

"I thought you said you weren't psychic?" Gil said, sitting up to wipe his eyes.

"Well, maybe just a little." Aunt Stella blushed and smiled. Gil reached for another cookie then stopped in mid-swipe and looked up at Aunt Stella first, the question in his smile.

She sighed. "All right, but that's it."

Gil stared at the Six of Swords as he chewed. "What else does it say?"

"I don't know. Why don't you turn over another one?"

He flipped a card to see a man hanging upside down, bound at the ankle by a snake hanging from an Egyptian Ankh. He dropped the card. "Am I going to die?"

"Ah, the Hanged Man," Aunt Stella said. "No, you're not going to die, but you have to forget about everything you are if you want to move past the ego to a place where things really start happening. Break old habits. Release your fear. You'll do great things."

"But I don't feel afraid of anything. I mean, sometimes I'm afraid of ghosts, but only the ones I don't know, and sometimes the dark, but only if Max isn't around." At the mention of his name, Max raised his head, opened his mouth, revealing a full set of molars, and yawned. Gil scratched him behind the ears. Max put his head down and went back to sleep.

"How about this? The only limitations on you right now — since this card deals with the present — are those you put on yourself. *Capice?*"

Gil nodded. "What's the last one say? The future card?"

"Turn it over."

Gil popped the last bite of cookie in his mouth and flipped the card.

"The Seven of Wands. Excellent."

"What's that mean?"

"It means stand by what you believe. Don't compromise. Trust your intuition and don't settle for less."

Gil sighed, folded his hands on his lap and looked at the cards. "Do they say anything else? Because I'm not sure I understand."

Aunt Stella smiled and reached for the deck. She handed them to Gil who wrapped his hands around them. "Concentrate," she said. He closed his eyes for several moments and then put the cards on the table. "Now fan them out and pick one."

Gil flipped over a card from the middle of the deck, The Star, a card from the major arcana. Aunt Stella smiled.

"This just iterates what we've already covered. Go forth and create. Be the conduit, the gateway for the light to come through you and out into the world. Trust yourself and don't be afraid to shine."

"Is that it?" Gil put his hands under his chin and slumped in his chair. "Aunt Stella, how can I do this by myself if I'm only ten?"

"What about Avery? Can't he help you?"

"Yes, but … ." Gil looked around behind him to make sure Avery hadn't suddenly appeared out of thin air and whispered to Aunt Stella, "I think I need more help than that."

"I don't know, Gilly. Let's see." Aunt Stella pointed to the cards. "One more."

Gil scanned the row of cards, his eyes running up and down, his fingers barely touching them until of their own volition they seemed to stop and hover above one card. Aunt Stella nodded, and Gil turned over the card.

"Ah, that's what you were looking for." Gil stared at the card. The Prince of Disks depicted a man with a strange helmet sitting in a chariot being pulled by a bull. "The architect has arrived," Aunt Stella said, consulting the Arien book. "See that double helix right there? It indicates an ability to build new worlds." She stopped and smiled. "Gilly, meet your new partner."

Gil stared back and forth between Aunt Stella and The Prince of Disks for a full minute before speaking. "Thanks, Aunt Stella." He threw his arms around her, kissed her on the cheek, and went upstairs to bed.

CHAPTER 55

A few days later, Kori was pulling out in Ruth's minivan when Jack cruised down the driveway, forcing her to slam on the breaks to avoid a head-on collision. He stepped out of his car, an impish smile on his face, and walked over to the driver's side.

"Better watch where you're going," Jack said. "You could hit somebody."

"Better you than me."

"Nice to see you, too." Kori stared straight ahead, ignoring him.

"How come you haven't returned my calls?"

"You called?"

"Very funny, Kori. What the hell's going on?"

"Nothing. Why do you ask?"

"I've been calling you all week is why I ask, and I know you haven't been home because I've driven by a dozen times. Then last night one of my buddies says he saw you and some flunky out having dinner."

"We're just friends."

"Oh yeah? When was the last time you lip-locked a friend?"

Kori shrugged.

"Answer me, dammit."

Kori stared at the woods to the side of the house. Jack tore open the driver's side door and yanked her out by the arm.

"Oww!"

"Oh, now I have your attention … ."

Kori shook loose from his grip and stalked off across the lawn. Jack ran ahead, hampering further progress.

"What in God's name has gotten into you? Why are you so angry?"

"Because you're a self-centered bastard. You waste your time watching sports when you could read a book. You prefer a night of drinking with your friends to the movies with me. You have no interest in my work. But most of all, because you wouldn't go to the damn public meeting with me!" She said the last with such venom that Jack thought she was going to strike him to hammer the point home, but she just turned on her heel and walked back toward the car. He stared after her, dumbfounded, before running to catch up.

"I'm sorry. If I'd have known it meant so much I would've gone with you."

"You did know."

"I didn't. I swear. Come here." Jack pulled Kori in and hugged her to his chest. "I miss you. Please don't do this."

Kori raised her face to him.

"Besides. Robbie told me to take care of you."

Kori grimaced and shoved Jack as hard as she could. He lost his balance and fell backwards.

"And Robbie told me to watch out for you," she said, "but not the way you think. Anyway, Robbie's dead. Gone. Just like you. Just like everybody."

Jack jumped up and grabbed the back of her neck. He pushed her chin up and kissed her gruffly. "C'mon, babe." He wound his arms around her, more gently this time, and whispered in her ear. "Don't walk away just so you can be the first to leave." He looked into her eyes. "You're happy with me."

"Are you happy, Jack?"

"Yeah, I'm happy." He kissed her again and this time Kori responded with her mouth and her body. After a minute, she released him. He was electrified.

"You win." She reached out and gave his dick a little squeeze. He shivered at the touch. "Call me, say, a hundred years from Monday. That should put us squarely in the next lifetime." She strode to the van, slamming the door after her.

Jack watched her drive through the small, forested grove to the side of the driveway and pull out onto the road before he even registered what had happened.

✦

Jack walked around to the back of the house and, hearing music, followed it to the barn. He banged on the door, but Gil didn't hear him over the bass. He peeked in the window and saw Gil holding Max up by his front paws and dancing to the Bacon Brothers, "Philadelphia Chickens." Jack knocked on the window, and when Gil saw him, he screamed and dropped Max to the ground.

Gil lowered the volume on the stereo and opened the door. "You can't sneak up on a person."

Jack laughed. "It's not like it was hard."

"Where've you been?" Gil demanded.

"Home. At work. Out. You want a list?"

"Why not here?"

"Your sister's not talking to me."

"So what? I'm talking to you."

Jack tilted his head, shrugged his shoulders and gave Gil a lopsided smile. "Gilly."

Gil looked askance at Jack, set his lips in a grim straight line, and closed the door.

"Gil, come on," Jack said, knocking again.

Gil locked the door and turned up the music.

Chapter 56

At dinnertime, Avery walked out to the barn, but Gil wouldn't open the door. After a few minutes, he walked away. He came back with a loaded tray and a bowl of dog food for Max, which he left on top of a fifty-five gallon drum next to the barn's entrance. Back inside the house, he checked the window every few minutes to see if the tray was still there.

"Would you stop? You're making me nervous," Kori said.

"Why won't he come in?"

"Because he's pissed at me.

"Why?"

"Well, let's see. I broke up with Jack so he's blaming me for Jack not coming around. I told Chris he could write the article about the TDU based on his suggestion that getting things out in the open would actually make it safer for us."

Avery cocked a single eyebrow, a technique he knew annoyed Kori because she couldn't master it.

"I didn't think it was bad to do that. I mean he did have his "revelation" after Aunt Stella read his cards. I'm not making him do anything he doesn't want to do."

"Kori, don't you think we have enough to handle. The minute that article is printed every guy with an engineering degree is going to be calling. And that's the legit ones. What about the scammers? We're paving the way for every kind of miscreant to show up."

"Oh, stop. You're just pissed because Gil thinks he needs more help than you can give him."

"That is so not true and you know it," Avery said. "I want this thing built as much as anyone." Avery checked the window to find Gil's tray gone. *Finalmente!* He loaded his plate from the pan of baked ziti sitting on top of the stove, grabbed a piece of garlic bread and took a bite before he even sat down. "Mmmmm." He turned and grabbed another piece. "So he's happy about the article then?"

Kori shook her head and loaded her own plate, set it down on the table and went to the refrigerator. "No, actually, he's mad because I gave Chris his school picture for the article."

"The ultimate geek picture?" Avery asked.

Kori nodded.

"No wonder he's pissed. I'd be pissed, too."

Kori set a salad, olive oil and balsamic vinegar on the table and threw up her hands. "I didn't have another head shot. They specifically needed a head shot." She grabbed the pepper mill and sat down.

"Let's just open up the lame file and plop that little excuse in," Avery said.

Kori shot him an arsenic-laced stare, but Avery didn't relent.

"You could have taken another picture. If you recall, we do have a digital camera."

"All right, I'm sorry. I panicked. Chris needed it right away, and Gil was at school." Kori forked a bit of ziti into her mouth.

"He'll get over it, I guess."

"You think so?" she said, her mouth full of pasta. "I don't know. He's very one-dimensional emotionally."

Avery shrugged, ground some pepper onto his pasta. "Like you're deep."

Kori frowned but didn't respond. "What's he doing out there anyway?" she asked, nodding in the direction of the barn.

"Getting the TDU ready for when 'the man' comes."

"I thought there was only a few hours of work left. He's been out there for three days."

"He's going over the entire machine, every nut and bolt. After Aunt Stella's reading, he thinks someone's going to be along any second. Have I mentioned lately what a good cook I am?" Avery took a bite and rolled his eyes dreamily, enthralled by his own culinary talents. "He even gave me the final specs for the patent. I sent it off this morning."

"Well, somebody might call," Kori said. She wiped her mouth and put her half-filled plate in the sink. She pulled her coat off the peg and put her shoes on.

"Where you going?"

"Out."

"With?"

"Who do you think?"

"You never went out this many nights in a row with Jack. Is it just the idea of dating a journalist that's appealing?"

"Yes I did go out with Jack this much. In the beginning. Don't you remember when he and Robbie had that fight?"

A shadow fell across Avery's face.

"What do you have against him, anyway? Other than he's not Jack."

"I don't know. He's like a bowl of alphabet soup with all the "A's" missing."

"What's that supposed to mean?" Kori threw her coat over her arm, grabbed her purse and opened the door.

"It means that he's not working with a full alphabet, what do you think? And a journalist, no less."

Kori rolled her eyes. "Now who's lame?"

Avery shook his head. "So, is Jack completely out of the picture?"

Kori smiled big at Avery, raised her eyebrows, shrugged her shoulders and left.

Avery stared at the empty space she left. "Women."

⅄

Avery threw on a light jacket and bolted out the back door, tripping the motion sensor and flooding the deck with light. The night was balmy, unseasonably so for the second half of winter. He inhaled deeply, identifying various scents, including the smell of new growth that predates the arrival of spring, as well as wet decaying leaves and cat piss. About a hundred yards from the house, the light from the motion sensor dropped off and with the moonless sky, Avery found himself walking in near-complete darkness. Gil worked by oil lamp this evening, and the barn threw off only the barest illumination. Avery tripped over a half-exposed tree root and went sprawling to the ground.

"Dammit." He brushed himself off and blinked several times, willing his rods — or was it his cones — to become more cat-like and vowing to bring a flashlight next time.

He reached the barn and rapped on the door three times. It was quiet inside and unless Gil had earplugs in, there was no way he didn't hear the knocking. "Gil. Open up. It's been like four days already. You're starting to stink. I can smell you from out here." Avery thumbed some paint peeling off the barn door. "How much more do you have to go?" He peeled off a few strips waiting for an answer. "Don't you think it's time to return to civilization?"

"No" came the monosyllabic reply. Avery smiled. That he answered the question meant that Gil was probably desperate for a shower.

"It would feel really nice, the water running all through your hair and down your back. Really, really hot water. You could stand in there so long there wouldn't be a steam-free inch of wall space." Avery heard some shuffling inside, but the occupants didn't emerge.

"Hey, The Matrix is on Bravo tonight. You can stay up and watch the whole thing," Avery said to the door. Nothing. "Well, at least come inside and sleep in your own bed. Kori's out for the night, and I want to go to sleep. I'd feel better if you were inside." He rested his head on the doorjamb and waited. "C'mon, Gil."

Avery waited so long for an answer that he dozed off, eyes popping wide when his head hit the barn door. He made one last attempt: "Well, don't come running to me if the boogie man comes after you." The lock clicked open but not the door. Avery waited, but after a minute, it clicked shut, the moment lost. He rolled his eyes and walked back into the house.

Avery left the kitchen light on in case Gil decided to come in during the night, and closed the door but didn't lock it. He also turned the backyard's motion sensor to the full "on" position so Gil would have a light to follow toward the house. Fixing your eyes on the motion sensor light helped navigate the dark parts. He also left the front porch lights on for Kori, then cast an uneasy glance around the perimeter of the house, lit up like a stadium for a nighttime game. He wished everyone would come home and go to bed already, then retired to his room.

At 2 o'clock, Avery's eyes flew open and he jerked up in bed. He touched his arm, still feeling the distinct sensation of someone shaking him awake. "Hello?" He looked around, but saw nothing in the shadows. "Mom?" As soon as he said his mother's name, a chill ran the length of his spine and his whole body shuddered. He shook his head to clear it then tentatively stepped out of bed. He peered out the window toward the barn.

A green phosphorescent light, barely visible, swept back and forth across the length of the structure. After several sweeps the light moved around to the other side. "What the..." Another chill ran through him, and he found himself pulling on his pants and shoes without any conscious effort. The light stopped, fixated on the door to the barn. Avery grabbed a sweatshirt off the chair and bolted from his bedroom.

He was down two flights of stairs and in the basement in twelve seconds flat, running to the cedar closet. He pushed through the off-season clothes hanging there: summer dresses and shorts, bathing suits, and Robbie's one-piece surfing suit clanged noisily on their hangers as he shoved them to the side. He lunged to the back of the closet where Robbie stored his gun cabinet. Avery tried the combination lock twice and failed. "Goddamn it!" He banged on the cabinet, took a deep breath and closed his eyes. "Please." Avery tried a third time and the lock clicked open. He grabbed the biggest shotgun without even stopping to load it. He reached the top of the stairs about the same time the roar of Gil's ATV and sound of Max's harsh barks flooded the silent night.

He made it outside in time to see the green light of the flashlight flick wildly across the copse and then burrow into the woods, disappearing into the blackness. Gil roared into the same abyss, Max running after him.

"Gil!" Avery ran, his heart pumping wildly with fear. Again, no flashlight. "Gil!!" He stumbled and cursed, found the trail and blindly followed the sound of the engine, propelled by instinct not eyesight, until he heard the sounds that made his legs buckle.

He couldn't distinguish one from the other at the time. It was only in recollection the sounds became clear: the breaking glass; the crunching metal; the creaking of a tree; the swish of dead leaves; Max's fanatical barking; and the most sickening sound, a dull thud, that of a body hitting the ground. "Gil!!" The tree rebounded, its sleeping branches swatting at the empty air.

The ATV lay on its back, its wheels spinning into infinity, the motor grinding on and on, while its tires searched for the missing earth.

Chapter 57

The alarm that Robbie and Jack had so meticulously wired tied directly into the police station, and when tripped, notified the dispatcher of the presence of an intruder at the Tirabi residence. The dispatcher put out the call, which was received by Officer Matheson and his partner, Officer Traecy, currently on their coffee break at the local diner.

Tony, the owner of the diner, was a young man in his late twenties taking on his first business endeavor. Looking to keep costs down, he worked the midnight shift alone, alternating between bussing tables, food, coffee prep, and customer service. Right now, he was out front wiping the counters and listening to Matheson's myriad stories of extended familial allegiances.

"I'm not kidding ya'. Bud is $3.75 a quart at Farrell's, my uncle's place," Matheson said. "He'll even give you a to-go quart cup if you want. I used to go in with my cousin, Huey. Three Hueys in one family. The dad, the grandfather and my cousin. Talk about branding. All part of the circle of punishing, I guess." Matheson and Traecy laughed while Tony restocked Styrofoam.

"Just like's Mom's," Matheson said, taking a sip of his coffee. His radio crackled to life. The dispatcher relayed the information regarding a potential break-in at the Tirabi's.

"We're on it," Matheson said, signing off. He signaled Tony for a refill, which he sipped with apparent satisfaction.

"Shouldn't we go?" Traecy asked.

"Nah. It's the Tirabi kids again. They set that alarm off once a month."

"Yeah, but what if … "

Matheson waved him off. "It'll be fine. Just let me finish this and we'll check it out." He forked down the last bite of an omelet.

"Hey, Tony. One to go, huh?" Matheson said, holding out his Styrofoam cup.

Traecy shrugged. Ten minutes after dispatch called, they were en route.

CHAPTER 58

A very dropped to his knees beside his brother and looked Gil over as best he could in the near-black woods by putting his face within inches of Gil's head. Because of the darkness, he gave over sight for touch, feeling the contours of Gil's face, his head, his neck. He noted a lump on the back of Gil's head that seemed to be growing. He performed a body check next, running his hands over every inch of Gil: torso, arms, legs. All appeared to be intact and at proper angles. He placed two fingers on Gil's neck. His pulse was strong. Avery finished by putting his ear to Gil's nose where he heard faint, but steady breathing. Gil was unconscious, but most definitely alive. "That's good," he sighed in relief.

Avery opened one of Gil's eyes; they were rolled back so Avery could only see the whites. He released the lid, and it flopped back into place like a dead fish. He had to get Gil back to the house and looked around for something, anything to help in that endeavor but he couldn't clear his addled brain, which seemed as dark and clouded as the night sky.

Avery stood up, ran his hands through his hair and began to pace. Gradually, the world returned to him. He could hear the whir of the ATV's motor and Max barking maniacally in the background, noises that had been emitting wavelengths of sound all along but which his mind in its hyper-focused state had blocked out. For a moment Avery had a brief insight into how Gil's mind worked during periods of intense concentration. He fumbled in the dark for the ATV's ignition and turned the key. The motor went silent. He sat down, legs crossed, on the ground. *What do I do? Tell me what to do.* Lie him down flat. Stabilize the neck. Avery concentrated on slow breathing, in and out the way he was taught in meditation class, trying to focus the mind. How am I going to get him back to the house? He looked over at the ATV sitting on its side.

Max's barking had reached such a fever pitch that he sounded like two dogs. *What the hell is he barking about?* The minute the thought crossed his mind, Avery's blood cooled. He took a few steps in the direction of the barking but was stopped by the sound of two successive pistol shots. Avery caught his breath. The barking resumed. On instinct, he grabbed the gun and took off running through the woods.

He used Max's voice as a guide and immediately regretted not taking the trail. Small branches whipped at his face and clothes as he tripped his way through the dense underbrush. A branch broke open his cheek and a bit of blood oozed from the wound. He cursed and smeared it away. Max's voice was growing hoarse, but he continued unabated. Avery was closer now and he could hear a man's voice straining with effort, cursing the dog and brandishing the gun as if Max would understand. The man's voice was muffled, drowned out by the consistency of Max's barking and growling.

Avery broke through to the clearing to see the man draped over a tree branch, shining a pale green light at the ground and trying to catch Max in the circle of it. Max leapt in complete defiance of the laws of gravity, making contact with the man's leg. The man yelped in pain and fired at Max. Avery fell, forced sideways and to the ground by shock and the wave of sound. Max yelped then resumed with a bark so ferocious wolves would run for cover. Max jumped and snapped again, inches from the man's jacket, then spun back and forth beneath the tree, a whirling dervish. The man pulled his gun and aimed it.

"Noooo!"

Avery turned to see Gil's shadowy figure stumbling toward him, paying little heed to the tree branches slashing at his clothes and face. At the sound of his master's voice, Max halted but did not leave his post beneath the bottom of the tree.

"Max! Come! Now!" After a moment's hesitation, he ran over to Gil who fell to his knees. Max licked Gil's face and rubbed his nose all over him, leaving a sticky residue. Gil dabbed at the gooey stuff. His hands flew to Max's snout, searching, until they fell upon the spot. A bullet had grazed Max's left ear. Blood dripped from the wound, and caught in Max's fur where it had coagulated.

The boys heard a thud as the man in the tree hit the ground. Max ran, his jaws wide, going for the jugular. Avery grabbed him by the collar just as Max tore the man's ski mask away. Recognition lit on Avery's face. *The driver?*

The man fired a wild shot and rolled to his side. Propelled by adrenaline, Avery reached for him. His fingers grazed the man's coat, but he eluded Avery's grasp and fled into the woods. Avery raised his gun, aimed, and pulled the trigger. It clicked. He stood that way for several seconds, wheezing and studying the blackness that had consumed the driver. Gil teetered forward, gripping Max's collar. Avery pushed back a wave of nausea and scooped them both into his arms. Gil's breath was short and ragged, the life force weak, as he slouched against his brother. Avery corralled his own erratic breath, lassoing the fear singeing his throat. He might have killed a man if the gun had been loaded.

He ran his hands over Gil's face and the back of his head, feeling for cuts and bruises. There were many.

"Are you all right?" he asked. Gil nodded and then proceeded to pass out. Avery caught him before he hit the ground. He tilted Gil's head back and checked his eyes.

"He just passed out," Avery said to Max. He rubbed Max's head, and Max returned the favor by licking his hand. "Thanks." Avery touched Max's ear. The dog winced; the wound was coagulating around the edge of his ear. "C'mon. We gotta get out of here."

He draped Gil over his shoulder, his knees buckling under the weight. They headed for the trail with Max leading the way.

Chapter 59

After checking the perimeter of the house, Matheson and Traecy crossed the backyard to the barn, their flashlights sweeping the yard like spotlights. The barn door was open.

"Hhmphh," Matheson said.

"What?" Traecy asked.

"Nobody's here." Matheson's raised eyebrow said: "I told you so."

"And your point is?" Traecy asked.

"These kids are messin' with us."

"You know, I think your brain's fried like those donuts. The house is lit up like the 4th of July, the barn door's flapping in the breeze, and you think these kids are messin' with you?"

"There's no signs of a struggle, is there? I've been out here half a dozen times responding to that alarm. Each time it was a different excuse."

"Yeah, well, we'd be remiss if we didn't at least look around." Traecy flashed his light inside the barn before walking in. Matheson followed. They scanned the empty room.

"What's that?" Matheson said. He strained to hear something off in the distance. The partners walked outside. A noise from beyond the copse was drawing closer. Matheson and Traecy pulled their guns and crouched down, tigers at the ready.

The ATV burst threw through the tree line, groaning and whining with the effort. The frame was bent and only one headlight worked, but it was running.

"Stop," Matheson yelled. Avery's eyes were dead-set ahead, and he would have zoomed right past had Matheson not jumped in front of the vehicle. Avery hit the brakes and stopped. The motor wheezed like a heavy smoker. Max yelped. Gil's head lolled on Avery's arm.

"Cut the engine," Matheson yelled.

"I can't. I have to get him to the hospital," Avery said, his voice gravelly and full of bravado. Matheson reached over and turned off the ignition.

"No, we have to go now!" Avery roared.

Matheson grabbed Avery's hands and held on tight. "Tell me what happened, son."

Avery recounted the story as quickly as possible, ending with their escape from the woods on the crippled ATV. When he was finished, Matheson grabbed his shoulder and gave it a gentle squeeze. Avery began to shake and then cry.

Traecy cleared his throat and shined his light at the trees. "He's long gone by now."

Matheson agreed. "Do you know what's wrong with him?" he said, nodding at Gil.

"Concussion, maybe," Traecy said.

"He's got epilepsy. He might be on the verge of something." Avery gave Gil a worried look and touched the lump on the back of his head. "He's been holed up in the barn most of the week so I'm not sure about his meds."

"Go get the car," Matheson said to Traecy who took off running.

"Where's your sister?" Matheson asked.

"Out."

Matheson checked his watch. "Kinda late, don't you think?" he asked, and shook his head. "I got daughters. Let me tell you, I'm not looking forward to these late night vigils." He looked back at the house. "Maybe you want to leave a note or something in case she comes home. We don't need another call to the precinct tonight."

Avery nodded, looked at Gil and then at Matheson. Matheson took Avery's place behind the wheel, allowing Gil's head to rest on his shoulder.

"Thanks," Avery said, and ran off toward the house.

Five minutes later Avery, Gil and Max were speeding to the hospital in the back of the patrol car.

⚔

It had been a slow night in the emergency room, and the boys were home in less than three hours, stitched up, patched up, wrapped up, and already on the mend. They both had several cuts on their faces and arms, but nothing that required stitches. The ER doc dressed the wounds with salve and put bandages over them with instructions to keep them dry for twenty-four hours. He even treated Max, completely against the rules, but Matheson had intervened, telling the ER doc that, but for the noble canine, the boys might not be sitting here tonight. Matheson admonished the doctor to report any patient arriving with teeth marks in his leg. The doctor agreed and sent the boys home with packets of Tylenol with codeine for the pain.

Avery sat cocooned in a blanket on the couch. Despite the medication, he couldn't sleep and decided to wait up for Kori. He had a spectacular view of the sunrise as it gained, then overtook the horizon, the explosion of color seeping into the dozens of smoky vapors dotting the sky, lending its luminescence to their whiteness and adding to the overall brilliance. When you looked at a sky like this there could be no questioning the existence of God. Although physically Avery felt fine, it was the pain in his heart that was causing him grief, and this view, all orange and red and resplendent, was doing its damnedest to alleviate that ache.

As if drawn by the intense beauty, Gil padded down the stairs in his stocking feet, reasonably alert under the circumstances. He had a bandage wrapped around his head, looking like the revolutionary war boy who played the flute fife and marched without proper footwear. Avery stifled a laugh and turned back to the magnet that was pulling all the angst from him.

"You hungry?" he asked Gil. Gil nodded, but Avery didn't even look. He knew what the answer would be. He began to rise, but Gil put a hand on his arm to stop him.

"Just wait until this is over," Gil said.

Avery flopped back down and offered Gil part of his blanket.

Gil sighed at the ongoing show out the window. "Did ya' ever notice how you stare and stare at something and it just blinds you? It's like you can't see it at all. But if you look away, even just off to the side a little, then you can see it clear."

Avery tucked the blanket up under Gil's chin. Max jumped up and sat on both of their legs. The last vestige of color wrote its name in the sky.

"Kori should be home soon," Avery said. Gil nodded.

The sunset faded, reminiscent of life's impermanence, into a new blue day while Avery and Gil stretched out on the couch, side-by-side and with their heads and shoulders touching, and fell fast asleep.

It was early morning when Kori came home to find her brothers sitting up and sound asleep. Max's massive head was curled up on Gil's lap, his body on Avery's. Two things were strange: the TV wasn't on, and Gil had a large white bandage tied around his head. She stood there, appraising the situation when Avery awoke.

"Hey."

"Hey."

"What the heck happened to you?"

"A lot. Where've you been?"

"Out."

"Well, that's helpful." Avery yawned and rubbed the sleep from his eyes. Kori moved in for a closer examination of Gil's contusions and abrasions.

"What's going on?"

Avery drew a breath. "Somebody tried to break into the barn in the middle of the night. Gil chased him down, flipped the ATV and suffered a minor concussion. Max picked up where Gil left off and had him pinned up in a tree until he got shot. I just picked up the pieces until the cops got here and took us to the hospital." Avery stretched his neck, sore from sleeping sitting up, and sat back matter-of-factly. "How was your night?"

Kori stared at him, silent and agape.

"I said how was your night?"

"Is this some kind of a joke?" Kori asked. Avery shook his head. Gil yawned, wide as Max ever could, and opened his eyes.

"No joke, sister," Gil said. "This is the stuff movies are made of."

"Oh yeah?" She studied Gil's ashen-colored face, touched the bandages to see if they were real. Gil flinched for effect. "What would you give it?"

"Four stars," Gil said.

"Four? You're kidding me."

Gil shook his head, slow and serious. "It was really scary." He pinched himself on the arm. "And we weren't even dreaming. We could have died, huh, Avery?" He looked at Avery and then rubbed noses with Max. "If not for Max we could have."

Avery shuddered involuntarily.

"Is somebody going to tell me what the hell's going on?"

"I'll tell you if you make us breakfast," Gil said. "A big breakfast. I'm starving."

Chapter 60

The funeral had been a splendid affair as funerals go, and Bicky personally greeted each of the four hundred mourners that had been appearing at the house since mid-morning to pay their respects. Now, twelve hours later, with the mourners gone, the caterers packed up, and the musicians disbanded, the house took on an eerie quiet, punctuated by the occasional clang of the dishes Mrs. Banes was loading into the dishwasher. Only Bicky, Hart and Jerry Dixon remained.

"Was anyone there when it happened?" Hart asked. They were alone in his study.

Bicky sat brooding in the study where he'd come often during the day to escape the crush of people with their endless outpouring of sympathy. Now, he stared at the fire's glowing embers, sipping a Chivas on the rocks, the distant look in his eye tipping Hart to the probability that Bicky's body might be here, but his mind was elsewhere.

"When I was young, this was years before we discovered oil on our land, when we didn't have two nickels to rub together that is, my father used to take me and my brother, Mason, trout fishing in the backcountry. I don't know if you've spent much time in West Virginia, but it had some of the most pristine and diverse eco-cultures of all our fifty states, California and Florida notwithstanding. We'd fish for two or three days, eating to fill our bellies and stashing the rest in the mountain stream. That water came flowing down just like nectar from Mount Olympus and was colder and clearer than any spring water you'll find on the market today. The fish stayed better there than in a fridge. We'd bring back what we caught, and my Mom would cook it up with some potatoes and kale from her vegetable garden. You can't buy fish like that today. Not even in the high-end food markets. They just don't exist anymore. So many things don't exist anymore." Bicky shuddered.

Hart grabbed a blanket off the couch and made to cover Bicky with it but, stopped short by embarrassment, left the blanket sitting on the arm of the chair and returned to his seat.

"Sonia used to do that all the time when she was a little girl," Bicky said. "Cover me. But that was before she learned to hate me. Of course, she always liked my money."

The day's events had drained Hart and didn't want to talk about Sonia now. "Maybe you need to go back to West Virginia for a visit. Some trout fishing might help with the … with all this." Hart waved his hand toward the study door where the sounds of dishes being stacked sliced through the silent hall.

"The West Virginia of my youth is gone. Just like everything else." Bicky sighed and took a big swig of whiskey. "Did you know they blow the tops off of mountains there now just to get at the seams of coal nestled underneath? They smother miles of streams with the rubble, pristine mountain streams, and call it progress. Altogether, in West Virginia, Tennessee, Kentucky, a couple others, the coal companies have buried over seven hundred miles of headwater streams with their little extraction business. Headwaters. That's where the stream starts. And they say oil kills wildlife."

Bicky gave a short, jagged laugh, drained his glass and threw it against the back wall of the fireplace where it exploded in a shower of sparks ignited by traces of whiskey. "Oopah," he said, deadpan, turning to Hart for the first time since they'd be sitting there. "That's what the Greeks say."

"What the hell was that?" Jerry Dixon came running into the study, followed by Mrs. Banes. Jerry's eyes were bloodshot. He was drunk.

"Are you all right, sir?"

"Yes, Mrs. Banes. I'm fine. I regret, however, that I've made a mess in the fireplace."

"Glass is it?" She stepped forward and gazed into the fire. "Shall I clean it out now?"

Bicky shook his head. "Tomorrow'll be fine. Why don't you go home now."

Mrs. Banes nodded in weary gratitude. "If you're sure you won't be needing me."

Bicky nodded. Mrs. Banes had been in the Coleman's employ for over thirty years, and although Kitty had come to treat her like family, Bicky rarely said a word to her unless giving an order. Mrs. Banes was wary of his silences, and his temper, having seen both in action.

"Well then, I'll take you up on the offer. Thank you, sir."

"Is anyone else still here?"

"No, sir. Last ones left about half an hour ago."

"I'll walk you out then," Bicky said. Mrs. Banes' eyebrows shot up, but she covered it over nicely by scratching her forehead.

"Goodnight, Mr. Hart. Mr. Dixon."

"Goodnight, Mrs. Banes," Hart said. He watched her move stiffly out the door, a baffled look on her face. Jerry sat down opposite Hart.

"How you doing, Jerry?"

"I've been better." Jerry pulled a much-used hankie out of his back pocket and gave a full-throttled blow. Deep circles hung like end-of-the-party streamers under Jerry's eyes, and the creases in his brow appeared etched in stone. Apparently, Bicky wasn't the only one feeling the pain of Kitty's sudden demise.

"Of all things to go. Her heart was bigger than anyone I knew." Jerry blew his nose again, a resounding effort culminating in a silence broken only by the crackling of burning wood.

Hart felt the hollowness of his own muscular organ, its ineffectiveness. That his eyes were dry and his breathing passages open came as no surprise. Given the sheer volume of bodily fluids that had passed through his nasal and ophthalmic cavities in the months following Sonia's death, he wondered whether he'd ever shed another tear.

There was something now, about Jerry's body language, about the way he rubbed his eyes so hard and rough they might pop out of his head that seemed scary, familiar. They sat in silence, Hart circumspectly watching Jerry, puzzling it out until he was struck with an analogy more solid than any wood or iron. He stared at Jerry in disbelief until Jerry wiped his nose, stifled a sob, and confirmed it for him.

"I loved her." Jerry coughed, covering the words that had escaped. "Too long. And yet not long enough."

The confession hung in the air like skunk spray, fetid and impossible to ignore. To Hart, Jerry appeared caricature-like, the undeniable look of guilt spread thin across his face. Jerry swallowed hard — Hart watched his Adam's apple wobbling under the strain — before continuing.

"I've been in love with her for over thirty years. There was nothing I wouldn't do for that woman." His eyes trailed off after his voice, and Hart could almost see time winding backwards to the point that even Jerry's voice changed, losing the throatiness, the slightly harder edge that comes with years of use.

"We met at a party Akanabi had for all its customers. In those days, they really knew the meaning of customer service. It was this swanky affair, and I was handling security. I was pretty new. Only been with the company six months. Kitty gave a little toast to honor all those customers that kept Akanabi in business and then one to honor all its faithful employees. She made eye contact with me. Later we chatted over the hors d'oeuvres. She was a knockout. The most beautiful woman I had ever seen. I made it my personal goal to find out everything I could about her. Even without digging, you could already see the cracks forming in their relationship." Jerry took a sip of whiskey and stared at the bottom of the glass straight through to the last few decades. "For over thirty years, I've loved her. And I'll keep on loving her long after that bastard has taken a new wife."

"So that was when they were first married?" Hart asked. "Before she had Sonia?"

Jerry stiffened. "Go ahead. Ask me," he said.

"Did you have an … did she love you back?"

"Yes," Jerry said, his voice small. "But I didn't know until it was almost too late." His face contorted. "God, it feels good to finally tell someone."

Hart heard footsteps behind him and jerked around to see Bicky walk into the room.

"Tell someone what?"

Jerry stared, wide-eyed at Bicky, but said nothing.

"About his Golden Retriever," Hart offered. "He was saying how he hasn't felt this bad since his Golden Retriever died." Jerry's look said he would lick Hart's boots clean with his tongue next opportunity he got.

"That's just like you, Jerry. Likening my wife to a dog." Bicky poured himself another Scotch, and Hart could almost see him dissolving in his chair, the energy draining from him in rivulets across the hardwood floor.

"Come to think of it, you always did enact a certain aloofness around her. Something I could never quite decipher. Bordered on downright rudeness, I thought." Bicky took a big slug of his whiskey without so much as a glance in Jerry's direction. "You couldn't say it was justified. Kitty might have been a lot of things, but rude wasn't one of them."

"I was never rude to her," Jerry replied. "I just ... Bicky, I want to tell you something." Hart looked at Jerry whose face had become an expressionless mask. "I ... ."

Bicky shot Jerry a withering look. The confession died in Jerry's throat while Anxiety and Guilt left a gaseous trail in their wake as obvious to the casual observer as a passing cloud. But Bicky was staring into the fire, dousing his own sorrow within the prescribed confines of his cerebral cortex and his whiskey glass. He had not a brain cell to spare for observation.

Jerry stood up, wavering. "I'm gonna head out."

Hart sighed, relieved. The male need to be territorial was pronounced even when the grand prize was six feet underground. The last thing Hart wanted was to watch a pair of middle-aged men go at it on the floor of Bicky's study.

"I'll see ya'," Jerry said. Bicky sat stone-faced without taking his eyes off the fire.

Hart walked with Jerry as he stumbled down the hall to the foyer.

"How about I call you a cab? You don't look like you're in any shape to drive."

"Death might be a welcome change," Jerry said, managing a weak smile.

Hart gave Jerry's shoulder a squeeze. "It's not you I'm worried about."

"I know. Always the other guy."

Hart punched numbers into his cell phone, but Jerry grabbed it and disconnected the call. He looked Hart dead in the eye for several moments before handing the phone back.

"You didn't know, did you?"

"What?"

"The last time you saw Kitty she had just had a stroke."

"Jesus. I thought something was strange, but … Why didn't anybody tell me?"

"You know Kitty. Doesn't want anybody knowing her business."

Hart noted the usage of the present tense as if Kitty were still alive. Jerry wavered, and Hart reached a hand out to steady him. Jerry grabbed the doorframe.

"Her right leg was gimpy after that. Little bit of paralysis. Bicky wanted her to fly to Europe — bastard that he is he still loved her — to see this neurosurgeon. Top guy in the field. She wouldn't go. She didn't leave the house much … after Sonia died." Jerry croaked.

"I visited with her everyday, and Bicky never even knew. Probably the best months of my life." Jerry pawed at his eyes and studied the toes of his cowboy boots. "Now she's gone and I'm lost."

Hart squeezed Jerry's shoulder and was surprised when Jerry's arms encircled him and held on for a long, fierce hug.

"I'm really sorry." Jerry pushed Hart away and called over his shoulder: "For everything."

He staggered to his car, leaving Hart standing in the open doorway, alone with his questions.

Hart returned to the study, heard Bicky's stifled sobs and took a reverse step, intent on backing out quietly, but bumped into an end table instead. One of Sonia's baby pictures rattled and crashed on the hardwood, shattering when it hit. Hart froze.

Bicky started then rose as if the movement caused him pain. He dragged himself over to survey the damage while sixty years of promises broken, of the shadow side of dreams, of futures never realized, all conspired to congeal, weighing down the sleeves and the collar and lining the pockets of Bicky's rumpled Armani suit. Grief, noticeably absent when his daughter died, now cloaked him in full regalia, aging him exponentially and adding decades to his countenance. In the months following Sonia's death, Hart had often wondered how Bicky hid his grief so well when Hart himself had been rendered debilitated. Perhaps Bicky hadn't cared about his daughter, as some had suggested, or perhaps he was just being brave for Kitty. But whatever threads had held him together, they'd all snapped now. Bicky was a wreck.

He stooped, picked up the picture and brushed away the broken glass, cutting his finger. He flinched, but didn't say anything. Instead he rubbed his finger across his baby's face, caressing her over and over as if the repetitive motion might raise the dead. Hart saw the blood oozing onto the photograph and left the room.

He returned a minute later with a wet towel and a trash can. Bicky knelt, crouched over the bloodstained photograph.

"I just hope that by the time I find the bastard, life hasn't wrung all the vengeance out of me. I'm getting old, you know." As if to prove it, Bicky grabbed the table and hoisted himself up, ragged and slow. Hart took the photograph, so stained with blood he could no longer make out the subject, and wrapped his father-in-law's finger in the wet towel. Bicky nodded once, acknowledging the gesture, and squeezed Hart's arm before shuffling over to the wet bar.

Bicky picked up a tumbler and filled it. "It's the least I can do for my favorite son-in-law." He tried out his famous scowling smile. It still worked.

"Bicky." Hart picked pieces of glass off the floor and threw them in the trashcan. "I'd say vengeance is overrated."

"Ah, but the momentary relief is as good as anything I've ever experienced." Bicky laughed, a dry brittle cackle. "Besides. Don't you want to know?"

"I do know," Hart said. "It was an accident. You saw the body. She slipped and fell. Hard. Hard enough to knock herself out. If I would have been home..." Hart dumped a big piece of glass in the trashcan and it shattered. He reached for a couple shards under the table.

"You said yourself you had the feeling that someone else had been there."

"I said a lot of things. You can't bank on anything I said then. If you remember, I wasn't very lucid." Hart was still smarting over Bicky's decision to dope him up for the two days following Sonia's death. The lost days. He shot Bicky a dagger, but Bicky was too preoccupied to feel it. Hart dumped the last bits of the glass into the trash and stood.

"I'd tell Mrs. Banes to go over this with a vacuum in the morning." Hart looked over at Bicky, but the man wasn't even in the same stratosphere. A profound feeling of fatigue settled over Hart. "Hey, Bicky, unless you need me, I'm gonna get going. I've got a bunch of stuff to settle at the house before my flight back to Philadelphia tomorrow night."

"You don't think I knew she was having an affair?"

The question startled Hart. "Who?"

"My wife, that's who."

"Jesus, Bicky. Ease up, would you?" Hart was not inclined to share the information Jerry had imparted. It wouldn't do any good. That Kitty chose to share the last months of her life with a man who obviously adored her over a man who rarely gave her the time of day did not come as a shock. What came as a shock was that she waited so long to do it. He was happy that Kitty had found a bit of happiness at the end.

Bicky shook his head in defeat. "I don't know. But if I find the son-of-a-bitch I'll kill him, too."

"Well, that's two people you're gonna kill. But hey, the night's young."

Bicky grimaced. "That's why she moved across to the other side of the house, you know. So I wouldn't catch on to her shenanigans."

Hart sighed, tired of arguing. "Enough, Bicky. Kitty loved you. Otherwise she would have left your flat ass a long time ago. 'Cause the way I see it, you had absolutely nothing to offer her." He smiled with the last words, meaning it as a bit of sarcasm, but immediately wished he could retract them. He searched Bicky's face to gauge a reaction, but there was none.

"Sorry. I gotta go." Hart squeezed Bicky's shoulder. "Call me if you need me."

Chapter 61

Hart spent the night at his house and woke before dawn after a fitful rest. He'd slept in his and Sonia's bed for the first time since her death, and his sleep had been plagued by eerie, disconnected dreams. Now he puttered around the house, coffee in hand, walking from room to room with no apparent direction, a wide-eyed somnambulist. He looked at each room as if seeing it for the first time. After about an hour, he took a nap on the couch.

He awoke in the still early morning with a start, a vivid image of a pregnant Sonia emblazoned in his mind's eye. He drank two full glasses of water from the kitchen tap then stood exactly over the spot where he had found her. He lay down there, hoping to embrace what remnants of her spirit were still caught in the tiles. He felt no trace of her, only the cold floor, more unsettling than a ghost. He turned over, folded his hands across his stomach and stared at the ceiling. He didn't move for an hour.

"That's it." He stood up and blew his nose. He dialed the number for a cleaning service and asked to speak to the manager. For an exorbitant sum, he arranged for a cleaning team to come that day to scrub and shrink-wrap the house. Then he called his father-in-law.

Bicky showed up a few hours later and scanned the place like a realtor performing an appraisal. The cleaning crew was well into it, and some of the rooms had already been "sealed off," vacuumed and dusted from floor to ceiling with the furniture draped as if the occupant would be absent for the season.

"What the hell's going on?"

"I'm catching a red-eye back to Philly tonight. I got an oil cleanup to close down."

"I know that. What's all this?" Bicky's arm arced out elaborately, a gesture that reminded Hart of float riders during the Thanksgiving Day Parade. "It's only going to take a couple more weeks, right?"

"It is."

Half a dozen cleaning people scurried around, dusting and draping. Hart had promised them double pay if they finished in four hours.

"Then what are they doing?"

"Come." Bicky followed Hart into the kitchen. Hart closed the door behind him.

"Do you want something to drink?" Hart asked. Bicky shook his head and sat down, but a second later changed his mind. Hart pulled a bottle of Dewar's out of the cabinet and poured himself two fingers. He made a face but took another swig.

"How do you drink this stuff?" Bicky walked to the fridge, tossed a couple ice cubes in his drink and poured a swig from the bottle to freshen it. Then he sat down on one of the bar stools around the island. "I'm all ears."

"I'm not coming back."

"What do you mean?"

"What word in the sentence didn't you understand?"

"You have to come back. You have two more years on your contract."

"So sue me."

"Now, how would that look if I sued you?"

"Is it always about appearances?"

Bicky shook him off and turned to look at the window. "What did you do last night? Catch a ghost or something? You sound like Sonia talking."

"She's been talking for a long time. It's only now that I've stopped to listen." Hart pulled up a stool. "I'll finish the job and I'll leave that river clean as technology can get it. But after that, I'm done."

"Hey, you listen to me. You can't just ... "

Hart raised his hand to silence his father-in-law. "Don't give me any grief about this, Bicky, and maybe I'll come back as a consultant. But it's a six-month sabbatical at least or no deal."

Bicky rolled his head around, stretching the tension out of his neck. "Fine," he said. He rubbed his temples. "I guess you finally figured out you're rich. If you sold all the Akanabi stock Sonia left you on the open market, you'd be very rich. Stinkin' rich."

"You think that's why I'm doing this? Because I suddenly have money?"

"Why else? You're not much of the powerbroker type, although you have your moments. You're more of the 'how can I serve you?' mentality. It doesn't do much for me personally, but I can see the necessity of it. We can't all be boss, right?"

Hart scoffed. "Your single-mindedness never ceases to amaze me."

"You're not going to find whatever it is you're looking for, you know. Not if you searched for a hundred years." Bicky drained his glass and rose to go.

"Where can I reach you if I need you?"

"Cell phone," Hart said.

Bicky sighed and stared at the spotless tile floor. "I still see her there, much as I try not to. I guess you do, too."

Hart thought he saw Bicky's eyes begin to water, but the old man turned before he could be certain. "You're trying to save a world that has no interest in being saved," Bicky called over his shoulder. "You'll call me when you realize it."

Hart watch him walk, stiff but proud, to the front door, an elegant man, even on the verge of defeat. Hart poured himself three fingers. The day was already turning out to be much longer than anticipated.

CHAPTER 62

Waiting on the tarmac at the airport in Houston, Hart tried reaching both Lapsley and Zenone but was unable to raise either on his cell. He checked his watch. Even OSCs deserve Sunday night off.

After takeoff, a flight attendant gave him a choice between *The Houston Chronicle* and *The Philadelphia Inquirer*. He chose *The Inquirer*, a nod to a new life, and dropped it onto the empty seat beside him. Hart stared out the window into the upper reaches of the troposphere, a stunning black freckled with starlight older than his entire lineage. He wouldn't say he was at actually at peace, but there was a calming feeling that came with his decision to take a leave of absence from Akanabi. He lowered his seat into the recline position, shut the overhead light and closed his eyes. But after an hour of chasing an elusive sleep, he flipped on the light and pulled out the Employment and Business sections of the paper.

He scanned the front page of Business first, but nothing caught his attention. He flipped through until he got to B-5 where his eyes met those of a smiling Gilliam William Tirabi, inventor extraordinaire. The headline read, *Inventor Turns Trash Into Gold*, a somewhat inflated view of the process as admitted in the first line of the article since alchemy was only involved figuratively. However, it wasn't the headline that caught his attention, but the face itself, and the feeling that he'd met this child before. The article, written by staff writer Chris Kane, recounted the tragic death of

Gil's parents and the MIA status of his older brother. It discussed Gil's re-luctance to complete the trash project until recently when he came to terms with his father's death and decided it was "okay."

Hart closed his eyes and thought about this kid's life. When he opened them again, the face of Gil Tirabi was staring right at him. Hart studied the picture until he thought he saw Gil's lips move. He shook his head, tossed the paper aside and shut the light.

At dawn, the plane touched down in Philadelphia. Hart grabbed his carry-on and moved into the aisle.

"Sir, would you like your paper?" the flight attendant asked.

"No, thanks," Hart said. But a moment later he turned, picked up the business section and stuck it under his arm.

Hart stopped at the "Jam and Brew" in Terminal C for a latte. He paid the woman, dropping the paper in the process. A customer behind him picked it up.

"Thanks," he said.

Hart took his change, shoved the paper back under his arm and stepped out of line. He stood, lost in thought for a moment, then walked to a nearby trashcan and tossed the paper in. He leaned over, staring after it, but the face of Gil Tirabi didn't move. Hart chuckled at his own ridiculousness and left the terminal.

Outside he flagged a cab, turned over his carry-on to the Indian driver, threw his briefcase into the back seat and climbed in after it. Another news-paper sat on the backseat.

"Where to, sir?"

"The Sheraton on 2nd Street." The cabby nodded and started the me-ter. Hart closed his eyes and slept until the cab pulled up to the hotel. He paid the driver, retrieved his briefcase and got out of the cab.

"Your paper." Hart hesitated before accepting the cabbie's offering, then shoved the paper in his briefcase and he walked groggily into the lobby of the Sheraton.

Once in the room, he unpacked his clothes, grabbed an Evian from the mini-fridge and sat down at the desk to work. He pulled a laptop out of his briefcase. On top was the Business section of the Inquirer and the smiling face of Gil Tirabi.

"Oh, Jesus. All right, already," Hart said. He huffed, polished off the Evian and dialed the operator. An automated response answered on the first ring.

"City and State, please."

"Philadelphia, Pennsylvania. I'd like the number for *The Philadelphia Inquirer.*"

CHAPTER 63

G il sat cross-legged on the floor watching *The Jerry Springer Show.* Today's episode centered around mothers who dated their daughter's boyfriends.

"Maybe we could get on the show," Gil said.

"For what?" Avery asked from his position on the couch.

Gil shrugged. "I don't know."

"Well they're not going to pay you to just sit there. They want something sensational."

"Well maybe we could just sit in the audience."

"Kori would bust a gut if we told her we wanted to see Springer. And she'd bust me for sure if she knew I let you watch this." Avery jerked his head toward the doorway suddenly afraid Kori might be standing in it.

"How much do you think they pay them to fight like that?" Avery asked. One of the daughters on the show swung a fist at her mother's head, making contact. The mother went down. A younger daughter, also on the show, went for the older sister's face and prime time fisticuffs ensued. Gil's eyes opened wide and he covered his mouth in shock.

"What do you mean?" Gil asked, his hand still over his mouth.

"I mean to keep the act going."

"It's not an act, Avery. It's real. Those people are really upset." Gil turned to look at Avery but didn't remove his hand.

"Gil. This crap is not for real. It's made up for television."

"Why would they make something like that up?"

"I don't know. Maybe it makes everybody else feel like they're not as bad off as they thought, especially when they see this kind of foolishness."

Gil stood up and flicked off the television, then walked to the door and threw it open, still holding the remote.

"Hey, you little turd. Why'd you shut off the TV?"

"He's almost here."

"Who?"

"The man who's going to help us."

Avery walked over to Gil and looked down the street. All quiet. A cold gust of February wind blustered in, overpowering the warmer vapors lingering there. Avery shuddered and closed the door.

"No," Gil said and put a hand up to stop him. "Just wait."

Avery rolled his eyes, turned the TV on manually and returned to his reclining position on the couch. Gil stood at the door, refusing to move. After a minute, Avery covered himself with a blanket. After several minutes, he yelled.

"Gil! Close the door!"

In response, Avery heard a car door slam.

Hart was halfway up the drive before he noticed Gil standing in the open doorway. He stopped several steps away.

"Are you waiting for someone?" Hart asked.

"You," Gil said.

"Me? How'd you know I was coming?"

Gil shrugged. "Aunt Stella told me."

"Who's Aunt Stella?"

Avery appeared in the doorway wrapped like a pig in a blanket. Gil held out his hand and Hart stepped forward to shake it.

"Gil," Avery said, pulling him back.

Hart introduced himself. "David Hartos. Akanabi Oil." He held a hand out to Avery who ignored it.

"The oil spill in the Delaware?" Avery asked. "So what are you doing here?"

"I saw your picture in the paper," Gil said.

"And I saw yours."

"I give your performance of the last month two and a half stars," Gil said.

"What's that mean?"

"He's got a rating system," Avery said. "Like the movies. Only he's much tougher."

"Actually, on the performance itself I'd go as high as three and a half, but you did spill the oil in the first place and so you get an immediate deduction for error."

Hart stood, mouth agape, until another gust of wind blew by and he shuddered. "Hey, do you mind if I come in? I'm from Houston and not really used to this East Coast cold."

Gil stepped back, but Avery blocked Hart's entry. They eyed each other a moment until Avery moved just enough for Hart to squeeze by him. The three stood in a tight circle in the foyer, Hart waiting while the boys stared at him, Avery still wrapped in a blanket, Gil still holding the remote.

"So what do you want?" Avery asked.

"I read where you discovered a way to change trash into oil." Avery narrowed his eyes. Hart gave Avery a tentative smile.

"Did you know that even a quarter-sized spot of oil on a bird's feathers is enough to kill it over time?" Gil asked Hart.

"Actually, I did know that. I spent a long morning at a de-oiling station."

"Yep. It breaks down their insulation and they can die from hypothermia. And it doesn't just happen in the winter. But you know what? I think it's 'cause they can't stand that one oily spot. It makes them crazy. They keep trying to get it off and it won't come off. It's like Ophelia in *MacBeth*. You know the one with Mel Gibson? 'Out, out, damn spot.'"

Hart stared at Gil, incredulous and wary. The kid was serious, and Hart wasn't sure whether to run away or hug the crap out of him. Hands at his sides and feet rooted to the floor, he did neither. Instead, he said to Avery: "You've got a smart brother."

Avery ignored the remark. "Do you have any credentials?"

Hart pulled out his Akanabi ID and handed it to Avery who looked it over coolly.

"Do you want some milk?" Gil asked.

"Love some," Hart replied. "If it's all right with your brother."

Avery gave Hart the hairy eyeball. "So you're the Chief of Engineering? What's that about?"

"It's about taking a lot of flak," Hart said, accepting his credentials back.

"How'd you know about the TDU? I mean, the Thermo Depolymerization Unit? Did somebody from Cooper's tell you? Or maybe it was your driver … "

Hart shook his head and reached into his back pocket. Avery took a step back and pulled Gil with him. Hart handed Avery the *Inquirer* article. In addition to the headshot, there was a photo of Gil, standing in front of the TDU.

"No way," Avery said.

"Let me see," Gil said, peering over the top to see his own face smiling back at him. "I hate that picture."

"Did you know about this?" Avery asked Gil.

Gil nodded. "But I didn't know when it was coming out. It doesn't matter though, right? Since he's here?"

"Who's he?" Avery asked. "Don't you understand, Gil? This was in the business section of the *Philadelphia Inquirer*. The Sunday paper. Not Monday, not Tuesday, freaking Sunday! The whole world's got our number now. He is just the first of many." Avery sighed and rubbed his brow. The blanket fell to the ground. "What was she thinking?"

"Look, if this is a problem, I can come back another time," Hart said.

"Good idea," Avery said, grabbing Gil's arm.

"No!" Gil grabbed Hart's arm and held fast. "It's okay, Avery," Gil said. "He's going to help us build it."

"Gil. You can't know that."

"It's him, Avery. I can feel it."

"Build it?" Hart asked. Now it was his turn to raise his brows.

"You're a trouble-shooter, right?" Gil asked. "Isn't that part of your job description?"

"Yeah, but … "

"Well, we need some trouble shot. So you can do that. Plus you can help us build a bigger machine, something really big that will save the world from suffocating under a gigantic pile of trash. Plus, if we make our own oil, people won't blow each other up for what's left."

Gil took a step forward and looked Hart directly in the eye. "My brother may be dead because of oil, but we're not sure because my father says we can't believe everything the government tells us. Plus, I don't think my brother would leave us yet because we really need him."

"Gil. Enough." Avery wrapped the fallen blanket around his shoulders and knelt down to eye level with Gil. "How did you know he was coming?"

Gil shrugged. "I just knew."

"Knew who was coming? Me?" Hart asked. Gil just stared at him.

"I'm going to kill Kori."

"Who's Kori?"

"Our sister. She likes this guy from the newspaper and she told him all about the TDU even though Avery told her not to tell. So he's mad at her."

"Gil!"

"But this is a fantastic discovery. It should be made public. I mean, what if Alexander Graham Bell kept the telephone idea to himself? What you need is someone to buy the technology from you."

"Somebody already tried to steal it from us. Twice. Once they blew up our porch and the other time they almost killed our dog. And our parents … " Gil stopped abruptly and looked at his brother.

Avery sighed and rubbed his temples as if he'd just developed a headache. He rose slowly, aging a hundred years in an instant and, still holding Gil's arm, turned to Hart.

"You have to leave. We can't talk about this anymore. Not to you or anybody else." He started shoving Hart to the door, but Gil intercepted, still holding tight to Hart's arm.

"No, Avery. He's the good guys."

"Gil. His company just spilled three hundred and fifty thousand gallons of crude in the Delaware River because they were using a forty-year old ship that, were it not for some medieval grandfather clause, would not pass half the safety requirements being imposed on today's vessels. He is most definitely not one of the good guys. He works for Akanabi."

"Not for long," Gil said, certain.

Hart felt an electric jolt shoot through him at this proclamation, but shook it off, still pondering something Gil had said.

"Wait a minute. You said someone blew up your porch looking for this machine?" Something about Gil's proclamation jarred his memory, but he wasn't sure why.

"Yeah. They took the drawings, but they got the wrong ones," Avery said. "Gil saw to that." Avery smiled at his brother.

"C'mon," Gil said. He grabbed Hart's arm with his free hand and led him out of the foyer, dragging Avery who was still holding fast to Gil's arm.

"What are you doing?" Avery asked.

"He wants some milk. We're going to the kitchen."

"Gil … "

"We have some cookies, too," Gil said. "Aunt Stella made them. She's an excellent baker." Avery shook his head and sighed but protested no more as he followed them into the kitchen.

⅄

Gil bustled about readying their snack. He served Hart himself — the first time he ever served anyone — and his pride and satisfaction wafted through the room like the aroma of breads baking, so much so, that even Avery's heart warmed. After much probing and prodding from both Gil and Avery, Hart recounted his own unfortunate events. By the time he'd finished, the trio felt as if they'd known each other forever, or at least for half of this lifetime. That's when a profound silence seeped into the kitchen, and Gil's discomfort with it prompted him to action.

"Let's go," he said and pushed them out the back door.

Gil gave Hart the tour of the barn where he explained the TDU in depth and encouraged Hart's examination of it. By the time Gil had finished, Hart was convinced that Marty Tirabi was a genius and that Gil was no slacker either. According to Avery, the actual breakthrough on the machine's salability came as a result of Gil's dream about oil and water. From the start, Hart sensed something otherworldly about Gil. It wasn't just the machine either: Gil himself stretched the boundaries of the human imagination.

After the barn, they drove Hart across the fields to Trash Mountain, as they'd taken to calling it, the primary feedstock for the TDU. It was a monstrous pile, even by landfill standards, but what impressed Hart even more was the means by which they arrived there: an ATV that pulled a series of connected trailers coupled like railroad cars and built by none other than Gil Tirabi. Was there no end to this child's inventiveness?

In the beginning of the day, if someone would have told him, as Gil tried, that Hart would be the one to help these boys raise the money to build the TDU on a grand scale, he would have laughed. Hart knew nothing about fund raising — that was more Bicky's bailiwick — and Hart had his doubts about a partnership with anyone. But by the end of the day, the little genius had sold him the farm, as it were, lock, stock and two technological barrels. Maybe he was going crazy, or maybe his alter ego, his "hero" persona as Sonia called it, was kicking in, but he really wanted to help these kids.

It was early evening when Hart finally left with a promise to return the following afternoon for more discussion. He was astonished with the ease at which Gil had taken to him and of the boy's certainty that Hart was their man. Avery was older and more measured than Gil, and Hart could sense his reticence. Whereas Gil was a full-on green light, Avery was a blinking yellow, reminding the driver to use caution at every intersection. Hart felt Avery was right. It could be that they were a perfect match but what they needed was a little time to get to know each other.

Chapter 64

On the evening of the thirteenth day, Hart returned late to the hotel. He had spent every afternoon of the last two weeks and all day on Saturday and Sunday brainstorming with Gil and Avery, reviewing plans, dreaming of possibilities, discussing permutations. Pizza and Chinese take-out had been the dinners of choice for the majority of those nights, but tonight Avery decided to cook. He made a fabulous dinner of moussaka, spanikopita, and Greek salad. They topped it off with a healthy helping of Aunt Stella's baklava. Aunt Stella adored Hart while Kori had become strangely silent about it all and by the end of the night, it seemed that she and Avery had discovered simultaneously what Gil had known all along: Hart was their man.

Back at the hotel, Hart grabbed a Sam Adams from the small refrigerator and sat down at the elegant desk. He drew a crude sketch of the TDU on the small Sheraton notepad and did some calculations regarding the square footage needed to house the machine. In order to bring investors to the table, he'd have to sell the complete package, not just the conversion from trash to oil, but on to refined oil and gas. The problem was going to be with the refining.

Refineries were dangerous beasts in and of themselves. To convince investors to ante up for the revolutionary TDU was one thing. There was more than a handful of nouveau riche with not only the collateral but also the common sense to invest in such groundbreaking technology. But would those same people also wish to invest in the construction of an oil refinery to complement the TDU, especially with several aging refineries already in the tri-state area? The reduction in air quality, the potential for spills and explosions, the astronomical construction costs, the staggering cost of liability insurance – all good reasons not to build a new facility. As far as he knew, the last new refinery built in this country was in 1976, in Louisiana.

Hart stared out at the shimmering city lights, his mind ticking through a list of possibilities when a broad smile crossed his lips.

"Of course."

Hart took his Sam Adams and the newspaper article about Gil and the TDU and headed down to the front desk in his bare feet. He handed the paper to the concierge and wrote down a fax number.

"Would you fax this for me? Now, if possible."

"Certainly, sir." The concierge retreated to the backroom. Hart stood at the counter and drank his beer, tapping his foot nervously. The concierge returned in a few minutes and handed Hart the newspaper article along with a confirmation sheet.

"Thanks," he said and returned to the bank of elevators.

⋏

Minutes later, back in his room, Hart telephoned Houston. Bicky picked up on the fourth ring.

"Hello," Bicky croaked.

"Am I waking you up?" Hart belatedly checked the clock. It was 2 a.m.

"No, I'm generally up at this hour," Bicky replied, his voice thick with sarcasm.

"Did you check your fax?"

"As is my habit in the middle of the night. What's up?"

"Well, I've been officially on sabbatical for two weeks and I've already found what will take us to the next level, economically, and environmentally. Want to hear about it?"

"Do I have a choice?"

"Everybody's got a choice." Hart said. Bicky took so long to reply that Hart thought he'd fallen back to sleep.

Finally, Bicky sighed. "Go ahead."

"How about this? A machine that converts trash into oil."

Bicky began a hack so violent, Hart had to hold the phone away from his ear.

"Hey, man, are you all right? Drink some water or something," Hart said. He heard the phone drop onto the nightstand as the cough receded into the background. After several minutes, Bicky picked up the phone abruptly.

"What the hell did you say?"

"I said, how about a machine that converts trash, you know, from a landfill, into petrol? Would you invest in that? And before you say another word, believe me, this is for real. I saw it with my own eyes."

"How? Where are you?"

"In Philadelphia?"

"I thought that machine was south of the city, out in Delaware County?"

"Huh? You heard of it before?"

"Ah — something about it, but I'm not sure from who."

Hart's eyes narrowed and his nose twitched involuntarily, probably because his body smelled a rat but his brain couldn't make the connection.

"You saw this machine?" Bicky asked.

"I did."

"You talked to the inventor?"

"Yep. Been hanging out with them for the last two weeks. Well, the actual inventor is dead. A tragedy in every sense of the word."

"How'd you find out about it?" Bicky's voice was coarse with sleep, which served to obfuscate his impatience so Hart didn't notice.

"I read a newspaper article on the plane. It was luck, I think. Something weird." Hart squinted into the past, trying to piece the events of that first day in Philly together, but like fragments of a dream, they scattered, leaving nothing but their fuzzy imprints.

"Bicky, I know you haven't had the time to think about this, but the implications. This is beyond breakthrough technology. It's downright mystical."

"I think you're cracking up. You better come back to work before you go over the edge."

"Listen to me. This machine eats trash. Do you understand? We install machines like this across the country and not only are our landfill problems eradicated but we're also no longer dependent on foreign oil. And I'm not talking about in situ burning that releases harmful carcinogens into the air. And not trash to steam. We're not replacing one problem with another. We're solving two problems at once. It even helps with greenhouse gasses since that trash won't be sitting in the landfill breaking down for a million years."

"Yeah, yeah. You said this was in the paper?"

"Yes."

"Which paper?"

"*The Philadelphia Inquirer.* Go check your fax machine."

"That means a lot of people know about it already."

"It doesn't matter. This kid wants to work with me. We ... bonded."

"Oh, Christ. Now I see where this is going. You don't have any kids of your own so you're out looking for some without parents."

"That's not it," Hart said. "I got the feeling that he chose me, but how, I'd be hard-pressed to say." Hart took another swig of his second Sam Adams and sat back in his chair. "If you think about it, you really can't write a check fast enough."

"Did you try buying him out? The board will want complete ownership."

"We can't buy him out, Bicky. He's only ten."

"Does the phrase 'candy from a baby' mean anything to you?"

"His father invented the machine."

"So you said."

"I did? I didn't think I said that."

Bicky started coughing again so Hart waited until he finished.

"The kid idolized his father. Now he's tweaked this machine to maximum efficiency. You should see it. It's a closed loop system that runs on supercharged water. It uses minimal energy for the process. It's, well, it's a beautiful thing."

Bicky sighed. Hart could sense the conversation was winding down.

"We don't need any investments. We're making enough money on the product we have which I don't need to remind you, this country needs to run. Without me, this country goes to hell in a hand basket."

"You're being short-sighted. What happens when your supply dries up?"

"It's not going to dry up anytime soon. The Middle East has plenty of oil."

"It's going to dry up, Bicky. Maybe not in your lifetime, but probably in mine, and definitely by the next generation."

Bicky was silent for a minute. "I don't have any grandkids. What the hell's it matter about the next generation?"

Hart felt the barb in the pit of his stomach. "Kids or grandkids, we have a moral obligation."

"Hey, maybe we'll find a cure for AIDS while we're at it," Bicky snarled.

Hart almost hung up the phone, but tried one more time. "Just think about it. From where we sit, with our dwindling resources, this invention rivals the Internet."

"Shut up, already. You're sounding like a National Geographic article. When are you going to stop worrying about everyone else and start worrying about yourself?"

"When you stop worrying about yourself and start worrying about *anyone* else."

"Very funny." Bicky coughed again. "I'll send somebody down to look at it."

"Don't send somebody down. I'm already down."

"You quit."

"I'm on sabbatical, remember?"

"Did you even ask him about selling?"

"They're not selling."

"I just want to know if you asked."

"Someone needs to help these kids, Bicky. Both their parents are gone."

"So are mine, but you don't see me crying."

"Oh, God's sake," Hart said, utterly exasperated.

"All right. Truth be told, I'm not interested. Now can I go back to sleep?"

Hart's anger rifled through the phone like machine gun fire. "Just so we're clear. I'm going to get this thing built, with or without you, and when it's done, my company's stock is gonna shoot so high you'll need a telescope to see me in the night sky." Hart could hear Bicky breathing into the phone, but no words were forthcoming. "Whatever. Go back to sleep. You always have been anyway."

"Damn it!" Bicky barked. "What are you going to do? Flood the market with Akanabi stock?"

Hart hoped his silence conveyed the fact that he was smiling.

"Go ahead, you little prick. I can withstand your assault, you stupid … "

Hart held the phone away from his ear so he didn't hear Bicky's last insult.

"You hear me, Hart?" Bicky screamed. Hart caught the echo.

He balanced the receiver on his index finger and watched it sway back and forth like the scales of justice. He could hear Bicky's disembodied voice yelling after him, his tirade continuing unabated. With his free hand, Hart lifted the phone and dropped it in its cradle. He sighed, like a man who has just taken his last bite of a memorable meal, sat back and folded his hands over his stomach. After allowing several seconds for it to disconnect, he took the receiver off the hook and laid it on the table. A minute later his cell phone started ringing. He switched the ringer to mute and opened another beer.

Chapter 65

Back in Houston, Bicky pulled the article off the fax machine and skimmed it. He huffed and sighed and stared out the bedroom window. He rubbed his head to stave off the headache that seemed inevitable.

"Dammit," he said to no one in particular. "God dammit." He dialed Jerry's number and waited. The phone rang half a dozen times before Jerry picked up.

"I thought I told you to get back East and get those damn kids under control," Bicky barked into the phone.

"What?"

"The inventor's kids! Did you check it out? No. You were too busy dicking around here doing God-knows-what." Bicky was so angry he was sputtering.

"Kitty died. Remember? You know. Kitty. Your wife of thirty-seven years. I was here for the funeral," Jerry said.

"Don't screw with me, Jerry."

"I'm not screwing with you, Bicky. I'm telling you that some things are more important than others, which is something you haven't learned in the last sixty years."

"I didn't call you for a psych session. I got a shrink for that. I called you about the kids."

"I sent somebody. He said there was nothin' going on."

"Who the hell'd you send?"

"Guy that used to drive for us."

"What guy?"

"The guy I fired a few months ago. You know. High strung."

"You are freaking kidding me. You sent someone who didn't work for us?"

"He was a good guy. And he had firsthand knowledge, and if he got caught, he wasn't one of us," Jerry said. "Jesus, I'll go check it out tomorrow."

"Forget it. I'll do it myself." Bicky slammed down the receiver, red-faced and huffing. He ran his hands through his hair and stared out again into the darkness.

⅄

Across town, Jerry hung up the phone and rubbed his eyes. An open book lay on the bed next to him and the light was still on. He roused himself and walked to the window. The night spread before him in varying shades of India ink, black on black, like a Hollywood wardrobe.

"Damn psychotic son-of-a-bitch," Jerry murmured.

He scanned the sparse room. A bookshelf filled to overflowing, a nightstand and lamp, a single chair, behind him the silhouette of leafless trees. "What the hell am I doing?" He closed the curtain, shut the light and crawled back into bed.

⅄

Jerry's office, located in the basement of Akanabi Oil, was a high techie's delight of an environment, encompassing ten thousand square feet and housing Akanabi's mainframe and various and sundry computer gadgetry. The whir and buzz of computer equipment was so intense that many of the technicians wore earplugs.

At the far end of the room, walled off from the rest of the equipment, was the closed circuitry monitoring station, Jerry's own personal fiefdom. The room had no windows and, if not for the door at the far end, would appear to be a wall. Hundreds of cameras graced the offices, hallways, elevators and common areas at Akanabi Oil. Some were in plain view, some were circumspectly installed; all of them were monitored from this room. The cameras were such a ubiquitous part of the decor at Akanabi that after a while people forgot they were being watched, an important plus from Jerry Dixon's standpoint. The most obvious cameras became part of the backdrop; the well hidden were rarely, if ever, noticed. Those cameras in the offices of mid-management were originally installed as a training mechanism. Monitoring could be done surreptitiously and suggestions as to tact and style could be made later without the need to embarrass the manager in front of the customer. The cameras had been "disabled," or so the managers thought, and could be brought back online with a few adjustments prior to a meeting should the manager request it.

But those managers didn't know what Jerry knew. That the company's fascination, its complete fixation with safety had morphed into something more sinister. Cameras and listening devices as small as buttons and earplugs graced every office, corridor, and waiting area of Akanabi, and the registered number of monitoring devices, somewhere in the 1300's, was more than twice as many. Jerry kept the real list locked in a vault for which only he and Bicky had the combination.

Some days Jerry would come down to this room simply to watch. Likely, his voyeuristic desire grew from his abject loneliness. Had you asked him, point blank, whether he was lonely he would have vehemently denied it. But the signs were there: the fastidiousness, the borderline obsessive-compulsive behavior traits, the need to control his environment and to have things "just so."

Kitty had the ability to curtail in him some of his more destructive tendencies simply by being in the room. But in the days since her death, he'd felt a welling up of those emotions and was at a loss as to how to channel the energy. He sat, staring at a computer screen, contemplating this very issue when Bicky burst through the door.

Jerry catapulted from his chair, rolled to the floor, drew his gun, released the safety and pointed it directly at Bicky's head.

"Are you crazy?" he shouted from a crouching position on the floor.

Bicky said nothing but jumped on Jerry like a feral cat, punching and clawing at his face. Jerry put up his hands to deflect the onslaught, but not before a right hook caught him in the temple. That was the last contact Bicky made. In moments, Jerry reversed positions and had Bicky pinned with a knee on one shoulder, his hand holding down the other, the gun pointed at Bicky's forehead. Jerry clicked the safety back into place and put the gun in his holster, hovering above Bicky, relishing the role reversal. He stepped back so Bicky could stand but offered no hand to help.

"Was that some kind of test?" Jerry sat down but did not turn his back to his boss. Bicky brushed himself off and straightened his suit and tie. He stared at Jerry so ferociously that Jerry's hand instinctively found his gun. Bicky threw a stack of papers at the ground.

"You're fired. Collect your stuff. Leave your keys, your combinations, your camera equipment, and all your other stuff with Phyllis. I want you gone by the end of the day. And if I catch you anywhere near here, ever, I'll rip your balls off with my bare hands." He stared at Jerry for a few seconds working his jaw as if to get the tension out before speaking again.

"You were like my brother, you little prick." Bicky spat at the ground, turned on his heel and left.

Jerry stared at the papers on the floor until his vision went soft and he leaned over to pick them up. The top paper was a codicil to the Last Will and Testament of Kitty McCain Coleman. The original will lay underneath. Jerry sat down to read.

The original will gave the portion of Kitty's estate that she brought with her into the marriage, substantial in its own right, to Sonia. In addition, half the shares of Akanabi left to Kitty by her father-in-law went to Sonia to do with as she pleased. The other half went to The Nature Conservancy with instructions that TNC's stocks should be sold and TNC given the fair market value of them. There were additional provisions on what TNC should do with the money. Jerry skipped over them and continued, flipping through the document until a specific provision caught his eye. First Bicky, and then Sonia, had a guaranteed thirty day right of first refusal on the TNC stocks. In this manner, Kitty assured that control of the company stayed within the family should the family still want it. Probably why Bicky agreed to this will in the first place. The mansion, in Kitty's family for generations, went to Bicky. "Straight forward enough," Jerry said to himself. He turned to the codicil and what he read made the hair on his arms stand up and his body shudder.

The codicil changed everything. Kitty had left her personal estate -- everything that would have gone to Sonia which included a good deal of jewelry and other family heirlooms as well as shares of various stocks and bonds – to Hart. The mansion she left to Bicky. The remainder which consisted solely of Akanabi stock and which should have gone to Sonia and TNC, now went solely to Jerry with instructions to sell it all and give half the proceeds to The Nature Conservancy, but only if he was so inclined. Notably absent from the codicil was the provision giving Bicky a thirty-day right of first refusal. The codicil was executed three months after Sonia died. Kitty had never said a word to him.

Jerry looked up from the papers and saw, as if for the first time, the drab, windowless office. Hundreds of images blurred, a thousand sounds merged into an incessant buzzing that seemed bearable only minutes ago, and for the last thirty odd years before that. His eyes followed the bundled cabling that sent millions of images through its wires every hour. He inhaled deeply, his first real breath in decades, and coughed out the breath, his body repelling it like poison. Jerry thought he could see the rejected breath, little dust clouds riding an imaginary wave of sunlight. The stack of papers in his lap looked very far away, like something on the horizon that you knew was there but couldn't quite make out. A giant teardrop fell and landed neatly on the page, spreading slowly, like lichen.

Chapter 66

The will had been on file in Bicky's attorney's office for years, and Bicky had full knowledge of it. He was well aware of the provisions it contained and had pestered Kitty relentlessly after Sonia's death for her to update the document. Otherwise, he'd argued, the disposition of more than a fortune would be left to the vagaries of Sonia's will. Bicky was reasonably sure that Sonia's will left everything to Hart, but he saw no reason to take the chance. Besides, Hart wasn't blood, and the events of the last few weeks had born that out in crystalline form. Unfortunately for Bicky, Kitty had ignored him. Soon after Sonia died, Kitty became sick and since his suggestions did nothing but further inflame her, Bicky let it drop. At the time, Bicky reasoned that with a little finagling he could fund a buyout of TNC's stock using his own assets as collateral and thereby retain ultimate control of Akanabi. But now? The stakes were a good deal higher and though he hated to admit it, there may not be a way to do this deal.

Bicky's father, that bastard, had set it up so Sonia and Kitty, operating together, could overrule Bicky's business decisions. Knowing Bicky's relationship with his wife and what the senior Coleman perceived to be Bicky's indifference toward his daughter, Bicky's father made it impossible for him to leave his wife and child without risking the loss of everything. For some reason, Sonia and Kitty never took advantage of their monopoly. Even more amazing, they stayed with him all those years when, had the tables been turned, Bicky would have taken his fifty-one percent and left.

Bicky ran a hand over his stubbled chin and rubbed his bloodshot eyes. The codicil was executed three months after Sonia died. Since Kitty possessed all her faculties up until the end, it would be difficult to argue that Jerry had put her up to it.

"Son-of-a-*bitch*, there's got to be a way around this mess," he said out loud. He punched the intercom for Phyllis.

"Yes?"

"Can you come here, please?"

"Certainly." Phyllis was in the door in moments. "What's up?"

"I don't know." He eyed Phyllis for a moment. "I think I need help." Bicky slumped back in his seat, looking older than Methuselah.

"Do you want me to call your doctor?"

"No. Not that kind of help." Bicky dropped his head to his hands and rubbed his face. His voice cracked. "I just need a friend, is all."

"Do you have any friends?" Phyllis asked, smiling. Bicky didn't return the gesture.

"Do you know anything about Kitty and Jerry?"

"You mean, for instance, Kitty was your wife, and Jerry has worked for you for about as long as I've worked for you, but now he doesn't?"

"How did you know?" Bicky asked. His face had assumed its mask-like qualities.

Phyllis's eyes grew wide, but if she had a quip she kept it to herself, limiting her retort to the obvious. "With so much cabling in this place word travels fast."

Bicky tossed a copy of Kitty's will across the desk. "Did you already read this?"

Phyllis stepped forward, reviewed it quickly, and nodded. It was her turn to put on the mask.

"Did you know?" Bicky asked.

"Know what?"

"That they were having an affair?"

"Well, if the question is, have I ever seen them hiding behind the water cooler, locked in an embrace, then no, I didn't."

"C'mon, Phyllis. Cut the sarcasm," Bicky replied.

"What's it matter now, Bicky? Kitty's gone. What would you do with the information?" Phyllis picked at a loose thread on her suit jacket.

"I just want to know, is all."

"Well, you're going to have to draw your own conclusions." She looked at him with an expression that relayed it to be her final word on the matter and stood to go.

"I just want your opinion." There was a remote quality to his voice, as if he were speaking into a fierce wind that blew all around him and sent his words to far off places. "Do you know you are the only person in my entire life that's never judged me?" Bicky said. "Or at least if you did, you kept it to yourself. If I've never thanked you before, I'm doing so now." The words had the desired effect. Phyllis sat down.

"Why did you torture her so much?"

Bicky responded in a voice that belied years of unrequited love. "Because she didn't love me. And I was too proud to show her why she should. And now, well, all that crap about it being too late would be appropriate here." Bicky coughed and rubbed his eyes dry. When he spoke again, his voice was level.

"This could ruin me, you know. A hostile takeover. I've not made many friends in this industry. I'd be out on my ass faster than stink. And if Jerry and Hart got together … "

"Ah, the truth comes out," Phyllis said. "Maybe it's time to take early retirement." The sarcasm was notably absent.

"Maybe. Just let go of it all." He traced his finger over the beautiful mahogany desktop. "That's been my problem all along, you know. Ever since my mother died. I was so obsessed with loss that I spent my life with my arms wrapped tight around everything I owned. Squeezing the air out of it all. Even my own wife."

Phyllis reached across the desk and patted Bicky's hand.

"I know I wasted a lot of time. Time I can't get back." He pulled his hand free and walked to the window. He stared out across Houston's skyline for several minutes before continuing. "But what am I supposed to do?

Roll over and die? Do you really think anyone will remember me?" Bicky slumped back in his chair looking frail and pathetic. Phyllis spoke softly, with tenderness.

"You have resources. Plenty of friends. People with fat checkbooks."

"Is that supposed to make me feel better?" Bicky snapped. Phyllis recoiled as if stung, all the goodwill of the last moments evaporating with a word.

Phyllis stood up and said in ice blue tones, "It's just an observation."

"Yeah, well keep your observations to yourself," Bicky huffed, steaming up the glass. "I could fight this for years, but he's still going to win. He'll bring on witness after witness that says my wife was of sound mind and body when she executed that codicil. Witnesses that will say I was a lousy husband. Hundreds of pages of briefs will be filed, and they'll have life expectancy charts and police testimony and psychological exams. My life will be on complete display for the gossip columnist, and at the end of the day, he still wins."

Bicky rested his forehead against the cool glass and stood as if cast in bronze.

"Well if you have nothing else to say, I have something," Phyllis said. Bicky didn't bother to turn around. "I'm tendering my resignation. As of today. I'm giving you two weeks' notice."

Bicky was stricken, a look Phyllis couldn't see. "Why?" he croaked.

"I want to spend more time with my family. Just like Christie Todd Whitman."

"Who?"

"The former, much beleaguered head of the EPA who had to step down because of philosophical disagreements with her boss."

He wanted to say something to change her mind, tell a joke, rehash the past, anything, but words had abandoned him. He felt the weight of Phyllis' stare aimed at the back of his head, but the profundity of his misfortunes rooted him to the spot; he couldn't even turn around. Finally, Phyllis left.

And for the first time in over thirty years, Bicky Coleman was suddenly and completely alone.

Phyllis sat in front of the computer reading her email when Jerry walked into the office. He looked pale and drawn as if he'd just come off an extended illness. She smiled warmly, stood and walked around to the front of her desk. They hugged, a bit stiff at first, like old friends who had served in the same war but hadn't seen each other since experiencing all the pain and suffering they had learned to forget. When they pulled away, they both looked sullen. Jerry nodded toward "the big door," but Phyllis shook her head.

Jerry walked back out into the hall and returned with a cardboard box filled with keys. "My instructions were to leave these with you." He set the box on the desk and backed away as if it were something extremely fragile or sensitive. "Guess that's it. Thirty years of loyal service," Jerry said in a voice redolent with sarcasm. He laughed, a dry mirthless sound emanating from his throat, and stared at the box as if he might see some part of those years replaying before him.

Phyllis touched him on the shoulder and he turned to her with a stare so savage she felt as if she'd been slapped. She bristled and looked away, breaking the connection. Jerry laughed, at first a small chuckle, which grew into a giggle and then a full-fledged belly laugh, ultimately careening into complete hysteria. Phyllis stared at him in mute horror, then turned and walked to the other side of her desk, her hand on the hidden button underneath, a button Jerry knew well, since he installed it. Jerry's laughter died down until he, too, became silent. If he noticed her hand on the button, he didn't say.

"I guess you heard about Kitty's will," he asked.

Phyllis nodded.

"I didn't ask her to do that, you know. I never asked her for anything. Except to just leave with me." Jerry stared at his well-manicured nails, his tone flat and even. "She couldn't do it. Never could bring herself to leave that son-of-a-bitch. Now she's gone and left us both." He looked up at Phyllis without emotion.

"I'm sorry for you."

"You think I was wrong, don't you? To love her like that."

"It's not for me to say, Jerry. Everybody has to live by the dictates of their own conscience. Otherwise you're not living, just going through the motions. But since you asked, no, I don't think you were wrong. Love is never wrong."

"Maybe if I'd have tried harder to convince her." Jerry shook his head. "It was always because of Sonia, you know. That she would never leave. She didn't want Sonia to lose out on what Kitty thought was rightfully hers and if the truth came out that ..." Jerry stopped his mouth still open, the unspoken words still on his lips.

"What?"

"Nothing." Jerry dropped into a chair as if he were suddenly very tired. "Right now it feels as if my whole life's been one giant lie."

"So make it right."

Jerry nodded, leaving Phyllis with the impression that the words were reaching him only after covering a great distance.

"How do I do that?" he finally said.

Phyllis shrugged. She'd said her peace.

Jerry turned to stare at Bicky's door. "You're right." He sighed and heaved himself up. The young, virile man was gone. An old, regretful man had taken his place.

"Thanks."

"For?"

"Always being an ally in the war against tyranny."

"You're welcome."

⅄

Hours later, Bicky sat in front of the fire, stone-drunk. He paced the room like a caged animal, wringing his hands in despair. He wailed, a deep, mournful, bellowing sound that started in the pit of his stomach and ascended, higher and higher, until it reached a screeching pitch that even he couldn't abide. He fell to the floor, covering his own ears, thrashing and hissing at the unseen demons that surrounded him, a man possessed. He banged his head on the floor, a rapid succession of syncopated rhythms.

He pulled his body in close and fell over on his side into the fetal position, wrapped his arms around his knees and began to rock like a baby. He cried, using the tears he'd stockpiled for the last thirty years, until he'd drained enough of the agony from his body that he no longer felt like throwing up. Despair and hopelessness were quick to fill the void, however, and he succumbed to the fresh onslaught.

When his body grew tired, he sat up, dried his eyes and cast an appraising glance around a room that for years had been shrouded in egotism and greed. He walked over to the side table and picked up a framed photograph of himself and Kitty on their honeymoon. The tears were back, and he was about to scratch them out with his own fingers but rubbed his eyes sharply instead, and, with so much pressure that he experienced a stab of pain, causing him to stumble backwards. He shook his head to clear his vision and Hatred, Anger's nimble first cousin flew in, replacing the light. He screamed, a horrible threatening sound, raised the photo above his head and threw the picture over the chair and into the fire. The glass in the metal frame shattered. Bicky stared after it, momentarily stunned, ready to accuse the perpetrator.

"Aaaaahhhhh," he yelled and ran to the fire. The edges of the photograph had begun to singe and without thinking, Bicky reached into the fire with his bare hand, his skin melding with the hot metal. He screamed again, this time from the burns, but he wouldn't let go of her, never let go. The skin on his fingers began to melt so he dropped the frame. It clattered as it landed on the hardwood floor. He grabbed a pillow from the couch and blotted out further incineration. His raw hand had already started to blister. He looked at the appendage as if it belonged to someone else, shook it twice then knelt down, hovering over the photo. He pushed aside the remaining pieces of broken glass with a pen from his pocket and pried the picture free, shoving the ruined frame away with his good hand. He knelt down on the floor, his chest to his legs and leaned in to kiss Kitty's face. He traced her body with his good fingers, the lovely creme taffeta dress flowing around her like a breeze, and kissed her now browned visage before starting to cry again.

At his apartment, Jerry packed a "cold" suitcase with winter clothes and a "warm" one with shorts, T-shirts, suntan lotion and other summer weather sundries. He walked over to the bookshelf and took down a dozen of his favorite titles along with a few he hadn't read yet and tossed them into the "warm" suitcase. He glanced around the room. Other than the floor-to-ceiling bookcase that lined one entire wall of his bedroom, there was nothing in this room he wanted.

He sat down on the bed and called Kitty's lawyer, giving him instructions to sell half the Akanabi stock Kitty had left him once the will was probated and to put that money in trust that named The Nature Conservancy as the recipient. The fund was to be placed under the direction of David C. Hartos with specific instructions to invest the money in either a private or publicly traded company as long as Hart had an affiliation with it. Each year, the dividends earned on such a phenomenal amount of money were to be turned over to TNC and used to purchase tracts of land in memory of Kitty Coleman and Jerry Dixon. Should the principal devalue in any given year, the dividend was to be reinvested, thus assuring the principal remained intact.

What to do with the rest of the Akanabi stock was the more difficult question. For now he'd instructed the lawyer to hold the stock certificates and gave him power of attorney so Jerry could access the revenue, should it be necessary, from anywhere in the world. Jerry himself had no use for the money. He'd lived a Spartan existence all these years and saved a ton of his own money because if nothing else, Bicky paid well. And other than the gobs of money he spent on books, Jerry had no real hobbies. For him to get this kind of cash now in his life meant nothing. Had he had it when she was alive, well, it may have made a difference. He shook his head. It didn't help to think about it.

He placed two firearms in the cold suitcase. He'd have to notify airport security and show them his permit. Likely it would be no problem as long as the guns were stowed in the cargo hold. He snapped the suitcases shut. Leather bound and heavy, they once belonged to his father. He knew today's models didn't take much in the way of coordination to carry and many came on wheels, but he liked the weight of them, the feel of the strength in his arms as he hefted them off the bed. He set one down, took a last look around the room, shut the light and headed out to put things right.

Chapter 67

Robbie and Amara lay on a tightly woven reed mat beneath an open window, the spare light of the crescent moon casting the faintest of shadows. His arm rested protectively on her belly. The thin blanket that had covered them lay crumpled on the floor, thrown off in the dead of the night's heat. A cool light breeze blew off the water and in through the open window, washing over their sleeping bodies in an undulating rhythm that kept time with their breathing. Waves lapped against the Quonset hut's foundation.

Robbie drew a deep, choking breath like one coming up for air after too long underwater. He coughed, waking himself, then bolted upright in bed, waking Amara.

"What is it?" Amara put a hand on his back. "Your heart is beating very fast."

Robbie took several breaths in rapid succession then pulled her to him. "You're cold."

"So are you." Amara grabbed the blanket and pulled it up over them. Robbie relaxed and they both lay down on the reed mat again. A rustle just below the hut refocused Robbie's attention; he was out of bed in an instant.

"It's only a mouse," Amara said.

"We're surrounded by water."

"Not everywhere. Much is just mud. The water is high now because of the spring rains."

"Well, how will he get out?"

"There's always a way out," Amara said. "Besides, mice are excellent swimmers. Please." She opened her arms and he snuggled closer to her.

"Sorry. Just a little jumpy."

"No one has been here for a long time. I'm sure it is very dirty in here."

"I thought you said it was a little fishing hut."

"Yes. It belonged to my grandfather's father. Of course, when he left he had no more use for it, but my uncles still used it." Amara's voice stumbled. "Now there is no one to use it." Robbie hugged her closed and smoothed her hair.

"Tell me about your dream," she said.

"I dreamt that American troops were driving their jeeps through the marshes. They were coming from Baghdad on their way to Basra and the most direct route was straight through the middle. The jeeps had these pontoons on them that kept them afloat when the water got deep. There was a place in the water where it rose about six inches like it was going over something massive below. The lead jeep got stuck on it. It turned out to be a remnant of one of Saddam's dams. Well everyone had to get out and engineer a different way across. They unloaded their mashufs, and troops started fanning out across the marshes in these canoes. I was watching from the reeds. Somebody came up behind me and grabbed me by the throat. I started choking … then I woke up." Robbie rubbed Amara's arm and she placed her hand over his heart.

"You're safe now. They won't find you until you're ready to be found."

Robbie kissed the top of her head. She kissed his lips.

"Dawn's coming soon," Amara said. "Please let's sleep. In the morning, I'll show you where you are."

⅄

At dawn, Robbie and Amara climbed into the mashuf they had borrowed from her uncle, a boat builder whose shop sat at the tip of what remained of the Al Hariz marsh. A mullet, small and bony by any standard, rose to the surface in search of breakfast. Robbie jumped at the splash that signaled its return to safe water.

"It's just a fish," Amara said, handing Robbie a paddle. "And a small one at that. They are returning now that the dam has been destroyed."

"Well, that's good, isn't it? I mean, about the dam." Robbie started to paddle in time with Amara.

"Yes, very good, but not enough. The Minister of Irrigation estimates that when the dam was breached, over one hundred and fifty quadrillion gallons of water flooded back into the channels, only enough to return the water to the two closest villages. At one time, there were hundreds of these villages. At this rate it will take a thousand years."

"Well, can't they just open another dam?"

"They have opened all the dams. The water is no longer here."

"Where is it?"

"Still in Syria and Turkey, being diverted for many projects. Agriculture, hydroelectric. Who knows what else? Saddam gave them our water. He stole it from his own people."

"We'll get it back."

"It's much more complicated than that. Here people fight over the right to use the water. Maybe not so now in your country, but you see the beginnings of it in your American west. One day people in America will fight over water just as we do."

The marshes were silent but for the lapping of the water on the shore and the slight rustle of the bulrushes. A fog had settled over the marshes and Robbie wiped at the drops of water that collected on his face. A bullfrog croaked. Robbie jumped, then relaxed.

Amara smiled and turned briefly to look at him. "You never fully get used to the noises that the marshes make. To live here is to constantly be on alert. So my grandfather has told me."

They rowed together in silence until Amara directed the mashuf through vegetation so dense and intertwined that Robbie felt they were inside a tunnel. When they emerged on the other side, the first rays of the day had filtered through the reeds, creating a mosaic pattern across the surface of the water. A blue heron caught breakfast and retreated to safer ground, flying directly overhead.

"A most beneficent sign," Amara said, bunching her fingers together and touching them first to her heart, then her lips and finally her forehead. She stopped paddling momentarily and squeezed Robbie's leg. "There it is. The house of my uncle, Sayyid. We will be safe here."

⅄

Robbie and Amara docked their boat on the small island where another hut stood.

"Who's there?" said a voice groggy with sleep. Inside, the occupants of the house stirred, the first rustling of the day. Amara tied the canoe and grabbed Robbie's arm just as Sayyid Sahain appeared in the doorway wearing the conventional robe and turban, but no sandals. In the misty morning light, Armara couldn't clearly see the face of her uncle, still pressed with sleep, his hastily donned turban slightly askew.

"Who is there?"

"It is me, Uncle. Amara."

"Amara! Is it you? I had word, but I did not dare hope. Allah be praised." Amara's uncle scrambled down to the dock and grabbed Amara by both elbows before crushing her to his chest in a warm embrace. "Allah has blessed me once again," Sayyid said. He held her at arm's length. "To look at you is to look again upon my brother's face." He wrapped an avuncular arm around her and patted her back before releasing her, then turned to Robbie, a question in his eyes. "And who is it that assures your safe travel?" he asked, sizing Robbie up.

"This is my friend, Robbie, Uncle. He is an American. He wishes to help our people. But first, Uncle, we must assure his safety. He has left his captain without permission." Sayyid raised his eyebrows in disapproval.

Amara continued. "The Americans believe he is dead. There was a car bombing and … they did not find him." Amara bowed her head and clasped her hands together. "I'm sorry, Uncle. I don't mean to bring you trouble." Sayyid studied Robbie's face then looked to his niece's bowed head.

"Amara. You could not bring more trouble than that devil Saddam has brought to his own people. Every day I ask Allah why he has allowed this.

But Allah has turned his face away from us." He lifted Amara's chin. "You were always the impetuous one. By the grace of Mohammed, had you been born a boy I believe you would have stopped the devil himself."

Amara smiled at her uncle and he stroked her cheek.

"Time has taught me many things," Sayyid continued. "For the memory of your father, but more important, for you, I swear I will keep your friend safe among us until the time he chooses to leave."

Sayyid turned to Robbie. "Welcome, sahib." He took Robbie's hand in one of his and with the other clapped him on the back. "You are safe here."

"Thank you."

"Call me Uncle as my niece does," Sayyid said.

"Uncle," Robbie repeated. Following Amara's lead, he bowed his head slightly to indicate his respect.

"Come, come," Sayyid said. "Let us go inside. You must be hungry. We will take a meal together and you will tell me of your plans."

 ⚔

Inside, Sayyid's wife Fawzia, was already grinding coffee. Sayyid made the introductions and Amara embraced her uncle's new wife before the woman retreated to the hearth to prepare a meal worthy of visitors.

"Fawzia is a good woman," Sayyid said. He directed them to several cushions scattered around a small round table barely a foot off the floor.

"I am sorry for you, Uncle. For my aunt. We had heard, but were unable to make the trip."

"Thank you, niece." Sayyid bowed his head and touched his bunched fingers to his heart, mouth and forehead. "She was a very good woman, dead now these five years."

"How did she die?" Robbie asked.

"From Saddam's poison water."

"Saddam poisoned the water? For real? Why isn't everything dead?"

"He is the devil," Sayyid said.

"I thought it was because of the dams," Robbie said. "I didn't know he used poison, too.

"He did not poison it with chemicals but with ideas," Sayyid said. "And revenge. Revenge for the part my people played in the Shiite uprising in Iran. We are Shiite Muslims. Saddam is Sunni. So he tried to kill us by taking away our water. When the water is not fresh, it dies."

"You mean it becomes stagnant?" Robbie asked.

"Yes. Stagnant. This water breeds cholera for which we have no cure." Sayyid's voice became soft. "When I see the problem, I take her by tarrada to the doctor." Sayyid turned to Robbie. "This is my large canoe, much bigger than my mashuf. It is more than thirty meters. Six people paddle while I hold her head in my lap, but it's not enough. By the time we see the doctor, it's too late." Sayyid wiped at his eyes as if he had an itch. Robbie looked at Amara who put her hands in her lap and bowed her head.

"Saddam killed my beloved wife with his dams. With his evilness. This I know." Sayyid adjusted his turban and straightened his robe. "My people lived here from the beginning of time. Now they live in refugee camps on the borders in Iran."

"That's why we've come, uncle," Amara said.

Fawzia appeared with a tray containing three demitasse cups, sugar, spoons, and an ebriki, a small brass pot with a long handle, used to cook the coffee directly over the stove. Steam wafted from the narrow opening of the pot. Fawzia set the tray down and smiled at Amara and Robbie.

"You are hungry?" She brought her fingers to her lips to indicate eating with one's hands.

Amara nodded and smiled. Fawzia squeezed Amara's hand and left.

"She speaks only a little bit English, my wife," Sayyid explained to Robbie.

Robbie nodded. "I'm sure we'll manage."

Chapter 68

Some saw it *coming, although they couldn't have predicted its speed. Both Syria and Turkey, and, to a lesser extent, Iraq, began dam building projects in the 1950's diverting the Marsh Arabs' water for their own agricultural projects. Their water, along with a five-thousand-year old way of life, had begun drying up. It would have happened eventually, but Saddam Hussein helped it come like lightning.*

For five thousand years, the Marsh Arabs were a self-governing people, managing to fly below the radar, breaching their own dams and flooding their homes, retreating to the marshes when the many conquering armies came through the region. But in 1980, following the revolution in Iran, many of the Shiite leaders sought refuge in the marshes. And the Marsh Arabs, themselves Shiites, hid these refugees. Afraid that a similar revolution would sprout among the Shiite population in Iraq, Saddam started a systematic campaign of arrests and executions removing the male heads of families and forcing the expulsion into Iran of the women and children left behind. That was his first attempt. The second was in 1991, and it was clearly more insidious, aimed not just at dismantling their families but the way of life of an entire region.

At one time there were as many as five hundred thousand Marsh Arabs living in the marshes. Today there are less than forty thousand, thanks to Saddam Hussein. He drove them out by drying up their marshes. Commissioning four drainage canals, several dams and a third "river" he called "The Mother of All Canals," he redirected quadrillions of gallons of water that fed the marshes, dumping them uselessly into the Persian Gulf. He claimed that the redirected water was to be used for agricultural purposes, but not a single project was initiated as a result.

It was really just a campaign of genocide against the Marsh Arabs for their part in the 1991 Shiite uprising, a three-week insurrection prompted by the Americans and the British following Desert Storm. The Shiite Muslims answered the American call, but when Saddam turned on them, so did the Americans. They were left stranded in the desert, and without their water that was being diverted to the Persian Gulf, they had no place to hide. Many were imprisoned, many others assassinated, and still others packed off to refugee camps in Iran where they still live today.

Chapter 69

After a breakfast of rice with buttermilk, chicken soup, flat bread and strong, bitter coffee, Robbie and Amara boarded Sayyid's flatboat and with Sayyid at the helm, set out on a journey to look at the recently refreshed marsh towns. Sayyid poled the boat through the water, skimming past huge clumps of papyrus and cattails.

Robbie watched the scenery change, enchanted by his surroundings. The fear that had sat in the pit of his stomach during their midnight exodus from Baghdad and had caused the bile to rise to his throat with every human encounter was finally in abeyance.

Robbie had cloaked himself in the customary robe and turban of the Iraqis, and upon Amara's urging, had remained silent the entire trip. Amara told the various drivers that she was taking her mute brother to Al Huwayr, a boat building town near the junction of the Tigris and Euphrates rivers where they intended to buy a mashuf and return to Zayad, their recently re-flooded ancestral home. Already, Amara said, their uncle, aunt, and three children had returned. The ruse had worked and here among the bulrushes and papyrus, Robbie rubbed elbows with the ghosts of the last five millennium along with a way of life he hoped wasn't dead, but merely on life support, and like the re-flooded marsh town of Zayad, could be resurrected and coaxed into thriving again.

"These are the biggest reeds I've ever seen," Robbie said.

"It is called qasab. It is a phragmites, like you see at your American bays. But these plants have been allowed to grow undisturbed, and without pollution," Amara said. "They can grow as large as twenty-five feet. We use them for many things, our mashufs, our huts. Too, we build our mudhifs from them. These are large buildings where many people can gather. Like your community center."

"This portion of the Al Hawizeh marsh is all that's really left of twenty thousand square kilometers of fresh water marshes," Sayyid said. "You know this measurement? It is maybe seven hundred miles. My people lived here for centuries. We believed we were comfortable. We believed we were safe."

"Here they raise cow and oxen and water buffalo and spend much time in prayer," Amara said.

"Water buffalo?" Robbie said. "I don't think I've ever seen a real one."

"The water buffalo are very important to our way of life," said Sayyid. "Early each morning the young boys take them to the feeding grounds. They don't return until the evening. They spend all day with the water buffalo."

Amara laughed. "My grandfather told me a story that once he was up all night with a sick buffalo. He covered it with a blanket and nursed it back to health with a bottle and songs."

"He sang to a buffalo?" Robbie asked.

"It's not uncommon. The Ma'adan depend on the buffalo for their existence. He gives milk, among a great many other things, and they thank Allah for this by treating the animals like family. It is not like in America the way you treat your animals."

"How do Americans treat their buffalo?" Sayyid asked.

"I won't tell you what happened to our buffalo," Robbie said. "But I guess the modern-day equivalent would be the cow. We have two kinds, dairy and meat. The dairy cows have a cushy life compared to the meat cows, but nobody sings to them. At least not that I know of. Although I did hear once about a farmer who played music to his watermelons."

Sayyid laughed, then grew quiet as he poled the boat through the water. "These marshes are all that is left. The Al Hammar and Central marshes are gone. Vanished. Like my people who inhabited them."

"They will come back, Uncle. When the water returns, they will come back."

"From your mouth to Allah's ears, niece," Sayyid said. "You know this group? Assisting Marsh Arab Refugees? The AMAR Foundation they call themselves."

"Yes. And I have read about another group," Amara said, "called Eden Again. The head of this group is an American, born in Iraq. They seek to return the water, to bring back the fish to the marshes. It is this group we come to work with. To offer our assistance," Amara turned to Robbie and squeezed his hand, "at great personal risk."

"How do you plan to help?" Sayyid asked. "No doubt you will use your schooling that was so important to my brother."

"Yes, uncle. I am sure they will need another biologist. And Robbie knows something about..." she turned to him for assistance.

"Environmental science. Back home I'm working on a degree," Robbie said. "For the first time I have a good reason for it."

"Uncle, may I?" Amara reached for the pole and Sayyid relinquished it with a smile, exchanging places with Amara in the boat.

"I know this group that you wish to find. Tomorrow I will take you to them. But today, we tour Al Hawizeh. It will be something for you to see," Sayyid said, turning to Robbie. "This place is like nowhere else in the world. What Saddam has done is a crime against Allah and against nature. He seeks to destroy the Ma'adan by destroying their way of life. But my people have inhabited these waters since the beginning of time. This is the Cradle of Civilization where the world began. Saddam thought to make history. And what has he done?" Sayyid spread his hands wide to emphasize his point.

"Not just genocide, but ecocide, uncle," Amara said.

"Yes." Sayyid turned to Robbie. "History will not be kind to him. But you caught him so there's hope." Sayyid returned his hands to his lap. "I don't dream it all will be returned. I'm not a naive man." Sayyid gazed after the reeds and bulrushes as the boat glided past. Robbie noted the comely, proud profile.

"Do you find it strange that they should take your name?" Sayyid asked Amara.

"Who, Uncle?"

The AMAR Foundation. Do you find it strange?" The marsh narrowed and Amara directed the boat toward a dense forest of reeds. "They say a man's name predicts his future." Sayyid raised his eyebrows in speculation. "Perhaps this is your destiny, Amara. To save your ancestors. To restore their lands." Sayyid stood and took the pole from Amara who resisted.

"I can do it," she protested. He motioned for her to sit down and reluctantly, she did.

"So much like my brother," he mused. Amara smiled, trailing her fingers in the water.

The flap of wings, the sounds of fish surfacing and retreating, the smell of dense, wet vegetation, and a million hues of green fanning out across the landscape all formed a backdrop to the peace rising up in Robbie's soul. He felt the adrenaline and terror ebbing away with each rhythmic pull of Sayyid's pole and that, coupled with a full belly, conspired to put him in a state of calm, the likes of which he had not experienced since he came to Iraq. A turtle jumped off the marsh and into the water. Amara pointed and turned to see if Robbie had seen it, but like the baby Moses adrift in a bed of papyrus, and the countless generations before him who had retreated deep within the marshes to hide from their aggressors, Robbie now lay hidden and safe, and in the safety of the marshes, he slept.

CHAPTER 70

Kori walked in the back door and dumped a pile of mail and the Sunday paper on the kitchen table. She shot Avery a dirty look, which he didn't catch because he didn't bother to look up from his magazine.

"Hi to you, too," she snapped. Avery took a bite of his cereal.

Kori got close to his face. "Hi!" she yelled.

Avery pulled the honey pot over, forcing Kori out of his immediate space. She crossed her arms and stared at him as he rolled the honey dipper around inside the pot. He pulled up a ball full and drizzled honey over his Cheerios, making little swirly patterns with the sticky golden liquid.

"Are you going to say something?" Kori asked.

He replaced the lid and pushed the honey jar away before turning his full attention to his sister. He scowled and squinted at her, contemplating his options.

"Yeah. I'll say something. Don't you think you're behaving outside the scope of what constitutes a good role model?" He took a sip of his juice, and rather than waiting for an answer, turned back to his magazine. Kori watched him, mouth agape.

"What the hell's that supposed to mean?" she shot back.

Avery pushed his chair back and crossed his legs. In that moment, he felt he'd become one with his father. He felt agitated and fatherly, a lecture for the child's latest transgression poised on his tongue.

"It means, you're acting like a … " His mouth formed a "wh" but no sound came out. Avery's face felt hot. He dropped his chin and looked at his stocking feet.

"What? Go ahead and say it." She threw a piece of junk mail at him. "Say it!" The envelope bounced off his shirt. "Say it, you little dweeb." She threw a stack of napkins at him. They fluttered to the floor like wingless birds. "Who the hell are you to judge me, huh? Do you know how hard it is being me? Keeping all this together?" She waved an arm behind her, a gesture so dramatic it may as well have encompassed the entire world, not just the pots and pans.

Avery rubbed the bridge of his nose, exactly the way Marty used to do to hide his smile, and mimed Kori's words back to her without looking up, a move Marty never made.

"Stop it, you little bastard." Kori lunged at her brother, but despite his lanky frame, Avery grabbed Kori with ease, stopping her in mid-slap, holding both of her arms, their faces inches apart. He looked closely at her now, at the worry lines on her face, at the dark, puffy circles below her eyes, and he softened. He released her and she sat down opposite him, looking pitiful and embarrassed. Avery returned to his magazine and pretended he wasn't moved.

"Just say it, would you?" Kori choked out the words.

"Okay. You need to be home more. Not just for Gil. For me, too." He pushed his cereal bowl away. "I can't remember everything. I have school, you know? And there's laundry everywhere and grocery shopping and Gil's homework to check, and I got my own homework. I mean, look at that." He waved his hand in the direction of the gargantuan pile of mail. "I think subconsciously I didn't pick it up because I know there are bills due and I've got no money to pay them with. I never know if there's going to be enough, and I keep hoping that Social Security will make a mistake and send us two checks so I can pay off some of these credit cards that I'm using, not to buy fun stuff, but to buy groceries." He dropped his head to his hands and stared at the floor.

Kori rubbed his back, but he shrugged her off and pulled himself together.

"You gotta get back to work. You have jobs waiting. Clients who can be tapped for other clients. Otherwise we're gonna drown here, Kori."

"Avery, I'm sorry. I didn't realize." Avery rolled his eyes.

"All right, I did. But I was trying to hide from it, too." She flopped down in the chair next to him. "Sorry."

"It's all right. Let's just get back on track, okay?"

"Okay." Kori slumped in her seat. "Anyway, I broke up with Chris."

"You're kidding. You and Mr. Wonderful are through?"

"He wasn't so wonderful."

"That's not what you said last week."

"Yeah well, last week my head was in a bubble of love, and this week the bubble burst. Life's much clearer without the filmy soap residue."

"What happened?"

"Same old, same old, I guess. My "last man on the totem pole" complex. He's so wrapped up in his work. I didn't see that the time he was dedicating to me had to do with the story he was researching. His interests have been slacking ever since the story ran on Gil. I got tired of ignoring it."

"What did Chris say?"

"Nothing."

"So you didn't tell him."

"I didn't think I needed to." Kori sighed. "Please don't beat me up about it."

Avery shrugged. "What good's it do to beat the animal that pulls the plow?"

Kori smacked him on the back. "Are you calling me a cow?"

"If the yoke fits," he said.

"Bastard." She smacked him again.

"Hey. Mr. Right'll come along. What did Mom say? For every pot there's a lid?"

"Are you calling me a pot now?"

"Geez, you're a bitch," Avery said. "Now leave me alone, please, so I can finish my gourmet breakfast." He pulled his cereal bowl over and took a bite but spit it out. "Uch. I hate soggy cereal." He dumped the offending mush, grabbed the cereal and was pouring a fresh bowl when the doorbell rang.

Kori looked at the kitchen clock. "Who's coming over at 9:30 on a Sunday morning?"

"Could be your new Prince Charming," Avery said.

"What if it's Chris?" Kori asked. "Will you get it?"

Avery laughed at the look on her face. "What if it is? You broke up with him, right?"

Kori didn't budge. Avery rolled his eyes.

"You better answer the door before the bell wakes Gil up."

"Just say I'm not here."

"In case you haven't noticed, I'm eating."

"Fine." Kori huffed, and stomped from the kitchen.

CHAPTER 71

Gil was under attack. He dodged a plastic missile and huddled under a small bush a few feet from the house. A large, old man, older than his father by a lot, was laughing. His laugh echoed, like it started down deep in the earth, and bulged and grew and clawed its way to the top where it became fearsome and overpowering. It made Gil's insides shake.

The man threw empty plastic water bottles at him: Perrier, Deer Park, Evian, Crystal Springs. The small bottles bounced off harmlessly, and he only ducked when the man launched the larger one-gallon bottles. He looked around for an escape route, and his eyes landed on the small plane parked next to the house. Kori would be pissed that he forgot to park it in the garage again, and that he was driving it without a license, but so what, he invented it. It wasn't a conventional plane but looked more like a giant egg laid on its side. Little claw-like chicken's feet descended from the main compartment and kept the body steady when the plane was grounded. The wings retracted into the body. Inside the egg were two seats, a cushion on the floor for Max, and a control panel. Avery wanted to sell these planes someday for a fraction of the cost of a Hummer.

Gil pulled a gas pump hose from an outlet below the kitchen window and crawled on his belly over to the egg, kicking plastic bottles as he went. He lifted the hatch and inserted the nozzle into the egg's fuel tank, dodging several bottles thrown in rapid succession. The hose connected to a small TDU in the basement and was fed by the garbage disposal and the trash bin, a complete in situ unit. After a few minutes, the filling stalled and the hose went limp in Gil's hand. He shook it but nothing happened. He crawled back over and kicked the wall of the house like a man kicking the tires of the car. "Oowww," he yelled, but the mini TDU failed to restart. "Dammit," he said, then covered his mouth and looked around to see if his sister was within hearing distance.

The large man started laughing again. Gil panicked and dropped the hose. He was crawling toward the egg when he heard Max at the kitchen door, barking like a crazy dog, so he crawled back to the house and let him out. Together they ran and jumped into the egg. Gil started the engine and the little chicken legs took off running at a fast clip. The wings fanned, the thrusters roared to life, and the egg was airborne, the chicken legs still running, but with no ground beneath them. When he retracted the legs, the egg shot straight up into the air. The large man bellowed, something between a laugh and a moan, and Gil accelerated. He turned around to see the man remove his Armani suit jacket, fold it neatly over his arm, and bend down to turn on an automatic ball toss machine.

"Where the heck did that come from?" Gil yelled to Max who raised his head to investigate. The machine began firing the empty plastic water bottles, pelting the egg mercilessly. Singularly, the bottles posed no harm, but collectively the force resulted in an erratic trajectory, throwing them off course while jolt after jolt caused the egg first to zig and then to zag. The large man laughed like a maniac, sending shock waves that caused the egg to tumble with each successive and inexorable guffaw.

"Hold on!" Gil yelled to Max who crouched down at Gil's feet, his paws over his eyes. Gil steered a hard right to avoid a fresh onslaught of plastic and came close enough to see the man's large mouth. And like the Cheshire cat, as the man's smile grew larger, his face shrank away until all that remained were his hideous radiating teeth, each half the size of the egg. The man threw a switch, converting the machine to fast pitch, and Gil was bombarded. The egg began to plummet. A bottle cracked the window. A hole emerged and grew. Air leaked out of the cabin. Gil flicked at the overhead switches.

"We're losing pressure," he screamed. He pushed a button and air masks dropped from the ceiling. He covered Max's large snout with one and was attempting to put his own mask on when the egg took another hit and rolled over. The mask flew out of Gil's hand and he lost control. He began coughing, choking for air.

Gil's eyes flew open and he coughed for a full minute before regaining his breath. Images of eggs and plastic swirled in the world behind his eyelids and he was cold and sweaty. He burrowed a hand under Max's furriness and laid his head on the dog's massive neck. Max yawned and put his head on the bed pillow. Gil closed his eyes, but the images still danced behind the lids, so he forced himself awake and sat up in bed. He yawned. His stomach growled rudely. He threw his feet over the side of the bed, put on his slippers and went downstairs to breakfast.

Chapter 72

"**D**o you have any collateral, Mr. Hartos?"

"As a matter of fact, I do." Hart opened his briefcase and displayed stock certificates for tens of thousands of shares of Akanabi Oil. The banker raised his eyebrows and picked up one of the certificates, analyzing it for authenticity.

"So what do you need me for?" the banker asked, setting down the certificate and folding his hands across his ample belly.

"I don't, actually," Hart said wryly. "Not if I sell that." He nodded toward the briefcase. "But I don't want to sell. Not yet." Hart opened Sonia's brown leather backpack and pulled out a thick business plan.

"I've been working on this all week," he said, pushing it across the table toward the banker. "I'm prepared to give you a twenty percent return on your money for the first five years in exchange for an unlimited line of credit."

The banker pitched forward in his chair and laid hands upon the document.

"Uh-ahh," Hart said, shaking his head. "Not before we make a deal."

"How can I make a deal if I can't examine the business plan?"

Hart pulled a confidentiality agreement from Sonia's backpack and placed it in front of the banker who read it.

"It bars you from even speaking about this matter to anyone who is not intimately involved in the release of funds, and then it's only on a need-to-know basis. After you read the plan, you'll understand the paranoia. This is revolutionary technology. The urge to steal it will be strong."

"This bank is not interested in anything illegal or immoral, Mr. Hart."

"It's nothing like that. But it will be the greatest invention since the advent of the industrial revolution. And you have the opportunity to be a part of it."

"What's the catch?"

"No catch. I need a line of credit. You're in business to make money."

"But why not do it yourself?" the banker asked, motioning toward the stock certificates.

Hart smiled and leaned back in his chair. "Once the first plant is built, that won't be enough to cover the cost of expansion. It's gonna spread like the wildfire, I guarantee you. Cities, states, municipalities, the Feds ... they'll all be clamoring for it."

Interest piqued, the banker signed the confidentiality agreement and opened the business plan. Hart watched his face change as he read the one-page introduction.

"Either you're a crazy man, or a genius, I'm not sure. But if it's true, I see your point. There's no telling how big this could get."

"So, we have a deal?"

"I need to look this over in detail, but my preliminary response would be yes, we most certainly have a deal." The two men shook hands.

"I'll look this over and call you later."

"No."

"I'm sorry, what?"

"I'll sit and wait until you've finished reading."

"Mr. Hartos, a line of credit of this magnitude will require the acquiescence of the bank's Board of Directors. And it's not going to be granted on a verbal request."

"That's fine. After everyone signs the confidentiality agreement, you get a copy of the business plan."

"Okay, well I've signed, so I can keep this copy."

"Not until you've approved the line of credit."

"But I just told you … "

"Look. I don't know how you're going to do it. Maybe only approve a line of credit manageable at the branch level and then take it to the board for an increase. In the interim, get everybody's signatures and I'll provide the literature."

The banker shook his head. "We just don't do business that way."

"There are plenty of banks on this street. Someone's going to lend me the money."

"Not without the proper paperwork."

"Suit yourself." Hart collected his papers and stuffed them in Sonia's backpack. "Remember. You signed an agreement. Not a word. Because if I hear one, I'll own this bank."

Hart smiled broadly. "Good day."

CHAPTER 73

As Gil's slippered feet hit the carpeted stairs, Kori was opening the front door. Gil froze. Sunlight blazed in through the door obliterating the man's visage, but Gil could see the silhouette looming and spreading across the space between the doorframes. Kori exchanged pleasantries, which Gil didn't catch because his ears were buzzing. She gestured toward Gil on the stairs, and the large man in the Armani suit stood in the middle of the living room moving his mouth, but with no sound coming out. The man smiled his giant toothy smile, waiting for Gil to say something, Gil was sure. Kori slammed the door behind the man, and Gil ducked at the sound, reminiscent of plastic bottles hitting their target. The man had one foot on the second stair now. Gil's throat emitted a strange noise, even by his standards, as the man held out his hand for a shake. Gil grabbed Max by the collar and ran upstairs, locking himself in his room.

↟

Bicky stood with his foot on the stair, his hand outstretched in the gesture of greeting. He watched Gil's lithe body retreat until he crested the top of the stairs and disappeared. Bicky turned to look at Kori, his arm still outstretched.

"Was it something I said?"

"He gets like that. He's really smart. It comes out in weird ways." She ran a hand through her hair and looked Bicky over, the Armani suit, the soft hands with nails more expertly manicured than her own. "Maybe you want to come back after breakfast? He's usually pretty communicative after a meal."

Bicky's face contorted into something that had the capacity to be a smile, but fell short somehow. Kori smiled back, feeling the draw of Bicky's gravitational pull, but only on one side.

"How about I talk to you for a while?" Bicky said.

Kori shrugged. "I guess that's okay."

"Maybe your other brother, too. Is he home?"

Kori narrowed her eyes and opened her mouth as if to speak.

"The newspaper article," Bicky said, intercepting her query.

"Oh. Okay." She turned and led him to the kitchen. Avery looked up from reading his magazine, but his expression did not change.

"Avery, this is Mr. Coleman. He owns Akanabi Oil. He wants to talk to us about the TDU." Bicky held out his hand for a shake, but Avery ignored it. Instead, he stood up, came eye-to-eye with Bicky and sneezed.

"Excuse me," Avery said and walked around Bicky holding a hand over his nose to hide the runny mucus. He sneezed again, grabbed a few tissues and blew out a nose full of snot. He tossed the tissues in the trashcan then held out his hand to Bicky who dropped his own hand to his side. Avery sneezed again, but it was only the first in a continuing series.

Kori counted ten sneezes before she said, "Why don't we go sit in the living room and wait until Avery's done." Bicky nodded and retreated. Kori glanced back over her shoulder to see Avery pulling out the tissues three and four at a time.

⅄

Bicky settled himself in an armchair as Avery continued sneezing in the kitchen. Neither Bicky nor Kori noticed Gil sitting in the shadows at the top stairs, peering through the banister.

"So, I read about you kids in the newspaper. I understand you've invented an amazing new piece of equipment."

"Actually, we didn't. My father did."

"Yes. I'm sorry about your father," Bicky said with as much emotion as he could muster. Kori nodded, sighed and drew a deep breath. "We don't know what we're going to do with it yet."

Bicky kept the emotion in his voice well checked and continued. "Perhaps I've come along just in time."

"In time for what?" Avery walked into the living room holding a box of tissues.

"You done now?" Kori asked. Avery nodded.

"Sorry. It's like I breathed in something toxic." He looked directly at Bicky's impassive mask.

"You sound all stuffy now," Kori said.

"I feel like someone sprayed caulk up my nose," Avery said. Gil giggled from his spot on the stairs and covered his mouth. Bicky turned toward the sound but said nothing.

"So, Mr. Coleman," Avery said. "I'm sure that as the head of Akanabi Oil you're acquainted with one David Hartos."

"Yes, I know one David Hartos," Bicky said, struggling against a full-fledged smile. "He works for me."

"It was my understanding that he's currently on sabbatical from the oil industry, so technically speaking, he is not working for you at all, but rather, for himself at present."

"You sound like every lawyer I've ever hired."

Avery held his smile in check with a stern, tight-lipped countenance. "Kori, can I see you in the kitchen for a minute?" Kori gave her brother a weird look but rose to go.

"Excuse us, Mr. Coleman," Avery said. "We'll be back shortly."

As soon as Avery and Kori left, Bicky smiled, his first genuine, un-planned smile in years.

🗡

Avery pulled Kori out the back door onto the deck, leaving the door ajar.

"What is wrong with you?" Kori asked. "First the gnarly sneezing and now you're being so rude. This guy's the head of a big oil company. He probably wants to buy the TDU and if that's the case, I say good riddance for all the trouble it's caused."

"What about Hart? We told him we'd work with him."

"You didn't sign anything, did you?"

"Listen to you!"

"No, listen to you, Mr. Lawyer. If you didn't sign anything, where's your obligation?"

"We made a deal to work with him, me and Gil. Gil thinks the guy walks on water. And I think we can trust him. He's out looking for financing, right now. I'm not going to call him up and tell him the deal's off."

"Spare me the drama."

"I'm serious."

"So am I. If the TDU is so fantastic, investors will be pounding down our door."

"Well it looks like that parade might have just started." Avery poked his head in the door and strained his ear toward the living room. He could hear nothing.

"He might be about to offer us some serious money, Avery. And I think we should take it. Wouldn't it be nice to be out of debt for a change? I mean, this morning … "

"We can't do that, Kori. I don't like him. And I don't trust him."

"You don't even know him."

"I know I'm having an allergic reaction to him."

Kori rolled her eyes. "That is the dumbest thing I ever heard. You're not going to take his money because of a few sneezes?"

Avery blushed.

"Give me one good reason why we shouldn't work with him, Avery."

"Dad." Avery said. "Dad would never sell out."

Kori stared at her brother and when she spoke, her voice was quiet, reluctant. "Well, Dad isn't here to provide for us anymore, Avery. And we need to pay our bills and keep food on the table and all those other things that parents do for their kids, but we now have to do for ourselves." Kori turned to go inside, but Avery grabbed her wrist.

Avery drew a deep breath. "All right. We'll listen to what he has to say. But no decisions until we talk to Hart. Okay?"

"All right." She sighed, squeezing Avery's arm. "Let's get back in there."

⋏

Gil strolled down the steps with Max. Bicky heard them coming, but acted surprised when they entered the room. Holding Max by the collar, Gil took a seat on the couch and stared at Bicky until even the unflappable Coleman became a bit unhinged.

"What?" Bicky finally said.

"What?" Gil replied.

"What are you looking at?"

"What are you looking at?"

"I asked you first."

"I asked you first."

"Is this some kind of joke?" Bicky shifted in his chair, annoyed.

"Is this some kind of joke?"

"You're not one of those idiot savants, are you?"

"You're not one of those … "

"Oh shut up, already. I get the game." Bicky huffed as if the very idea was ridiculous to him. "My own daughter used to play it all the time. I didn't like it then and I … "

"What happened to your hand?" Bicky covered his bandaged hand with his free hand in response.

"What are you doing here?" Gil asked.

Bicky looked Gil over, the piercing, intelligent eyes, the purposeful posture, the fact that he had his own hand resting lightly on the neck of a seventy-five pound ferocious looking dog with a mean set of teeth. In that instant he knew this child, for that was what he was, could not be trifled with, and moreover, that it was more than intellect working in that compact, graceful body. He decided instantly, subconsciously, that truth was the best course of action.

"Well, I'm not here to help, obviously. I'm a businessman and businessmen do not become successful by helping," Bicky said. True confessions.

Gil nodded, a beneficent king waiting for his subject to continue.

"But I'm not here to steal anything from you either. I'm willing to pay the fair market value for the product you've invented, and should that not be possible given the scope and reach of the product, then I'm willing to bring you in as a partner, to a limited extent, of course, given that I'm taking all the financial risks, and to make sure your family receives money from the development and sale of this product for years to come. You'll never have to worry about money again, that's for sure."

"I'm ten. I don't worry about money now. That's for Kori and Avery to worry about."

"Well, what do I have that would interest you? I'm sure there's something I can give you to make this deal not just acceptable but attractive to you."

Gil shook his head slowly back and forth. "We don't need you. We have Hart."

Bicky smiled slightly, relishing the delivery of this news. "Hart works for me."

"I know that. But he's not doing this with you. He's doing this with us."

"Hart can't give you what I can give you."

"He can get as much money as we need to build a factory."

"Hart's a very rich man, and I'm sure he'll be true to his word. But have you thought about the expense of not only developing your machine but building, staffing and maintaining an oil refinery? It's not just the cost but the labor that's very intensive. The insurance alone on a facility like that'll kill you. I can offer you a fully functional, completely operational facility. Already built and running and only a scant thirty or so miles from here."

"We already have one in the backyard," Gil said.

Bicky's raised his eyebrows, but he didn't say anything.

"They're not hard to make if you know what you're doing."

"Surely you don't think you're going to build something of this magnitude in your backyard?"

"I told you. I'm only ten. That part's up to Avery." As if on cue, the backdoor slammed, and Bicky heard strangled whispers and two sets of footsteps approaching. And given the brief time he'd spent in the presence of the sixteen-year old — for God's sake, was everyone in this family a prodigy? — Bicky knew he needed to make his move now or lose his chance forever.

"The plant will be a monument to your father. I'll even rename the refinery after him. By the time we're finished, not just the U.S., but the world will know how great he was. We can even market some of his other inventions. I mean he didn't create something like this in a vacuum. The man was obviously a genius." Bicky paused for effect. "I'll leave it up to you, of course, whether you want to pursue those other avenues."

"Hey, Gil," Avery said, coming into the room. "I see you've met Mr. Coleman. He … "

"He's taking us on a tour of his oil refinery this morning," Gil said, before turning to Kori. "Do we have any pop tarts? Me and Max are starving."

"Ah. Okay," Bicky said. "Shall we take breakfast on the road?"

Chapter 74

Gil, Max and Kori sat in the back seat of Bicky's Lexus so Avery could sit up front and "talk business." Bicky set the cruise control and the car glided north on I-95 at seventy-two miles per hour.

"Why seventy-two if the speed limit is sixty-five?" Avery asked.

"The police don't stop you for a five-mile transgression," Bicky said. "I like to push it the extra mile or two."

"Guess you get a lot of tickets."

"I haven't had a ticket since I was twenty-five."

Avery raised an eyebrow. "Guess you're lucky, then."

Bicky raised an eyebrow of his own and smiled wryly.

"So. Have you figured out the parameters of the deal you're offering or are you waiting to see how sophisticated we are? The 'Louisiana Purchase' comes to mind."

"I'm not trying to bilk you with a handful of beads, I assure you. My money's as good as the next guy's. I just have more of it."

Avery checked off a note made on a small legal pad. "If we made a deal, we wouldn't be interested in a lump sum payment. We'd want royalties. And if the stock goes public, we'd want dividends. We'd also want to retain a large portion of the interest. The controlling interest."

"I'm confident I can meet all your needs." Bicky's eyes didn't leave the road.

"Max, knock it off," Kori snipped from the back seat. Max flipped his giant fluff of a tail in Kori's face, his hair snaking its way into her mouth and nose. She pushed his tail aside and rubbed the itch from her nose.

"What about the requirement that Hart still be involved?" Avery asked.

"I told you, Hart works for me. He's my Chief Engineer right now. Perhaps I could move him up to Chief of Operations for this project. Let him work solely on this."

"You ever going to give this dog a bath?" Kori asked Gil.

"Let's see how it sounds to Hart before we make any decisions," Avery said.

"Because he stinks," Kori said.

"He doesn't stink," Gil said. "He just needs a biscuit for his breath. He had garlic last night."

Kori shoved Max's tail out of her face again. "Get that dog's tail out of my face, before I cut it off," she snapped. As if in response, Max whacked her in the face again. She sneezed. "Gil, I swear to God … "

"Your sister sounds annoyed," Bicky said.

"She broke up with her boyfriend this morning," Avery said.

Bicky nodded slowly as if all had been revealed. "I know a little about that."

"Come here, Max," Gil said, pulling Max down to him with one hand. The other hand gripped an open package of pop tarts, which Gil bit into two at a time. He broke off a piece and handed it to Max who inhaled it, swallowing without even chewing. Gil then stuffed Max's tail underneath his body. Thus, both chastised and sated, Max put his head on Gil's lap and went to sleep. Gil took another pass at the twin pop tarts. "I'm thirsty," he said with a mouth full of wild berry.

"You should have brought a bottle of water with you," Avery said.

"But I didn't."

"We're on I-95," Kori said. "Not a Wawa for miles. Guess you're just going to have to suffer." Kori flashed a smug smile and turned to the window to watch the industrialized landscape glide serenely by. Gil flashed his food-laden tongue at her, but she didn't see it.

"I can't wait, Avery," Gil said. Avery turned around and gave Gil a sympathetic shrug. Bicky watched Gil in the rear view mirror, clutching his pop tarts and looking retched. He grabbed his own bottle of Perrier, sitting in between the console, and handed it back to Gil.

"Thanks," Gil said with a full mouth. He took a swig and handed it back to Bicky. Bicky took one look at the minute traces of pop tart swirling around in the bottle, suspended in crystal plastic and shook his head.

"You keep it," Bicky said.

Gil nodded and smiled. When he finished the last bite, he said to Bicky, "Do you know that bottled water is responsible for an increase in tooth decay?"

"Well it's a good thing you didn't bring any with you. We wouldn't want your teeth rotting on the way," Bicky said.

Avery chortled. Even Kori smiled at Bicky's quick retort.

"Did you know that in 1990, a little over two billion gallons of bottled water were sold in the U.S, and that it's going to hit over seven billion gallons by the end of 2005?" Gil asked. "And that retailers sell more bottled water than coffee or milk or even soda?"

"That's a lot of water," Bicky said.

"Yeah, and you know where it comes from?"

"From natural springs?"

"Yep. From natural springs fed by groundwater that belongs to everybody," Gil said. "Did you know you were paying for water that already belongs to you?"

"How's that make you feel?" Avery asked.

"Cheated," Bicky replied.

"That ground water that used to be going somewhere else, like to somebody's well, or to feed a wetland is now being diverted to a little plastic bottle that sells for $1.19 in Wawa." Gil held up the bottle by way of demonstration. Pieces of pop tart floated in silence.

"Whoever came up with that name anyway? Wawa?" Bicky asked.

"I think it's the name of a type of Canadian goose," Avery said.

"Still, what's that have to do with a convenience store?" Bicky said.

"Don't you even care that you're paying $1.19 for somebody else's groundwater, and that *that* somebody isn't even getting the money?" Gil asked. "Instead some multinational corporation is."

Bicky turned to Avery. "Is he always like this?"

"He's just getting warmed up," Avery said.

"Fascinating," Bicky said. "Maybe there's a way we can bottle him."

"What kind of water do you prefer, Mr. Bicky?" Gil asked. "This?" Gil held up the Perrier bottle.

"It's true. I confess. I'm a Perrier man."

"Did you know that Perrier is a defendant in citizen suits in five different states? People are mad because they say Perrier's using up all their groundwater. Perrier says that doesn't make good business sense — to use up all of the resource that they're selling — but how do we know what they're thinking?" Gil mused. "They sell fifteen different brands of water, you know, and pump it from about seventy-five different spring-fed locations. They sell more bottled water than anyone else in the country which means they pump more water, in some cases as much as five hundred gallons per minute from their sources — taxpayer owned, of course."

"Do you know who owns Perrier?" Avery asked.

Bicky shook his head.

"Nestle. The largest food company in the world. A multinational mega-corporation."

Bicky looked at Avery as if he'd just thrown up a hairball. "What is wrong with you people? You're children, for God's sake. Children don't behave like this. They talk about things like baseball and the latest creature feature at the Cineplex."

"You don't have to dry up the entire aquifer in order to dry up your neighbor's well," Avery added.

"Did you know that after a certain point an aquifer loses the ability to recharge itself?" Gil said. "Do you think it's possible Nestle knows what that point is?"

Bicky glanced in the mirror to find Gil looking at him with large owl eyes, unblinking and full of certainty, the way Bicky envisioned an owl's must look before it's about to pounce on a tasty bit of prey. For the first time in years, Bicky thought he might be out of his league.

"The thing is if you watch a water commercial, they're selling health. Health, health, health," Avery said. "Pure, crystal-clear, uncorrupted health."

"Did you know one company was pulling water from a well in a parking lot adjacent to an industrial facility that at times had traces of hazardous chemicals in it?" Gil asked.

"Oh, come on. Now, you're making this up," Bicky said.

"Am not," Gil replied.

"I'm sure there are water quality standards," Bicky said.

"Huh! You wish. The EPA regulates tap water which, except for a very few places, is safe. But it doesn't regulate bottled water. The companies regulate their own selves. Get it?" Bicky saw Gil wink at him in the rearview mirror, an action so exaggerated it looked like his whole face was winking.

"The FDA's supposed to regulate bottled water, but they don't interpret the rules the same way and even worse, they don't even have a full-time staffer dedicated to overseeing the whole bottled water craze," Avery said. "EPA employs hundreds of people whose job it is to regulate tap water. Do you see a dichotomy there?" Avery pointed a finger at Bicky. "On any given day a water authority has to give you a list of what's in the tap water you're tied into. It's required by law. Not so for the bottlers. They don't even have to answer your letters. And tap water isn't allowed to contain even traces of e-coli, where bottled water has a limit."

"Oh, this is ridiculous. You're telling me that bottled water contains e-coli," Bicky said.

"I'm telling you it may contain traces, and it wouldn't be prohibited by law," Avery said. "The National Resources Defense Council, that's the NRDC, tested a hundred and four brands of bottled water over four years and found a third of them contained things like arsenic and other carcinogenic compounds. Odds are, tap water is safer than bottled, but people don't find it as appealing."

"It's because the water authorities don't advertise," Kori said.

"Another country heard from," Bicky replied, glancing in the rearview mirror at Kori who didn't take her eyes from the window.

"She's sort of in advertising," Avery said. Bicky shook his head and huffed.

"They say that if bottled water sits on your shelf for more than a year, it might go bad. Whoever heard of water going bad?" Avery asked. "I think it's the plastic leaching."

"Do you know the worst part?" Gil asked.

"No, but somehow I think you're going to tell me," Bicky answered.

"The worst part is that thirty million bottles a day go to landfills. Only one out of ten bottles is recycled. Did you know that it takes a thousand years for plastic to break down?"

"Enough. I get it. You've managed to depress me sufficiently to last for the rest of the millennium. So can we talk about something else?"

"Sure," Gil said. Name a topic."

⋏

By the time they arrived at the Akanabi refinery, Bicky was more thoroughly drained than a kitchen sink after a visit from the Roto-Rooter man. The car ride with an adolescent, a teenager, and, from what he could tell, a scorned and scornful young woman had left him jittery and out of sorts. Hart was right. That these weren't normal kids was abundantly clear. Perhaps he'd need to rethink his plan to woo and wow them and turn to contingency plan B. Now he just needed to devise it before the sister — the putative leader of the group from what he could figure, because of age, not intellect — got bored and called the whole thing off. Bicky felt his blood quicken as he stepped out of the car. His mouth was dry, his tongue felt thick and spongy, and he wished for about the third time in the last half hour that he hadn't given his bottle of Perrier away even if the little Einstein was right and the bottle, because of its very existence, would smother the earth's surface. Who the hell cared? We may be unearthing and chopping down our collective resources at unprecedented rates, but he'd be dead by the time we managed to pave over the entirety of the Eden we called the United States.

Bicky parked and checked the rearview mirror. Kori was asleep with her head resting against the window, her eyebrows furrowed in concentration. On the opposite side, Gil stared wide-eyed at the tank farm directly across from the parking lot. Bicky cut the engine, but made no move to get out, just continued watching the sleeping Kori and insatiable Gil.

"We ready?" Avery asked.

Bicky turned to the third of the triumvirate. "You know what? Since your sister's asleep, let's drive the tour route. You can stop me whenever you see something you might want to investigate further."

"Okay," Avery said. "*Vamanos.*"

Chapter 75

"All this," Jack said, placing his hand on Kori's heart, "is highly combustible. When things heat up like this, it always gets a little dicey." Jack removed his hand from Kori's heart and pulled her to him. "It's all about chemical reactions, Kori," Jack said. "The most dangerous part of the process is starting up and shutting down. That's when things are the most precarious." He squeezed her hand and smiled. "But you already knew that." She smiled back despite herself.

"Are we starting up or shutting down?" Kori asked. She hoped her voice didn't belie the need in her.

"That depends. Can you take the heat?" Jack asked.

"Well, how hot's it gonna get?" Kori asked.

"As much as thirteen hundred degrees Fahrenheit for some of these processes," Jack said.

"What processes?" Kori asked.

"Refining processes," Bicky said.

"What are you talking about?" Kori asked. She took a deep breath and surfaced to consciousness, opening first one eye and then the other. When she realized where she was, she groaned and squeezed both eyes shut.

"Boiling points, my dear," Bicky said. "The beauty of crude oil is that it's not just a single chemical compound but a mixture of hundreds of them. They're hydrocarbon chains and they each have different boiling points. Refining is simply heating the crude to higher and higher boiling points and pulling off the vapor through the process of fractional distillation. Then you condense the vapor through cooling in the distillation column." Bicky glanced in the rearview mirror. Kori scowled at him but Bicky continued. "Each different hydrocarbon chain is useful for something. With a chemical process called conversion you can convert the longer chains to shorter chains depending on demand. You can also combine fractions to give you yet more usable products. Of course, much of it needs to be treated, but that's a small price to pay. There's a reason why crude oil's called liquid gold. It's one of the most versatile compounds known to man. Actually it's a shame that so much of what we make with it is gasoline."

"Now who's showing off?" Gil asked.

Bicky smiled. "Don't blink now, ladies and gentlemen, or you'll miss it. To the right is the crude oil distillation unit and to the left is the delayed coking unit. Beautiful, aren't they?" Bicky asked.

"What a geek," Kori mumbled under her breath. Max's tail brushed her nose and the combination of smelly dog and too much expensive perfume from the pedantic idiot up front was making her head hurt. She sneezed and turned back to the window.

"Hey, Sleeping Beauty," Avery said. "Have a nice nap?" Kori stared at Avery long enough to convey her distaste before returning her gaze to the storage tanks that looked like hundreds of giant white gum drops floating by her window. "You were snoring," Avery said.

"And drooling," Gil added.

"Shut up," Kori said. Avery held his hand up for a high-five and Gil whacked it.

"I just want to go back to sleep," Kori said, desperate to see how her dream would end.

"That's the tank farm on the left, if you're interested, Kori," Bicky said.

Kori couldn't be less interested. She yawned, rubbed her head and smacked Max's twitching tail away from her face.

"Knock it off, Kori," Gil yelled.

"I told you to keep his tail out of my face, you little brat."

Gil scowled at Kori and pulled Max closer to him. "You better watch it or I'll set him loose on you."

"Yeah, right," Kori snarled.

"No blood, please," Bicky said. "It's a rental." Both Kori and Gil stared out their respective windows.

"So. As I was saying, there are many different processes that occur in a refinery. There's separation and conversion and treating and blending. Crude oil gives us lubricating oil, tar, asphalt, petrochemicals, which are used to manufacture plastics. And, it's a model for recycling since many of the end products are used as feedstock to create new products." Bicky craned his neck to look out the window. "See over there? That's the catalytic reforming unit. And over there's the catalytic cracker," Bicky said.

Kori rolled her eyes and mumbled "freak" under her breath. She looked over at Gil to gauge whether he heard her, but Gil was listening with rapt attention, apparently enthralled with every word that came out of Bicky's mouth.

"So far the TDU only makes oil and gas and some mineral byproducts. But we could make other stuff," Avery said.

Gil nodded.

"Are we going home anytime soon?" Kori whined.

"That's the hydrofluoric acid alkylation unit," Bicky said. "And over there is the sulfuric acid alkylation unit. And that, I believe, is the light ends distillation unit."

"Do you know how all these units work?" asked Gil.

"Years ago, when I first started out, I devoured chemistry and I knew the ins and outs of all these machines," Bicky said. "It's been awhile, though. I think I may have forgotten."

"You don't ever forget, really," Gil said. Bicky looked at him in the rear view mirror and when their eyes met, Gil smiled.

⋏

At Gil's insistence, they had stopped at Wendy's for dinner, because Gil wanted a frosty. Although Bicky detested fast food of any kind, he acquiesced after Gil reported he was prone to carsickness, almost always brought on by a lack of snack food. Bicky smiled inwardly. The kid was clever, that was for sure. Bicky watched him in the rear view mirror, Gil's countenance serene in sleep.

Recognition lit Bicky's brain like a fireworks display and a bolt of adrenaline shot through his solar plexus as memories of a ten-year old Mason came flooding back to him. Although Gil looked nothing like Bicky's brother who had died around Gil's age, Gil's canny mind, crooked smile and clever dialogue lent him an aura reminiscent of Mason. A shiver ran through Bicky's body, as if Mason himself had reached out beyond death to whisper in his brother's ear. Bicky squeezed his eyes shut to quell the flood of memories, then opened them and focused on the lines in the road.

It was after 10:00 p.m. when Bicky pulled into the Tirabis' driveway.

"Sorry about the time," Bicky said. "I didn't realize it was so late. You'll be tired in school tomorrow."

Avery shrugged and looked at Bicky with kind eyes. Any malice he was still holding for the man was evaporating like distilling crude oil. "Thanks for showing us the refinery … how everything worked."

Bicky dismissed the thank you with a wave of his hand. "You're most welcome."

"Kori could probably have done with something less than a marathon tour," Avery said, but she'll get over it."

They turned to glance at Kori who, along with Gil and Max, was fast asleep in the backseat.

"He's got a huge appetite," Bicky said, watching Gil.

"Oh, yeah. Thanks for dinner."

"Stop thanking me already. That's actually not what I was talking about. It's his voracious appetite for knowledge." Bicky turned back to Avery. "You all have it."

Kori snored, a small, inconsequential noise, but a snore all the same. Avery raised his eyebrows and looked at Bicky for confirmation.

"Yes. Even Kori," Bicky said.

Kori issued another strange, guttural sound, waking herself up.

"We're home?" she asked.

"You spent most of your day sleeping," Avery said.

"I dreamt we were little. Before Gil was born. The three of us were asleep in the backseat and Dad said he and Mom should carry us all in at once so no one would be left alone. Mom said she'd wait with two while he brought one in, but Dad said that still left someone alone, but on the inside. He hated to see anyone be alone." She rubbed the sleep from her eyes and yawned wide. "Mom had Robbie and Dad already had you Avery, and was leaning in, trying like hell to pick me up one handed. I peeked and he saw me, so I shut my eyes real quick, waiting for him to say I should walk inside since I was awake. But he didn't say it – just carried me in, pretending I was still asleep." Kori's gaze grew wistful and her head lolled back against the seat. "Weird. The stuff you dream about." She got out and offered Bicky her hand. "Thanks for dinner. Sorry about how I acted before."

"My pleasure," Bicky replied, his gaze falling once again on Gil. "How about I carry him?" He looked at Avery and then at Kori and smiled. "You, on the other hand, will have to walk."

PART THREE

Chapter 76

Hart sat on the bed in his hotel room reading the newspaper behind closed eyelids. Two sharp raps on the door startled him awake.

"Hold on," Hart called. He rubbed his face with one hand before rising to look through the peephole.

"What the ... ?" Hart said, throwing the door open.

Bicky held up a hand to silence him. "May I come in?"

Hart stepped aside to allow Bicky in. Bicky headed straight to the window.

"I've been calling you all day," Hart said. "What the hell are you doing here?" Hart grabbed two beers out of the mini-fridge, popped the tops and set one down on the windowsill next to Bicky. "And what happened to your hand?"

Bicky appraised the offending appendage as if it were an alien species but said nothing. Hart switched topics.

"I've secured financing. But it means I have to sell out. Completely sell out. Every last stock certificate." Hart gave this information some time to sink in, but Bicky didn't answer, just stared out the window, his face glued to the view. "Look, I know what that could do to you ... to the company. And I'm not trying to undermine you, Bicky, so if you can get the money together ... ."

"I spent the whole day with the kids." Bicky stood as still as Billy Penn atop City Hall Tower, staring out over the Delaware, watching the ships come in. "She came back nicely, didn't she?" he said, nodding toward the river. "Not even a trace of the spill is visible to the naked eye. And it's only been what? Two months? He picked up his beer and raised the neck to tap Hart's own. "To the healing power of nature." Bicky took a seat on the windowsill and turned to Hart, his entire body engaged.

It was the atypical nature of the gesture that made Hart uneasy. "I'm guessing you didn't come here to talk about nature."

Bicky shook his head. "I was wrong. Too many times over these years I've treated you with less than the respect you deserved." Bicky picked up the beer but did not drink. "You're a fine engineer and a fine son-in-law. Probably the best I've ever seen in both categories." He set his beer down and stood up. "I just wanted to tell you that."

Hart stared at Bicky, mouth agape. In the ten years he'd known his father-in-law, Hart had received more than his share of the booty for a job well done: new cars, six-figure bonuses, vacations in exotic settings, even a boat once, but this one small comment, mixed with confession, was the most profound and heartfelt gesture Bicky had ever made. Perplexed and more out of sorts than when Bicky first walked in, Hart stood up, too.

"Thanks," he said. He looked at Bicky queerly for a moment until Bicky's words sunk in. "The kids? I guess you're talking about my kids?"

"Very fascinating family. I've been thinking about this all day, and I'm prepared to make a deal that benefits everyone. Truly benefits everyone."

"I'm listening."

"Tomorrow. Let's meet at the Tirabis' in the morning. Say ten?"

"You want to give me a glimpse into the future?"

"The thought struck me that you could benefit from an existing facility, not just for refining purposes, but for transport. We have pipelines all over the country bringing raw crude into our refineries. What if we reversed the process? Instead of pumping to us, we send the finished product, the stuff you distill from trash, away from us to be either sold or further refined around the country. We're set up to run with this without the additional capital cost and I predict..."

Hart's smile was so wide Bicky stopped in mid-sentence.

"What?" Bicky asked.

"Had you given me the chance on the phone that night ... "

"Oh. You already thought of that, is that it?" Bicky smiled, his trade-mark half-smile. "Well, thanks for humoring an old man." Bicky patted Hart on the back and walked to the door. "Tomorrow."

"The Tirabi kids know we're coming?"

"Yes." Bicky stood face-to-face with his son-in-law, his hand on the doorknob. "They are one loyal group. They wouldn't deal with me at all until you were at the table. You should be proud of that. The ability to engender loyalty is a lost art."

Hart couldn't formulate a response because of the boulder in his throat. Bicky squeezed Hart's shoulder and shook his hand at the same time.

"See you tomorrow, son."

Chapter 77

At exactly 10:00 A.M. the next morning, Bicky arrived at the Tirabi residence uncharacteristically dressed in a pair of khaki pants and a polo shirt. Kori and Jack were sitting at the kitchen table when he knocked at the front door. Kori jumped.

"You expecting company?" Jack asked.

"No." She had called Jack the minute Bicky pulled out of the driveway the previous night, and Jack had picked up on the first ring as if waiting for her call. They'd talked into the small hours when night blurs into day and the grandest of ideas are born. After a marathon phone session, Jack showed up on the front step looking hanged-dogged and hopeful. Kori invited him up to her room where they'd continued their conversation, among other things, and now they were both sated and pleasantly exhausted. Maybe it was the sleep deprivation, the fact that they hadn't seen each other in a while, or that Jack had made sufficient reparations along with all the right promises, but whatever it was, when Jack proposed that they get back together, Kori acquiesced. And she hadn't again thought, until this precise moment, about Chris Kane. So while she sat, still as garden statuary, wondering about the odds of him being on the other side of the door, and if so, how to explain it away, Jack got up and answered it.

"Kori's in the kitchen," she heard Jack say as Bicky entered. Kori let out every cubic inch of breath she'd been holding and smiled.

"Good night, I see," Bicky said, smiling back at her.

Kori introduced the men and Bicky extended his hand, his smile wide, and like the khaki's, both uncharacteristic and real.

"I heard all about you yesterday," Bicky said.

Jack shot Kori a quizzical look and she blushed. "I was dreaming," Kori said. "I'll tell you about it later."

"And I'll keep all further comments to myself except to say that's a very special lady," Bicky said. "Should you have the good fortune to have her unwavering gaze upon you, I suggest you rise to meet it."

Kori popped up and planted a kiss on Bicky's cheek. "I take back all the bad thoughts I had about you yesterday" Kori said. She gave Bicky a squeeze, which he accepted stiffly, clearing his throat.

"It's like hugging Gil," Kori said to Jack. Bicky blushed at his own ineptness.

"They're out in the barn," Kori said. "Just Gil and Hart. Avery's at the library working on the patent."

Bicky nodded and whispered into Kori's ear, loud enough for Jack to hear, "I think, my dear, that a mid-morning nap might do you wonders," and he closed the door behind him.

"I think it's an excellent idea," Jack said, pulling Kori close. "No time like the present."

⅄

The strains of Yo-Yo Ma's cello on the soundtrack to *Crouching Tiger, Hidden Dragon* filled every crevice, corner and cobweb in the barn. Gil practiced the martial arts techniques he learned from the movie using a broomstick and Max as his opponent. Hart reclined on the hammock, reading a backdated version of *Omni Magazine*, one that waxed prophetically about the brilliance of a little known scientist by the name of Marty Tirabi who harbored radical theories and an insatiable appetite for breaking down paradigms. The article, written in 1983, donned Marty the proverbial new messiah of the scientific world, said his star was quick and rising, and it was just a matter of time before he stood the scientific community on its head with some scintillating new breakthrough.

Hart stopped to watch Gil who executed first a side and then a round-house kick, both flawless. He poked the air with the broom handle while Max chased the other end. Waves of tenderness started in Hart's chest and rippled outward to his arms and legs, his fingers and toes, and kept on rippling until he felt the room go electric with it. God had given him back something that he'd been horribly denied, something minute yet infinite. He breathed in the smell, like the air after a lightning storm, both burnt and wet at the same time, and gratitude filled him up so much that he felt vertiginous. He tossed the magazine aside and planted his feet on the floor. He felt like he had received a divine download, a specific, yet wordless instruction from a source higher than himself. With guidance, this child could pick up the mantle his father was so unexpectedly forced to set down. *And you'll guide him … .*

The knock at the door made Hart jump and set Max to barking, but both relaxed when Bicky walked in. Hart walked over to greet his father-in-law, but Gil bumped past, throwing his arms around Bicky's neck and his legs around his waist. Bicky reeled then caught his balance, holding firmly to Gil with one arm and a support beam with the other. It was a light gesture, yet it landed in Hart's stomach solar plexus, threatening to detonate with the import of it.

"What took you so long?" Gil yipped in Bicky's ear.

Bicky grimaced, patted Gil clumsily on the back, and set him down, slow and deliberate.

"You guys had a good day yesterday, I see," Hart said. He lowered the volume on the stereo.

"Thank you," Bicky said, rubbing his ears. Gil's smile was a flower in full bloom.

"He's got all kinds of ideas for marketing the TDU," Gil said to Hart, "and he said that we can build a special wing in Akanabi and dedicate it to my Dad. Maybe even rename part of the company. But whatever we do, people are going to know all about him. By the time Bicky's done, he'll be as big as Thomas Edison."

"Bigger," Bicky said.

"Who do you think made the bigger contribution?" Gil said. "Edison or Bell?"

"Those are just the common names." Hart said. "What about all those physicists, toiling away in anonymity? The ones who come up with the big theories that advance our understanding of the universe. Somebody needs to thank them. It can't all be about the light bulb."

Gil sat on his stool, set his lips in a tight line and moved them back and forth across his teeth in deep concentration. "I think it's got to be about the light bulb. Without that invention, everyone else is in the dark. Eating in the dark, swimming in the dark, making phone calls in the dark, even inventing in the dark." He looked up at Bicky as if for confirmation.

"Then we won't stop until his name is synonymous with Edison. How's that?"

"Excellent." Gil smiled and jumped off his seat. "Let's get started then. C'mon over."

Bicky followed Gil to the TDU and stood in front of it. "So this is the machine with a hundred and one uses," Bicky said. He pulled open the metal door and was met with a full blast of hot air. "Whoa," he said and took a step back.

Gil nodded and raised his eyebrows. "Should have warned you. It gets pretty hot in there. Let me show you how everything works, and then we can sit down with the drawings."

"You joining us?" Bicky asked Hart.

"Go ahead," Hart said. "Gil and I have already talked this through a bunch of times. I would like a fresh pair of eyes, though, in case there's something we've missed." Bicky nodded.

"Okay, Mr. Bicky." Gil said. "This machine is small for what we want to do with it. In a real facility, the scale could be increased as much as you want. Twenty to one. Fifty to one – whatever." Gil said. "In here," Gil opened the TDU's door and another blast of heat escaped, "is where we feed the beast. My dad excavated it twenty feet down to a fully lined pit. Those side doors over there slide open," he said, pointing to a wall of the barn. "We back the ATV into the barn. It's got this little hydraulic cylinder that raises the front of the trailer bed – just like a dump truck – so the trash slides off the trailer right into the machine."

"By the way, I called the bank and told them I no longer needed the financing," Hart said, returning to the hammock to watch and wonder.

"Thanks," Bicky said, giving Hart a full smile instead of his usual lopsided grimace. "I mean, really — thanks."

Gil went over every square inch of the TDU. For his part, Bicky was unwavering in his focus and seemingly enthralled, both in the presence of genius and in that which genius had wrought.

⅄

Over two hours later, Gil finished his tutorial and sat down on the swivel stool. "So. What do you think?" he asked. He pushed off and began spinning.

"I think," Bicky said, "that this may be one of the single most important, money-making inventions I'll see in my lifetime. It'll reshape the world. Maybe even put us in Bill Gates' league."

Gil's stopped spinning long enough to scrunch his nose at Bicky, clearly not the answer Gil had wanted.

Bicky let out a long sigh. "I'm sorry that I never met your father. What vision. And now his dream a reality."

"More like his nightmare, you mean."

Gil jumped. Everyone turned around to see Jerry Dixon emerging from the shadows in the corner of the barn. "Because if you had the opportunity to shake his hand, well then that would mean he'd be alive, and you wouldn't be taking his product to market for him."

"What the hell are you doing here?" Bicky hissed.

"Where did you come from?" Hart asked.

"How'd you get in?" Gil said.

"Through the door, buddy," Jerry said. He walked over to Gil and tousled his hair as if he were a toddler. Gil grimaced and leaned away.

"I've been hanging out listening to all this lovey-dovey crap. It is indeed heartwarming." He glanced over at Hart. "No pun intended."

Gil smoothed his straight hair over to the side and scowled at Jerry.

"Just came by to see how it all turns out now that everyone's become such fast friends."

"Hart, get him out of here," Bicky said.

"Bicky, what's going on?" Hart asked.

"I fired him a few days ago."

"Fired?"

"Fired. Just like that," Jerry said. "Can you believe it, Hart? After thirty-three years of loyal service. And for what?"

"I'm going to give you five seconds, and then I'll remove you myself."

"I'll tell you for what. Because Bicky Coleman, our Commander-in-Chief, the man we'd follow blindly into battle without a care for the consequences, was disappointed in me. Who knew disappointment carried such a huge price tag?" Jerry huffed, walked over to the wall phone and pulled the receiver from its cradle.

"Hello, Operator? What's the number for disappointment?" He smiled at Bicky, a sardonic, dripping thing, and yanked the phone off the wall, tossing it to the ground. "She doesn't know," he said. He shrugged, walked over to Gil and shooed him off the stool.

First confused, then obstinate, Gil refused to give up his stool until Jerry gave him a shove, which sent him spiraling to the floor. Max lunged at Jerry, nipping the fleshy part of his hand before Jerry managed to put Max in a chokehold and press him to his chest. Max stood with two paws off the floor, alternating between sucking air and baring his teeth.

"I'll break his neck."

"No!" Gil yelled.

Hart grabbed Max's collar and Jerry released his grip. Max collapsed on the floor, panting for air. Hart picked him up, all seventy pounds, and deposited him in the hammock.

"Jerry, what the hell is your problem?" Hart was at Gil's side, pulling him to his feet, dusting him off. He scooped Gil up and placed him in the hammock next to Max. "Stay," he said to both of them. Bicky stood in the corner, eyeing the bulge in Jerry's trouser leg.

Jerry rubbed his temples with both hands as if he had a headache. "Because I had a little dalliance with a woman that he cared nothing for, other than to control her," Jerry said, responding to a question that no one had asked.

"Dalliance, my ass," Bicky quipped. "She left you billions of dollars. Billion does not equal a dalliance. Just how long were you screwing her?"

"It really doesn't matter, does it, Bicky? What matters is money. It's all that matters."

"You son-of-a-bitch," Bicky said. He lunged for Jerry, swung and caught him with a glancing blow to the side of the jaw. It was like hitting granite.

Jerry neither reeled, nor blinked but caught Bicky squarely with a punch to the mid-section. "Oh, does that feel good," Jerry said on contact.

Bicky groaned and doubled over then pulled up and swung again. Jerry blocked Bicky's fist and returned his own jab while Max barked in time with the punches. Gil watched in fascination as if these were the recorded antics of daytime television. Jerry's military training gave him the upper hand, but Bicky's years spent working out with a personal trainer made him a worthy opponent. Hart stared at them, momentarily stupefied, before his brain roused his body to action. The men were locked in an angry embrace, each fueled by years of swallowing their own bitter disappointments. Hart broke up the fight and held them at arm's-length, a referee between two boxers.

"Knock it off, dammit. There's nothing to be done," Hart said.

Bicky and Jerry stood glaring at one another, less than a few feet between them, inhaling each other's fury, fueling their own. The ambient air, dank and fetid with the ghost of so much lost love, reeked of hate and hopelessness.

"She's dead. You both lost."

"Why'd you come here, Jerry?" Hart snapped. "You have a hefty inheritance. Take it and go buy an island somewhere. Have some respect and leave the man to his grief."

"Grief? The only thing Bicky Coleman grieves for is a bad investment," Jerry said. He spat at Bicky's feet, splattering the warm Italian leather. "Nothing else matters to him."

"Why don't you say something back," Gil said to Bicky, a note of pleading in his voice. He walked over from the hammock, Max in tow. Both fear and loss were reflected in Bicky's crystal blue eyes. "Don't let him say those mean things."

"It's you he needs to say something to," Jerry replied. "Isn't it, Boss?" Jerry smiled grimly. "Something he's going to have a hard time telling." Jerry shook Hart off and sat back down on Gil's stool.

Hart turned to Bicky. "What's he talking about?"

"Still didn't tell him?" Jerry asked. "Why am I not shocked?" Gil stared wide-eyed, alternating between Bicky and Jerry. Hart moved Gil and Max back to the hammock.

"Get out," Bicky said.

"You know, son, here's a lesson for you. Before you go into business with someone, make sure you have a good idea of his character. And barring that, make sure you get yourself a damn good attorney," Jerry said. "At least do a background check."

Jerry picked at his nails as if he had all the time in the world before looking Gil straight in the eye. "Do you know if it wasn't for this guy, you'd still have parents?" Jerry smiled at Gil as if he'd just relayed the home run hitter's batting average. He reached down to the leg of his trousers.

"What does that mean?" Gil asked. He turned to Bicky. "What does he mean?"

"Get out! Get out! Get Out!" Bicky yelled in a sputtering rage. He took a step toward Jerry just as the former head of security for Akanabi Oil stood and pointed a 9 mm. at Bicky's mid-section. Bicky halted in mid-stride.

"I mean, Bicky ordered me to have someone tail your parents the night they were killed. He really wanted those papers over there," Jerry said, motioning toward the desk. "Told me to use all means, which, of course, I paid extra for." Jerry cleared his throat. "It was me, by the way, torched your porch. I'm real sorry about that. In hindsight, it was sloppy and uncalled for."

"You're lying!" Gil screamed. He jumped off the stool, grabbing the closest weapon he could find — a snow globe. It sat on a pink base, its clear plastic hemisphere filled with water and faux snow. Plastic tropical fish swam inside, stirring up snow. Marty had purchased it for Gil during a family trip to Florida and for two months after, Gil slept with it every night. Now he heaved it across the room as hard as he could. It glanced off Jerry's shoulder, hit the floor and landed with a distinct thud. Water leaked from the newly formed crack in the plastic and spread into a small, round puddle.

Bicky grunted and lunged for Jerry's gun. Jerry fired and for an instant the room went quiet, the only sounds a whoosh of air as the bullet hurtled through time and space to its target, and the sickening sploosh as it made contact. Hart pulled Gil and Max back. Bicky screamed in pain and collapsed. Gil's head poked out from behind Hart's back, his face a mixture of horror and awe.

Jerry smiled at Bicky, heaped on the floor like discarded packaging, clinging with both hands to his oozing thigh. Blood spread out, soaking into the fine cotton twill of Bicky's pants, the smell of it acrid and strong. Jerry raised the gun to Bicky's head and started to laugh, a maniacal, full-bodied thing that showed no signs of relenting.

CHAPTER 78

Fifteen minutes later, Bicky sat leaning against the wall of the TDU, his leg wrapped in a tourniquet that Hart was tying off. The tourniquet, made from pieces of an old ripped bed sheet turned rag, was streaked with dirt and motor oil. Jerry had refused to allow anyone in the house to get medical supplies. Bicky flinched as Hart secured the whole mess in place with a finishing nail.

"There are more civilized ways to get retribution, Jerry," Hart snapped.

"Don't tell me it's not something you thought about yourself from time to time, Mr. Chief of Engineering. You know, Hart. You and I? We're a lot closer than you think."

Hart snorted. "I have no idea what you're talking about."

"Death. That's what I'm talking about. From the minute we're born it's always right here," Jerry said, "starin' you in the face." He held his hand up to his own face, examining it for clues. "You don't see it is all."

Jerry dropped his hand to his side. "You know what surprises me, Hart? What surprises me is that a thousand freaking people a day don't just get up out of bed, strap on a semiautomatic, and blow the crap out of something. That's what surprises me." Jerry's voice cracked. He cleared his throat and scratched the barrel of the gun against his scalp. "And everywhere there's death. People dying."

"People are always dying, Jerry. It's just the one that's got you upset. But you're not alone, man. Let's get some help, huh? I got someone you can talk to … "

"Actually, it's two. And if you give me a minute, I'll tell you about it. But first I want to clear some things up with your boss, here. Before he passes out, that is." Jerry stooped down next to Bicky and held the gun to Bicky's heart.

"You proved your point, man. You're in control," Hart said. "Now let me call an ambulance."

"And then what? Have me arrested? I'm a rich man now. Rich men don't go to jail."

"Look, Jerry," Hart said, watching Bicky. "Given the extenuating circumstances, I'm sure we can work things out." Sweat poured from Bicky's ashen face but he managed a nod.

"I want to tell you a story first," Jerry said. "Sit down," he said to Hart. "Keep the kid over there on the hammock. Take the chair over next to him."

Hart laid a hand on Gil's shoulder and pushed him toward the hammock.

"And get that beast outta' here."

Gil snarled at Jerry but did as commanded. "Come on, Max," Gil said. Max ran over and stood next to Gil, wagging his tail. Gil walked him to the door and ushered him out. "Stay," Gil said. Max started barking as Gil shut the door.

"You better shut him up or I'll shut him up for you," Jerry said.

Gil's eyes watered, but his voice didn't waiver as he opened the door again. "Ssshhh! Sit, Max. Be quiet. Understand?" Gil raised his index finger to his lips, and Max whimpered once but sat down as instructed. Gil's sad, brown eyes blinked once and Max sighed. Gil took a seat on the hammock. A soft low growl rolled in like a wave through the crack under the door.

"You did the right thing," Hart said, squeezing Gil's hand. Gil returned a brave smile. Jerry's face clouded with something akin to regret. He rubbed a rough hand over his eyes and it was gone.

"Story time, eh?" Jerry folded his arms across his chest, facing Hart and Gil, the gun poking out from under his arm.

"You see, one night, I'm sitting outside your house … "

"My house?" Hart narrowed his eyes at Jerry.

" … and I'm watching, and I'm waiting, and I happen to see a familiar car pull into your driveway, and lo and behold, who gets out, but your father-in-law. That means kin-by-law, you know, and brings with it a certain degree of responsibility, which a lot of people don't take seriously enough, I think. It's not just about a seat at the holiday dinner table." Jerry fixed Bicky with an accusatory; Bicky returned his own.

"Anyway, he doesn't knock, just goes right in like he owns the place. You know what I'm talking about, right?" Jerry tilted his face toward Hart for emphasis but wouldn't break eye contact with Bicky. "So I get out of my car and I walk around to the kitchen window to see what's happening. Bicky's in there and Sonia's got the kettle on for tea and it's steaming, but not whistling yet. She's putting a tea bag in her cup, and she's got her back to him. The windows are open, which I don't understand because it's hot as hell out."

"Sonia didn't like air conditioning," Hart said, his voice thick.

Jerry nodded. "And if not for that small fact, I wouldn't be relaying this story to you now as I've witnessed it," Jerry said to Hart, his eyes still glued to Bicky's face. Anyway, I hear bits and pieces of things. Bicky says: 'Sonia, enough,' and then something something. And Sonia says: 'Where's what?'" and Bicky says, 'You know what,' and the tea kettle starts screaming and I can't hear a thing for a minute, but this ear-splitting whistle and Sonia and Bicky stare at each other and words come out of their mouths, but I can't make them out until finally, he yells at her to 'shut the kettle' and she very calmly walks over, grabs the kettle and pours herself a cup of tea." Jerry smiled at Bicky as if he had just one-upped him.

Sweat poured down Bicky's face and scalp while his face changed from pale grey to pale green. Bicky squeezed his right leg but did not avert his eyes.

"You never could back her up, could you? That's what always pissed you off about her," Jerry said. "How did it make you feel, Boss, to finally have no control over something?"

Using his hands for balance, Bicky tried to stand, winced in pain and dropped to the floor, both hands wrapped around his thigh just above the entry wound.

"Kind of like now?" Jerry asked, the pleasure of the moment apparent on his face.

"Dammit, Jerry. What the hell are you talking about?" Hart said.

Jerry sidled over to Bicky and put the gun to his face. "You want to tell them?" Bicky shoved the gun away, breaking eye contact.

"Uh oh," Jerry smiled and patted Bicky's face. "You lose."

Jerry sauntered over to Gil and Hart. "He's quiet tonight," Jerry said, a note of mock concern in his voice. He let out a long, labored sigh. "So, Bicky whirls on her, like this." Jerry grabbed Gil by both arms and gave him a violent shake.

"Hey!" Hart said, jumping up. Jerry dropped Gil's arms, stuck the barrel of his gun in Gil's ribs and held up a single finger. Hart froze.

"Tsk, tsk, tsk," Jerry said, shaking his head and motioning for Hart to sit down. He grabbed Gil again.

"He was in her face, squeezing her arms, saying a bunch of what, I'm not sure, and it must have hurt because Sonia finally let out a yelp. So what's the son-of-a-bitch do? He loosens his grip, but still doesn't let her go." Jerry shot Bicky a murderous look.

Jerry dropped his voice, his face taut with recall, one hand tightening around Gil's arm, the other still poking the gun in Gil's ribs. "I wish now I had gone through the window after him."

"Oooww!" Gil said. Jerry jerked on Gil's arm as if to bring him back in line, but when he looked at Gil's small, pinched face, he released his grip.

"Sorry," Jerry said. Gil inspected his reddened forearm, already forming a bruise.

Jerry's eyes misted over, but he continued: "'I don't have it,' she said. 'Don't lie to me,' he said. 'What you sent wasn't what you took,' he said, and then a bunch of stuff I didn't hear." Jerry swiped at his watery eyes with his free hand, then rubbed his forehead with the barrel of the gun, leaving a bright, red welt. He pushed Gil toward Hart and motioned them back to their seats. He shook his head like a wet dog, before pointing the gun at Bicky. "Son-of-a-bitch," he said, drawing back the trigger.

"Jerry!" Hart yelled, and pulled Gil behind him.

Bicky braced for the bullet, his face scrunched and tense, but his eyes were unwavering in their gaze. Jerry leaned back, inhaled slowly and fired, lifting his gun slightly before pulling the trigger. The bullet drove harmlessly into the wall above Bicky's head. Bicky began shaking and sucked in a long, raspy, breath.

Jerry stood up and walked over to the drawing table where Gil had laid out a blueprint of the TDU. He thumbed through the drawings using his gun as a finger to turn the pages. He turned back to Bicky.

"What were you thinking that day, Boss? Did you understand? Were you resigned? I'll never get why you so uncharacteristically backed up. Why'd you leave without it, huh? When you knew she had it? 'Cause you know, she'd be alive today if you would have just done what you always do which is not take no for an answer."

"I was with Bicky at the Union Club that night, Jerry," Hart said. "I left before he did. So he couldn't have been at my house."

Bicky looked at his son-in-law, his lips forming into a slow, sad smile.

"Loyal to the end, aren't you, Hart?" Jerry sat down on Gil's stool, pointed the gun and spun around once. The moment he was in a direct line of fire with Bicky's head, he planted his feet on the ground with authority.

"I tell you your wife would be alive today if not for him, and you defend him. You've been duped. We all have." Jerry spun around again and came to another abrupt stop in direct line with Bicky. This time he fired. The shot went into the wall just above Bicky's right shoulder. Bicky heaved out a lung full of air but refused to utter a sound.

"'Just tell me you didn't go to the newspapers,' he said, and she shook her head. Just the way he looked at her, trying to see inside her, to see what she was up to. But he never could, never did understand her. Not like I did. Jerry swiped at his eyes and stared at the floor.

"What happened next?" Hart asked.

Jerry spun around a third time and once again pointed the gun at Bicky who was now sobbing quietly, the muscles in his face tight with pain. "I'll tell you what happened next." Jerry fired and the shot drove into the wall less than an inch above Bicky's left shoulder.

"Bicky left."

CHAPTER 79

Bicky moaned and squeezed his leg above the wound.

"But you said he killed her," Gil said.

"He did," Jerry replied. "He just wasn't in the room at the time."

"He's already lost a lot of blood, Jerry. If he dies … " Hart stood up. Jerry fired the gun into the floor near his feet. Hart started then froze in place.

"Sit down and don't ask me again. Sit down and let me finish my story," Jerry said, waving the gun at Hart. "Sit down!" Hart sat.

"I was about to cross the street to my own car. I wasn't really comfortable spying on Sonia." Bicky snorted, and Jerry fixed him with a vaporizing glare. "I had to jump back behind the house when the other car came. This one belonged to your mother-in-law."

"What? Did the whole world visit that night?" Hart said sarcastically.

Jerry's impatience released itself in a huff. "May I continue, please?!" Hart snorted and looked away.

"Pay attention," Jerry said. "Because you never get a second chance."

Hart rubbed his face as if deciding something and turned back to Jerry.

"I went back to the kitchen window. Good thing your neighbors aren't close by, because the girls were screaming at each other. Seems Kitty also wanted that report."

Hart chuckled once, then twice.

"Go ahead, laugh," Jerry said. "It's ridiculous, right? Everyone running around like chickens for a few inches of paper. But it's true."

Bicky moaned in pain and passed out, his head hitting the floor with a thud.

"Oh! Can't have that." Jerry walked over and kicked Bicky in the injured right leg.

Bicky roused, bellowing.

"This is the best part, Boss. Don't fall asleep now."

Tears streamed down Bicky's cheeks. With great effort, he propped himself up on one elbow. His head lolled against the cool stainless steel siding of the TDU.

Jerry knelt down and patted Bicky on the cheek. He grabbed Bicky under the chin and rolled his face from side to side. "It'll all be over soon, Boss. Don't worry. I promise." He gave Bicky another smug pat and returned to his seat.

"He's fading," Jerry said. "We better jump to the end."

Bicky sputtered and began convulsing as if freezing.

"Jerry, please," Hart said, watching his father-in-law.

"Hey, kid, that machine throws off a lot of heat, right?" Jerry asked. Gil nodded.

"Go open the door. It'll be better than a blanket."

Gil grabbed his water bottle, walked over and held it to Bicky's lips. Bicky tried to drink, but with his shaking, spilled half a swallow out the sides of his mouth.

"Hey, Florence Nightingale, I didn't say do that."

Gil set the bottle down next to Bicky, pushed back the outside grate, and slid open the door of the TDU. A blast of heat burst up and out, and Gil recoiled from it. He walked back to his seat, an impetuous glare at Jerry as he did so.

"Ah, whatever. I guess it's good to show a little compassion to your enemies now and again. Keep 'em close. That's what I say. You're a good kid." Gil held Jerry's eye, but said nothing.

"Okay, where was I? Oh yeah. Kitty wanted the report, too. To bargain with him," Jerry nodded toward Bicky, "for her freedom. That night, she finally told Sonia the truth. It was a secret she'd kept for thirty-two years. Nobody knew. Not even me. I got it all after the fact these last few months," he said to Hart, "or I probably would've told her." Jerry nodded as if in agreement with himself. "She didn't believe it. Called Kitty a liar. I gotta think it wasn't because of me, per se, but just the shock of it."

Jerry furrowed his brow and stared at the back wall of the barn, his voice taking on a somnambulistic quality. "I should have walked in then and stopped it... all that pent-up emotion flying out like machine gun fire. Kitty hit her. She didn't mean to. I just don't think she realized the toll all those years had taken on her. On them. I mean, if she wouldn't have had Sonia, she would've never stayed in the first place. I would've seen to that."

Jerry cleared his throat as if to dislodge the memory. He shook his head. "Sonia went nuts. I never saw her like that. She threw her teacup at her mother. Kitty put her arm up – it was still steaming – and it broke all over the floor. Tea everywhere." Jerry snorted defiantly. "She got a couple nice second degree burns on her arm because of it. Next thing I know she's running from the house, and I'm running after her."

"What about Sonia?" Hart's voice was cracked and tinny.

"I didn't see her fall. 'Cause if I did, I would've gone back. She was crazy with rage. I think she slipped on the wet floor, maybe banged her head on the counter. I heard a noise, but I thought she just threw something else.

"You didn't go back to see if she was okay?" Hart was on his feet.

"I couldn't. I had to go after Kitty."

Hart lunged for Jerry who was unprepared for the attack. He toppled Jerry from the stool and the gun clattered to the floor. Gil reached to pick it up, but Jerry's foot kicked it away along with Gil's hand in the process. Gil winced and dropped to the floor.

The two men struggled, punching, kicking, biting, clawing, rolling up, around and over each other. Bicky crawled toward the center of the floor toward the gun, a painful, slow propulsion. With each inch forward he risked being trampled by the fighters, first a finger, then an arm, and finally his leg, the last of which caused him to lose consciousness for half a minute, passing out where he lay. Gil watched the fight in relative safety from his position in the corner, holding his injured hand, his body following every punch and kick.

Hart's pent-up anger launched him like a heat-seeking missile, and he pounded Jerry inexorably with the full fury of it, but anger is not a thrifty shopper and after spewing it all over the room, Hart spent himself, leaving Jerry with the edge. Several minutes later, Hart sat in a heap in front of the TDU, with a black eye, blood dripping from his nose, and a variety of scrapes and gashes that would be telling their story for days to come. Jerry emerged with a gash over his right eyebrow, which bled profusely, a broken pinky finger, jutting out in an unnatural position, and the gun. Both men had given and received more than a few blows to the stomach and now prodded their tender midsections. Jerry spat out some blood, turned to Hart, and pulled the trigger. It grazed Hart's elbow. Hart howled and cradled the injured arm.

"Now you sit," Jerry said to Hart. Blood oozed from the cut above his eyebrow, dripping into his eye. He blinked it away, but it was pervasive.

"I am sitting," Hart spat back. Jerry raised the gun again, but Gil grabbed a rag and shoved it in his free hand. The gesture grounded Jerry who retreated by lowering his gun. He wiped at the wound before nodding at Gil to take his seat on the hammock, then walked over and dropped the bloodstained rag in front of Hart.

Hart ignored it, ripped off a sleeve of his shirt, and bandaged his elbow. He was sweating because of his injury and the rise in temperature since the door to the TDU had been opened.

Jerry walked over and peered inside to the wide, gaping mouth of the giant stainless steel tank below. "How far down's that thing go?"

"About two stories," Gil said.

"Probably what hell looks like." Jerry took a step back and wiped at his brow. "You can't build this machine. It'll ruin the only good thing we got left to us."

"What are you talking about?" Hart said.

"It'll kill the oil industry. Akanabi's stock price'll go way down, and my money'll be worthless." Jerry whirled around to face Hart. "Kitty left me all her money, you know." Jerry smiled sardonically at Bicky who was trying to stand up.

Bicky grabbed the stool for balance but fell back down with a sickening "oaaaaw."

"And you know what I'm doing with it, Boss? Huh? Turning a profit, you say? Noooo. I'm giving it all away. To the Nature Conservancy. Just like she wanted. And it'll be in our names. Together on the same legal document. Like a marriage license or a birth certificate. Together forever in history."

"I don't care what she does with the money, Jerry. I never did."

"Hhmph," Jerry grunted.

"I just wanted … " Bicky croaked in a voice like splintering wood, "her." Bicky took a faltering step up, his weight bearing on one leg, his arm leaning on the stool for support. "And the baby."

"My baby," Jerry growled. "Did you know that, Boss? That Sonia was my baby?" Jerry wiped at the dripping blood now mixed with tears that cascaded down the side of his face. "We may not have always known it, but we belonged to each other," Jerry gushed.

A strange gurgling noise arose from deep in Bicky's throat. He doubled over, first coughing, then hacking, then vomiting. When he was finished he stood taller.

As the fire in the TDU diminished the available oxygen in the room, Bicky began a slow march toward Jerry, stopping intermittently to suck in a raspy, labored breath. He leaned against one of the barn's dozen posts for support. "I don't know … what I knew. I just wanted … " Bicky grabbed his stomach and started hacking again. His pant leg, now a dark, saturated red, was plastered against him, the pain drawing him down from the inside. Bicky leaned against a post while gravity, always one to side with a downward spiral, forced him to crumple.

"Kitty said she had always been petrified you'd find out who it was. That's why she never told me."

"This is a bunch of crap," Hart barked in disgust. "Bicky, set him straight, please."

"Doesn't he wish. Tell him, Boss. Tell him how you tried and tried to get her pregnant."

"Shut up." Bicky said. He pulled himself up by inches, a slow torturous ascent. He grabbed the post with both hands and pushed off, a ship leaving port.

"Finally went and got checked out by a fertility doc a few years after Sonia was born. Check the records for Mason Coleman."

"Shut up!" Bicky hollered.

"It was Bicky's brother's name. The one who died. He used it as an alias. Didn't want the highbrow Houstonians finding out that the great Bicky Coleman's sperm don't swim too well. When d'you figure it out, boss? When she left me all the money?"

"Shut ... up!" Bicky roared. He collapsed in a spasm, clutching his leg.

Hart rolled to the side, ready to stand, but Jerry motioned him back with a wave of the gun. Hart ignored him, pulling himself up into a crouching position.

Jerry fired a bullet inches from Hart's face. There was barely a sound, just the friction in the air as it passed, and Hart fell onto his haunches. With one big breath, Gil sucked in his fear and covered his mouth.

"She wanted you to believe it was yours, but after a while you knew better, right. You just didn't know who, huh? Well, me neither." Jerry grunted and shined his gun on his pant leg.

Bicky crawled to the next post and laid his head against it, catching his breath.

"You coming after me, Boss?" Jerry asked, humor and malice mixed. "Well, come on then. I promise not to shoot you."

Bicky rose and took a slow, halting step, and then another, his face contorting in pain with each one. "This machine ... will ... be ... built. With or ... without you," he wheezed. "It's time ... has come. You won't ... stop it." He cleared the debris from his throat and spit on the ground.

"Watch me." Jerry's face contorted and he raised the gun to Bicky's chest; Bicky continued his funeral march.

Jerry growled and squeezed the trigger. The bullet lodged in Bicky's forearm. A shot of blood squirted out. Bicky grunted, more than screamed, and stood, eyes closed, swaying in the middle of the room. He pitched forward but latched onto a beam forestalling the crash. He panted like a dog, trying to steady himself before walking, slow and stiff toward his nemesis, a plane locked on autopilot, unable to alter its course. Jerry may have had the gun, but Bicky had the upper hand.

"Why didn't you let her go?" Jerry said, years of anger and longing bubbling up to the surface like a spring.

Bicky stood within inches of Jerry now. The two men glowered at each other, breathing in rage, breathing out hate.

"I did. She didn't want to."

"You lying sack of … " Jerry raised the gun to Bicky's heart, but Bicky just smiled. Unsteady on his feet, yet undeterred, his ragged breath flowing more easily as adrenaline started a quick trot through his body.

"She said you wouldn't let her go. That you'd disown Sonia if she left you. She didn't want her daughter to grow up with no father and no money."

Bicky shook his head. "You were her father. You had money. Not as much as me, granted, but you could have provided for … "

"But I didn't know!" Jerry screamed.

"Stop it. Just stop it!" Gil yelled, and covered his ears. Jerry whirled to face the boy, raised his gun and shot him. The bullet hit him in the shoulder and came out the other side. Gil hit the floor without uttering a sound. His eyes rolled back in his head and his lids fluttered.

"Noooo!" Bicky grabbed onto Jerry for balance, and the two men began an awkward choreography. "Damn you," Bicky yelled, a strangled curse. He tried striking Jerry with his fist, but Jerry deflected the hit. Each held fast to the other's arm, pushing, pulling, a scant few feet from the miracle machine, as exhaustion and heat coaxed the sweat from their pores.

"You could have let us go?" Jerry sobbed. "Why didn't you?"

Bicky glanced over at Gil who was lying on the floor in a pool of his own blood. Hart crawled to him and checked his vital signs. Jerry and Bicky struggled, edging ever closer to the open door of the TDU. Inside, the fire raged without apology at thirteen hundred degrees Fahrenheit.

"Gil," Hart said. "Gil. Can you hear me?"

"Maybe the time just wasn't right, Jerry. Unlike now."

Bicky broke free of Jerry's grip, and with all the force remaining in his battered body, shoved him.

Gravity stepped in again, bolstered by its cousin, Entropy, and Jerry started to fall. But like a magnet, or a mirror that reflects what we truly are, Jerry pulled to him that which was most like him. He grabbed onto Bicky's shirt tail, and together they plunged over the small lip of the TDU. Jerry only had time to scream once, falling as he was at a rate of thirty-two feet per second per second, an angst-ridden, shrilly noise that reverberated in the barn even after the men had bottomed out.

Hart shuddered. The flames danced, then roared, eating all the remaining sound in the room until there was nothing left but silence.

人

"Gil? Are you all right?" Hart squeezed Gil's hand. "Gil?"

Gil opened his eyes and blinked at Hart. "Am I dead?"

"No, but once the shock wears off, you'll wish you were." He knelt down at Gil's side and wrapped his good arm around Gil's boyish, angular shoulders.

Gil hid, rabbit-like in the crook of Hart's arm, scanning the room, assessing the casualties. "One hundred and two," he said, a muffled observation.

"One hundred and two what?" Hart asked.

"One hundred and two uses."

Hart laughed once and squeezed Gil, crushing him to his chest. He tore off the remaining sleeve of his shirt and wrapped Gil's shoulder.

Gil flinched. Sweat had plastered his hair to his scalp so that he looked like a preformed plastic *Ken* doll. His complexion was the color of ash. Tears fell in careless, random fashion down Gil's cheeks, and Hart felt the steel grip on his heart loosen. He squeezed Gil again and brushed back his hair. Hart staggered over to the TDU, slid the door closed, but didn't look inside.

"Kori can take us to the hospital," Gil said.

"I'm surprised she hasn't been out her yet with all the noise." Hart said, helping Gil up.

"She's a heavy sleeper," Gil said.

Hart laughed for real this time and threw his good arm around Gil's waist. "Can you walk?" He asked. Gil nodded. They breathed in tandem, heavy and erratic, and walked to the door, a pair of contestants in a three-legged race.

Chapter 80

Robbie sat on a small reed mat, his back propped against the base of a date palm tree. He ate dates and took sips of water from a canteen. The sun scorched the earth almost everywhere else in this Godforsaken country, but right here in the Al Hawizeh Marshes, life was lush and fecund. The river teemed with otter and minnows, and date palms lined the banks. An auger lay next to him and a cylindrical shaped mass of soil next to the auger, and a Munsell soil chart so he could identify the soils. He squinted against the harsh sun and scanned the horizon.

Something small and swift approached, a mashuf with a single occupant, poling the boat through the marsh water. A light breeze blew across Robbie's face, and he raised his nose like a dog to sniff at it. He stood to get a better look at who was coming. The figure was closer now; he could see it was a woman. She didn't wear the abayas, the traditional black head-to-toe coverings of the Iraqi women, but the garb of a western university student — jeans and a t-shirt. He hesitated a moment before sitting back down. The way the military came through this place, one could never be too careful, but the military wouldn't send a civilian or even an officer out of uniform to arrest him. It was probably somebody from *Eden Again* coming to help him take soil samples.

He popped another date in his mouth and waited as the boat drew closer. If this country had taught him anything, it was patience. Life seemed to have all the time in the world here. But the truth was, here, like everywhere else, time was running out.

The sun cast a glare on the water making it impossible to see the woman's face as she alighted onto the shore. She towed the mashuf another two feet out of the water so it wouldn't drift away, and Robbie thought he should stand or call out, offer a greeting of some sort, but his arms and legs felt weighted to the ground and his voice a sorry deserter. The woman walked right over to Robbie as if she'd known him forever, as if she'd known he'd be sitting under a date palm tree in the middle of the Al Hawizeh Marshes, eating flat bread and hard cheese, waiting. He held his hand up to shield his eyes from the sun. Within a foot of him, her silhouette eclipsed those rays and he was able to make out her features. The vision made him choke on a date.

"What are you doing here?" Robbie asked. "I thought you were … "

Ruth raised her hand to silence him. "We don't need to say the 'D' word, Robbie. It's so … inconsequential. I mean, compared to other things." Confusion swept across Robbie's face like a push broom, leaving ragged trails in its wake. He started to wheeze. Ruth grabbed his canteen and handed it to him.

"Are you all right?" Robbie took a long drink off the canteen and rubbed his eyes.

"You looked wonderful, baby," Ruth said. "Could it be this work agrees with you?" She knelt down and touched his cheek. He flinched. She drew him in, wrapping one arm around his neck and patting his back with the other, just like she used to when he was little.

For the next few minutes, Robbie cried tears of grief and joy as big as dates, long lodged in his heart — tears that carried the sum total of his collective heartache, and of the absolute terror he'd felt every day since his plane touched down in this dry wasteland and that only the last few weeks in the marshes had helped to dissipate; tears that every child saves up, be it for minutes or weeks or lifetimes, to drop in their mother's lap because only she knows how to dry them. Had he channeled those tears, Robbie could have re-hydrated the Central and Al Hammar Marshes. Instead he stopped, dried his eyes and look into his mother's eyes.

"Better?" Ruth asked.

Robbie nodded, took a deep breath. Ruth pushed back his hair and cupped his cheek in her hand. A small splash denoted a school of minnows nearby, and Robbie turned toward the noise. The midday sun sat high in a cloudless sky, unblinking, unmerciful and most undervalued. Robbie pulled the turban down to his eyebrows and mopped the sweat on his brow before its saltiness stung his eyes.

"What a completely underused resource," he said, looking up at the sun. "Why doesn't anybody do something with it?"

"They are actually. It's just not funded properly."

"Why?"

"There are a million reasons, or at least a few big ones, and they mostly revolve around money. And the old adage, 'If it ain't broke, don't fix it.' Right now it's not broke. But when the oil runs out, the need will be imperative and great minds will go to work."

"With that kind of solar energy, Dad could have powered the world." Robbie snorted, stood up. "It's not fair. None of it." He kicked the dirt with the toe of his sandal.

"Mind if I ask what happened?"

"You mean to me and Dad?" Ruth said. Robbie nodded.

Ruth searched his face before responding. "Does it matter? If you knew, you'd want to do something about it, right? And there's nothing you can do. We think we're in control. We strive and struggle and build our little empires to assure our safe passage. But life wrenches control from you every time." Ruth stood up to face her son. Robbie shrugged, picked up a spade and plunged it into the moist, fecund ground. Ruth watched as he dug a small hole.

"Six months ago, this dirt was dry as the Sahara. We did this. The Americans. By getting rid of Saddam, some of these people got their water back. A few anyway." He dropped the spade and picked up the auger. "So it couldn't have all been for nothing, right?" He twisted the auger back and forth, pushing it deeper and deeper into the ground.

Ruth shrugged. "On its face, nothing is good or bad. It just is. It's up to each of us to live according to the dictates of our own conscience. The operative word being conscience."

"That's not what you used to say."

"I used to not be as smart as I am now," Ruth said. "You can only do what feels right for you here." She placed her hand over his heart. "And let the other guy do what feels right for him. Wouldn't it be funny if we discovered that at the end of it all, it wasn't one religion over another, or one political ideology over another, but the simple acts of tolerance and forgiveness that were the most important?"

She pulled Robbie to her, wrapped him in a bear hug. "The only constant in life is change, Robbie. Have the wherewithal to go with the flow." Ruth waved her hand over the flowing, abundant marshes. "I suspect you might learn a great deal about it here." She smiled and kissed her son on the cheek, then turned and walked to the mashuf.

"Amara's pregnant!"

Ruth nodded. "I know."

"Don't leave, Mom." Robbie dropped the auger and ran after her to the canoe. "I don't know what I'm doing."

"Of course you do."

"No. Honest."

Ruth smiled, smoothed back his hair. He accepted the gesture with clenched eyelids the way he did when he was small and scared.

"Not all who hesitate are lost," Ruth said.

"Tolkien?"

"Joseph Campbell."

Robbie drew a deep breath. "That's nice, Mom, but it doesn't really help me. I'd rather you tell me what to do."

"And deny you the opportunity of figuring it out?" Ruth said. She kissed Robbie's cheek. "You have lots to do, mostly in service to others, and don't forget your brothers and sister need you. Especially Gil. His road will be particularly difficult." Ruth picked up the pole and pushed the mashuf back into the water. "He doesn't even know yet what he's being asked to bring forth into this world. But he'll need your support and protection to do it." Ruth climbed into the mashuf and held it steady on the shore with the pole. "There's nothing else to tell."

"What if I need to talk to you? How will I do that?"

"Robbie, my first born." Ruth's eyes locked on his. "I'm as close as your next thought." She blew him a kiss and pushed off the shore.

Robbie watched her turn the mashuf around and pole away. He waved until she melded into the horizon.

⚄

Robbie returned to the auger, pulled it out of the ground and laid it down carefully. He released half a cylinder's worth of soil, making sure to keep the column intact and went back to the hole for another half, sniffling all the while.

"What's the matter?" Gil asked.

A startled Robbie jumped and held the auger forth as a weapon. "Jesus. First Mom, now you. What the hell's going on today? You're not dead, are you?"

Gil shrugged. "I don't know. I don't think so."

Robbie looked at the water, but there was no canoe. "How'd you get here?"

Gil nodded in the opposite direction.

"But that's the desert!" They both looked toward the desert as if waiting for some mode of transportation to materialize. When he turned back, Robbie noticed Gil's sling. "What happened?"

Gil shrugged. "I came to tell you we're okay. It was scary for a while, but it's over."

"What are you talking about, Gil? Talk in English."

"Maybe I shouldn't go into it now." Gil looked around, surveying the area. "I mean, you might have some problems of your own."

"Thanks a lot."

"You'll be okay, though. I know it. Call us when you get in trouble. You know. When they catch you. I've recruited some outside help. A trouble shooter ... "

"Mom said ... "

"You talked to Mom, too?" Gil asked. "I'm not totally sure what she was saying. Something about choices ... "

"Do you need me to come home?"

"I want you to come home, but I don't want it to be like a Frank Capra movie with you going Jimmy Stewart on us. I'm no Clarence, you know."

Robbie couldn't suppress the smile. "I don't know if it's the time I've been away, but it seems I may have lost the ability to interpret whatever the heck it is your saying."

"I know." Gil toed the marshy soil with his foot. "Can you come home when you're done?"

Robbie took off his turban and stuck it on Gil's head. "First thing. I promise."

ʎ

Amara watched Robbie sleeping in the stern of the mashuf. In the time he'd been in Iraq his skin had turned a deep golden brown, weathered by sun and wind, a fact that probably saved his life on more than one occasion. That he looked like one of the Ma'adan when wearing the traditional robes and head scarf, and that he'd mastered the language in his short time here had helped him escape unnoticed from the various American and British troops that periodically patrolled the area. Amara knew his life was in danger. She had no doubt that he'd be subjected to a court martial and forced to stand trial for going AWOL, or worse, letting the army think he was dead. And so she brought him here among her people, her father's people, these people who governed by consensus, people who the Americans and Europeans considered lawless, people who desperately needed Amara's and Robbie's help before they were wiped off the face of the planet. Robbie murmured something in his sleep and Amara pushed at him with her toes. He mumbled again, opened his eyes and looked at her blankly.

"Huh?"

"Such a dreamer," Amara said, and tugged at Robbie's headscarf. You were speaking in your sleep." She tossed a canteen to him. "Perhaps you have sunstroke." Robbie said nothing, just smiled and took a long drink from the canteen.

"Thank you," he said, handing it back to her.

"What were your dreams?" Amara asked.

Robbie stared blankly at her for several seconds. "I honestly don't remember. But somehow I feel ... better."

"Then it was a good dream."

"Allah be praised," said Sayyid. "Our dreams are how we navigate the course of our lives. A good dream signals that you are following Allah's path for you, and He is pleased."

Robbie smiled and raised his head to see where they were going. "How about I drive for a while, Uncle?" Robbie said.

Sayyid nodded and handed off the pole. Robbie took his place at the stern.

CHAPTER 81

Gil coughed and opened his mouth, pushing with his tongue. His eyes flew open, and he found his face pressed against Max's coat, a mouthful of the course bristly stuff, dry as cotton, poking at the insides of his cheeks. He coughed and spit the hair out, whacking at it with his unencumbered hand. The bushy mane turned like a giant rock rolling away from the opening of a cave and yawned. Max lay on his back, paws in the air, and whined, waiting for Gil to rub his belly. Gil grabbed his water bottle from the nightstand, took a big swig and swished it around in his mouth.

"Yuck." He sat cross-legged next to Max, adjusted his sling then began to rub in slow, deliberate circles with his good hand, putting them both in a trance. Max pawed the air in ecstasy until Gil stopped in mid-stroke.

"Oh my God." Gil looked at Max. "I had a dream, Max. I had a dream." Gil got up on his knees and bounced. "I had a dream, Maxie. A dream!" Gil stood up on the bed and began jumping up and down, then dancing in a strange, cohesive rhythm, singing all the while. "I had a dream. I had a dream." He danced and sang and twirled, "I had a dream. I had a dream." until his foot accidentally landed on the discarded water bottle and he toppled to the floor. He bounced once upon landing. Max stared over the side of the bed after him. For a moment Gil looked at him with wide-eyes before bursting into peals of laughter.

"I gotta tell Kori and Avery." He leaped up, and in two giant awkward strides, he was at the door. "C'mon, Max. Let's go."

⚔

Hart sat on the couch, studying the computer screen on his laptop, a cup of coffee in his hand. Avery sat at the other end reading *The Philadelphia Inquirer,* the Sunday edition. Kori and Jack snuggled together on the recliner. They could hear Aunt Stella, whistling in the kitchen while she made breakfast.

"I still can't believe it's a week already," Avery said.

"Can we not talk about it please?" Hart asked. "I'm better if I just don't think about it." Hart sighed. Had Bicky, in a single and unlikely courageous act, not saved Gil from probable extinction at the hand of a man whom Hart had at one time considered to be his close friend and ally, things would be vastly different right now. For the past week, Hart had struggled to redefine his relationships with both men, but the matter was too close, the parameters too large, so he filed it under the category of *Life's Mysteries and Conundrums*, the kind that need time and space for disentanglement. Kori's yelp roused Hart from his reverie.

"Aaaah, your feet are cold," she said to Jack.

Jack rubbed his bare feet against Kori's calf. After a few seconds of squirming, she wrapped both legs around him.

"God, I love you," Jack said, nuzzling Kori's neck. "I come to you with cold feet and you embrace them." He hugged her to him and whispered in her ear, "I really love you."

"I love you, too," Kori whispered back.

"No, I mean I really love you," Jack said. "Really, really love you."

Kori poked Jack in the ribs, and he grabbed both her hands, trying to pin her just as Gil came running down the stairs, Max barking in his wake.

"I had a dream," he said, jumping up and down. "I had a dream." He stopped in the center of the room and did a little jig. Max jumped around Gil's feet, barking until Gil picked him up by the front paws and danced with him.

Hart stared at Gil and Max, a smile gracing his lips. Drawn by the commotion, Aunt Stella waddled into the room.

"What was it?" Kori asked, sidling up next to Gil. Used to the last week's worth of uber-mothering, Gil stopped his little dance and raised his face to Kori so she could feel his forehead with her chin. "No fever," she said and shrugged.

"He's alive," Gil said. "Robbie's alive."

Aunt Stella covered her mouth and folded into an armchair. Kori yelped as if she'd been poked and dropped to her knees. "Tell me."

Avery dropped the paper and joined Kori on the floor. Gil sat down next to them, wrapping his good arm around Max's neck to keep him still.

"He's someplace with a lot of water."

"Water? Iraq's a desert," Jack said.

Gil shrugged and ran his closed lips back and forth over his teeth. He looked at Jack.

"Ssshhhh," Kori said to Jack. "More," she said to Gil.

"Well, there was a desert in the background, but there was so much water everywhere that I'm just not sure." He scratched at Max's ears and drifted off, back toward the dream.

"More," said Kori.

"Robbie was wearing a robe and one of those head thingies," Gil said, rubbing Max's wide side. "And the people traveled by boat. Well, really by these little canoes. And they used poles instead of paddles to move the canoe through the water."

"Interesting," Hart said. He assessed Gil with his brilliant hazel eyes before typing something into the computer.

"More," Kori said. Her eyes didn't leave Gil's face.

Gil thought for a moment, his mouth animated, his eyes and nose scrunched in concentration. "Oh yeah. He was digging a hole. He was using a little shovel and this long cylinder thingy that was open at the top and bottom and some of the sides."

"An auger?" Jack asked. Gil shrugged. Aunt Stella fanned herself with a dishtowel.

"Got it," Hart said. "Is this what you saw?" He turned the laptop's screen toward Gil who jumped up and ran over to look at it.

"That's it! That's it!" Gil said.

"Where is that?" Avery asked. Everyone leaned in to peer at the screen.

"That, is the Fertile Crescent," Hart said. "It's in southern Iraq. And if you believe the Bible, this is where civilization got its first leg up."

"Wow," Gil said.

"Are you sure that's where he is?" Kori asked.

Gil nodded. "Looks exactly like it."

"So how do we find him?" Kori asked.

"Depends. He might not want to be found," Jack said. "He's supposed to be dead, remember?"

"Which means ... " Kori said.

" ... that he faked his own death," Avery finished.

"He doesn't want to see us anymore," Kori said, a crack in her voice.

"No. It's not like that. He'll come back," Gil said. "When he's done." Gil nodded his head with enthusiasm.

Kori gave Hart a look that he interpreted as a need for deliverance.

"I'll put feelers out," Hart said. "See what I can come up with. I have some contacts in Iraq."

"Is that safe?" Jack asked.

"I'll be discreet," Hart said. He looked to Kori. "Okay?"

"Okay," she said, hugging him. She ran over to Aunt Stella whose eyes appeared to be leaking and hugged her as well before floating back to her spot on the recliner.

Avery grabbed Gil by the shoulders and looked into his eyes. "You sure?" Gil nodded, and Avery let out a long, haggard breath that sounded like it came all the way from Iraq.

"Of course he's sure. He's a vision guy," Hart said, smiling. "Okay," Hart said. "Now, Gil. You feeling up to a little work?" He patted the seat next to him.

"Sure," Gil said and flopped down on the couch.

Hart smiled and gave Gil a brief hug, avoiding the sling. Gil, startled by the gesture, sat very still for a moment before awkwardly patting Hart on the back. Hart broke into a fit of laughter.

"I give you four stars," Gil said and sat back looking pleased with himself.

"Who? Hart?" Jack asked. "Why does he get four stars?"

Gil looked at Hart with admiration. "He just does. And if he moves in with us for good, I'll give him four and a half."

Hart cleared his throat, blinked his eyes and stared at the screen, suddenly at a loss for words. Gil leaned against him on the pretense of following Hart's gaze.

"Okay," Gil said, "show me what you got."

CHAPTER 82

Four months later, Gil, Avery, Kori and Hart walked the perimeter of a building inside the Philadelphia Naval Business Center. After careful deliberation, Hart and his "team" had decided not to use Akanabi's existing plant but to build fresh. The day before, Hart signed a ten-year lease. He walked slowly, surveying the area, while the Tirabi children followed him like sheep behind the shepherd.

"I've got the contractors lined up. We'll start construction next week. We'll have to sequester the blue prints. No one gets a full set. Just bits and pieces. Enough to keep them working on their part."

"But we already have a patent," Gil said.

"That we do," Hart said. He winked at Avery who blushed. Avery's endless hours at the library had paid off several days earlier with the arrival of the official seal of the United States Patent and Trademark Office.

"We have affirmative rights," Avery said to Gil. "But that doesn't mean somebody couldn't steal the idea, or maybe improve on it and get their own patent. Even if they incorporate it wholesale, we'd still have to sue them to get them to stop."

Hart turned to Kori. "I'll need Gil to take a little time off from school. He'll have to be on the floor while we're in the construction phase, just to trouble shoot." Kori frowned.

"No worries. We'll get a tutor," Hart said. He wrapped an arm around her shoulder. "It'll be all right. I promise." Kori nodded, relaxed a bit.

"Can we have ice cream?" Gil asked.

Kori checked her watch. "It's only 11:00."

"I know," Gil said. "But I'm hungry."

"Tell you what. Let's go down to 9th and Catherine. There's a little deli called Sarcone's. They make the best hoagies you ever ate. It's all in the bread. They got a veggie one – spinach and roasted peppers." Gil turned up his nose and looked the other way. "You gotta try it. If you don't like it, we'll go to Geno's and get you a cheesesteak."

"But I want ice cream," Gil said.

"Ah, but you didn't let me finish. Afterwards we'll go to John's and get the world's best water ice."

"Like Rita's Water Ice?

"Rita? Never heard of her. But I can assure you, Rita don't know nothin' about nothin' when it comes to water ice. I'm tellin' ya'. This is the stuff."

"Okay, but I want half kiwi-strawberry, half mango."

"You got four flavors. Chocolate, cherry, pineapple and lemon. They may have added one in the last twenty years, I don't know, but if they did, it won't be kiwi-strawberry," Hart said.

Gil frowned and crossed his arms. "Whatever. Can we go now? I'm starving."

"Why am I not shocked?" Avery said, following Hart out.

Gil stole a last glance around the deserted floor and ran to catch up.

人

Hart started the car and pulled out of the parking lot.

"Estimated time of arrival, sixteen minutes," Hart said. Avery sat next to him in the front seat, Gil and Kori in the back.

"I don't think I can wait sixteen minutes," Gil said. "I'm so hungry, my stomach is soon going to eat the rest of me. I'm also thirsty." Gil made notes in the blue folder on his lap, his head bowed in concentration.

"Why didn't anyone remember to bring snacks and libations for this child?" Hart kidded Kori.

Kori rolled her eyes and rummaged around in her purse, coming up with an old, yet edible peppermint, which she handed to Gil. Gil tried ripping the paper off, but it had melted in sections and the job was too tedious. He handed the mint back to Kori who yanked it out of his hand.

"Can't you do anything yourself?" she asked, picking lint off the stale, hard candy. Gil shook his head and she handed him the mint. He popped it in his mouth and crunched it to bits within seconds, then looked again at his sister.

"That was it. I don't have anymore," she said.

Gil went back to his notebook. Several minutes later he raised his head, capped the pen and closed the folder. "Hey, Hart?" Gil said.

"Yo."

"Did you ever hear about the Zero Point Field or Torus energy?"

"No, but I'm sure you're going to fill me in," Hart said. Gil smiled and looked at Avery before grabbing Kori's purse.

"Hey, you little brat," she said, but made no effort to retrieve it. Gil began routing around, looking for more candy.

"The Zero Point Field is a constant backdrop in all physics equations. The theory is well known," Avery said, "but not in the way Gil is working on it. Because it's a constant, it used to be something that physicists subtracted out of everything."

Gil found another peppermint, this one more tattered than the first. He handed the peppermint to Kori and she peeled the plastic off in strips. He grabbed it from her outstretched hand, picked off the last few pieces of lint, and chomped it up as quickly as the first one.

"But for the last thirty or forty years, a few pioneers have been tinkering with the idea that there's more to the Field than the need to remove it from a few equations," Avery said. "Some of the brave ones have begun a series of experiments, mostly in isolation. Collectively, their results point to a phenomenal result. It turns out that the Zero Point Field, what used to be thought of as empty space, is this massive, cohesive unit of energy that runs through everything, not only on the planet, but in the entire universe."

Gil licked the sticky peppermint off his fingers. "Anything can happen in the Field," he said. "That's why sometimes they call it the Zero Point Field of All Possibility."

"Sounds like science fiction," Hart said.

"Yeah," Gil said. "Did you ever see on Star Trek when they heal somebody without medicine and without surgery? They were tapping into the Field." Hart laughed out loud and Gil blushed.

"He's not kidding. Our modern medicine will become obsolete," Avery said.

"If you get shot or a tiger bites your arm off and you want somebody to reattach it, then you'll still need a doctor," Gil added.

"Yeah, but not for the stuff like cancer or arthritis or Alzheimer's," Avery said. "You won't need to take drugs."

"Yeah, because you can just go back in time to the "seed moment" and fix it before it gets to be a problem," Gil said. He stuck his hand in Kori's purse and fished around for more candy. She yanked it away.

"Enough," she said.

"What's a seed moment?" Hart asked.

"Well, these physicists who are studying the Field say it's the time of the conception of a disease. Or actually, the exact moment before when all the pathways are coalescing to form what will become the disease."

"And you're saying you can go back in time and cure it even before it manifests itself just by accessing this mysterious Field," Hart asked. Gil nodded.

Hart mulled this information over for a moment before speaking. "What if it wasn't a disease, but an accident. Could you change it then?"

Avery looked at Gil who shrugged.

"Does it involve more than one person?" Gil asked.

"Yeah," said Hart.

Gil thumbed through his folder and rubbed his chin just like his father used to do. After a minute he closed the folder. "Too many variables," Gil said. "You can talk to God, but you can't have his job."

Hart's expression sank as he exited the highway. Gil caught Hart's eye in the rear view mirror and smiled, forcing Hart to do the same. Hart shrugged.

"Anyway … " Gil handed Kori the blue folder. On the cover, in large type it read: "Plans to Solve the World's Health and Energy Problems Using the Zero Point Field and the ABHA Torus," by Gil Tirabi. At the bottom of the page in smaller type it read: "I give this five stars."

Kori read the cover and turned to stare at her brother. "You … are kidding me. You never gave anything five stars." Kori flipped through the folder. "What? Did you prove the existence of God or something?"

"Something," Gil agreed. He fidgeted in his seat and made a goofy face, one that belied the intelligence lurking beneath.

Kori dropped the folder on the seat next to Hart who, at present, was maneuvering deftly around a car double-parked in the driving lane. He cast his eyes down to the folder lying next to him and read the title. He looked at Gil in the rearview mirror.

"Are you serious? Because if this is true, Gil, we better hire some better security, and pronto."

"Well," Gil said, "maybe you should start interviewing."

THE END

ABOUT THE AUTHOR

Pam Lazos' passions run deep and wide but, they are mainly: her family, writing, and the environment. She is a former correspondent for her local newspaper (*Lancaster Intelligencer Journal*); a literary magazine contributor (*Rapportage*); on the Board of Advisors for the *wH2O Journal, the Journal of Gender and Water* (University of Pennsylvania); an editor and ghostwriter; author of a children's book (*Into the Land of the Loud*); creator of the literary and eco blog www.greenlifebluewater.wordpress.com; an environmental lawyer by day; and because it's cool, a beekeeper's apprentice. She practices laughter daily.

Made in the USA
San Bernardino, CA
11 September 2017